Praise for
FREEDOM'S TEARS

"A gripping historical treasure trove of a story for those who thought they knew about the Civil War. *Freedom's Tears* pulls you into . . . a plantation community of enslaved people in South Carolina as history lands on their doorstep and the war reverberates through their lives. Rich in detail, grounded in real events, this sweeping landscape of what took place in the heart of the South during this time is vividly portrayed. A riveting read!"

—Leslie K Simmons, author of *Red Clay, Running Waters*

"Captivating historical fiction! Olsvig writes with passion and empathic authenticity. Her words poignantly capture the emotional nuances her characters would have experienced in the situations she portrays. The accuracy of her historical references and terminology withstands scholarly scrutiny and conveys a deep understanding of the time of which she writes."

—Richard E Thomas, founder and president, Legacy Leadership, LLC; chairman, History Department, Heritage Library; lecturer, Osher Lifelong Learning Institute–USCB; author of *Backwater Frontier: Beaufort County, South Carolina, at the Forefront of American History*

"As a historical fiction novel, *Freedom's Tears* is both vivid and gut-wrenchingly accurate. From the climate-setting background to the Civil War through Emancipation Day, Josie Olsvig paints a picture of abducted Africans few dare approach, and many would like to forget. 'One should remember, at this point in history, the Republicans were liberal and anti-slavery, while most Southern Democrats, or what later became known as Dixiecrats, were conservative and pro-slavery.' Was it cotton, or was it greed? The reader will have to decide as they unpack this unvarnished study of slavery's marrow during one of the most divisive periods of American history."

—Riccoh Player, CEO and founder, Parade Deck; retired base commander, Parris Island Marine Base

"Go grab your personal copy TODAY of an extraordinary historical fiction book by my friend and fellow author Josie Olsvig. Her latest novel, *Freedom's Tears*, is a compelling story set during the Civil War and eventual emancipation that will literally keep you on the edge of your seat. Let the pages of this award-winning novel draw you into a very chaotic and complex period in our nation's history."

—Greg Estevez, president, Hutchinson Heritage Foundation; Edisto Island author, historian, and genealogist

"Extremely well researched and beautifully written, Josie Olsvig's novel *Freedom's Tears* will haunt you for years to come."

—Kim Poovey, author of *Shadows of the Moss* and other Southern novels

Freedom's Tears:
The History of the Civil War in Charleston,
South Carolina & Port Royal Sound

By Josie Olsvig

© Copyright 2024 Josie Olsvig

ISBN 979-8-88824-436-4

All rights reserved. No part of this publication may be reproduced, stored in a retrieval system, or transmitted in any form or by any means—electronic, mechanical, photocopy, recording, or any other—except for brief quotations in printed reviews, without the prior written permission of the author.

This is a work of fiction. The characters are both actual and fictitious. With the exception of verified historical events and persons, all incidents, descriptions, dialogue and opinions expressed are the products of the author's imagination and are not to be construed as real.

Published by

köehlerbooks™

3705 Shore Drive
Virginia Beach, VA 23455
800-435-4811
www.koehlerbooks.com

JOSIE OLSVIG

Freedom's Tears

THE HISTORY OF THE CIVIL WAR IN CHARLESTON, SOUTH CAROLINA, & PORT ROYAL SOUND

a novel

VIRGINIA BEACH
CAPE CHARLES

I do not pretend to understand the moral universe;
the arc is a long one, my eye reaches but little ways;
I cannot calculate the curve and complete the figure by the experience of sight;
I can divine it by conscience.
And from what I see I am sure it bends toward justice.

~Theodore Parker

Author's Note

Our country is going through a most peculiar time, marked by many firsts: the first time a former president was indicted and then convicted of multiple felonies, the first time fellow Americans attacked our nation's Capitol, and the first time an attempt to thwart the will of the American people by undermining their vote in a presidential election occurred. Multiple acts were committed against the rule of law. Yet, many pundits and scholars predicted that a wave of such action, incited by fiery speeches, was coming, something akin to a second civil war. The Lost Cause Doctrine had been rearing its ugly head for a period of more than five years. Racial hatred has escalated, along with xenophobia, the hatred of groups, such as Asians, Jews, and other minorities.

Over the past decade, I felt compelled to try to develop books to enable readers to gain a better understanding of our often-complicated past, as it directly impacts the period we are living through now. The principal vehicle I used was the historical fiction novel, yet standing alone, I found it inadequate. I believe it is necessary to insert sections of historical information likely unknown to the reader, along with photographs. Believing that a historical fiction novel would reach a broader audience than just a textbook or nonfiction guide, I chose the former format. Bringing history alive in a novel puts the reader in the historical context, to feel the texture and understand the mood of the time. Whether you lived in the North or the South, the textbooks available were intentionally distorted and flawed. The truth was hidden from us for more than a century. Now, when the truth tellers started to reveal the ugliness of our past, books were pulled from the shelves.

I believe it is time we faced our past, particularly with regard to one of the most divisive periods in our history, the Civil War, and those years that led up to it. Just recently a US representative stated that the "red states" should divorce the "blue states," and we should split our country in two again. Such words should not be taken lightly. More lives were lost in the Civil War than in all wars put together. Let us hope that we never experience such a horrific event again. It is only through enlightenment that we can avoid such tragedy.

To that end, I have provided a historical addendum that chronicles the people and political forces fueling the uprising that divided and nearly ended this country. As with today, there was a cadre of segregationists who advocated creating a separate country where Blacks would be enslaved. That agenda masqueraded as "states' rights," a euphemism, once again, being used to culturally divide this country. The South Carolina uprising and succession leading to the Civil War is a harbinger of where this country may once again be heading. It happened once; it can happen again.

Lucy Stanton, "A Plea for the Oppressed" Delivered in 1850, Oberlin, Ohio

Lucy Stanton Day Sessions,
I Shall Have Your Sympathy, If Your Judgment Refuses Me Your Support (1864)

Courtesy Papers of Ellen Lawson and Marlene D. Merrill, Oberlin College Archives

Lucy Stanton was probably the first African American woman to complete a four-year collegiate course of study. Stanton, the daughter of John Brown, a Cleveland barber active in the Underground Railroad, enrolled in nearby Oberlin Collegiate Institute (now Oberlin College) in northern Ohio. The institution would soon be noted for its abolitionist politics and admission of both male and female African American students. In 1850, Stanton completed the "ladies' course," which, unlike the bachelor's degree program, required no Greek, Latin, or higher mathematics.

As president of the Oberlin Ladies Literary Society, Stanton was invited to offer a graduation address at the commencement exercises on August 27, 1850. Delivered just two weeks before the enactment of the Fugitive Slave Act, a time when Black and White abolitionists felt the cause was experiencing its greatest difficulty in years, Stanton bravely called upon her fellow female students to embrace the antislavery campaign. She also envisioned, perhaps to the surprise of many in her audience, the day in the not-too-distant future when slavery would be abolished. Stanton read her speech to the crowd:

> *When I forget you, Oh my people, may my tongue cleave to the roof of my mouth, and may my right hand forget her cunning! Dark hover the clouds. The Anti-Slavery pulse beats faintly. The right of suffrage is denied. The colored man is still crushed by the weight of oppression. He may possess talents of the highest order, yet for him is no path of fame or distinction opened. He can never hope to attain those privileges while his brethren remain enslaved. Since, therefore, the freedom of the slave and the gaining of our rights, social and political, are inseparably connected, let all the friends of humanity plead for those who may not plead their own cause.*
>
> *Reformers, ye who have labored long to convince man that happiness is found alone in doing good to others, that humanity is a unit, that he who injures one individual wrongs the race;—that to love one's neighbor as one's self is the sum of human virtue—ye that advocate the great principles of Temperance, Peace, and Moral Reform will you not raise your voice in behalf of these stricken ones!–will you not plead the cause of the Slave?*
>
> *Slavery is the combination of all crime. It is War.*
>
> *Those who rob their fellow-men of home, of liberty, of education, of life, are really at war against them as though they cleft them down upon the bloody field. It is intemperance; for there is an intoxication when the fierce passions rage in man's breast, more fearful than the madness of the drunkard, which if let loose upon the moral universe would sweep away*

everything pure and holy, leaving but the wreck of man's nobler nature. Such passions does Slavery foster—yea, they are a part of herself. It is full of pollution. Know you not that to a slave, virtue is a sin counted worthy of death? That many, true to the light within, notwithstanding the attempts to shut out the truth, feeling that a consciousness of purity is dearer than life, have nobly died? Their blood crieth to God, a witness against the oppressor.

Statesmen, you who have bent at ambition's shrine, who would leave your names on the page of history, to be venerated by coming generations as among those of the great and good, will you advocate the cause of the downtrodden, remembering that the spirit of liberty is abroad in the land? The precious seed is sown in the heart of the people, and though the fruit does not appear, the germ is there, and the harvest will yet be gathered. Truly is this an age of reform. The world is going on, not indeed keeping pace with the rapid tread of its leaders, but none the less progressing. As the people take a step in one reform, the way is prepared for another. Now while other evils in man's social and political condition are being remedied, think you that Slavery can stand the searching test—an enlightened people's sense of justice? Then speak the truth boldly; fear not loss of property or station. It is a higher honor to embalm your name in the hearts of a grateful people than to contend for the paltry honors of party preferment.

Woman, I turn to thee. Is it not thy mission to visit the poor? to shed the tear of sympathy? to relieve the wants of the suffering? Where wilt thou find objects more needing sympathy than among the slaves!

Mother, hast thou a precious gem in thy charge, like those that make up the Savior's jewels? Has thy heart, trembling with its unutterable joyousness, bent before the throne of the Giver with the prayer that thy child might be found in his courts? Thou hast seen the dawning of intelligence in its bright eye, and watched with interest the unfolding of its powers. Its gentle, winning ways have doubly endeared it to thee. Death breathes upon the flower, and it is gone. Now thou canst feel for the slave-mother who has bent with the same interest over her child, whose heart is entwined around it even more firmly than thine own around thine, for to her it is the only ray of joy in a dreary world. She returns weary and sick at heart from the labors of the field; the child's beaming smile of welcome half banishes the misery of her lot. Would she not die for it? Ye who know the depths of a mother's love, answer! Hark! Strange footsteps are near her dwelling! The door is thrown rudely open! Her master says—"There is the woman!" She comprehends it all—she is sold! From her trembling lips escape the words—"my child!" She throws herself at the feet of those merciless men, and pleads permission to keep her babe, but in vain. What is she more than any other slave, that she should be permitted this favor? They are separated.

Sister, have you ever had a kind and loving brother? How often would he lay aside his book to relieve you from some difficulty? How have you hung upon the words of wisdom that he has uttered? How earnestly have you studied that you might stand his companion—his equal. You saw him suddenly stricken by the destroyer. Oh! How your heart ached!

There was a slave-girl who had a brother kind and noble as your own. He had scarcely any advantages: yet stealthily would he draw an old volume from his pocket, and through the long night would pore over its contents. His soul thirsted for knowledge. He yearned for freedom, but free-soil was far away. That sister might not go, he staid with her. They say that slaves do not feel for or love each other; I fear that there are few brothers with a pale face who would have stood that test. For her he tamed the fire of his eye, toiled for that which profited him not, and labored so industriously that the overseer had no apology for applying the lash to his back. Time passed on: that brother stood in his manhood's prime as tenderly kind and as dearly beloved as ever. That sister was insulted;–the lash was applied to her quivering back; her brother rushed to save her! He tore away the fastenings which bound her to the whipping post, he held her on his arm–she was safe. She looked up, encountered the ferocious gaze of the overseer, heard the report of a pistol, and felt the heart's blood of a brother gushing over her. But we draw the veil.

Mother, sister, by thy own deep sorrow of heart; by the sympathy of thy woman's nature, plead for the downtrodden of thy own, of every land. Instill the principles of love, of common brotherhood, in the nursery, in the social circle. Let these be the prayer of thy life.

Christians, you whose souls are filled with love for your fellow men, whose prayer to the Lord is, "Oh! that I may see thy salvation among the children of men!" Does the battle wax warm? dost thou faint with the burden and heat of the day? Yet a little longer; the arm of the Lord is mighty to save those who trust in him. Truth and right must prevail. The bondsman shall go free. Look to the future! Hark! the shout of joy gushes from the heart of earth's freed millions! It rushes upward. The angels on heaven's outward battlements catch the sound on their golden lyres, and send it thrilling through the echoing arches of the upper world. How sweet, how majestic, from those starry isles float those deep inspiring sounds over the ocean of space! Softened and mellowed they reach earth, filing the soul with harmony, and breathing of God–of love–and of universal freedom.

Contributed by BLACKPAST
Posted on January 24, 2007

Table of Contents

Author's Note ix

Lucy Stanton, "A Plea for the Oppressed" Delivered in 1850, Oberlin, Ohio xi

Character Key 1

Chapter 1
Cully Out Hunting for the Family 6

Chapter 2
The Lynching of Christmas Luke 16

Chapter 3
Hentie and Big John's Life at Twin Oaks Plantation 37

Chapter 4
Patrick Pringle and Fitzwilliam Langdon, Citadel Cadets 57

Chapter 5
Fitzwilliam's Pregraduation Ceremony from the Citadel 72

Chapter 6
The Shots Over Fort Sumter: The War Has Begun 90

Chapter 7
The South Awakens from its Long-Contented Sleep 105

Chapter 8
Farewell to the Ninety Days' War 118

Chapter 9
Issac Runs from the Confederate Encampment 140

Chapter 10
Flag Officer Samuel DuPont's Great Armada 152

Chapter 11
The Battle of Port Royal Sound Commences 163

Chapter 12
DuPont Walks Through Beaufort;
Robert Smalls Liberates Himself 174

Chapter 13
Can the Union Army Recruit African American Men? 191

Chapter 14
Getting Settled in After the Big Skedaddle 200

Chapter 15
Juba Meets Susie King Taylor from Savannah 216

Chapter 16
Harriet Tubman is Called to Serve in the
Port Royal Experiment 233

Chapter 17
The Weeping Time in Savannah 247

Chapter 18
Emancipation Day 268

Chapter 19
The Combahee River Raid 288

Genesis of the Civil War 307

Acknowledgments 348

Discussion Questions
For Book Clubs 351
For College Classrooms 353

Select Bibliography 356

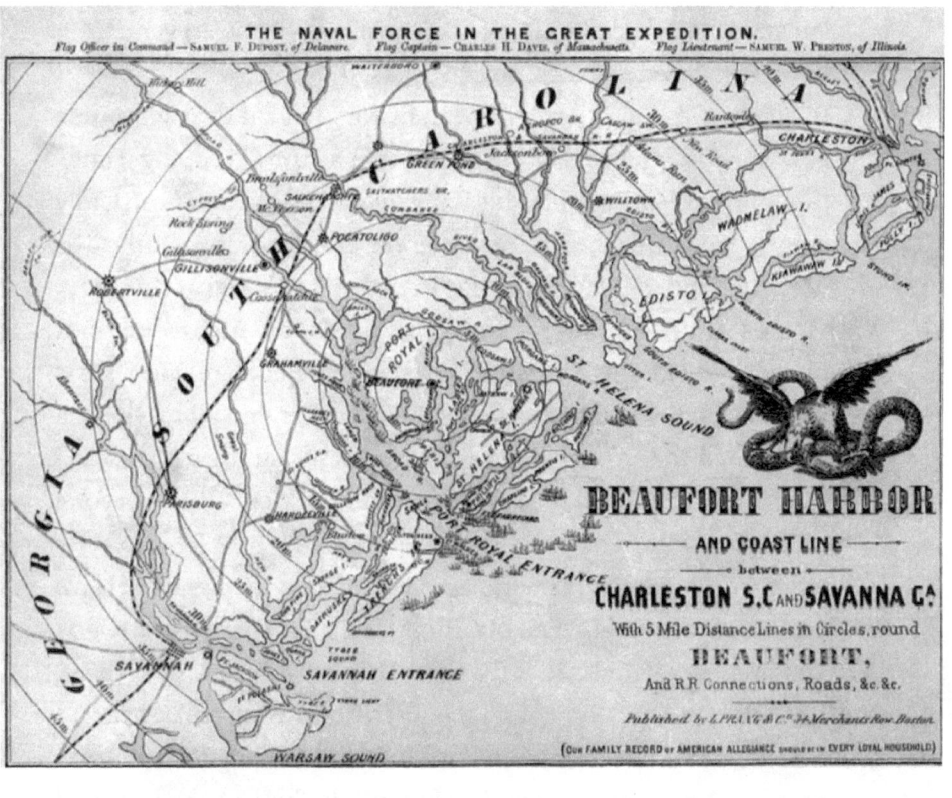

Character Key

Big John: The manservant and closest adviser to Master Langdon of Twin Oaks Plantation in Mount Pleasant. Big John is literate and quite clever but never reveals the full scope of his knowledge to the master. He is a middle-aged man about six foot, five inches tall with bulky muscles. Despite his size, he is a kind and gentle spirit. He is married to Hentie, an enslaved house servant.

Cully: An enslaved teenage boy purchased by Master Langdon at the largest slave sale in American history held at the racecourse in Savannah, Georgia, an event known as the "Weeping Time." Big John takes him under his wing and acts as his mentor. Cully subsequently becomes a carpenter on the plantation. Cully lives with Big John and Hentie and is informally adopted as their son.

Christmas Luke: A deeply religious enslaved man who first introduced Hentie to the Praise House and Gullah religion. He is an older man who has worked for Master Landon all his life. He is assigned to the stable where he maintains all the buggies and grooms the horses. He is an endearing soul loved by everyone on the plantation.

Cuffee: Juba's deceased husband who had died at the hands of slave catchers in the final scene of *Gullah Tears*. He was unaware Juba was pregnant with Issac at his death. His spirit lingers over them.

Doll (Baby Doll): Young, biracial (octoroon mulatto) enslaved herbal doctor and concubine of Mr. William Langdon. She was murdered by way of drowning in *Gullah Tears* at the hands of Master Langdon. At the time of her death, Tobias was a toddler and was present when she met her demise.

Duke: Black driver, an enslaved worker responsible for monitoring the work of the field hands. He lives in the slave village with the other enslaved workers.

Emily Trenholm Langdon: Wife of William Paul Langdon, the plantation owner. She is several years younger than her husband

and his second wife. She bears him a son, Fitzwilliam. She is temperamental and lonely. Often estranged from her husband but forced to live in the same household. She has no close friends and feels insecure, always believing she is lesser than the other women.

Elliott Chase: Son of Sarah Chase, cousin to Mrs. Langdon. The Chase family lives a far more modest lifestyle than the Langdons. They owned a small farm in Pennsylvania near Gettysburg that they struggled to maintain. Mr. Chase was killed in a farming accident just before the War of Northern Aggression. Elliott attends the Citadel on a hardship scholarship.

Fitzwilliam: Mr. and Mrs. Langdon's son, a Citadel cadet who graduates as the Civil War commences with the cadets firing on Fort Sumter. Fitzwilliam looks very much like his father; he is tall with blond hair and fair features. He is a child of privilege and, at times, is resented by others for his pompous behavior and how he puts on airs.

Flora: An enslaved servant who initially works in the laundry house and then is reassigned to the main house to assist with various household duties and the care of Mrs. Langdon.

Hentie: The main character, was brought to America on a slave ship by slave traders via the Middle Passage and sold into slavery near Gadsden Wharf in Charleston. Master Langdon bought Hentie at the slave market; Big John accompanied the master on that day. She was in her early thirties at the time of her capture and is now middle-aged. Hentie is a house worker, assigned to work in the kitchen house and the main house.

Issac: Son of Juba and her husband Cuffee. Because Juba was owned by Master McKee when her baby was born, he was also considered chattel property at birth pursuant to law. As a teenager, he was sent to work in the cotton fields at the McKee plantation, Ashdale on Lady's Island, but was later brought back to the city house to work in the stables where he handled the tack, buggies, and other items. It proved to be a much easier life and it allowed him to be closer to his mother, Juba. At the outbreak of the war, Juba and Issac are rented out to Confederate soldiers. Juba acts as valet and laundress; Issac helps with gathering food, cooking, and cleaning up after meals.

Juba: A young, enslaved woman with a caramel complexion, and average height. Apprehensive, substantial trauma. In *Gullah Tears* she was purchased in Georgetown, SC, to work in the kitchen house. Married to field hand Cuffee; held ceremony in which they jumped the broom. Sold to the McKee (who also owned Robert Smalls) family in Beaufort, SC, after she had accidentally spilled a pitcher of milk on the master. She was severely whipped after the incident and then taken to the slave mart for sale. Her husband ran away on the Underground Railroad trying to find her at her new owner's home. The husband was gunned down by a slave catcher. She swears revenge.

Lydia: Slave girl and Octavia's sister. Former slave at Twin Oaks, then sold to a family on the Battery, where she became a house slave and seamstress.

Mimba: An older enslaved woman and root doctor who practices hoodoo/conjure.

Nellie: An older enslaved head cook in the kitchen house at Twin Oaks.

Octavia: Enslaved house servant and lady's maid to Mrs. Emily Langdon.

Sarah Chase, cousin to Emily Trenholm Langdon. Sarah had darker hair and was a bit taller and hardier than her cousin Emily. She had married down so to speak out of love, something that Emily couldn't fully grasp. Sarah was devout, kindhearted, and gentle-spirited.

Simon McBride: Overseer at Twin Oaks. An illiterate man of Irish descent who is an alcoholic. Plump, dirty, and unseemly.

Tobias: Enslaved biracial son to Master Langdon, born of an enslaved negress, Baby Doll. He is tall, muscled, lean, and handsome with curly blonde hair and light-colored eyes, but like his parents, eyes that seem to change between blue and green, and even gray, depending on what he is wearing.

William Paul Langdon: Master and plantation owner at Twin Oaks, husband to Emily Langdon. A tall handsome man, with curly blonde hair, and blue eyes. Mercurial, he can be kind, but then quickly turn violent. His first wife died of yellow fever; the spirit of this first wife haunts his current wife. Only one legitimate son, Fitzpatrick, by his second wife.

Those who fail to learn from history are condemned to repeat it.

Winston Churchill's speech to the British Parliament, 1948

Chapter 1
Cully Out Hunting for the Family

Mount Pleasant, South Carolina, 1860

On the Langdon plantation, the sun was setting behind the shacks in the slave village. Some of the enslaved workers were slowly trudging home. They spoke in hushed tones, weary from the day's work in expansive fields at Twin Oaks. Their backs were bent, and their heads hung due to their exhaustion.

Despite his tiredness, Cully readied himself to go into the woods and hunt. The family needed more meat for the week. He sat on a small stool he had crafted that was situated in the middle of the slave cabin. He tightened the leather laces on his dark-brown brogans and tucked a sharp knife into his coarse wool trousers. He then prepared a bag to take on the hunt. He shoved in some twine and a length of rope, along with a few rudimentary weapons to catch small game. As darkness blanketed the cluster of small whitewashed wooden cabins, he headed out to the woods.

Cully had previously set a couple of homemade traps nearby,

which he planned to check, hoping he'd snared a rabbit or an opossum. The man who had become his new father, Big John, had taught him how to hunt and trap animals. He was very patient in teaching Cully how to track small animals, where to look, and signs that they had passed through, such as animal skat, broken branches, shelters, and their paw prints. As the master never gave them much more than a pound of meat a week, the family had to hunt to survive. The enslaved field hands needed far more calories to live, laboring for twelve to fifteen hours a day. It had been that way as long as anyone could remember. The enslaved workers weren't supposed to leave their assigned areas or venture off the grounds of the plantation, but in situations like this, it was necessary for survival.

As Cully entered the woods, he tried to mind which direction he was traveling so he could maintain his bearings. As he penetrated the wild thicket, he felt the temperature drop. He took in the woodsy smell, particularly the heady scent of the surrounding oak trees and loblolly pines. Leaves and small twigs crunched under his feet as he progressed into the forest. He tried to remain quiet.

Once in the belly of the wilderness, he realized he had gone astray. Even though he was quite familiar with the woods, he felt disoriented and didn't recognize his surroundings. Cully had tried to stay close to the outskirts of Twin Oaks plantation but thought he may have veered off a bit. He tried to regain a sense of direction. First, he walked toward the main road to gain his bearings, and then reentered the woods. As he continued his travels, he noted the sun had skipped away and the moon was coming out.

Adjacent to this part of the plantation Sally, a free woman of color, lived alone in a small shack. Her man, Titus, an enslaved field hand at Twin Oaks, often snuck off to visit her. According to the White man's laws of South Carolina, enslaved Negroes were considered chattel property, not people, more like horses or cattle. They were forbidden to marry. The master wouldn't even let the couple jump the broom, an act of matrimony which was largely symbolic. Master said if he allowed Titus to marry the woman, their children wouldn't be his. They would be born free since she was free. The child always acquired the status of the mother. Didn't seem fair, two people in love for years, always loyal to each other, couldn't marry. *Just ain't right,* Cully reasoned.

After orienting himself, he turned back toward the woods but walked parallel to the road. Suddenly, Cully thought he saw a flash, maybe a rabbit, so he crouched down and listened very carefully. At first, only crickets and an old owl.

Cully hissed, "Shush now, owl!"

Cully stayed still, hoping to see the animal again. He held his breath and swayed a little, almost dizzy from his hunger and the long workday. Just then, a swamp rabbit rushed by him, the small animal leaping in the air with the grace of a deer as it hustled off. It splashed into a shallow swamp, and in the moonlight, it sent ripples as its webbed feet swam away. The only cottontail with such size and unique abilities, it could swim and run with unparalleled athleticism. He tried to steady himself as he felt his heartbeat increase. *What's out there?*

Cully continued onward but then thought he heard another movement. It was like a writhing sound across the dead leaves. The slithering animal caused a chill to tiptoe up Cully's spine. He hated snakes and reptiles; they were creatures of the devil. He felt the creature push by his boot, and his whole body jerked. He could hear the movement, now just inches away. The sound caused his body to quake, in turn spurring his hands to tremor and his belly to tighten. He let out a restrained yelp and jumped to move away from the creature, backpedaling with dramatic speed, his lungs pumping. Birds, previously dormant, were sent flapping up into the air, and an owl hooted in disgust. It was then that Cully caught sight of the copperhead snake slinking away, the moonlight glistening off its jeweled back. *Jesus! A snake! I hate snakes! Why are there so many here in the Lowcountry?*

Then he heard something new; it sounded like the clanking of a chain or metal striking against something. Cully drew in a breath. Was there an animal caught in a trap? He hadn't checked yet. He opened his eyes wider, trying to take in as much as he could in the pale moonlight. Cully wondered if he had passed Sally's cabin without realizing it. Perhaps it was cloaked in darkness. *Am I closer to her cabin than I thought? I know it's around here somewhere.*

Then he heard the sound of commotion, not birds or animals. Cully drew closer to the road; it wasn't anything he could identify at first. But whatever it was, it seemed to be coming closer. He peered out onto the road and took in the images. It was the sound of horses clomping slowly down the road toward him. Riders carried glowing lamps that illuminated them.

Just in time, Cully dove back into the bushes and froze.

Cully's body tensed; he felt a needling beneath his skin as the blood coursed. What if the master or overseer caught him away from the plantation? He would be beaten for sure. Small droplets of perspiration formed on his upper lip as he adjusted his eyes to darkness. He listened carefully, stiffened his body, and clenched his hands as the clopping of hooves approached. There seemed to be more than one man's voice. Frozen, Cully could only hear his own rapid breathing. He tried to slow it down, quietly taking in deeper breaths, wondering whether the approaching horsemen had seen him. Peering through the bushes, he could see them now, dark, slowly moving shapes going in a direction that would eventually take them past Cully toward Sally's house. They carried two lanterns and a couple of torches that illuminated them and threw light onto their path.

All the riders were White. They proceeded past him, then turned into the woods just a few feet beyond him. He watched and waited, keeping absolutely still, not knowing what was about to happen until they had all gone past. *Why would a group of five men be out this way?* They proceeded onward to Sally's cabin. *What do they want with her? Why so many?*

After a moment of indecision, Cully got up and followed them, moving carefully from tree to tree. He carefully placed each footfall so as not to make a sound. Cully was afraid of them, yet curious. He quickly rolled differing notions through his mind as it darted from one idea to another trying to figure out what they were up to. *Do these men belong to one of those Southern rights groups, like the master?* He had heard about the Langdons belonging to the Knights of the Golden Circle, which was common knowledge in the slave village. Those White men met from time to time under the cover of darkness. They wanted to preserve slavery.

Dangerous as a group of White men on horseback could be, Cully stayed still and watched, viewing the threatening intruders through the branches as they moved closer and closer to Sally's cabin. Sally's small wooden home was in a moonlit clearing in the woods. The men pulled to a stop outside her door and began to shout to one another. As they seemed preoccupied, Cully used the opportunity to draw near and crouched down in the surrounding bushes.

The men were brusque and crude, speaking in deep, gravelly voices. It was hard for Cully to make out exactly what they were saying, but he caught bits and pieces of their conversation.

"You know the dirty bastard is in there with her. Why else would he leave the plantation and take off for the woods?" huffed one man. He held up a lantern and tried to look in a window.

"Probably in there making little niggra babies right now. Babies the master will never be able to own," chuckled one man.

"Well, that's why Langdon sent us. Wants to breed this buck with some other woman. Best get on with it," said the man as he dropped down from his horse.

Sally was a good woman, a free Black. Her father, now dead, had bought their freedom years ago. She worked hard as a seamstress and sometimes took in laundry for folks around the area, sometimes even for Twin Oaks. She was goodhearted and hardworking.

Four of the riders dismounted and went up to the door of the cabin. One man struck the door with his fist, then kicked it with his heavy boot. When no one answered his pounding, another man stepped forward and the two began trying to break the door down. It looked like a heavy door, one more likely to break the men's shoulders than to give way. Then, followed by one more blow, the wood splintered. Apparently, the latch wasn't as sturdy as the door itself. The four men rushed into the cabin. Sally screamed and objects crashed into the cabin walls. Cully shook with fear wondering what they might be doing to the woman.

Two people were shoved out of the door and thrown toward the ground in front of the cabin. One was Sally, wrapped in a blanket, and the other was her man. The last rider, who had been waiting outside, dismounted, apparently expecting that they would find the two alone in the cabin. The slave catchers—Cully figured that's who they were now—began tossing comments to one another. Cully could make out a few of the words, but some of the exchange was more like inarticulate throaty sounds, almost like growling.

"No pass," said one of the riders. "Titus here must have snuck off."

"No sir," pleaded a dark figure from the cabin to the men who encircled him. "I had a pass! I had—"

Without warning, one of the White men punched the jittery bondsman in the face, propelling him backward. Stunned, Titus tried to steady himself. Then the two others lunged forward and grabbed hold of him, and Titus sagged between them. The men continued to berate him.

"If you had a pass, where is it?" demanded one man.

"Don't know sir. I must have dropped my ticket somewhere on my way here. Must be somewhere in the woods, I expect."

"Don't believe this lying dog for a moment," exclaimed one of the men. "He snuck off to be with his woman. He'd be stealing what should properly belong to a White man. I say we slice off his manhood." He pulled out a long bowie knife to handle the task. "This will stop him from visiting that which he ought to leave alone."

"Put that knife away! Master Langdon doesn't want his property harmed that way. The master has plans for old Titus here. He wants to mate him with one of his Negro broodmares and spawn some new niggra babies. He'll lock them up together in a breeding shack before too long. Won't let them out until the niggra woman is with child. Now come on over here!" The White man who seemed to be in charge of the group motioned the slave catcher toward him.

The two men holding him on either side hustled Titus to a nearby tree, so close that Cully fell to the ground, stiff with fear. Cully knew these men were out to draw the blood of a Black man and that he could be their next victim. Cully inched back, alarmed, so terrified he could hardly breathe. His mind raced.

Titus was forced to hug a tree, and his hands were tied to prevent him from letting go. The man was naked, having been dragged from the bed he had shared with Sally.

Cully managed to crawl away from the tree, as the men had their attention fully on Titus. After Cully found his new position, he glanced over to where Sally stood, still wrapped in a blanket near the cabin with a look of horror. One of the men took long strides toward her and tore off the wrap. Sally said something in a tone so low Cully could not distinguish the words.

"Shut your mouth, Negress!" The man clutched the blanket, then threw it to the ground. "Just who in the hell do you think you are, anyway? You ain't got no rights, not here with us."

The other man strode toward her and exclaimed, "Ha! What do you think you got that we ain't seen before?"

The first man said, "Yeah, I have seen a lot more and better!"

There was raucous laughter followed by growling and obscenities. One man reached forward and squeezed Sally's large breast, then whooped in amusement.

Titus was securely tied to the tree, and the man who appeared to be the lead slave catcher went to his horse to retrieve a whip. He cracked it once over the men's heads, then cracked it again for effect, loosening his arm as he strutted. He cracked it a third time, seemingly for his own amusement. Then, he laid his first blow. Titus convulsed with the lash, but the only sound he made was an audible gasp. The White man continued to lay blows, one right after the other. He put his whole body into it, trying to use more and more force, hoping to break the bound man. Titus took the blows with no outcry, but even from a distance, Cully could hear his breathing, hard and quick.

Sally, like her man, remained silent, tears rolling down her cheeks; yet she remained stoic. She focused her eyes on the front of her cabin, looking away from the brutality unfolding before her. She didn't utter a word, not a sound. She wouldn't give into the terrorizing slave catchers. As the beating continued, she looked upward to the heavens. Perhaps she silently prayed to God to make this all stop.

After a while, Titus' resolve broke. Cully had lost count of how many blows he had taken; three dozen perhaps. Titus began to moan, a low gut-wrenching sound emitted against his will. Then, finally he began to scream as the blood poured down and part of his flesh lay torn on his back. The flames from the torchlight glistened on his bloodied back.

Cully, now in a state of terror, began to quake in fear and at the stench, which was like the smell of blood of slaughtered hogs. He could hear every jagged breath coming from Titus, every cry, and every cut of the whip, Titus' body jerking, convulsing, straining against the ropes. His screaming went on and on. Cully tried to cover his ears; he was afraid he would cry out himself, powerless and unable to take the brutality of it any longer. His stomach heaved and tears flowed. *How could one human being do this to another? God have mercy on us all. Why won't they stop?*

Titus cried out, the sound bursting from him, "Please stop!" he begged. "For God's sake, please."

Yes, God, please stop this. Stop this man's agony. Cully closed his eyes tight, praying. He tensed his muscles against the urge to vomit, the taste of bile coming up from the back of his throat. *God, please make this stop!* He wanted to scream but found no voice. Sweat rolled down his back; tension constricted his entire being.

Cully lay there, focused on trying to stay quiet and keep himself from sobbing. Then he realized the beating had stopped. He waited a moment, then peered through the branches. The patrollers were untying Titus who continued to lean on the tree and gasp for air, his body still heaving.

After a minute, one of the men reached out and pulled him from the tree. Another man tied Titus' hands in front of him. Titus was still swaying, overcome from the beating. They paused just another minute, then one man nodded to another, and they began to walk toward their horses. They pulled Titus along on the rope as one might pull a dog. They spoke in low voices for a minute or two, as if to further plan their deed.

The man holding the rope tied to Titus turned his horse, then shouted, "Come now, niggra, you about to face your master!"

The White men were mounted now, save one, who was left back by the cabin having a low-voiced discussion with Sally. She covered her breasts as they spoke as if in a defensive posture. Evidently, the discussion didn't go the way the man wanted, and he threw his torch to the ground. He then pulled back his fist and punched her in the face, much like Titus had been punched earlier. She fell backward to the ground. The torchlight glowed near her. She remained there, limp. The man jerked his head in approval of his own handywork.

"Time to go," the head slave catcher shouted. "The missus has supper waiting for me. Leave that niggra woman alone and come on!"

The patroller spat at her, then said, "Just remember, you Black bitch, I don't need no stinkin' permission from you. And I can come back at any time." He leered at her, then smiled revealing gray teeth. He turned to spit out a stream of brown juice, a fleck of chewing tobacco on his cracked lip. He turned on his heel and marched away. As he mounted his horse, he glanced back at Sally once more with a stare so evil it lingered in the air and seemed to land in Cully's heart, piercing it.

The patrol and their stumbling hostage started toward the roadway. Cully could hear the men's voices grow fainter, as did the sound of the horses' hooves. After it all seemed quiet, Cully crept forward, remaining on his belly as he slithered across the ground.

"Sally!" Cully called softly.

She rolled to one side, then stopped and peered at Cully through the darkness. Unsure of who owned the voice, she called out, "Who's there?"

"It's Cully, Big John's boy." His voice was strained and hoarse from the bile he had swallowed. He wiped away the moisture from his eyes and blinked to see her more clearly. Then, he inched forward, holding his body upright while still on his knees, fearful a White man might yet be near.

"It's okay, boy, you can come out now. They gone," she struggled to say.

With that, Cully moved toward her, helped her to her feet and the two entered the cabin.

"It's just not right . . . not right. Why can't you be with your man? Why they beat him like that just cause he wanted to be with you? It ain't right. Ain't right at all. White man shouldn't be able to tell you who to love and who to marry!"

"All we can do is hope for a better day, Cully. There may be a war coming. Maybe things will get better for us Black folks. Till then we just gotta do what the White man says. Ain't got no choice, just remember that, Cully. You got to accept things the way they are. Gots no choice."

"Someday I hope I can do something to make it so we got a choice. It just ain't right Sally. A Black man needs to have a choice!"

Chapter 2
The Lynching of Christmas Luke

Mount Pleasant, South Carolina, 1860

Mimba, a dark-skinned, enslaved seamstress, exhaled and glanced across the workroom at the spinning wheel and large, imposing weaving loom. The old woman was small and slightly hunched from decades of strenuous labor, almost gnomelike in stature, but with a mind as sharp as a bowie knife and as quick as the overseer's bullwhip. Her fingers had grown numb from all the mending she had done that morning. She carefully set her mending on a small roughhewn table beside her chair, then splayed her fingers out, trying to relieve the stiffness. She worked them back and forth to limber them up. Mimba sat back in her chair to stretch her torso, then decided to try to stand to work out the crick in her back. She planted her feet squarely on the floor several inches apart and slowly pushed herself out of the chair. Her small frame gradually unfolded, and her simple, blue, course-cloth shift dress fell below her knees. She placed a hand on her lower back to urge her body to stand fully upright.

As Mimba lumbered along, she chuckled to herself, shook her head, and mumbled, "Sure gettin' harder to get out of a chair these days, but at least I'm able to shuffle around this place."

Another enslaved woman working at the loom shot a smile at Mimba and said, "But at least your movin', thank the Lord for that."

"That's for true!" Mimba nodded in agreement.

Inching along, she tucked a few loose gray hairs up under her indigo-blue head wrap. Her homemade moccasins, crafted by one of the other enslaved workers, dragged across the wooden slates of the spinning house as she moved. Mimba reached down and touched the carefully organized colorful spools of thread as she exited through the doorway. Clutching the threshold as she cautiously stepped down onto the work yard, she gasped when she touched the solid ground.

Still trying to work out her stiffness, she continued to flex her fingers. Mimba moved along the edges of the work yard, past the livestock pen, the noisy workshops, the dairy, and smokehouse. The smells from the work yard wafted up to her—the burning wood of the blacksmith's hearth, the slop that had been thrown down for the hogs, the lye soap concoction boiling in the laundry house caldron, and the animal dung in the pens. Hoping to snatch the remnants of the morning's buttermilk biscuits or a bit of dried pork from the kitchen house, she picked her way across the work yard.

The bright sun shone down, and she tilted her head upwards to catch more of its warmth. As she got closer to the kitchen house, the fragrance of jasmine and the blossoms from the lemon trees tickled her nose. She breathed in deeply, taking in their scent. Springtime in the Deep South was heavenly. Suddenly, jerked from her temporary respite, the clucking sounds from a handful of hens drew her attention. She stopped abruptly, dropped her hands by her sides, and waited for the chickens to pass. Then, still relishing the idea of one of Nellie's biscuits, she picked up her step and headed to the kitchen house.

The kitchen house, a modest, separate brick building, was set directly behind the mansion but at a good distance from it so as not to risk setting fire to the Langdons' dwelling house, with its valuable house furnishings and treasures imported from Europe. It was where all the cooking for the Langdon family took place. The kitchen house's covered walkway, sometimes called the "whistle walk," allowed the enslaved workers to carry the food into the main house with limited exposure to the elements. The ill-tempered and miserly mistress of the plantation often forced the house servants to whistle as they carried the prepared dishes to the warming kitchen. This task rendered them unable to knick food off the serving dishes and eat it as they proceeded to the main house.

The kitchen space was compact and functional; on the wall opposite the main door was an open fireplace with a large black kettle on a swinging wrought iron arm. To the right of this, two recessed baking ovens with black iron doors were fashioned like cubby holes in the brick. The ovens baked loaves of bread, corn muffins, biscuits and roasted various types of meat. Mimba hoped that something was baking in there. She scanned the tightly built workroom for signs that Nellie was making up the fresh dough or about to pull something delicious out. Sensing that no baked goods were about to appear, she exited and headed back out to the work yard, leaving undetected. Nellie had not noticed her brief presence as she scurried about doing her work.

As Mimba stepped back onto the sandy soil of the work yard, she looked up and noticed another one of the enslaved workers heading toward her. Christmas Luke, a shorter middle-aged man with a mocha complexion and graying hair, was walking with his leather driver's gloves in one hand. Mimba assumed he must be preparing to drive one of the plantation's rigs somewhere.

"Yo' headin' somewhere, Christmas Luke? I see yo' got your special gloves wit' yo.'" Mimba nodded at his hand.

"Yes, gots to take Master Adrian into Charleston to do some

shoppin' for 'em. He's wantin' to buy hisself a new frock coat and a matchin' waistcoat. Seems he's getting as fat as a stuffed pigeon nowadays. Guess he's eating a little too well 'round here." He paused and chuckled as he spoke. "It will all go on da master's account, of course."

Mimba cocked her head and said, "Yes, Ma'sa Adrian been enjoyin' his good life 'round here on his uncle's plantation, don't he? I thought he was supposed to be off studying at Yale or sumthin'. What's he doing back here?"

Christmas Luke lowered his voice and took a step closer to Mimba to speak in a hushed tone. "I think Adrian was asked to take a semester off by the college president. Da ma'sa saved dat boy from bein' thrown out permanently from Yale. He got hisself into trouble there actin' up somehow. Ma'sa promised dat college some large gift, lots of money, if Adrian was allowed to come back next year."

Mimba shifted her stance and put one hand on her hip as she spoke. "Well dat boy thinkin' he's entitled to everythin' Master Langdon owns, includin' all us slave women and chillun. He thinks they's all his little presents."

"Yes, that boy does seem to enjoy his good life, don't he?" smiled Christmas Luke.

Mimba flashed a stern look. "I think he does a bit more than that. He forced hisself on Sally, that young colored girl who works up to the big house just a couple days after he got here."

"Oh no, I hadn't heard." Christmas Luke furrowed his brow.

"He beat her so hard to make her give in, she done lost a tooth. Then he made her please him again and again, all night long. Poor gal was all tore up." Mimba looked down and shook her head.

Christmas Luke remained silent as he listened carefully to Mimba.

"Then earlier this week, little Ginny was sent down to the creek to rinse out some dirty work clothes, and didn't that man snatch her up once she got out of ear shot? She just went into some of the brush where you couldn't see her from the big house, and he grabbed that poor chil' by her hair on the back of her head. That baby hadn't even had her first blood yet."

"Oh no, that poor chil'. Why does he have to pick on our babies?" Christmas Luke drew back with a hand on his hip and scowled.

Mimba went on. "She didn't understand what was happening to her. Afterward, Master Adrian just left her there. Someone came across her hours later. Her mama worked for hours to quiet her. Her face was all swelled up where he had punched her in the head. Her eye was swollen shut. Ginny bawled all night long 'til she cried herself to sleep."

Christmas Luke looked Mimba in the eye to try and quell her anger. "That poor gal. But you know, Mimba, ain't nothin' we can do about it. Just gots to accept it. You know that."

Mimba scowled again. "I know we gots to put up wit it, but it don't make it right."

Christmas Luke looked down and shook his head. He kicked at the dirt. "I know that, Mimba. The White buckra gets their way. Ain't nothin' us colored folks can do 'bout it. All we can do is hope freedom comes to us one day. Just pray 'bout it; dats all we can do."

Mimba whispered as she shook a finger at him, "Maybe a war is a to comin', Christmas Luke. We can pray our people gonna be set free. We may not see the end of it, but it's a comin'. I knows it. I feel the trembling in the land."

"Mimba, I know you're a holy woman who can speak with the spirits. You know what's coming better than me. Whatever hoodoo magic you got, you need to use it. Let there be a way we can see freedom come to us. It's going to have to be the work of the spirits or the hand of God that liberates us." Christmas Luke nodded and walked away.

Mimba nodded back and called, "Christmas Luke, I talk to the spirits 'bout it every day. Every *single* day."

Mimba headed on toward the kitchen house where she could hear Octavia, Hentie, and Nellie engaged in a conversation, along with a clamor of sounds—the beating of batter in an earthen bowl, the cracking of nutshells, the chopping of vegetables and a small child humming. She stepped inside the kitchen house where a young toddler child with caramel-colored skin and green eyes sat on the floor playing with a homemade doll. She was singing to herself as she gingerly manipulated the doll.

Mimba joined in the conversation and took in the aromatic odors of baking bread and chopped onion. She greeted the other women warmly.

"How you gals doin' this morning? I can smell that bread baking right now. I was in here a spell back and I couldn't smell nuttin' bakin' then. You got any biscuits a'goin'?"

"Not yet, Mimba, you're goin' to have to wait until dinner time for that. Master always wants those biscuits right outta da oven. And you best not let the ma'sa or mistress catch ya snatchin' one. You know how crazy she is 'bout thievery. She'd have us all whipped!"

"Oh, hush. That crazy woman don't scare me none. I'll just cast another hex on her to make her bark like a dog!" Mimba heaved with laughter picturing the mistress crawling around on all fours when she put that fix on her a few years back.

"That was something, I'll have to tell ya Mimba. That conjure was the best fix you ever done!" Octavia chuckled.

Mimba stepped back outside to watch Christmas Luke and Adrian get ready to leave the plantation.

Outside, Christmas Luke brought around the rig he was taking into town. He noticed Mimba standing outside the kitchen house but focused on the horses and making sure everything was carefully arranged in the bed of the wagon. He checked that the three empty barrels were secure and that he had remembered to bring extra ropes to tie down supplies for the plantation. He wanted it all in good order before Adrian jumped on board.

Mimba watched Adrian take long strides toward the buggy. He was immaculately dressed, his hair pomaded back, and a stiff collar on his white shirt. She looked upon him with hatred; she despised him for his brutality to the enslaved women. She quietly mouthed the words of a hex and poked her index and pinky fingers toward Adrian to force the dark spirits in his direction. Adrian was smoothing out his coat, unaware of Mimba's hex. As Mimba continued with her incantation, she reached around her neck and rubbed her gris-gris (mojo bag), which she had packed just a few weeks before. She had great skill as a root doctor and used that prowess in assembling the magical amulet. The bag held a combination of herbs, roots, and the feather of a great horned owl. The talisman held powerful magic that she hoped would inflict vengeance on Adrian for his cruel acts against the enslaved women on the plantation.

When Adrian finally glanced in Mimba's direction, he only caught her cold malevolent glare. Unaware of its significance, he dismissed her gaze and jumped onto the rig. Shortly thereafter, Christmas Luke snapped the reins and the two were off. Christmas Luke nodded at Mimba and waved at her as they passed. Mimba smiled knowingly as the buggy drew by her. A bit puzzled by Mimba's beaming gaze, Christmas Luke shook it off and proceeded on the journey.

Christmas Luke initially drove the buggy around to the front of the estate grounds and the entrance of the big house. Adrian shouted to Langdon who stood on the front portico as they passed by on the buckboard.

"Heading into Charleston to shop on King Street, stopping by Berlin's for some suiting," Adrian called out to his uncle.

"Fine, fine. I will have Nellie hold dinner for you if you're late," Langdon called back. "Christmas Luke, don't forget to get the salt and flour while you're in town. We're nearly out."

The two nodded at one another and the rig took off down the lane under the craggy oak trees draped in long swirls of Spanish moss. The air was pungent with the scent of the cavernous trees. Enjoying the shade of their large branches, the cooled air wafted over the two men as the team of horses trotted down the lane and onto the main road. Passing a neighboring planter, they waved to him as they continued down the thoroughfare.

The day was sunny with only a few clouds dotting the azure-blue skies. Adrian inhaled deeply to partake of the pleasant aromas of the magnolia trees, wisteria, and crepe myrtle. As the two men progressed down the road by the orderly rows of orchard trees, Adrian felt assured that all was right with the world. They first passed the pecan trees, then the adjacent peach orchard; the trees were vibrant and lush. Adrian was soothed by the scenes about him, occasionally jolted from his soothing thoughts by a rut in the road. Such privilege he was able to enjoy under the sheltering wing of his uncle. He wished it could go on forever, enjoying the life of a Southern planter, but not really having to work for it.

Suddenly, Adrian was thrust from his daydreams. The horses pulled against their harnesses, snorted, and roared like a trumpet. Their necks arched as they reared with fear. Christmas Luke pulled on the reins to control the team spooked by a copperhead slithering across the road. The large coppery-orange viper had a muscular, thick body over a yard in length with a triangular head. Christmas Luke recognized the venomous snake immediately. Trying to pull the team to the side of the road to avoid the viper, he looked down into the vertical pupils of the serpent's reddish-brown eyes that seemed to exude evilness, sending chills down his back.

While the snake progressed toward them, Christmas Luke was sitting on the left-hand side of the rig and attempted to veer the horses out of its way. The horses stomped and showed the whites of their eyes in terror. Crossing a bumpy stone bridge with waist-high flagstone walls at such high speed, the wagon was thrown off balance. The snake jerked upward and struck one of the horses, sending its poisonous venom into its leg. The horse snorted and reared, causing the entire rig to tilt to one side. Christmas Luke held onto the reins for dear life and attempted to calm the horses, to no avail. Simultaneously, Adrian slid to the end of the bench seat, throwing the wagon out of balance. It tipped over toward the water, rolling. Adrian was catapulted toward the river rocks below, his arms flailing as he flew through the air, wailing and unable to stop. The empty barrels were tossed into the air; one hit the rocks below, while the other two plummeted to the water and floated on the swift current. Adrian crashed on a large dark rock on the water's edge, his shattered body sprawled across a large slab of gray rock. His head tilted at an unnatural right angle. The commotion and banging sounds further frightened the horse team, and with adrenaline force, the pair pulled away from the wagon, snapping the breeching and traces to the rig. With frenetic energy, the horses galloped down the road.

Christmas Luke had been jolted from his seat, but due to his strong grip on the reins, was able to catch himself on the side of the rig, causing him to fall unevenly. He was pressed between the wagon and the stone wall. He had been battered, bumped, and bruised with a gash on his temple, but was otherwise all right, managing to hold onto the bridgework during the commotion, stopping a fall into the water below. He slowly slid and squirmed out from between the wall and the wagon, then called to Adrian.

Christmas Luke saw the horses in the distance still dragging parts of the breeching and front axle further down the road. Stretching out the cramping from his impact, he trudged back across the bridge, scanning the area for Adrian among the craggy trees and scrubby bushes. Finally, he looked down to scan the water's edge and saw Adrian crumpled on the rock below.

"Dear Jesus! What happened?" screamed Christmas Luke.

I bet that Mimba put a hex on that man. That's why she looked at Adrian that way. I knew that woman was up to something by the look on her face.

A few minutes later, a White planter, George Sneed, traveling in a surrey came upon the accident. Along with him was his wife and her cousin Amanda Rose Fripp who was visiting the family from Saint Helena Island. Mr. Sneed jumped down from his rig and offered to help. Christmas Luke was still panic-stricken, trying to find the words to explain what happened and motioning to Adrian's body on the rocks below.

"Oh, Good God! How could this happen?" exclaimed the White planter. "It doesn't make sense."

Christmas Luke was becoming alarmed that the White man thought it was a purposeful act.

"A snake! A snake scared the horses. I tried to lead the team away, but the snake struck out and bit one of the horses! There was nothing I could do!" he pleaded.

Mr. Sneed rushed down to Adrian and put his fingertips on his wrist. Not detecting a pulse, he looked upwards toward Christmas Luke and shook his head.

Quash, a young enslaved Negro, overhearing the commotion, jogged over to the scene. He was a half-hand worker at Twin Oaks plantation who had been collecting tinder wood and berries in the woods. Christmas Luke recognized the boy and asked him to run back to the plantation to get help. He said either Big John or Hentie would know what to do and to try and find them first. If he couldn't find them, he said to locate the overseer, but he thought he would be out in the fields somewhere and harder to find. Christmas Luke suspected Big John would be closer to the main house and easier to find. Quash dashed off for help, running as fast as he could, sucking in air as he sped through the woods.

While Christmas Luke paced, the tension between him and the White planter started to escalate. Other travelers began to come upon the scene; a man with dark hair in his early thirties, clad in a deep red shirt riding a mount. Then a rig holding three White men on their way to the waterfront to fish arrived. They looked to be working-class men in more modest attire, probably recent immigrants. It appeared they had been drinking spirits while on their trek.

Mr. Sneed asked, "Why didn't you reach out and save your master? You were able to save yourself? Look, you only have a gouge on your head and a few scratches, and that man has a broken neck."

Around the same time, two slave catchers approached the scene on foot. The role of the slave patrol was to enforce the laws governing Blacks, whether free or enslaved. There was a federal law, the Fugitive Slave Act, which controlled the movement of Negroes away from home, plus, there was the much more restrictive Black Code of South Carolina. The statute created the local slave patrols.

The men were rough and dirty and had obviously been traveling for some time. Their breeches were soiled, and their shirts were discolored with what appeared to be red wine stains and tobacco juice. The larger of the two men grunted, then turned his head and unapologetically spit a long stream of dark-brown juice out the side of his mouth, nodding as he wiped the remaining tobacco adhering to his lip with his already soiled sleeve.

"Hey boy! Whatcha been doing to that White man?" he bellowed toward the terrified Christmas Luke.

The dark-haired man with a straggly beard was the epitome of evil. He thrived on his work and doling out pain to helpless colored victims.

Frozen with fear and his eyes wide, Christmas Luke merely shook his head side to side.

The slave catcher shouted again at Christmas Luke. "Boy, what did you do? Did you kill that White man? Sure the hell looks that way to me!"

"No sir! I was ridin' into Charleston with my ma'sa and the horses got scared by the snake. We tried to calm em, but the copperhead struck one of em. You can check the horse. It must have a bite mark."

The slave catchers looked skeptical. "I don't see no snake 'round here. Don't see no tracks either."

"Sir, the horses may have covered them with their stompin' of their hooves. They were so scared," Christmas Luke pleaded.

The White men dismounted and began to encircle him. The slave trackers shouted their accusations calling him a "murderin' niggra." It was like the devil cast a dark heinous cloak over them; they were out for blood.

"You can never believe no stinkin' niggra. He done in his master plain and simple," shouted one of the slave catchers.

The White man wearing the deep red shirt who had approached on horseback thought he would clarify the controversy before him. He conceived it to be a fairly simple matter.

"We can't let no spook get away with killin' a White man, you know that, right?" He tilted his head as if he were asking the group to see reason. He glanced over to the three White men who were on their way to fish in the nearby Horlbeck Creek. One hooked his thumb in his belt and shook his head in the negative. One of his companions pulled a bottle of whiskey out from under the seat of the rig, took a long gulp, then passed it on to the third man seated up on the rig. He wiped his sleeve across his lips and let out a satisfied sound.

One of the White fishermen slipped his knife from a leather holder attached to his belt and said, "We can take care of this."

His traveling companion walked around to the back of Christmas Luke's rig and grabbed a couple of the lengths of rope he had spied.

"This here rope should do real nice." He nodded and looked over to his comrades.

"But I didn't do anything wrong! I swear to God. The horses reared and caused the wagon to turn over. I didn't kill this man. Believe me!" Christmas Luke pleaded.

From the nearby surrey owned by the White planter, two White women watched the exchange. One of the ladies wearing a pale green outfit, Amanda Rose Fripp, who was visiting from Saint Helena Island, became agitated. She shouted over to the men.

"You know you can't let a darkie get away with killing a White man. Robert Barnwell Rhett warns us about that all the time in his newspaper the *Mercury*. Those Negroes will have an uprising and kill us as we sleep! We can't let them get away with this kind of thing!"

While the White men turned to listen to Mrs. Fripp, Christmas Luke tried to run from the cluster of men. He managed to get several yards away, but the man in the red shirt pulled out a pistol from his waistband and shot him in the leg, propelling him forward as he fell flat onto the road. The shooter caught up with him and kicked him in the ribs with his heavy riding boot causing Christmas Luke to yelp.

"That was a stupid move there, boy! Might have thought about just slicing off an ear, but now you have forced our hands." He tucked the pistol between his scarlet shirt and trousers, then looked over to the other men with a crooked smile.

"We ain't got no choice now, men. I say we start by taking his ears for my special strand here," said one of the slave catchers, holding up his trophy necklace of human ears he had collected from runaway slaves. He sauntered toward Christmas Luke, his large girth encumbering his gait. The slave catcher wanted to make a long, drawn-out, tortuous event for the onlookers, a spectacle to entertain the gathered White folks with this poor Black man caught in this inescapable quagmire. A bit like a cat toying with a small rodent snapped up in a mouse trap with no means of escape. It was a barbaric display of the power.

The group closed in on Christmas Luke as he covered his head and begged for mercy from the malevolent group.

The slave catcher looked out to all those about him, turning his body as he did so. He pulled a long bowie knife from his belt and held it high up in the air for everyone to see. An audible gasp came from Mrs. Fripp. Apparently, she had never actually witnessed a torturous event such as this. Such deeds were done away from the sight of a proper lady.

"Mighty men and women of the South, we will not stand idly by and allow a niggra to take the life of a White man, especially a young man such as this, one of aristocratic blood. From the family of a planter! Nay! The Bible says that all slaves shall obey their masters! Isn't that right?"

"Yes, that's right! We all know that. It's written right in the Good Book!" shouted one of the men from the fishing party.

Cheers rose up from those gathered.

"I am here to demonstrate to you what will happen to those who disobey the law and God's plan. I have the righteousness of God behind me!"

"That's right! Do justice to him!" shouted one of the men.

"Punishment for Negroes who dare go against God's plan and the Black Code of this land. How dare he go against our institution!"

Christmas Luke pleaded for mercy. "But I did nothing wrong! I swear I did nothing against Master Adrian. Please believe me. I am a man of God!"

Christmas Luke began sobbing as two men rushed him and held him down. His piercing screams echoed through the trees as the slave catcher severed his ears, then some of his fingers.

Mrs. Fripp began to sob and walked back to the rig. She was muttering, "Oh, how could they do that to another human being?"

It was nearly a half hour later when Quash came again upon the overturned wagon and shouted back to Hentie, who was struggling to keep up with the young boy. She was getting older and not able to run as swiftly as a fit and nimble youth.

Initially, Hentie saw the wagon on its side, wedged against the stone wall. One of the horses had wandered back and was standing idly by the edge of the bridge, casually grazing on some grass. She scanned the scene quickly, looking for the crowd of White men that Samuel had described. But all was eerily quiet by the wagon, with no voices or discernible activity. Then Hentie began to look in earnest for Christmas Luke.

She noticed a length of rope hanging off the back of the wagon. It was odd, as she knew Christmas Luke would have taken a handful of ropes with him to tie down crates and barrels of goods for the trip back home. Puzzled, she looked off down the road.

About fifty yards down the road she spotted a light brown object. *What could that be?* A small animal, perhaps a rabbit, hiding in the grass?

As she approached it, an electric shock of recognition suddenly jolted through her as if it were a lightning bolt. *Oh no! This is a bad sign. That's one of Christmas Luke's shoes lying on the side of the road. They must have dragged him off.*

Hentie recognized the uniquely colored tan brogan he had received last Christmas when the slaves received their annual allotment of clothing. The shoes were an unusual shade of beige that everyone in the slave village noticed. They were good, store-bought shoes the Langdon had rewarded Christmas Luke with for his decades of loyal service, and his never-ending devotion to the lord of the plantation.

Hentie turned to Quash and said, "Oh God! Where did they take that poor man? Maybe they took Christmas Luke back to the plantation for the master to deal with there?"

"Don't know, ma'am. Them White men sure was mad."

"Let's hope he wasn't taken down to the sugar house. God only knows what might happen to him there. They'll whip that man until the skin comes off his back. He is an old man now. He'll never survive an ordeal like that," Hentie said with terror in her eyes.

Hentie took several steps forward, then stopped dead in her tracks. She saw a vague shadow ahead. Gently swaying, something dangled from a tree. At first, she thought, or at least hoped, it was a broken branch hanging down, or perhaps a clump of Spanish moss.

Frightened for Christmas Luke, her eyes welled up with tears. She knew what had likely occurred. An eldritch sense of foreboding tiptoed up her spine.

Hentie turned to Quash and said, "You go back to the wagon and wait for me there."

Hentie forced herself to move forward several steps, but then unable to propel her body any farther, paused and almost sensed a negative energy in the air, like pinpricks. Frozen in terror, her heart dropped to her stomach. After a few beats, she regained her composure and slowly moved forward, looking upon the hanging massive form.

As she approached, she could discern what appeared to be a dangling lifeless form. In this massive ancient oak tree with branches angling in all directions was a human being, a man of God who had at one time been full of vigor, now dangling at the end of the rope; a colored man with a stout frame, graying hair, and deep facial wrinkles from working in the sun and from his frequent smiles. But now, his head was twisted at an unnatural angle.

Hentie couldn't avert her eyes. Stunned by the gruesome sight before her, she gasped and covered her mouth; she could feel vomit surge up into her throat and felt herself begin to gag. The man's swollen face made it difficult to recognize him at first; his body was battered and bloody. Nonetheless, Hentie knew it must be Christmas Luke. She recognized his shirt and of course, Christmas Luke's familiar shoe. The one remaining tawny-colored brogan that Langdon had given to Christmas Luke during the holiday season. It was well-worn with a homespun shoelace.

There was little sign that just minutes before, this lifeless form had contained the soul of a God-fearing man who did so much to share His word. Hentie looked more carefully at the scarlet streaks that ran down from the sides of his head onto his oatmeal-colored Negro cloth shirt. His ears had been hacked off. Some of his fingers were missing. Stunned by the brutality of his death, she stood engrossed, fixed on the lifeless form. She could hear the echoes of his screams; such pain and horror must have erupted from him just minutes ago. Such unspeakable cruelty. *How could men do this to another man?* His hands had been tightly bound together; there was nothing he could do to fight off his attackers.

Knowing his gentle soul must have risen to the heavens, Hentie shook her head and hoped that God could offer him the comfort he so deeply deserved. Tears streamed; she wanted to somehow put him back together and bring him back to life, but knowing she had no power to do so, she just sobbed. She stood staring at him, shamelessly weeping aloud. He was gone.

Christmas Luke's mouth was agape as if he were still trying to take in his last gasp of air, or perhaps, beg his captors for mercy. One could almost still hear him pleading for his life and the final, deep, guttural sounds of pain lingering in the air. The panic he must have felt in those last moments. His eyes had remained open, focused on the White buckra who had condemned him to die in such a manner, staring into their demon-like souls. As his soul slowly leaked out of its battered vessel, he must have looked on the men with contempt, knowing that one day they would be judged as they had judged him when they faced their maker. Unable to dispel this image from her thoughts, Hentie shook her head as if she could somehow jar it from her own mind's eye.

The following day, Big John, Hentie, and Octavia were in the warming kitchen talking about Christmas Luke and the horrible way his life had ended. Some of the enslaved workers had gone to the site, cut down the body from the large branch, and brought it back to the plantation so that what remained of this godly man could be buried in a slave cemetery.

"It was horrible what they done to Christmas Luke. I could barely recognize him with his face all beaten and his ears hacked off. What come over them men to do that to him? They knew he wouldn't kill a White man." Big John scowled as he looked downward.

"I don't know, Big John. I think dat White men around here are just getting' all worked up. I tink they're 'fraid of da idea that Black folks might be free one day. It scares dem. What if a war do come? I think dey worry about Black folk rising up against them."

"I know the master been havin' some of those meetin's down to our lower storage barn. Dey call themselves the Knights of the Golden Circle, and dey wear some fancy robes 'n silky aprons. I've seen dem through a knot hole in the barn's boards. Juba and Cuffee told me about their meetin's too. Dem White men come here to the plantation and talk 'bout states' rights and keepin' slavery going. Dey think dey are being secretive, but how can you not notice when all their buggies are here? I know dey move around to different plantations, and sometimes 'dey meet over in Charleston. I think dey are gettin' all worked up 'bout things. I hear dem hollerin' when their meetin's are going on."

"I suppose dey be scared. Dey don't know what dey will do if they don't have their slaves to do their work for them. How will all that dang cotton get picked and their fields be tended to?" Hentie waved her hand as if to erase the idea and then piled some of the dirty dishes from supper.

With a heavy sigh, Big John started to speak. "Master Langdon had me go down and retrieve Master Adrian's body from the riverbed. I made sure to take a couple of White men down with me when I did it. I wanted them to look at his body first so they could see if there had been anything other than a rearing horse that caused him to fall. Both men carefully looked over the body before we carried him off. They agreed. Didn't look like there had been a fight or a struggle. There weren't any weapons like a gun or knife found, neither. It was just an accident. That's all."

The three enslaved house servants heard the doorknocker on the front door to the mansion house. They paused momentarily and looked at one another, concerned as to who the caller might be. Big John, Hentie, and Octavia quietly stepped toward the front hallway waiting until the butler, Samuel, answered the door. Hentie wiped her hands on the skirt of her pinny and drew in a deep breath as she tried to steady herself. Big John placed his warm, comforting hand on her shoulder to calm her.

Two gentlemen callers stepped into the foyer as Samuel bowed and lowered his eyes in their presence.

"Good evening, gentlemen. May I be of service to you?"

"Yes, we are here to speak with Mister Langdon. Is he at home?"

"I will check. May I ask your names? I believe you are planters from the area?"

The two planters responded, "Yes, yes. He will know us. Just tell him Pinckney and Drayton are here."

"Yes sir, would you like to come into the parlor while you wait?" Samuel guided the two White planters into an adjacent room.

"Yes, of course," one responded as he looked about the fine carvings in the entry way and the heavy mahogany doors with brass fittings and heavy glass transoms. He glanced downward at the polished black-and-white marble flooring as he walked across into the parlor.

"What do you think they here about?" asked Hentie as she turned to the other two enslaved workers.

"Lord, it could be anything. I wonder if it has anything to do with Christmas Luke," whispered Octavia.

"Those men are part of that Knights group. I wonder why they are coming to the big house this time of night," Big John said with a puzzled look.

After a few minutes, William Langdon came out and greeted the men and then asked them to come back to his library. Hentie stepped out from the butler's pantry to see if her master might want libations for his guests.

"Yes, bring some brandy and port. I know these men will be needing some evening spirits."

"Yes sir. I will bring it right away." Hentie was quick to give a brief curtsey and dipped her chin to her master and his guests.

Hentie turned quickly. Her skirts swished about her as she scurried to retrieve a silver platter and crystal stemware.

"Put a few biscuits and cheese on a china plate and some nuts in a bowl too, Octavia. We better do all that we can to please dat master. Dem men can't be up to no good," scowled Hentie.

As the men walked back to the library, Hentie could hear the heels of their booted feet thumping against the floorboards. Their heavy footsteps conveyed the gravity of their impending discussion. Once the men entered the library, Langdon solidly closed the door shut.

Hentie took a deep breath, knowing she needed to carefully carry in the tray to the men, attend to them politely, and melt into the background of the room. She shook out her hands as she felt her heart flutter and tension build in her chest. Running her hands down the front of her skirt, she hoped that would help to soothe her nerves.

As Octavia set down the tray, Hentie straightened her back. Once Octavia stepped back and nodded at her, Hentie bent her knees, drew in a breath, and lifted the tray onto her palm. She took careful, measured strides, trying to loosen the tension in her body as she progressed toward the study. Once she came to the door, Hentie hesitated, licking her lips and moving back and forth on either foot. Then drawing in a breath, she tapped on the door and entered when the master acknowledged her.

"Yes, you may enter," bellowed Langdon.

"Good evening, sir. I brought you and your guests some brandy and port. Got some fresh crystal glasses too, sir. Octavia done put together some small toasts and cheese for the guests, Sir. She was thinkin' they might enjoy some 'bout now." Hentie then carefully set down the tray on a side table and turned to her master and inquired, "Shall I serve, sir, or shall you?"

"No, I'll handle it."

Hentie gave a quick curtsy and nod, then assumed her position against the wall. Hentie knew it was her role to remain ready to serve her master but to remain inconspicuous. She found it best to stand near the heavy damask draperies where she could melt into the background. She stood with a tea towel over her arm, ready to step into action when summoned.

"Well, it was unfortunate that you lost a favorite niggra slave today, but things got out of hand, William. Those slave catchers got the White men all riled up, and they felt compelled to do something. Remember, a White man was dead. The only other person there was a darkie. They just assumed he had something to do with it. It was just a quick judgment, could have happened to anyone." Drayton looked at Langdon as he carelessly tossed back some port.

Hentie turned her head the other way and blinked to stop from tearing up. She couldn't believe the topic of discussion was the brutal beating and lynching of a dutiful slave and kind man.

Just a quick judgment call? A mistake anyone could make? Did that include slicing off his ears and cutting off his fingers before they watched a man strangle and die?

Langdon drew in a deep breath, looked away from the gentlemen and gazed out the window. He exhaled brusquely. After pausing a few beats, he drew in a long sip of amber liquid from his brandy snifter and pensively considered his words. He turned back to his guests.

"I understand the need to keep the darkies in check, but Christmas Luke was one of my most highly trained slaves. He was a good valet and loyal servant worth over a thousand dollars! Who is going to compensate me for that? It's like losing fine gelding. One cannot readily replace such stock."

The two visitors looked at one another puzzled by the query as though they had never contemplated such a question.

"It had to be done, William. What can I say? We need to keep the niggras scared and in line. You can't question what's gone on here for generations. It's a loss you have to take, for all of us. You just need to assume it."

Langdon just looked down, shook his head, and threw back the rest of his brandy.

Chapter 3
Hentie and Big John's Life at Twin Oaks Plantation

Mount Pleasant, South Carolina, 1860

A dark cloud hung over Twin Oaks plantation following the brutal death of Christmas Luke. A kind, righteous man of God, he had been beloved by the slave community. It had been several days since his burial, and Hentie still felt a heaviness in her heart. The image of his mutilated body hanging from a tree haunted her day and night. Feeling the gravity of it all, she was still forced to carry on her duties. Black folks were never given time to grieve.

A few weeks before, Langdon allowed a few of the enslaved Black men to take an old wagon to the hangin' tree to retrieve Christmas Luke's grisly, blood-soaked body. For their protection, they were accompanied by a White overseer and a White neighbor. It about ripped their hearts in half when they had to cut down Christmas Luke's mortal remains. If they hadn't known it was him, they wouldn't have recognized him. His body and face were all bloated from the beating he had taken; one eye was sunken back in his skull. Most of his fingers were missing; nearly all were bloody stubs. All of the Black men who retrieved Christmas Luke's body had tears streaming; Caesar, Christmas Luke's closest friend, openly wailed and couldn't stop sobbing. They carried his corpse back to the wagon where they prepped his body. The men covered Christmas Luke's face with a cloth and wrapped the rest of his body in oatmeal-colored Negro cloth, then drove back to the plantation. The enslaved workers down in the village had to wait until the workday was done before they could bury him. Langdon wouldn't allow the Negroes to take the workday off for a funeral, no matter how loyal a servant Christmas Luke had been.

After a twelve-hour day in the fields, the enslaved workers were hungry. After returning to the slave village at first dark, the bondsmen choked down fish stew and bread as fast as they could before they started their solemn funeral procession. Langdon wouldn't give up any valuable land for the burial of the enslaved, so at the rear of the plantation in a secluded area where the brambles and underbrush grew lush was a cemetery for enslaved Blacks. It was far away from the public eye where White folks wouldn't have to look upon it. Here, unable to afford proper headstones, hand-carved grave markers and simple crosses dotted the land. Traditional hymns were sung by all the enslaved as they made their way to the hallowed ground. Four men, including Big John and Caesar, carried the wrapped remains, walking in the center of a procession lit by torches being carried by others.

For the Gullah-Geechee people, it was important that graves be near the water, whether it be a marsh, a river, or the ocean. This allowed the spirit of the decedent to travel back home to Africa and be at peace. It was believed that the spirit, like the sun, traveled from east to west; therefore, the body of the dead was oriented eastward. Graves weren't marked in the traditional ways the White buckra used. Enslaved Negroes didn't have the money for headstones and didn't know how to spell. So, the Gullah would outline the grave with conch shells that represented the ocean that the Africans had crossed during the Middle Passage from their homeland to the Deep South.

Once the shells were in place, someone would announce, "The sea brought us, and the sea shall take us back."

Those from the slave village marked the site with a plant and items that were personal to the decedent, such as a button from their shirt or a lock of hair. Or perhaps they would mark the site with the last thing the person used, such as a cup, which their next of kin would break, symbolizing the ending of things in this world.

Nellie, the plump, dark-skinned cook, dropped a heavy iron pot on the stove. The clamor caused Hentie to snap out of grieving over Christmas Luke and return to work. Hentie and Nellie had already been up for several hours tending to matters in the kitchen house. They had baked a variety of sweets and biscuits for later in the day. Hentie had been back and forth between the mansion and the warming kitchen house to assist with setting up for an event. The mistress had invited her lady friends to the plantation for afternoon tea. Mrs. Langdon also had her cousin, Sarah Chase, and her son Elliott, from Pennsylvania, visiting for a few weeks. They had come for Adrian's funeral service, but any company always sent the missus in a tizzy.

As they were working, Nellie made more room to allow the baked goods to cool by moving some of the pots and pans around on the worktable. Then, Nellie held up a jug, one that had often been used to carry milk from the dairy house. She paused and told Hentie, "You see this here jug? I ain't never used it ever since Juba got sold for bumping into the ma'sa and spilling milk on him all those years ago." Nellie stared at it for a long moment, remembering the day it happened.

"Oh Nellie, what a sad day that must have been. That poor colored girl. Juba never deserved to be whipped so badly . . . then sold." Hentie looked down as sadness overcame her.

"The master was evil as a serpent that day, just lookin' for someone to take his anger out on. Course, like always, it's us colored folk who takes it. He was still vexed cause he done in Baby Doll, strangled the woman with his own hands. He regretted it but couldn't take it back. Juba just happened to be in his way, and he threw his rage all on her," Nellie huffed.

"Gots to watch the ma'sa. You don't have to do wrong to get whipped. Just be 'round him when he in a mood," cautioned Hentie.

"Don't I know it! That man can turn on you in a second. He was carryin' on with Baby Doll for a long time when he kilt her. Mmm mmm. Such a sad endin'." Nellie shook her head and shuffled over to the oven to check on some scones.

Hentie added to the story. "Ma'sa had a baby with her. Now his son, Tobias, born of a negress, don't have no mama. He done kilt her. Ma'sa knew little Tobias was his, even though he never owned up to it."

"Dang, that boy was the spittin' image of the ma'sa and his own son, Fitzwilliam. People used to confuse those boys all da time." Nellie chuckled at the thought of how they confused a slave boy for the master's legitimate White son.

Hentie spoke softly as she recalled nearly twenty years ago. "Yes, I 'member when Baby Doll passed. We all knew what musta happened. Gettin' different treatment all those years and gifts from him, carries a burden with it. Doll was always his special gal, but she was still a mulatto slave. Wasn't no changin' that. You never know when a White buckra master gonna tire of a Negro mistress."

"She wasn't no mistress. You mean that child was forced to be his whore, don't you? She wasn't much more than a child herself when the ma'sa started up with her." Hentie's eyebrows scrunched together, and her forehead wrinkled as she shot a scowling look at Nellie.

"Yeah, s'pose your right 'bout dat," Nellie nodded in agreement.

Hentie carefully stacked up the hobnobs, bourbon biscuits, and Cornish fairing cookies in neat stacks on a colorful Delft blue china serving platter, then brushed her hands on her apron. She stood back and admired the array of treats on the fine Dutch platter coated with the shiny tin glaze that glittered so nicely in the sunshine.

"We'll have to put this platter on the table right in front of the main window. It looks so fancy. The missus will love it. I'll make sure to put a blue linen cloth under it to show it off," smiled Hentie.

"Yeah, you know how the missus loves to show off in front of those fancy friends of hers," snorted Nellie.

"I know, just once I'd love to drop a glass of punch down her finest dress the way she has us run 'round here for her events. No wonder the master kept a woman like Baby Doll who used to act like he hung the moon!"

"Gots to say, Baby Doll was a beautiful young woman. But she shouldn't have pushed the ma'sa like she did for her freedom papers. Just cause he treated her special and had a child with her and all, she started to forget her place. Black folks can never do that." Nellie waved her finger and shook her head as she scraped off a baking sheet.

"Well, he knew he done wrong. Drowning his special mistress, then leaving her dead body with her crying baby right there. No wonder he felt so much guilt." Nellie shook her head and kept working the dough with her flour-covered hands. Then he never treated Tobias right his whole life. Such a good boy and lookin' just like his daddy, the ma'sa."

"Well, none of it was right. Guess it was about a week after he done in Baby Doll that Juba bumped into the ma'sa while tottin' that milk."

"Poor Juba come runnin' in here to the kitchen house to figure out what the ma'sa was shoutin' about. She musta thought a cookin' fire got outta hand or somethin'. Just the ma'sa having a fit like a spoiled child. Stupid White buckra shoulda been happy she was tryin' to save his damn house," Nellie huffed. She dropped more dough on the worktable from a higher-than-usual height. It made a loud thud when it hit. She pounded it with a floured rolling pin, then rolled it out.

"I 'member Big John carrying poor Juba to the sick house after her whippin'. Skin was near lifted off her back. Dang near put her eye out too. She musta turned at some point while the bullwhip was in the air. We weren't sure if she'd live. All over a little damn spilled milk." Hentie furled her brow and continued to arrange the delicate pastries on an English bone-china platter.

"The master was just havin' a fit and needed a dog to kick or a slave to beat, and Juba happened to show up first. Juba didn't know what was happenin' when she heard all the bangin' around. She ran in to help and bumped the ma'sa while she was carrying this here jug. Ma'sa found hisself an excuse to wallop a colored gal, is what he did. Plain and simple," Nellie jerked her head to reaffirm her account of what happened and lifted the jug in the air.

"Not right, Hentie. Just not right," Nellie said.

"I know, none of it right." Hentie dropped her fist into the center of a heap of dough as she released a ragged exhale. "Worst part of it is the ma'sa split up Juba and Cuffee when he sold her off. They was just newlyweds." She yanked out a rag, wiped her hand, and started to assemble small tea sandwiches made of cucumbers and special cheeses.

Nellie stepped a bit closer and lowered her voice. "You ever hear what happened to them? I know that Big John hears lots of things down on the waterfront. He talks to a lot of folks down there. He gives folks good information and gets some in return through da watermen."

Hentie nodded and stepped around the worktable. "There's a whole web of men down on the waterfront who share information, you know. Big John been a part of that for years. He's been helpin' with the Underground."

Nellie lowered her voice another notch. "You know I would never tell a soul Big John can read, but that man probably know more about what goes 'round this here plantation than any of the White buckra. So many people rely on him, including the ma'sa. Poor Ma'sa doesn't even realize that his dang slave knows more than he do!" Nellie laughed and slapped her thigh.

Hentie looked down as she arranged the food. "I know, my

man knows so dang much from lookin' over the plantation ledgers, glancing at the ma'sa's mail and all his papers. And the ma'sa has no idea Big John can read! Then he hears so much down on the waterfront from the colored men workin' on the boats and wharfs. They's a number of conductors on the Underground. Big John's the hub on the wheel in this network. Men tell him lots of stuff. Seems when ma'sa had Juba taken into Charleston to be sold, some man from down in Beaufort bought her. I think she livin' in a city house there. It's down around Port Royal Sound in some of them Sea Islands. I believe it's about seventy miles south a' here by water."

"Poor girl. Such a dreadful thing to bust up a family, 'specially man and wife. They was so in love. It hadn't been too long after Juba and Cuffee had jumped the broom." Nellie sprinkled some flour on the worktable to start another batch of scones.

"They were so happy when they found each other. I was so happy for em. Ain't sure what happened to Cuffee after he left here lookin' for her," Hentie said.

"I know he started out with help. Conductors got him part of the way. I 'member Big John managed to trade and get him some new boots and socks 'fore he ran." Nellie rolled out the dough as she spoke.

"Yeah, folks helped him hide and get him along his way to Juba, but I ain't sure how it ended up. I believe some minister down in Beaufort said he'd let em hide out in a shed or barn." Hentie shuffled to the oven and slid in a pan of blueberry scones.

"Guess we'll never know. Dem poor folks. Let's just hope the Lawd God watchin' over dem," said Nellie.

"Well, let's hope so. I'm going back over to the big house and see how things are going there. You okay here?"

"You go on, girl, I'll be fine. I'll head over in a bit." Nellie nodded and turned back to her work.

Hentie headed outside and ambled toward the mansion house, taking in the surroundings as she did so. The low gray clouds overhead, filled with moisture, were beginning to roll out toward the river, then onward to the sea. In the distance, Hentie heard a dog barking at the rumbling thunder, but his objections trickled down to a whimper, then silence as the storm moved out. The recent rain made the air heavy with moisture, laden with the earthy scent of wet soil and the sweet scent of saturated blossoms.

Hentie paused for a moment to breathe the aroma as the sun winked out from behind the clouds. She inhaled deeply and held her breath for a few seconds, leaning on a fencepost and recalling for just a moment the rich floral smell from her childhood in her homeland of Africa, the image of her and her mother holding hands in the sunlight, taking in the morning's aromatic scents. Dewey drops hung from beautiful bursts of color—scarlet, magenta, and deep red. The warmth of the sun and the richness of the colors surged through her memory.

Her thoughts were suddenly invaded by the scene of her capture decades ago back in her native Sierra Leone. On that day, all had seemed right with the world. She had been carrying out her daily chores wholly unaware that marauders were watching nearby. Hentie's mother was standing not too far from her, chatting with another villager. They winnowed rice in large round fanning baskets. Hentie's husband and a handful of other men from the village were cleaning wild game from the morning hunt. All were in good humor from the success of their outing, jesting with one another, laughing. Hentie's beautiful young daughter, Amahle, walked by and gently touched her on the arm as she passed, then turned back and gave her a warm smile.

Seemingly from nowhere, a hostile tribe appeared and ambushed the villagers. Hentie winced at the memory of it. The abductors threw nets over them, gathering them up like a school of fish. After their capture, they were all marched in a coffle while in fetters to the African coast, where a British slave trader and his ship awaited.

Their bindings cut into their flesh causing swelling in their hands and feet and bleeding where they cut into their ankles and wrists. Many were barefoot and suffered cuts and gashes along the march through the interior of Africa. If they were rendered incapable, they were abandoned, tossed aside as useless merchandise. Typically, up to half perished on the march to the coast.

Ugly memories of the slave ship came to her in flashes. Hentie recalled Amahle's long, sleek body being held down by three large White men as they branded her with a red-hot iron, her head jerking upward as she screamed in agony. Hentie's heart skipped beats and blood rushed to her head as she pictured the lewd captain who walked over to Amahle, reached down, and cradled her face, his thumb caressing her smooth skin. "You'll be mine, precious girl. You'll be mine." As he chuckled, he revealed gray rotting teeth. It made Hentie squirm even now.

Hentie's last memory of Amahle was her final act, when she seized an opportunity to end the captain's near-daily sexual assaults on her. On that particular day when the prisoners were brought up from the hull of the ship, Amahle acted on a plan she had hatched days before. The captain grabbed Amahle by the hair on the back of her head and pulled her from the cluster of other captives. He pinned her against the side of the ship with the weight of his body while he started to fondle her breasts. Amahle decided she had endured enough. Seized with rage, adrenaline gave her the strength of a bull. She wrapped her arms and legs around the captain and flipped her body backward over the railing of the ship.

Hentie recalled the glimpse of the horror that passed over the captain's face, his mouth agape, his eyes wide and terrified as both fell overboard. His arms started flailing in mid-air as he howled.

After the captain hit the dark blue-green, choppy ocean water, he momentarily became submerged before his head bobbed above the waves. An awaiting hungry shark surged toward him as his arms started slapping the water, the sleeves of his uniform visible. In a few beats, he disappeared under blood-reddened water.

Amahle dogpaddled nearby trying to remain afloat. She took a few gulps of water as she went under a swell in the blue abyss. She appeared again, but soon, the same fate befell her. She wailed as she was pulled under by a large, silver sea creature. Hentie wept but accepted that her daughter chose this end, allowing her spirit to return across the waters to Africa.

Abruptly, Hentie was flung back to the present. She shook off those ugly memories and prodded her body back into motion.

I best get back to my chores here. I can't get caught daydreaming like this. I might get whipped but good for dawdling. If I want to stay alive, I gots to keep my mind on my work. I have been fortunate so far. I never had a bull whip used on me. Been slapped by that crazy mistress, had her throw books at me and call me filthy names, but ain't never had nothing but some cuts and bruises from a crazy lazy. I's lucky.

She shook off the thoughts and focused on the missus' afternoon tea party.

⁓

Hentie hurried onward to the big house and entered through the rear door into the warming kitchen where Octavia, the mistress' lady's maid, and Nellie, the head cook, were fussing over silver serving trays and setting them full of tea sandwiches, scones, and various cookies and chopped nuts. They were preparing high tea for Mistress Langdon and some of her gossipy lady friends. The White ladies in the fine garments would be arriving later that afternoon, and a perfect presentation of the food and teas was a must.

The enslaved house servants wore their best house dresses and long white aprons. Their ensembles were recently pressed and brushed with herbal leaves to freshen them. Looking at their crisp appearance, Hentie peered down at her rumbled apron and smoothed it with her calloused hands, catching them on its fibers.

Suddenly, Octavia dove toward her and started fussing with Hentie's hair and retying the bow on the back of her apron.

"Octavia! You like to knock the air out of me!" Hentie hissed.

"It's better I knock ta air out of you then that crazy mistress has you whipped for lookin' like such a sight in front of her friends."

Hentie stopped fidgeting, knowing Octavia was right. She had to look neat and pressed or the missus would throw a fit.

They would be serving in a large parlor that overlooked the rolling front lawn with its freshly trimmed ornamental garden. Plantings had been brought from Europe years before to fill out the design of the landscape, the colors perfectly coordinated for the greatest impact. The parlor was perfect for entertaining with its large, overstuffed chairs and long settees. It provided an ideal setting for the ladies to gather and gossip.

Octavia spun on her heels and quickly moved in the opposite direction. "I best get upstairs now and make sure the mistress' hair is lookin' fine and still perfectly pinned up. She'll be wantin' to get that new gown on 'bout now." Octavia turned and started up the back stairwell to the mistress' bedroom.

Flora, one of the enslaved workers, suddenly appeared at the back door of the big house looking for Nellie. Her deep brown eyes were full of pain as tears flowed down her coffee-colored cheeks. She held her right hand upright, bent at the elbow and wrapped in a rag. Her arm was tense, emphasizing the definition of the muscles from years of physical labor.

As she swiftly entered the back door, she looked into Nellie's eyes with a pleadingly. "You got some salve that can help my burns? I done spilled some boiling water with lye on my hand. It's eating my flesh off!"

"Oh, you poor child! Come with me. Did you already flush it with some cold water?"

"Yes ma'am," Flora answered brusquely with pain in her voice as she bobbed her head.

"We'll flush it again and put some pokeweed salve on it," Nellie said. She swiftly but gently guided Flora along and headed to the sick house where Nellie kept a stash of homemade remedies to dress the cuts and burns of the enslaved workers. The Gullah workers didn't have any White-man medicine, but Nellie had a variety of herbal remedies, including salves and oils from African and Native American traditions.

Big John walked in through the back door with a large pitcher of freshly made brewed green tea for the mistress and her lady friends. Hentie and Big John were finally permitted to marry two years ago after years of mutual service to Langdon. They casually brushed up against each other as Hentie retrieved the pitcher from him. She looked up and smiled at his kind face.

There was a casual ease between Hentie and Big John. They were very bonded and comfortable as man and wife. Big John had been smitten from the outset; Hentie had taken a while to come around. She had been anxious about gaining her master's consent for their union. Langdon might have thought she would somehow hinder Big John's work, but instead, she supported him however she could, and fortunately, the master realized that fact.

Langdon relied heavily on Big John. Even though he wasn't his overseer or driver, Big John was Langdon's valet and closest adviser. Langdon's son, Fitzwilliam, had never shown much interest in the plantation. He always knew his life would be away from running Twin Oaks; Fitz would have others do it for him. This only increased Langdon's reliance on Big John, who held great influence over him, more than Langdon realized.

Big John was very crafty with his approach. He was always careful to allow his master to think new ideas were his own, not the suggestion of an enslaved Negro. He made sure to give his master credit for an innovative idea he had planted, then he would congratulate his master for his cleverness. Langdon was a planter of English descent, an aristocrat that thought very highly of himself and his lineage. Tall, broad-shouldered, fair-haired with pale blue eyes, a man who considered himself a descendant of a race of masters, intended by God to rule over the lesser Negro slaves.

⸻

While Big John lived in the Caribbean as a young man, he had surreptitiously learned how to read before he landed in Charleston. The wife of his former master had taught him the alphabet and the fundamentals of reading during his Bible lessons, as she believed it was her Christian duty. Due to his literacy, Big John could casually check what his master recorded in his ledgers and the content of the letters Langdon penned. Big John never revealed his vast knowledge of accounts, inventory, cultivating crops, and the annual harvest.

Most importantly to Hentie, Big John was able to plant the idea of his marriage to her with Langdon, so that he thought it was his own notion. Langdon grew to believe that marriage would lend even greater stability to Big John's life, keep him anchored, and ensure he would remain grounded at Twin Oaks. While the Black Code did not actually recognize the lawful marriage of two enslaved Negroes since they were regarded as chattel property, ceremonies and rituals sometimes marked the occasion. Thankfully, Langdon permitted the union in the formal garden and a large celebration down in the slave village at the rear of the plantation. Due to the special affinity Langdon had for Big John, he had even allowed a barrow pig and two hens to be slaughtered to add to the feast. Rarely did food rations extend beyond the typical one pound of meat per slave per week, along with rice, corn meal, lard, and flour. Slave rations were carefully doled out on Saturdays after the day's work was completed. The wedding of Big John and Hentie was an exception.

Due to their informal union, now Hentie and Big John could progress through life with some level of confidence that they were recognized, at least by their master, as man and wife. The two enjoyed some assurance that they could remain with one another without being sold off to another plantation, a feat most never accomplished. The warmth and affection of Hentie and Big John had only grown over the years. Big John was a good man, smart, warm and caring. He was also immense, well over six feet tall with big hands and fingers like sausages, but his touch was gentle. He appreciated Hentie's kind spirit and understanding ways.

While Big John continued to linger in the warming kitchen to pull out some of the larger silver pieces stored on the higher shelves, Octavia came rushing down the stairs with her eyes wide open and her face full of fury. Obviously, the mistress had said something to perturb her, as she often did these days.

"I swear dat woman is crazier dan a bed bug, and one day I'm gonna to quit coverin' for her. I'm gonna let her refined friends know what a nutty lady she done is. Do you know what she just done to me? She had me chasin' all dem little haints out da upstairs. Like I ain't got nothin' better to do right 'fore a party at dat mansion house. She had me pourin' salt in front of all dat windows and beatin' two sticks together down all da damn hallways to scare away da boo-hags. I felt like a damn fool!"

Big John and Hentie paused for a moment, wanting to be supportive to their good friend, but looked at one another and burst out laughing.

"Now what y'all laughin' 'bout? Next time I'm going to tell dat crazy woman she should have you do it, Hentie, cause you're so much better at it. Or better yet, I'd like to see Big John beating dem little sticks down da damn hallways. We'd all get a good laugh outta that!" All three broke up laughing at the thought of Big John's huge frame bent over with little sticks chasing haints down the hallway.

"It would be like Big John chasing chickens outta the hen house!" Octavia was holding her stomach from laughing so hard.

But then they all heard a loud thud and the laughter stopped abruptly. God only knew what the mistress might have done. Octavia gasped and pounded her fist on the counter. She let out an exclamation as she gathered up her skirt in one hand, turned, and ran up the back stairwell. Big John and Hentie turned to each other with a questioning glance, then quickly followed Octavia. They were afraid that the missus might have become unsteady on her feet again from taking too many opium drops. Perhaps her nerves were acting up since company was coming and her cousin had been at the house for a handful of days now.

When they entered the mistress' large bedroom suite, they saw her cousin, Sarah Chase, bent over Mrs. Langdon. Sarah's cheeks were bright pink and her face full of horror.

The missus' cousin blurted out, "I've never seen her like this! Her eyes just rolled back, and she crumpled on the floor. What's wrong with her? Did she have a fit or something?" Mrs. Chase shrilled.

Big John walked toward the missus and propped her up, then started to lift her, but the missus objected.

"No, I don't need anyone's help. I'm just fine . . . REALLY, I am." But then her eyes rolled up into her head and she fell backward.

"Y'all go ahead, Big John. Us womenfolk can take care of her. You best let the ma'sa know what has happened." Octavia nodded at him with a knowing look.

"Yes, I expect so. Guests are due shortly." He hurried out of the room to try to locate Langdon.

Hentie rushed to Mrs. Chase's side, while Octavia did her best to rouse Mrs. Langdon. Believing that she had the right to touch a White woman under these circumstances, Octavia scooped her up in one sturdy arm. Grasping the woman's upper arm, she began to tap her face with her other hand. Mrs. Chase stepped back, still horrified that her cousin was either having a fit or was inebriated.

"Mrs. Langdon. Mrs. Langdon. Wake up. You've got guests a comin'. You need to open your eyes now and get ready," Octavia urged.

Octavia glanced over to Hentie and said, "Go over to her side table and pour some water from that pitcher. Give me a glass of it." She pointed her finger in the direction of the porcelain pitcher and wash basin.

Hentie sprang into action and quickly retrieved a glassful of cool water and brought it over to Octavia. While Octavia still supported the mistress with one arm, she dipped three of her fingers into the glass and spritzed the water into the mistress' face. The mistress twitched, and Octavia repeated the act, this time with more water. The mistress' eyes flapped open, and her mouth gaped.

"What? What happened?" The mistress shouted at Octavia in an accusatory tone.

"Well ma'am, I'm thinkin' you may have took too many of those drops again. 'Member, we talked about this before? I found this little bottle by your side," Octavia calmly spoke as she held up the mistress' small blue bottle of laudanum drops. She tilted her head downward as she stared into the mistress' eyes and pursed her lips.

The mistress acted much like a small child who had been caught with her hand in the cookie jar. She looked at the floor and only said, "Oh, I see."

"Emily, I can't believe you did such a thing right before your guests are expected! What were you thinking? A lady doesn't behave in such a manner!" the mistress' cousin blurted angrily.

"I just get so nervous. These women, they judge me," Mrs. Langdon shouted defensively. She then attempted to sit up but slumped back again.

Octavia helped to pull the mistress up by the elbow but found that the missus was unable to make it off the floor. She tried to smooth things over. "That's okay, we all have our bad days. We can all overlook such a little thing as this." She shot a glance to the mistress' cousin and Hentie to calm the situation, knowing that her master and Big John must be on their way.

The ordinarily calm and reserved Sara Chase panicked. "A lady can't present herself like this," she said with one hand on her hip and the other palm open and directed toward Mrs. Langdon. She walked about the room taking in some air and making a clicking sound with her tongue against the roof of her mouth. While Sara Chase currently held a much more modest station in life than her rich cousin, she had grown up in great wealth and was reared with the skills of aristocratic young women. As such, she was well aware of social expectations.

Mrs. Langdon looked downward in shame while Octavia continued to try to position the mistress into a steady sitting position on the floor.

Mrs. Chase paced the floor and pressed the side of her hand to her temple. "Well! We must say that Emily has suddenly fallen ill. If she appears at this event, her guests will think she is a lowly drunkard. I know how a proper lady should carry on in these circumstances. I was raised on a plantation. I know what these guests will expect."

"Don't know if it's gonna be all dat bad. She's been able to 'come round sometimes 'fore and nobody knowd the difference," offered Octavia.

"What? She's done this before? Oh, dear Lord! She can't show herself like this. She'll be ruined! More importantly, she'll bring shame to her husband and son." Mrs. Chase turned bright red as she grasped the top of her forehead and turned on the threesome.

"We still have a little while before the guests arrive. Let's see if we can get her to come 'round. She might not be as bad off as she's lookin' right now," Hentie offered.

"Oh, but it is! It's a disaster! Emily and I have taken lessons on how to behave as proper wives and hostesses ever since we were young girls. One simply doesn't accept callers in such a condition as this. Not when she is living at this social ranking." The cousin's panic continued to escalate, her face taking on an almost burgundy hue. Beads of sweat formed on her upper lip. She pulled out a lace hanky and began to dab her face.

Suddenly the women heard the clomping of heavy footsteps

coming down the hallway and all four fell silent as they looked toward the door. The ladies held their breath waiting for their master to explode.

"What is this? What happened?"

"I'm sorry ma'sa, but while I was fixin' the trays for the missus' tea, she musta got into her drops. I didn't think she'd do such a thing on a day like today," Octavia pleaded.

"Oh, dear God." Langdon pivoted on one foot and locked eyes with Big John. He then rolled his eyes upward and stretched his hands outward. "What am I supposed to do with a woman like this?"

"I'm not sure, sir," said Big John as he shook his head.

"Of all the days for her to do such a thing!" Langdon paced the floor for a few moments, exhaling loudly out of frustration. He slapped his hands on his thighs.

Then he turned to his wife's cousin and said, "Sarah, it should be incumbent on you to act as the hostess this afternoon and entertain Emily's guests. A woman should do this, not a man. It's not my place. You manage the guests."

Sarah Chase, shocked by this demand, plopped into a side chair and gasped, "Me? Why me? I'm merely a visitor to this house. I've only casually met a few of these women. I haven't lived on a plantation or entertained guests of this caliber for years. I am not sure I am prepared."

Langdon stopped dead in his tracks and locked eyes with Sarah. "You are a lady and HER kin."

"Yes, but—" the cousin sputtered.

"This is an afternoon tea for dignified women of good breeding from this area. You should be honored to be counted among them, let alone be the hostess of this affair. You have blood ties to Emily and shared much of your early life with her. Now show her that you are a lady of integrity that won't let Emily's good name be forever scarred," Langdon stated forcefully.

Mrs. Chase sat up in her chair, apparently having seen some reason to Langdon's argument. She planted both palms firmly on her legs.

"All right then, I shall, but it is because I am a good Christian woman, one of good breeding, even if I live in humble circumstances. Not because I condone a lady consuming intoxicants, but because I am called to forgive in Christ's name and move forward. The Lord never intended for us to rely on such devices, only on our moral fiber and inner strength."

"Yes, whatever." Langdon waved off her banter and looked in the opposite direction, then facing the enslaved women said, "Hentie, help Sarah get ready for our guests. Let her borrow whatever frock or jewels Emily owns that she wishes to wear. I want Sarah to be glowing with confidence by the time the guests arrive. Do you understand?" Langdon paused and looked directly at Hentie.

"Yes, Master. I think I know exactly what gown would look becoming on the missus." Hentie nodded and dipped quickly in a curtsy.

"Octavia, put my wife to bed and make sure she doesn't sneak out. For God's sake don't let a soul see her in this condition." He threw a beseeching hand skyward.

"Yes, ma'sa. I'll make sure she stays put." Octavia nodded at Master Langdon and bent one knee in his direction.

"Good, then. Big John, you and I need to get back to updating my ledgers and confirming some deliveries. I also need to send off a few letters today. Let's get going," Langdon demanded, pushing Big John toward the bedroom door and never looking back toward his encumbered wife.

"Yes, Ma'sa. Let's get to it. I'll go check to see if we got those supplies you been expectin'. I believe I done heard they come in a bit ago." Big John nodded and quickened his step. He then shot back a look at Hentie and winked.

Hentie captured the look and smiled lovingly back at him. She reflected again on her good fortune to have him in her life.

I sure is lucky to have Big John in my life. Never thought I could love another man after my husband, Abenti was killed over in Africa. My heart done broke in half when I was taken from my home, Abenti died, then my daughter was eaten by sharks. Never thought I'd get over it all. But Big John helped me heal. Dem angels musta sent him my way. Thank you, Lawd God!

Chapter 4
Patrick Pringle and Fitzwilliam Langdon, Citadel Cadets

The Citadel Academy, Charleston, South Carolina, 1861

Patrick awoke with a start. Warm beneath his woolen blanket, snuggled down in his pillow, dreaming of his mother's fresh, hot buttermilk biscuits and grilled ham, he was reluctant to leave the comfort of the dreamland womb.

"Hey, Tomato Head! You better move it. You'll be late," shouted Fitz, knowing that Patrick should have been up and dressed at least ten minutes ago.

Patrick's roommate, Fitzwilliam Langdon, had thrown a hefty calculus book at his roommate, barely missing his head as he exited the room. But on this morning, Patrick had wanted to snooze just those few extra minutes. His wavy red hair sunk deep into his feather pillow; covers pulled tight around his neck.

Patrick, Fitzwilliam, and a few other lads had the good fortune of nicking a bottle of whiskey the night before. They sneaked the booze into the infirmary to dispose of it in secrecy. It had been a hilarious time, and the otherwise regimented cadets got to blow off some steam.

One of the other cadets, Elliott Chase, snatched a nurse's cap, white uniform, and navy cape. Elliott donned the ensemble and took on the character of a nurse with such authenticity that he had everyone in stitches. He portrayed a nurse checking in new plebes trying to take everyone's temperature, orally and otherwise. Cadets were scampering every which way, sliding down the hallways and bumping into walls.

Elliott, Fitzwilliam's cousin, was decidedly different from his fair-haired kin. They had the same bloodline, but their connections stopped there. They seemed to be of entirely different breeding, the antithesis of one another. Their mothers were cousins and had been close companions as children but had gone on to lead contrasting lifestyles as grown women. One, Emily Langdon, had married for money and social status but was forced to endure her husband's philandering and mercurial temperament. The other cousin, Sarah Chase, gave up a more opulent life and married for enduring love, fidelity, and a close marital relationship. The latter cousin, unfortunately, was widowed at a young age.

Fitz was the son of a wealthy planter and was used to finery and hearing the jingle of coins in his pocket. As an only child, he had been overindulged and could be quite a hellion at times—even pompous—but he always landed on his feet. He was tall, fair, and athletic. Elliott was shorter than Fitz with darker features and a slighter build. He was an ordinary fellow, kindly and goodhearted. Elliott was from a farming family in southern Pennsylvania and was better able to get along with the other cadets as he was far more amiable, always had his fellow cadets' backs, and was able to join in the fun. Fitz tended to think only of himself.

On the night the boys snatched the booze, they managed to drink it down before they were caught by the officer in charge that night.

The bottle was empty when they heard someone coming. Provincially, they had managed to ditch the bottle in with other empty vessels of medicines. Hence, there was no real evidence of wrongdoing. They were merely trespassing in a restricted area. Fortunately, the officer of the day decided to overlook the incident. God must have been on their side, seeing their way through to graduation.

But Patrick didn't know if he could continue to stay in God's good graces if his wayward behavior persisted.

I best get a move on if I want to make formation. Not that much longer until our commencement ceremony. Got to make it until then.

Patrick jumped out of bed with an extra oomph and hit the floor scrambling. He grabbed up socks, uniform pants, shirt, and jacket. He slid on his socks as he grabbed for a comb. He had to get down to lineup and fall in. As he was pulling the comb through his tight, copper-colored curls, he suddenly heard a piercing shriek, almost like a banshee cry.

"Awwwww! Snake! Snake!" followed by the sounds of heavy wooden furniture being knocked over and a body hitting a door. The screaming continued as a plebe ran down the hallway screaming, "Snake! There's a snake in my room!"

Patrick yanked open the door to see the poor plebe with one boot on still pulling up his pants. Howling laughter erupted from the stairwell at the end of the hallway as the heads of five senior cadets peered out. They cracked up at the sight of the poor plebe in obvious distress. Patrick merely rolled his eyes at the prank and continued to ready himself.

"Sidney! You scream like a schoolgirl! How can you go out and fight the damn Yankees with a screech like that? Besides, that little garden snake isn't going to hurt you. You damn big chicken! Haven't you ever seen a garden snake before?" shouted the prankster.

As the plebe slowed his pace, his face turned a burgundy red. He gave the cadet a steely gaze as his steps tapered off and he came to a stop in the middle of the hallway. Momentarily allowing his eyes to burn into the face of the cadet, he yanked up his pants to make himself more presentable and jolted to attention, saluting the senior cadet.

"Sir, unfortunately, I did not take the time to examine the snake. I was still half awake. I felt it slither up my leg from inside my boot. I didn't know if it was poisonous or not. I apologize if I alarmed anyone, sir."

"Yes, well, make yourself ready for roll call and get down to courtyard immediately," shouted the senior cadet as he turned and walked down the stairwell, winking at his comrades.

Fortunately, Patrick was able to push by the other fellows and fall in line unnoticed as the officer in charge was dressing down another cadet who was a member of the Lamp Squad for his lackluster execution of duty. Assignment to the Lamp Squad was considered a special honor to be carried out with expediency and care. The cadets in that squad were given special uniforms and expected to collect the oil lamps proudly and quickly from the cadets' quarters, deliver them to the lamp room for replenishment with kerosene.

The sergeant, just inches from the cadet's face, blasted him. "You lazy knob! Don't you realize you have been given a special honor? Your fellow comrades rely on you to get their lamps and get them filled so they have light by which they can study in their quarters. We have a war brewing. You need to become a reliable soldier. Can you hand your comrade a rifle that hasn't been primed, then see him shot down by the enemy? You are here to be trained as a soldier, not a mama's boy! You're acting in a manner unbecoming the uniform! And someday that behavior may get you and a cadet near you killed! Do you understand me, boy?"

All the poor lad could do was stare straight ahead and sharply belt out the words, "Yes sir!"

As Patrick coolly fell into line, he let out a sigh. "Oh, thank God," Patrick whispered to the cadet next to him. "I thought I was doomed."

"You might have been if Barnwell hadn't tripped over his own damn feet joining ranks," Duncan hissed. "He's such a clumsy oaf."

"Well, the poor bastard has feet the size of wooden paddles. I'm surprised he made it to adulthood!" Patrick rolled his eyes as he spoke.

"Well, that's true I suppose. Poor bastard." Duncan just shook his head.

The bane of morning check-in was otherwise painless, and the cadets were off to breakfast. There was plenty of shoving and pushing as the young men lined up. Some of Patrick's classmates could put away a pound of sausages and a dozen eggs for breakfast. Unfortunately, there was nothing that glorious on the menu. Just fatback, mush, and beans. Not very appetizing, but it was all that was offered. At least the cook had made her melt-in-your-mouth buttermilk biscuits. Perhaps tomorrow, they might enjoy the cook's wonderful sausages and Johnny cakes.

Fitzwilliam and Patrick grabbed a table off to the side of the large mess hall wanting to avoid the other knobs. Across the cavernous room Fitz spotted his cousin Elliott with his usual energetic stride. Elliott waved at Fitz and shot him a broad smile; Fitz merely returned a nod of acknowledgment. He did not indulge his cousin or invite him to join them for lunch, as was his habit. He knew he was blood kin, but believed he was a bit above the less-than-athletic farm boy. Suddenly, Fitzwilliam's attention was drawn back to his red-haired roommate, Patrick.

"Fitz, we need to talk." Patrick looked earnestly into his roommate's eyes.

"Sure, buddy, what's bothering you?"

"It's all the mucking around we've been doing. Like nicking the alcohol and sneaking off to the infirmary. We're seniors now. I can't afford to get kicked out of the Citadel, at any point, but particularly now. We're weeks away from graduation. There's a war coming for Christ's sake! You know as well as I do that South Carolina has been pressing to secede from the Union for a long time. Well, I think it could happen any week now. It's not a game anymore with Carolina seceding. It's all been good fun, man, but this fool-heartedness has to cease."

"Oh, Patrick. You worry too much. And secession—well, it may come soon, but the Yanks have been sitting in our harbor for months and not much has gone on. We'll leave the Union and life will go on."

"Yeah, right, Fitz."

"In the meantime, let's enjoy our senior year. You're with me. You know I can always slide by. My old man will fix things for us. He and the commandant are friendly. You'll see, my red-haired friend." Fitzwilliam reached out and squeezed Patrick's forearm as he chuckled.

"No, Fitz, I'm serious. I think I've used up all of God's good graces. You're from a wealthy family. Your father can fix things for you. You're tall, good looking, and bright. They will undoubtedly make you an officer," Patrick said.

Fitz looked down a moment, smiled, and blushed, knowing everything Patrick said was true. "I know I'm lucky, Patrick."

Patrick realized Fitzwilliam couldn't grasp the reality of his roommate's life. Patrick's father ran a small farm, not a sprawling plantation with nearly a thousand acres and hundreds of slaves like the plantation owned by the Langdon family. Fitz lived in a mansion and rarely saw the fields beyond the well-manicured gardens surrounding it. He was removed from the work and the toil of farm life. Conversely, Patrick was from a poor Irish farming family with ten children. His father sent him to the Citadel on scholarship so there was one less mouth to feed at the dinner table.

"Fitz, I don't have all those things going for me. I need to make sure I am successful here so that I can leave and make my own way in life." Patrick looked intensely into Fitz's.

"I get it, buddy. Someday I will need to run a plantation or some business. My father works hard too," nodded Fitz.

"Your father's not a laborer. My father uses his hands. He gets dirty. He farms and he does some blacksmithing work, but he's in competition with skilled colored men who do that work. They do the same thing for dirt cheap. My old man struggled to feed our family and keep his kids clothed. Meanwhile, your mama's buying gowns from France. It's different worlds we live in. I need to watch myself. Do you get it?"

"I hear you, but I still think you worry too much, Paddy Boy." Fitz shook his head and looked away.

Patrick went on. "We have about four hundred cadets enrolled here. More than half of us are here on scholarship from the state of South Carolina. We have to tow the line and avoid demerits. My folks can't afford the full tuition."

"How much does it cost to go here anyway? I've never heard how much tuition is."

"Of course you don't know, buddy. That's my point! The regular fee here is eight hundred dollars a year. Plus, if you're not on a scholarship, you have to buy your own clothing. I can't afford to lose my special scholarship. It pays for damn near everything, right down to my cotton drawers, shoes, and winter coat. I'm damn lucky to have clean kecks to cover my butt and a coat that fits me." Patrick struck his fist on the table for emphasis.

"Wow. I guess I never realized, I mean, I never had to deal with tuition," Fitz sputtered.

"You're different. You accept me even though I'm from a family as poor as church mice. You know there are cadets who resent a man like me from poor folk in the Upcountry of South Carolina and other poor Southern states. We, poor farm boys, come from families grateful to send off a son to the Citadel where they can be fed, clothed, and cared for. They're damn grateful to be relieved of the burden of providing for yet another child."

"I have some understanding. The same kind of thing goes on with my cousin, Elliott. I think they sent him here for much the same reason. His mother and my mother are cousins, very close. They wanted their boys together, and this way, Elliott was taken care of through his scholarship. He gets clothes, food, and a good education." Fitzwilliam nodded.

"Up until this past year when I started sharing a room with you, my record had been flawless," Patrick said. "No report on the Book of Delinquencies, nor on the sick list. Now, I've been showing up tardy and have turned in late assignments. I can't keep this up. I have to make it to graduation and get out of here."

Fitzwilliam looked away, knowing there was truth in what his friend was saying, but not wanting to acknowledge it. He was aware of Patrick's circumstances but wanted to have a good time in Charleston, away from plantation life and the drudgery of it.

Fitzwilliam reflected on what he had learned when they were assigned to share their dorm that year. He remembered seeing Patrick for the first time, such a poor, unfortunate soul. Patrick was an ivory-skinned boy with curly red locks, a bit gaunt and unsure of himself. He had a bad leg that had been broken in a farming accident. It had never been set properly by a trained physician, causing it to be a bit shorter than the other. As a result, he had to make his way through the Citadel to become a scholar in a particular academic discipline or acquire a new trade. It was critical that he be successful while at the military academy.

Patrick seemed to thrive being Fitz's sidekick. The red-haired cadet worked hard and tried to be compliant with all the rules and rigid structure of the Citadel, but Fitzwilliam often led him astray.

Patrick touched Fitzwilliam's wrist and raised his voice a bit. "I know you might not see it now, but we are getting a good education here. We have the same curriculum as West Point."

Fitz looked over at his roommate with surprise. "I never knew that. We're modeled after West Point? I just thought I went here because it was close to our plantation in Mount Pleasant and that's what my father wanted."

Patrick exhaled in exasperation, "Fitz, you idiot. Don't you check out anything? Do you just go where your father tells you? Yes, this is a fine institution just like the military academy in New York. The one and only West Point. Look at all the fine officers that have come out of West Point."

"Egads, nearly every great military officer in America came from West Point!" exclaimed Fitz.

"When the Founders established our academy back in the 1840's, they looked to what they thought was the best model in the country and built the Citadel after that institution. The Founders developed us as a four-year program. Our coursework includes science, mathematics and one modern language. At the time, it was a definite departure from the classical education that other colleges were offering. The goal of the Founders was to make us into officers and gentlemen."

"Well, buddy, I'm glad you told me. Kind of makes me feel better about this place." Fitz looked around the room, broke into a broad smile and chuckled.

"Fitz, you've had years of private tutoring throughout your life, and you do so well academically. We need to quit all our antics from here until graduation. Come on, buddy, let's make a promise to each other." Patrick reached out and grasped Fitz's forearm.

"Okay, Patrick, I hear you. Let's try to buckle down until graduation. I think you're right. You've got a good point, my red-haired friend. My world is different. I'm lucky." Fitzwilliam rose from the table with his tin dishes with a sincere look and nodded at his friend.

The two left the dining hall and headed on to the classroom for the remainder of the afternoon. Surprisingly, Fitzwilliam was alert and complained the entire day. No jokes, no shenanigans. The day passed without incident, and the week wore on much the same. Patrick observed the mandatory evening study hours. He was in his quarters as required and in bed at lights out.

Early Friday morning, Fitzwilliam awoke and threw his pillow at his roommate. "Hey, buddy! It's Friday! Only a matter of hours and we will be outta here! Out of the damn classroom and onto the streets!"

"What? What are you saying?"

"Come on, buddy, this is the best day of the week. We're gonna be free men able to grab the food of normal human beings, not the slop they serve here!" Fitz announced.

"Well, you can do that. I'm not sure I can afford that this week." Patrick curled back up around his pillow.

"Oh, buddy. Would I ever let a good man down? I'll share my good fortune," Fitzwilliam smiled at his bunkmate.

Patrick, keeping his thoughts to himself, merely smiled. He didn't mention that his roommate had abandoned him just last weekend. Fitz was not accustomed to thinking of others. If his attention strayed to other matters, such as pretty ladies, he was out of luck.

"No, buddy. You're the best roommate a cadet could have, you know that." Patrick nodded.

The boys hurriedly dressed and made it down to formation. Determined to make it through the day without incident, they made sure to adhere to the code of conduct down to the letter—staying alert in class, walking hurriedly between classes, and showing the utmost respect to officers. The time seemed to tick by ever so slowly, but at last, lunch hour arrived, and then finally the afternoon passed.

The glorious weekend was upon them. The anxious cadets poured out of the classrooms like scurrying crabs poured out from a fishing net and dancing on boat's deck. The gray-and-white uniforms spilled into the hallways and out the front steps to the civilized world at Marion Square. The lads had been cooped up at the installation located at Meeting and Boundary (later to become Calhoun) Streets but could quickly make their way to the shopping district on King Street and all the activity of Charleston.

The cadets walked briskly along pulsating city streets and the buzzing shopping district. Ladies strolled down through the business district in fashionable attire, carrying out their shopping and stopping to gossip when the opportunity arose. The lads took the opportunity to admire the scenery and point out beauties to one another with a quick upward jolt of their chins. They had been admonished to act as gentlemen when on the streets and comport themselves so as to be worthy of the uniform. So, they did a lot of looking, but no touching.

Patrick, Fitzwilliam, Elliott, and the other lads enjoyed a variety of escapades as cadets. Sometimes the things they did were minor infractions, bending rules more than breaking them. But then other times their pranks were more significant. Some acts were clearly against the code of conduct. For instance, what they were scheming that very afternoon. Fitzwilliam, having just made a promise to Patrick to stop his illicit behavior, had not let him in on their plan.

Patrick, a good Catholic lad, felt like he was stuck in the middle between the persuasion of the devil and the firm guiding hand of Mary Ever Virgin. As he listened to his mates discuss their proposition to surreptitiously remove a vendor's sign from a storefront on King Street, he mumbled, *"Hail Mary full of grace. The Lord is with thee..."* The cadets loved to collect signs from local stores and decorate their dormitory rooms with them. Fitzwilliam was dying to get such a sign into his clutches. The boys tried to act casual, size up the situation, and see which store appeared the most vulnerable. Then as Patrick was finishing his fifth Hail Mary, he saw Fitzwilliam jump up and grab a sign from its display post.

"Fitz! What did you do? It's broad daylight, you idiot!"

Patrick glanced in the storefront window and saw the proprietor looking aghast. There was only one thing to do—run as fast as hell and try to ditch the old geezer. As the cadets raced down the street, the chill of the air burned the young men's lungs.

"Damn it, Fitz!" Patrick screamed. "I'm going to kill you!"

The young cadets pushed by Lydia, the enslaved servant who lived on the Battery, and her mistress as they ran down the street.

"Why I never! What are those young men up to?" challenged the mistress.

"I think they stole something from a store. I thought I saw one cadet carrying a sign," answered the servant.

"What? Why would they want that?" Mrs. Simmons tipped her chin upward, her eyes following the lads racing down the street.

"What do young men want with any number of trinkets? I think they just collect them for the fun of it," proposed Lydia. "These young cadets just need to blow off some steam. They coop them up and structure their lives all week. It's Friday afternoon. They want to have a little fun."

"And these are the young soldiers who will protect us from the Yankees? God help us all!" The mistress turned her eyes heavenward and stepped into a shop.

Another woman dressed in finery of a deep olive tone overheard the matron's comments and said, "Let's hope our men can protect us from a Yankee invasion. I hear that they've been trying to ship in supplies and are building up fortifications at Fort Sumter."

"I've heard much the same. They're trying to sneak Yankee ships into our harbor. Those heathen dogs!" snapped Mrs. Simmons.

"Those Federals want to ruin our way of life! What business is it of those Yankees if we have slaves. They're like our family members. We take care of them like they are our children. We need our servants for our more agrarian way of life," hissed the woman cloaked in green.

"We don't have factories like the Northerners. Why can't they let this state make decisions for its people and leave us alone?" Simmons angrily tossed a scarf down as she spoke.

"Yes ma'am, them Yankees should just leave us alone," said Lydia as she carefully folded the scarf her mistress had just tossed aside.

"So much of our rice and our cotton require extra labor. We need the servants to keep plantations productive and keep our fine homes looking their best. Those Yankees are just jealous of our more refined way of life," complained another shopper.

While the ladies continued their discussion in the fashionable millinery shop, the cadets continued to bound down the street, Patrick's anger only adding steam to his pace as he ran faster than he ever thought he could.

Fortunately, they had lost the storekeeper and were now safely back in their dorm rooms. They locked the door and fell on their beds laughing. A couple of minutes later, Patrick peered out the window to see if they'd been followed. *Damn!* The proprietor was downstairs speaking to the officer in charge down in the sally port. Undoubtedly, he was complaining that two cadets in the standard issue gray-and-white uniforms just stole his sign. With Patrick's wavy red hair, he was a dead giveaway.

"We're doomed. That's it. I'll be pushing a plow in just a few weeks. Back to the farm for me. God forgive me, I'll never graduate now." Patrick looked at the floor, knowing he was done.

Fitz offered up a brilliant idea. "No, mate! We'll burn this sign up in the fireplace. With no evidence, how can they court martial us?"

Thank goodness there had been a chill in the air and the fire had already been going. They broke up the sign and put the pieces in the flame. The embers quickly took hold, the black-and-white sign now roasting away.

As they watched the sign dissolve, the officer in charge pounded on the door. "Open up, boys! Did you steal this merchant's sign?"

The boys fell to their knees and Patrick started reciting all the childhood prayers he could recall.

Fitzwilliam, quite used to deceiving his superiors, said in a calm, but measured tone, "We're saying our evening prayers, Sir. Patrick is finishing the rosary. That takes a while to complete."

The lads kept their eyes on the sign, watching the flames swallow it up. At a slow, consistent pace, Patrick continued with his prayers, "Glory Be to the Father and to the Son and to the Holy Spirit . . ." muttering, "Hail Mary full of grace. The Lord is with thee . . ."

At last, the sign was nothing but ashes. Fitzwilliam jumped to his feet and opened the door.

"Yes sir!" blurted Fitz, standing at attention.

"This gentleman here says you two were in front of his store and grabbed his sign. He saw a boy with red hair in a Citadel uniform."

"No, sir. We've been here reading and then we did our evening prayers. You can check our room if you like. We don't have any signs here."

"Humm." The officer stepped into the room and started pulling back blankets and checking under the beds and behind the desks. He then held his hands out toward the shopkeeper and said, "I don't see anything."

"I could swear one of them had bright-red hair."

"Maybe it was just the sun playing on someone else's hair. Who knows?" offered Fitzwilliam.

"Well, I don't know, but that sign wasn't cheap!" barked the proprietor.

The officer in charge said, "Come with me, sir. I'll see what we can do." The two men then left the room.

The two cadets looked at each other in awe. Their eyes were wide open in surprise. Patrick held up a finger. "Wait. Don't say anything." He then leaned toward the window to see where the two men had gone. Apparently, they were going to confront other cadets on the grounds.

"We did it!" Patrick exclaimed in a hushed voice. "It's the luck of the Irish. I swear it is."

"It's that damn red hair! It's a blessing and curse." Fitz roughed up his buddy's hair and squeezed him.

Patrick fell to his knees again and said, "Glory be to the Father, and to the Son, and to the Holy Ghost. As it was in the beginning, is now, and ever shall be, world without end. Thank you, Lord, for your kindness. Thank you for saving me this day. I swear I'll behave myself from here on out. I'll be good. I'll be good. I'll be good!"

In a matter of weeks, these young cadets, still in their teenage years, would be called to serve in one of the bloodiest conflicts known to humanity. Some of them would be made officers before their twentieth year simply because they were able to survive on the battlefield longer than their older superiors. These boys who were playing pranks on one another just months before would be forced to confront their counterparts on the battlefield under horrendous circumstances. The enemy, who looked like them, spoke like them and had the same worldly desires, was the target they were called to annihilate. Literally, it would force brother against brother and cause a loss of life more than all other wars combined.[1]

---

1 The story depicted in this chapter was based on the journal of a Citadel cadet and other archival documents held at the Citadel Military Academy.

Chapter 5
Fitzwilliam's Pregraduation Ceremony from the Citadel

The Citadel Academy, Charleston, South Carolina, April 1861

The spring air in Charleston was heady with the fragrance of magnolia trees and Confederate jasmine as the group from Twin Oaks plantation strolled along the city's streets. The heavy heat and humidity of the summer had not settled in yet in the Lowcountry; temperatures were pleasant, the humidity low by South Carolina standards.

The Langdon family and a few of their enslaved workers had come to Charleston to see their son, Fitzwilliam, attend pregraduation ceremonies at the Citadel. Fitzwilliam, their only child, had once barely made it through an early childhood disease. The remedies of Rosa, a clever Gullah herbalist who worked at the plantation infirmary, and her young assistant, Baby Doll, saved the boy's life, and also spurred Langdon's interest in Baby Doll. Their subsequent liaisons later resulted in the birth of a son, Tobias, who looked nearly identical to Fitz.

Big John, Langdon's trusted manservant, was in tow. Hentie was attending to the missus on this trip. Hentie was patient and possessed far more tolerance for the missus' flighty behavior than Octavia, her lady's maid. Hentie was chosen to come on this trip due to perseverance and restraint. She was an "old African" and had gone through the seasoning process long ago.

The group was led by Langdon and his wife, Emily. She looked rather pinched as she worked to keep step with her much taller husband, a particularly painful endeavor due to her tight new ankle boots. She was wearing a newly acquired frock in a tawny gold hue. As she walked, her dirndl rustled while her dome-shaped skirt with rows of flounce and intricate embroideries swayed back and forth. The layers of skirting and her artificial cage crinoline added ten pounds to what she was forced to bear, while her stiff corset with boning limited her capacity to breathe. Her drawstring bag held in the crook of her arm flapped against her hip as she labored along. She was clearly made miserable by the ordeal and wished she had remembered her small vial of drops.

Hentie looked down and quietly smiled, mildly amused by her missus' plight. Hentie's own modest osnaburg cotton dress and plain brown shoes were much more simplistic, consistent with her station in life, and far more comfortable. The deep shade of rose flattered Hentie, highlighting her high cheekbones. Pressed and neat, but not ostentatious, she silently followed the missus.

Hentie's outfit had been made for her the previous season when she and the Langdons visited White Sulphur Springs, the grand resort in West Virginia, later known as the Greenbrier, where the family vacationed nearly every year. This renowned retreat situated in the cool Allegany mountains was a respite from the heat and humidity of Lowcountry summers, and the mosquito-borne diseases. It was the social scene for the aristocratic families of the South, a place where marriage matches were made, and business deals were sealed.

The Langdons had new garments made for Hentie and Big John

every two years, then had them rotate their clothing. They didn't want the other guests to notice that new outfits weren't made for the entire staff on an annual basis. The women at the resort viciously gossiped. At times, the social pressures were so great that Mrs. Langdon took to her bed with dreadful headaches, only treatable with her trusty laudanum drops. At times, even the sulfur springs, so well known for their healing qualities, couldn't settle her mood.

"Emily! Keep up," William Langdon barked at his wife. "I don't want to be late for the ceremony. It is an important day for the whole family. I want a good seat where we can see Fitz receive his awards and be able to see the other families."

"Yes, dear. I'm walking as fast as I can. It's just that these boots are so tight. It's so difficult to walk, dear," she whined as her face became strained and reddened.

"Yes, well, perhaps you should choose more wisely when you know you'll be walking in the city. We've been planning this little excursion for months now, Emily. Couldn't you have selected a finer pair of slippers for this event?" He sighed and shook his head in exasperation.

The missus, having been scolded, turned her head away from her husband and let out a mild harrumph as she shuffled along.

As the Langdons approached the chapel near the Citadel campus, others were likewise joining the procession. Many were parents, sweethearts, and siblings, but most were the young cadets in their gray woolen uniforms with a black stripe down the front midsection. The trim young men walked hurriedly, as disciplined cadets always do, arriving in a timely fashion. The others kept a more leisurely pace. The ladies sashayed along haltingly to show off their latest fashionable ensembles. The trendy frocks were in pleasant hues of yellow, gold, and a rich green. A few other ladies wore various shades of blue ranging from a pale sky blue to a deep azure.

Hentie and Big John casually brushed up against each other as they turned and entered the grounds of the small chapel, just a short way from the Citadel. They continued to follow behind the missus as she labored along, warmly smiling at each other as they strolled. Meanwhile, Emily Langdon continued to noisily exhale and flap her bag against her thigh in anger.

Several feet down the street, Mr. Langdon stopped to converse with the other White aristocratic planters milling outside the chapel. He seemed to tower over another man from somewhere outside Charleston who was dressed impeccably in a gray woolen suit and stylish black boots that gleamed in the sunlight.

"Hello, sir. I don't believe I have had the pleasure of your acquaintance before. May I introduce myself?" Langdon extended his hand, nodding and smiling downward at the much shorter man. "I am William Paul Langdon. I live outside Charleston where I have a plantation named Twin Oaks. Are you from the area?"

The smiling man, perhaps a bit intimidated by the much larger Langdon, stood upright, and said, "No sir, I am William Randolph. I hail from Richmond, Virginia. My grandson, whom I have reared since he was a young boy, attends the Citadel and will be graduating this year. My grandson's name is Charles Randolph. I felt that sending my grandson to the Citadel would be much closer to us than West Point and make traveling a great deal easier."

"Oh, yes, I would think it would be much easier. You could take a train here and ride in comfort."

Langdon momentarily turned and acknowledged a few Citadel parents walking past, smiling as he tipped his hat to them, then turned his attention back to Mr. Randolph.

"Yes, when we heard the Citadel was established more recently and modeled on West Point, I thought it would be ideal." Mister Randolph smiled brightly and nodded. "How is it that Charleston came to establish this academy? It turns out that it was a good move to have a Southern military school."

Langdon nodded. "Indeed, particularly now, we are blessed to have a military academy almost in our backyard. This military installation was built shortly after the 1822 attempted slave uprising. Did you hear about it? Planned by a free man of color named Denmark Vesey?"

"Oh, yes, I did hear about that. Weren't hundreds of Negroes involved in that scheme?"

"Yes, Vesey had been plotting it for years apparently. Black men from all over the area were involved. The Negroes greatly outnumber us in this area. They're needed to run our plantations. The landowners grew fearful of another uprising, so all kinds of measures were taken to protect homes. Here in the city, homeowners installed *cheval-de-frise,* or high fences with razor-sharp protrusions, to keep the darkies out."

"Oh my, city dwellers must have been scared out of their minds to do something like that. I don't think I have ever heard of such a thing." The Virginian's eyes opened wide as he touched his fingertips to his mouth.

Langdon continued. "Yes, well, it was a frightful time. We strengthened our Black Code and developed tighter restrictions on Negroes. A curfew was put in place calling for all coloreds to be off the street by ten o'clock. Other limitations called for restrictions on the number of enslaved workers who could hire out their time. They also limited their freedom of movement around the city. We had to do things like this to protect ourselves, don't you see?"

"Yes, we allow the hiring out of slaves, too, but I am not sure we ever had any issues with it. They are monitored," Randolph noted.

Langdon drew in a breath as he explained the most restrictive step taken under the Black Code. "We found it necessary here in South Carolina to incarcerate any free Black sailors, foreign or domestic, upon landing until such time as their departure was assured. We feared that sailors, who travel around the world, might spread ideas about liberty and freedom. They would have seen other lands and opportunities. We didn't want them spreading notions about living independently. So, when they come into port, we have them arrested and put in jail until the ship is about to leave. Of course, there are some unfortunate souls who never rejoin their crew. Mistakes are made down at the jailhouse, you know. Completely unavoidable." Langdon looked down and dragged his shoe in the crushed shell-and-sand street.

The other gentleman, a bit shocked by this assertion, drew in a breath and said, "Oh really? That's rather novel, isn't it?"

"We found it necessary to take other measures, as well, to keep our peculiar institution of slavery intact. We wanted to keep the darkies scared. Strike terror so they wouldn't try anything like the uprising in Haiti. So, we have layers of protection—the patrolmen, guards, and penal institutions–to control them. When we do have to discipline them, we have found it more effective to do so publicly. Often, they are restrained in a public place, and then their discipline is administered before the Negro population."

"Oh yes, I can see how that might have more of a quelling impact on them," the visiting gentleman offered.

"They might be hanged, beheaded, or set on fire. We leave the heads on the pikes for weeks all along public roads as a reminder. The same when we have a burning. We burn them alive at the stake and leave the corpses there so no darkie gets an idea to strike out against a White man. That's how you manage them here in South Carolina. I know it may sound ugly, but it is necessary, you see. We need to do all that we can to avoid an uprising. We've been in agreement about this for decades. Robert Barnwell Rhett, who runs our local newspaper, has been our biggest proponent."

Others walked by the two men as they continued their conversation. A pious woman in dark clothing carrying a large drawstring bag that concealed a copy of former Charlestonian Angelina Grimké's booklet titled *An Appeal to the Christian Women of the South,* raised an eyebrow when she caught a bit of the conversation. She looked upon Langdon with scorn and hurried past.

The man from Virginia had fallen silent. While pro-slavery, he had never heard such an ardent discourse.

"Well, you here in South Carolina have certainly refined the system, haven't you? Now if you'll excuse me. I must find my seat." With that, the older gentleman tipped his hat to Langdon and hurried off.

Little did the Virginian know that just across the street from the military academy is what would later become Marion Square, an exhibition site for the yet-to-be-erected statute of the statesman and favorite son of the South, John C. Calhoun. An outspoken proponent of race-based slavery, he contended that the South's "peculiar institution" was actually doing a positive good for Negroes. Benevolent masters provided food, shelter, and clothing to the otherwise heathen savages in their charge, Calhoun would argue, and their heathen souls were placed under the guiding hand of a White Christian master allowing Negroes a chance at salvation.

Langdon puffed out his chest and walked in toward the chapel. He grasped the lapels of his dark frock coat, drew in a deep breath of fragrant spring air, and stepped with purpose toward the chapel doors. This was a great day. They were here to celebrate the graduation not only of their son, but also that of Mrs. Langdon's kin, Elliott Chase. He hadn't fared as well academically as Fitzwilliam, who would graduate with honors. But of course Elliot did not have all the special privileges granted to a Langdon, including tutoring and the encouragement pressed upon Citadel instructors to give good marks to Fitzwilliam if they wanted academic recognition and special favors from the administration. All the years of special tutoring that Fitz had received seemed to have engendered an astute mind and active thinker. He had grown into a tall, handsome man who looked much like his father. Broad shoulders, flaxen waves of thick hair, and pale blue eyes. While he had a propensity for drink and hijinks, he seemed to be able to get away with a bit more than other lads due to his good looks, persuasive manner, as well as the Langdon name.

Mr. and Mrs. Langdon indulged their precious boy who had nearly died during childhood. They could never enforce discipline on the boy, who knew how to push limits.

Mr. Langdon was so very proud of his son and the award he would be receiving for his accomplishments in math and science. On this evening they would be dining at the nearby Planter's Inn, a well-established restaurant in Charleston that had attracted some of the city's most well-heeled aristocrats. It was a good venue for William Langdon to network with other wealthy planters.

As the Langdons made their way into the Citadel's chapel for the brief prayer service and awards ceremony, Mrs. Langdon glanced about, looking anxiously at what the other guests were wearing. Her gloved hand tensed on her new amber fan, recently acquired from the Far East. She nervously jerked it back and forth, as much to cool herself as to release her strain. Her hair had been meticulously swept upward with a fresh blossom carefully tucked into her coif and securely pinned down. To this, she added a unique Parisian bonnet with velvet ribbons and a large feather, a recent acquisition. Never mind that it blocked the view of those seated behind her; she paid them no mind.

As she approached middle age, Emily Langdon felt as though she had at long last achieved the status she had so earnestly desired early in life. As a younger woman, she lacked self-assurance and often relied on the reddish-brown laudanum kept in a small vial to relieve her anxiety. While she still made liberal use of this crutch, she didn't think it was as necessary as in previous years. Not at least in her mind. What started as a nervous irritation eventually evolved into anxiety, dread, and a deeper depression. She often kept a small vial tucked into her dress pocket and two small bottles on her dressing table. She tapped her bag to feel if she had some safely hidden at the bottom of it. *Ah, good!*

As Mrs. Langdon progressed up the center aisle of the chapel, she surveyed the crowd, carefully checking the pews on either side of the aisle to see who was present and worthy of her attention. Her eyes landed on Anna Trenholm, who was married to a wealthy merchant and plantation owner from John's Island. She was actually a distant relative of the woman.

"Why, hello, Mrs. Trenholm. I didn't think you would be here. Do you have someone participating in the ceremonies today?" Mrs. Langdon smiled nervously as she flicked her fan. She noticed Mrs. Trenholm's finery, probably a frock shipped all the way from London. It was a deep plum color with ornate trim, nothing like what she had seen locally.

"Why yes, we have a nephew who is receiving an award today. And you?" She raised an eyebrow as if she were uncertain why Mrs. Langdon might come to such an event.

"It's our son, Fitzwilliam. Surely you remember him. He's tall and quite handsome, just like his father. He's being given an award for his science and math achievement. He's such a bright boy, you know. And then tomorrow he will receive his commission at graduation." Mrs. Langdon glowed with pride, a rush of pink rising up her cheeks.

"Oh, really? I hadn't been aware of that. Humph, I wonder how that skipped my awareness." Pausing, wanting to be more mindful of her social graces, Mrs. Trenholm added, "Oh, and by the way, I must compliment you on your gown. It's lovely and really offsets your golden hair." She dipped her head in approval.

Shocked by her compliment, Mrs. Langdon was momentarily speechless. A woman so prominent had never remarked about her attire before in this way. She flushed all the way to her scalp; feeling the heat rise, she began to fan herself furiously.

"Oh, well, thank you. Thank you very much. That's so very kind of you. We just had this made up with fabric and patterns brought from London. I thought it would be appropriate for Fitzwilliam's special day."

"Well, you certainly look lovely, dear. Congratulations to your son," the woman nodded at Mrs. Langdon and then looked away, dismissing her from their conversation. Even though she could only see the back of Trenholm's head, Mrs. Langdon nodded and strolled away, trying to ignore her abrupt dismissal.

As she walked onward down the chapel's aisle, she heard from behind her someone apparently trying to gain her attention.

"*Psssst*. Emily, wait," came a hushed woman's voice.

When Mrs. Langdon turned to look, she saw the familiar face of her cousin from Pennsylvania, Sarah Chase. She was walking hurriedly behind her, trying to catch up. Emily hadn't seen her cousin since she had visited more than a year ago.

Mrs. Langdon paused and broke into a warm smile, a rare occurrence, but something that frequently occurred with this special cousin. In greeting, she leaned into her, tucked her arm under hers and kissed her on the cheek. Sarah's gentle spirit enveloped Mrs. Langdon and caused her to drop all of her defenses. The two got on like schoolgirls.

"Dear cousin, I'm so happy to see you. Isn't this a glorious day? Our sons are graduating from the military academy. Such a proud day for our boys and the family!"

"Oh dear, I know. I almost never thought this day would come." Sarah's cheeks blossomed into a rosy pinkish hue. "My dear boy, Elliott, is becoming a military officer. I just wished his father had lived to see this day." He had been killed on the family farm. "He worked so hard, always. He would have been so proud of his son." Sarah's gleaming smile showed her deep pride. The two continued to walk forward and grabbed seats near the front of the chapel, making sure to allow space for Mr. Langdon.

"Well, Sarah, as I told you before your wedding day, one doesn't marry for love. You marry for what a man can provide for you and the children God bestows on you through that marriage. You know that is why I married William. We have a beautiful mansion house, a productive plantation, and a handsome son. What else could I have wanted out of life?"

"Yes, dear cousin, you have been very blessed. I realized I was blessed in a different way. God sent me down a different path. I was wrapped in the warm love of a kind man. I was joyous every day with him. Our farm is much smaller than your beautiful plantation, but I got to enjoy all that plentiful life in my youth. You and I were so fortunate to have the rearing that we did, Emily," Sarah squeezed her arm. "I am grateful for the bounty we enjoyed as young girls, too."

"Yes, I suppose that's why I always wanted all the private tutoring for Fitzwilliam. I wanted him to learn foreign languages, geography, history, and so much more. Just like we used to enjoy. He started riding lessons quite young. Of course, his father could afford all these things and so much more for him. He's a very calculating planter, and he's acquired great wealth over the years. I'm *so* lucky!" Emily smiled and winked at Sarah, then giggled.

"Well, Julius was a man of God who was fair and honest. He never harmed anyone, never cheated a soul. He came home to me every night and slept in the marital bed with me and me alone. I have no regrets."

Her cousin's snipe at her was a rarity, but Emily must have brought up her great wealth one too many times to her humbler cousin. She knew exactly what her cousin was referring to, her husband's propensity to have liaisons with enslaved Negro women, and even adolescent girls, on the plantation. Emily withdrew her hand from the crook of her arm.

"Yes, well, I know we all need to make our choices in life. I am just glad I have all that I do. The sacrifices are of no mind to me. I thoroughly love my life at Twin Oaks. I could never survive in a farmhouse in Pennsylvania." She turned her head from her cousin and flicked out her fan furiously. Fortuitously, the organ music changed its tenor, becoming a bit louder as if to signal the crowd to take their seats. The women sat in the pews and redirected their attention to their programs.

In the rear of the chapel in the anteroom, the graduating cadets at the Citadel were charged with excitement. They were anxious to get through the ceremonies and awards so they could see their way clear to graduation and their pending officer appointments. They were eager to join the fight and push the country to a decision recognizing states' rights and being uninhibited at self-rule.

Patrick was elated to have made it to this day. He was on the brink of graduation, and he would no longer be dependent on his already burdened Irish immigrant father or the Citadel.

"Hey, buddy, we made it. We're here and before you know it, we won't just be cadets, we'll be damn officers!" Patrick's face was so scrunched up that his freckles all seemed to become one giant mass.

"Yeah, I wonder who the hell allowed that to happen! Musta been my charming personality!" said Fitz with a puffed chest.

"No, you pompous ass. It's the luck of the Irish! I'm tellin' you. I've been your lucky charm all along." He slapped Fitz on the back and dashed off to greet other cadets before they walked out to begin the ceremony.

Fitz took the opportunity to torment his cousin, Elliott. As Fitz walked toward him, Elliott turned to another cadet and said, "Oh, Christ, here he comes. Undoubtedly, he wants to remind me that he is the smarter, quicker, more athletic, and better-looking cousin."

"No doubt," replied the other cadet.

Fitz loved to one-up his cousin, knowing he would always win. Today was no exception.

"So, Elliott, where do you think you'll go after graduation? Have they hinted at an appointment for you?" Fitz taunted.

"Yes, I think I will get something. I'm just not sure what," admitted Elliott.

Fitz took a few long strides around his cousin. "And me? Oh, I'll probably stay on as an instructor, say mathematics. Or perhaps if the war breaks out, as we all assume it will at some point, I'll get an assignment as a field officer, perhaps a lieutenant."

"Yes, Fitz, you're very good at mathematics. I'm sure you will get a fine appointment. It'll be whatever your father wants for you," moaned Elliott as he rolled his eyes.

"Yes, perhaps they will send me out to the field as an officer. Give me a stallion to ride. Don't you think that would be fine, Elliott?" Fitz poked him in the stomach.

"Ugh! Yes, Fitz, just great. Can't you find someone else to torture?"

"Of course, I can, but I only have another week or so to torment you, cuz," chuckled Fitzwilliam as he smiled broadly. He tugged down his gray uniform jacket and pulled back his broad shoulders to emphasize the four inches in height he had over Elliott.

"Don't worry, buddy, you still might grow." Fitz slapped Elliott in the stomach and slid down the hallway, laughing.

"Bastard," Elliott mumbled to himself when Fitz was out of earshot.

"Yes, he is a bit of a ratbag, isn't he? Don't worry, if he didn't have his old man's money, he wouldn't be quite so bold," offered another classmate. "A few more days, and you won't have him to needle you anymore."

"Yeah, I suppose you're right, but he is such a self-centered bastard," groaned Elliott.

"Can't argue with you there, mate."

As the music for the ceremony started, the young men lined up and stood at attention. When given the signal, they marched in, standing tall and in an orderly fashion.

The Federals were holed up at Fort Sumter in Charleston's harbor. It was a three-story fortification just recently built, and Lincoln was anxious to try to hold onto it. Federal boats navigated through the waters of the harbor, eager to get supplies to the new fort in the event of an outbreak of war, but they had been largely unsuccessful. The cadets were full of excitement, eager to start a fight. There had been skirmishes for weeks now, and they hoped the much-anticipated conflict would erupt and they would be there.

Hentie and Big John had ascended to the gallery of the church to observe the ceremony from the only section of the church where they were permitted to sit and observe. Of course, the seating was much coarser and cramped, but it did allow them to rest their feet during the proceedings. They looked down on the crowd of White folks, all trying to outdo one another in their fine clothes.

"Ain't it amazing how much Fitz has grown to look like Tobias? I know dey really half-brothers, but dey sure was different as chillen. More so as young mens. Tobias is the gentle soul," Hentie pointed out.

"I expect Tobias got the soul of his mama, Baby Doll. Dat's where he got his kindness," said Big John.

Hentie pointed to a few of the White ladies sitting in the fifth row of pews. "Missus Langdon has tea with dem women down at the Hibernian Hall on Meeting Street. I hear dem call demselves the St. Cecilia Society. It's some group dey put together a hundred years ago. dey some musical society, but I hear how those ladies talk about each other, and it like to burn ya ears off! Um-hum. The way they gossip 'bout one 'nother. I don't see how they call themselves Christians. It's like a bunch of hens clucking away and peckin' at one 'nother."

Big John's kind face broke out in a broad smile. "Well, sometimes the White ladies can get like that. I think it's because they ain't got nothing better to do than make ugly comments 'bout other women."

"Such idleness they have. Those White women just drink tea and fret 'bout others. Dey got us to care for their children, clean dey houses, cook dey meals, and run dey plantations. Seems to me dey would find somethin' better to do with their time." Hentie scowled as she looked toward Big John.

Big John patted her hand and smiled. "Ain't nothing we can do about how White women spend their time. So long as they leave you alone, we just got to put up with it. We have it a lot better than others down in the slave village. We can thank God for that."

Suddenly, their attention was drawn away as they heard movement downstairs in the chapel. Everyone became quiet as they waited for the ceremony to start. Then, a tittering went through the crowd as some of the cadets with flags entered. Behind them were the commandant, the chaplain, and other academy officials. The flag officer shouted out a few commands, and the procession started.

Emily Langdon scooted in her seat and giggled like a little girl with excitement, anxious to see all the pageantry. Mr. Langdon shot her a scowl to settle her, which ultimately proved futile. As the young men in their gray woolen uniforms filed by, they continued their stiff military posture with eyes forward. Even though Fitzwilliam never glanced at his mother, she nonetheless sent him a glowing smile and a small wave.

As the ceremony progressed, a handful of cadets were recognized for their academic achievement. Fitzwilliam was called up to receive recognition as first in his class for achievement in the sciences. His mother let out a small yelp of excitement when they announced his name, then caught herself, covering her mouth with a gloved hand, but she still bounced in her seat.

The ceremony went on and a handful of others were recognized for their prowess in Romantic languages, Latin, military history, and the humanities. Then came an award for mathematics. Once again, Fitzwilliam's name was announced. This time, under her husband's watchful eye, Emily Langdon tried to be more restrained and politely applauded, all the while beaming with pride.

The ceremony concluded a short time later, and the cadets, clearly uncomfortable in their scratchy woolen uniforms, did their utmost to maintain a stiff military deportment. As they exited the chapel, mumbling began throughout the crowd, and guests started to exit the chapel. Mrs. Langdon noticed another planter's wife across the room, Mrs. Legare, and nodded at her. She then noticed Mrs. Mary Chestnut, who was always quite gracious to her and waved toward her. The two then stopped and chatted briefly before exiting the chapel.

Langdon paused and waited for Mr. Randolph from Richmond to exit. He wanted to speak with him further before leaving the area and going to dinner at the Planter Hotel. He was curious what the

Virginian thought about the impending war.

"Congratulations are in order," William Langdon said. "I heard your grandson was recognized during the proceedings for his leadership and bravery within the South Carolina Corps of Cadets." Apparently, they had recently been called into action.

"Why yes, they've been called down to help out with the Federals who've been circulating through Charleston Harbor. They're trying to quell their activities," noted Randolph.

"I hope we can count on you Virginians to support us should we need to stand up to those Yankees. You know trouble is brewing with them." Langdon looked deep into his eyes as he pulled on the lapels of his overcoat.

"Richmond is a city not too dissimilar from yours, sir. We are somewhat smaller than your fine city, but we hold many of the same values dear. We pride ourselves in Southern gentility and enterprise. Our social structure is critically important to us, and it is imperative that we keep it. Our identity as Southerners is crucial to us," Randolph tapped his walking stick on the ground to punctuate his point.

Robert Barnwell Rhett, overhearing the exchange, sidled over with his chest puffed out, ready to enter the discussion.

"You know our peculiar institution of slavery is at the core of our way of life here in the South. We rely on the labor of slaves to keep our plantations running. Slavery is the lynchpin of our economy. It is crucial to our agricultural life here . . . the cotton, rice, tobacco."

Langdon chimed in. "It certainly is. I couldn't manage my large plantation without my slaves. I have over two hundred now. I need that labor to plant the seed, tend to it as it takes hold, and then harvest it at the end of the season. Plus, I rent out some of the skilled laborers for extra income. Don't you?"

"And what white man would pick cotton with those sharp shards? They slice your fingers to bits!" Rhett looked to the visitor from Richmond for a response.

"True, we rent out enslaved workers, too. They keep a number of our industries running, like our iron industry. However, gentlemen, I am not sure that our citizenry could engage in some of the practices you seem to hold dear here, such as what you call 'public discipline.' Others might find that a bit offensive." He shook his head and shifted his feet.

Langdon barked, "Our slaves are necessary. We not only have agricultural interests, but many other commodities come from here. I make good money from renting out darkies to mine phosphate. It's a good reliable income for me. If I have a poor harvest, the income from phosphate helps balance it out. I can always rely on it."

Langdon paused, trying to contain his rage. Randolph looked on, somewhat intimidated. Rhett pounced.

"Our slave economy keeps things humming along. It's what God intended. Those unfortunate Negroes aren't able to care for themselves. They need our paternal care and guidance. It's part of God's divine plan. We are merely benevolent caretakers for them. Should the North push the question of slavery, we will be forced to secede." Rhett smiled and shook his head.

Langdon became emphatic. "Everyone in the South benefits from our economy. Our wealth gained from the planters keeps others employed: the merchants, the manufacturers, the shopkeepers, the public houses, and the inns. It's a symbiotic relationship. They live off our fine productive plantations. Without it, we'd all face ruination. Therefore, we must bind ourselves together as Southern brethren."

"Gentlemen, I hear your points," Randolph said calmly. "However, I cannot agree to the full course of your lifestyle. There must be limits, there must be some regard for humanity."

Langdon took a step closer. "Oh, there is. For White men of good breeding, there is. We simply do not consider darkies worthy of such consideration. As our fine statesman John Calhoun pointed out decades ago, they are inferior to us. We are doing them a service by keeping them as our slaves. We give them a chance at salvation by working under men who serve the Lord God, men who provide them with shelter, clothes on their backs, food to eat, and a trade. That is why we need to perpetuate our peculiar institution. Don't you understand?"

"Yes," said Rhett, we only have one choice should we be pushed. We must secede from the Union to keep slavery thriving. It will keep the economy thriving and expanding."

"Indeed," nodded Langdon.

Randolph's face began to redden. He stepped back a bit as his chest puffed up. He raised his voice defiantly as he glared at them. "Gentlemen, you have a queer way of thinking. I simply cannot agree with your ideas and your barbarity. You are not men of God, but followers of some malevolence masquerading as Christianity. In time, you will face God's wrath for your sins. It will happen all in good time and all your wealth will no longer matter." The Virginian poked a finger at them and turned on his heel, swiftly walking away from them.

The two Charlestonians were left standing on the street as their heads swiveled toward each other in amazement, their mouths ajar.

"I don't understand it. Why would he say such a thing?" gasped Langdon.

"Well, he is not from South Carolina, William. His thinking is different."

Chapter 6
The Shots Over Fort Sumter: The War Has Begun

The Lower Peninsula of Charleston, South Carolina, April 1861

With a crystal snifter in hand, William Langdon strolled along the piazza of the stately home of Joseph Manigault. Located on Meeting Street in the heart of Charleston, the eighteenth-century home was a fine example of accumulated Southern wealth. In the distance, Fort Sumter rose just across the harbor where there were scores of ships and vessels of various sizes—schooners, sloops, rigs of various kinds as well as paddle-wheel steamers, and small fisherman boats. The harbor was the South's economic juggernaut, a gateway to the world that created markets for Carolina's crops and goods.

From street level, Manigault's home appeared narrow, but it extended back quite a distance, a work yard and slave quarters behind it. To the side of the exquisite house was a carefully crafted garden with lemon trees, rose bushes, and other ornamental flowers. Swanlike blooms covered the plentiful gardenia bushes. The magnolia trees with their creamy blooms as big as dinner plates would later leave unopened pods on the ground, where they would burst with red seeds that stained the streets of sand and crushed oyster shells.

Manigault had inherited great wealth and married well. This French Huguenot family had worked as merchants and planters for generations. They owned several plantations and over two hundred enslaved servants. Manigault was first married to the daughter of Arthur Middleton, a signer of the Declaration of Independence, then later married Charlotte Drayton, who was also from a prominent family.

Langdon and Manigault had been friends for years and socialized with some frequency. Manigault hosted a party in honor of his good friend's son, Fitzwilliam. The Manigault home was situated much closer to the Citadel and convenient for their mutual guests.

It was a beautiful evening. The moon was starting to rise over Charleston with breezes gently wafting in from the harbor, gas lanterns flickering along the streets. A fluttering draft set the palmetto leaves clicking like crickets. Spanish moss dappled the streetscape as it waved at pedestrians from the branches of the magnificent oak trees.

Langdon proudly strutted about the grounds of the Manigault home, having seen his son graduate with honors from the Citadel and receive an officer's appointment. Socializing with like-minded Southerners, he felt confident about his and his son's futures. Fitz relished the attention he garnered from the eligible young ladies of Charleston at the various Citadel functions and galas thrown by Charleston's elite. William Langdon could only admire the boy for his charm. Fitzwilliam breezed through with a crystal champagne flute in his hand, and with a broad smile, joked with the host while keeping one eye on a fashionable young maiden.

Langdon had just gone through another favorable planting season, having opened up a tremendous amount of additional acreage for the growth and development of profitable Sea Island cotton. He was looking forward to a monumental season and even greater wealth. Others were circulating around him, and the champagne was flowing freely. Other Charlestonians were feeling optimistic about the future, too, despite the festering disputes between the United States and the nascent Confederacy. Whether the threat of a conflict with the Yankees would erupt into open warfare was yet to be seen.

As Hentie and Big John assisted in serving the guests, they took the opportunity to look around this fine city house. They were dazzled by the ornate furnishings, decorations, household accessories, and collection of artifacts from other countries. Obviously, the owner was well-traveled and spared no expense for his creature comforts. While emptying her tray in the warming kitchen, Hentie noticed a large alkaline-glazed stoneware jar. It was tan and had script on it. She poked Big John who had just entered the room and pointed to the pottery.

"What does that say on it? I've never seen anything like that."

Big John recognized the earthenware straight away. "Oh, that's special pottery made by a colored man named David Drake. Edgefield pottery, I think. David makes that pottery right here in South Carolina. He's owned by some man who runs a newspaper. I think his name is Landrum. We figure that's how he learned to read and write. Folks love it cause he always writes a little poem or rhymes on what he makes, then signs it. Crates of it come in on the waterfront. Folks talk about him a lot."

"How's he do this? How's he put these sayings on the pots?" asked Hentie.

"Well, after he forms the stoneware out of clay, he thinks up a little poem. Then he takes a sharp stick and makes an inscription on the side of the pot, then signs it. He really comes up with some clever stuff." Big John chuckled.

Stunned, Hentie said, "His master knows about this? He knows he can read and write? I wonder why he lets him do that. Couldn't they get into trouble?"

Big John just smiled. "I think folks love it so much that police look the other way. I also think his master may pay them a bit for overlooking it. His master makes a lot of money off that pottery, so he can afford to pay off those men."

"We best get back to serving the guests, Big John, before the master misses us. You know he wants this party to go well. You walk out first, and I'll carry a tray out with drinks for the master, mistress, and other guests." Hentie nodded at Big John as he turned and walked toward the parlor.

Hentie loaded up her tray with beverages and appetizers, then followed Big John out through the library and onto the piazza. She handed out the refreshments with politeness, making sure to nod and curtsy to each guest as she moved through the crowd. Having already emptied her tray, Hentie came to rest against the railing of the upstairs piazza.

Suddenly, the sounds of cannon fire rang out. Hentie, jolted by the reverberating boom, dropped her serving tray. Fortunately, at the moment she was not carrying any china or crystalware. The commotion spurred party guests to spring to their feet to look out over Charleston Harbor. Others were jarred by the sound and stood with their mouths agog, wondering whether they should take cover.

Manigault, harkened by the commotion, shouted from the first-floor piazza, "Our boys are firing on those damn Yankees at Fort Sumter. Look, they're firing the cannons lined up on the Battery! They are going to chase those damn Yankees out!"

"At long last! Chase those devils out!" shouted another guest.

"I say blow them out of the water and chase them back north!" Langdon raised his glass as if to toast the occasion.

"*Whoo hoo!* Our day has come. Take the fight to them!" shouted Fitzwilliam.

Other residents took to their rooftops to watch the spectacle. There was cheering and gaiety. People were smiling and laughing, springing to their feet in excitement. Crowds gathered on the streets and rooftops surrounding the Battery and White Point Garden as if it was a circus attraction or fireworks display.

The Confederate soldiers under the command of P. G. T. Beauregard had ordered Yankee Major Anderson to surrender along with his eighty-five men. He refused, so the forty-seven howitzers began to reduce the recently constructed fort.

As the bombardment continued, Charlestonians began to travel down to the waterfront by buggy, horseback, and afoot to see the show. The cast-iron Columbian cannons continued to roar as they shot cannon balls that arched through the air at a high trajectory. Balls made of fifty pounds of solid iron slammed against the fort's timber and stone walls. The explosions shook the fort like earthquakes.

Joy for those around Hentie, but not for her. A chill skittered up her arms and her stomach lurched. As if it were a premonition, she saw idealistic young men wounded and dying, their twisted bodies lying about in battlefront towns and fields. Hentie felt a quivering down her spine and tingle on out to her hands. No, this was no tournament or sporting event, but the end of a way of life. Hentie could hear the soldiers' cries as their suffering persisted, echoing through her mind. Freedom might come to Negroes, but at such a cost to the entire nation.

As Hentie began to pray she asked, *God, please bring a swift conclusion to the war we have just entered into.* She paused as her heart was momentarily lifted by the notion of freedom.

Dare one even pray for such an outcome? Might I one day be free? Big John and I can go where we want to and live as we please.

Hentie clasped her hands so tightly in prayer she left fingerprints near her knuckles. It was her ardent wish that God could hear her and embolden her in the months to come, as she knew it would be a long and turbulent road. "God, please grant us freedom. Please, God. Let our people be free and protect us from the conflict that has only just begun."

Hentie picked up her embellished silver tray and slowly walked among the guests. She remained distressed by the enthusiasm shared by all the guests regarding the outbreak of the conflict. *Don't they understand what this means?*

One guest, a middle-aged man with auburn hair pomaded back, leaving a rather shiny expanse of forehead, spoke with vigor. "Our boys fired right from the Battery at those loathsome Yankees. At long last, the Confederate Army proudly bombarded the Union troops who had been stockpiling supplies for months. Fort properly belongs to South Carolina, not the Federals."

A portly older man in a dark suit responded, "The Yankees, of course, by their mere presence provoked this whole matter. All this time the Union Army held possession of the fort. It's truly not theirs. It belongs to us. This has been brewing for quite some time. I'm glad it's come to a head."

"Yes, I'm glad we're finally kicking those devils out!"

Hentie returned to the interior of the house and stood in the emptiness of the butler's pantry, folding white linen napkins, and trying to contemplate what this all meant. Her fingertips brushed against the fine-combed threads that would later touch the lips of the master and mistress of the household along with their guests, an indulgence she would never know. As she stood there, she heard the tinkering of the small brass bell that the missus kept in her skirt pocket, to summon an enslaved servant to attend to her latest whim or desire. Fortunately, another nearby house girl from the Manigault house waited on her. Hentie sighed with relief.

While all the confusion was going on, Hentie thought she might slip out with Big John to hear the chatter among the enslaved workers on the peninsula. She asked the other house servants to cover for her in her absence. Octavia, the lady's maid to Mrs. Langdon, had asked her to try and make contact while in Charleston with her sister, Lydia, if she was able, as she lived just a few streets away from the Manigaults. Lydia used to live at Twin Oaks and was enslaved by Mr. Langdon, but he had sold her due to disagreements with his wife. Lydia now lived with a wealthy family on Rainbow Row near the Battery.

Hentie quickly scanned the house and located Big John. He agreed to go with her. William Langdon had been drinking and was otherwise engaged in the excitement. Emily Langdon had been mixing her drops with sips of champagne. Surely, she would be caught up in the excitement and not miss them for a few minutes. One at a time, they slipped out of the house, past the mansion's dependencies, initially past the kitchen house, then the stable, through the courtyard, and silently exited through the back gate of the property. First, Hentie slipped out the gate while Big John kept an eye out. Then he gradually followed. The two hurried down the street, then ducked into the alleyways toward Lydia's home.

Lydia's mistress and master had already left the house to watch the cannon fire upon the fort. They would be absent for the duration of the onslaught. In their absence, Lydia had likewise slipped out and was scurrying down an alleyway when she ran into Hentie and Big John.

As Lydia cautiously looked around, she saw Hentie and Big John. She couldn't believe her eyes. Such good fortune. Over the din, the three stood against a back fence to a mansion house and chatted. The three talked about their fears regarding the bombardment and their conflicting excitement over the idea of prospective freedom should the Yankees prevail.

"Lydia, what will you do if the Federals take over Charleston? You know if there are reinforcements they will destroy the city. Do you have a place to go?" Hentie's eyes were full of concern.

"Yes, I have friends who are free people of color who live up around the neck. I'll go there if need be. We can make our way on our own. If we have to, we can leave the city. I've been improving my skills as a seamstress. Should freedom come, I think I'll be able to support myself. You two will be fine out at Twin Oaks, at least for the time being." Lydia clasped Hentie's forearm to reassure her.

The three gossiped about Mrs. Langdon who was declining, continuing her reliance on her laudanum drops and how her husband dealt with it by turning his back on his inebriated wife. He relied on his servants to deal with her.

The friends decided they had best get back to their respective masters before they were discovered missing and quickly said their goodbyes. Lydia slipped along the back walls of the alley toward her home. Big John and Hentie scampered the other way toward the Manigault home. They took turns entering the back gate, looking through a knothole before appearing in the work yard behind the house. Folks were still in a tizzy about the cannon fire and didn't seem to notice their absence.

"What shall we do if the Yankees come marching through? Where will we go?" Mrs. Langdon slurred as she spoke to her husband.

"Oh, don't be ridiculous! Those Northerners will never march into Charleston. God would never let contemptible Yankee dogs have control over our city!"

Emily briefly turned away and harrumphed at his cross words. Another male guest with large mutton-chop sideburns and a thick mustache joined in, the notion seemingly so absurd to him, added, "This is just a little skirmish. It will be over soon. Surely, those Yankees will realize we want to keep producing crops and Sea Island cotton for them. Our cotton and all our crops keep this country going. They'll come to their senses. You'll see."

William Langdon countered, "Yes, don't be naïve, woman! We're seceding from the Union. We are forming our own country! We need to preserve our noble way of life in the South. They need our cotton. They want us to keep our way of life with all our laborers. They'll come to their senses and drop to their knees. Those damn Yankees have no idea what we can do to them! They may have their machines and factories in the North, but we have all the food, the labor, and the know-how. We have superior breeding and wit. They are helpless without us."

A resounding explosion then erupted; a momentary pause washed over the crowd. It appeared the engagement might be escalating. Big John and Hentie then heard a succession of local gunfire. With their eyes open wide in amazement, they looked at each other.

"But, sir, what if this little skirmish becomes a war?" Terrified, Hentie looked toward the Battery. "What if this turns into a war like the Revolution? That went on for years! What do we do then?"

"Oh, that will never happen, you'll see," Langdon waved off her concern and walked back toward the railing of the piazza.

Hentie, still stunned, looked over to her husband and said, "I don't know, Big John. I have a bad feeling about this. I think we're in for something terrible."

Partygoers were elated that the bombardment had commenced. The revelers thought it was something akin to a fireworks display, never realizing the true gravity of the moment. The months of tension had erupted; the conflict exploded in a barrage of artillery fire. From the rooftop of the Manigault's home, they watched cannon fire pelt the fortification.

Confederate General Beauregard had brought the fight to the enemy, and the Rebels were giving the Yanks a black eye.

Following a mere thirty-four hours of artillery fire, the Union forces surrendered. The Yanks were being starved out and running low on munitions; they had no other choice but to concede. The battle seemed to end quickly enough. In less than forty-eight hours, the War Between the States appeared to be over. The Federals waved a white flag and acknowledged that they could not continue without reinforcements, supplies, and armaments. They were permitted to leave peacefully as the Rebels held their fire. There were celebrations everywhere as Charlestonians assumed this conflict had been blissfully short and that the Union had conceded. Little did they know, it was merely the beginning of what would be one of the bloodiest conflicts known to mankind. Charlestonians and other Southerners believed the war had come to a glorious end. They never suspected that President Lincoln would swiftly recruit seventy-five thousand militia volunteers to answer the call to arms and preserve the Union at all costs.

Upon graduation from the Citadel, Fitzwilliam Langdon was appointed a second lieutenant in the Confederate Army. However, within a matter of months, he was promoted to the rank of captain. Many of the Confederate officers were well along in their years at the outbreak of the War for Southern Independence. Numerous officers had fought in the War of 1812 and the Mexican American War. These more seasoned field officers were being either killed or wounded in great numbers on the battlefield. As a result, young men were swiftly promoted in the Confederate States of America, or CSA.

As the hostilities continued, lists of the dead were posted on a near weekly basis in towns throughout America. For many, these battles were being fought far away from home, and it was easy at times for Charlestonians to deny that the United States was engaged in a mighty conflict, but reality kept sinking in, either through newspapers, letters from the front, the wounded returning home, or soldiers being granted furloughs. Despite the South's denial, the truth was leaching into its consciousness, as evidenced by the last letter from Major Sullivan Ballou, written to his wife leading up to the battle at First Bull Run.

> *Headquarters, Camp Clark*
> *Washington, D.C., July 14, 1861*
> *My Very Dear Wife:*
>   *Indications are very strong that we shall move in a few days, perhaps to-morrow. Lest I should not be able to write*

you again, I feel impelled to write a few lines, that may fall under your eye when I shall be no more.

Our movement may be one of a few days' duration and full of pleasure and it may be one of severe conflict and death to me. Not my will, but thine, O God be done. If it is necessary that I should fall on the battle-field for any country, I am ready. I have no misgivings about, or lack of confidence in, the cause in which I am engaged, and my courage does not halt or falter. I know how strongly American civilization now leans upon the triumph of government, and how great a debt we owe to those who went before us through the blood and suffering of the Revolution, and I am willing, perfectly willing to lay down all my joys in this life to help maintain this government, and to pay that debt.

But, my dear wife, when I know, that with my own joys, I lay down nearly all of yours, and replace them in this life with care and sorrows, when, after having eaten for long years the bitter fruit of orphanage myself, I must offer it, as their only sustenance, to my dear little children, is it weak or dishonorable, while the banner of my purpose floats calmly and proudly in the breeze, that my unbounded love for you, my darling wife and children, should struggle in fierce, though useless, contest with my love of country.

I cannot describe to you my feelings on this calm summer night, when two thousand men are sleeping around me, many of them enjoying the last, perhaps, before that of death, and I, suspicious that Death is creeping behind me with his fatal dart, am communing with God, my country and thee.

I have sought most closely and diligently, and often in my breast, for a wrong motive in this hazarding the happiness of those I loved, and I could not find one. A pure love of my country, and of the principles I have often advocated before the people, and "the name of honor, that I love more than I fear death," have called upon me, and I have obeyed. Sarah, my love for you is deathless. It seems to bind me with mighty cables, that nothing but Omnipotence can break; and yet, my love of country comes over me like a strong wind, and bears me irresistibly on with all those chains, to the battlefield. The memories of all the blissful moments I have spent with you come crowding over me, and I feel most deeply grateful to God and you, that I have enjoyed them so long. And how hard it is for me to give them up, and burn to ashes the hopes of future years, when, God willing, we might still have lived and loved together, and seen our boys grow up to honorable manhood around us.

I know I have but few claims upon Divine Providence, but something whispers to me, perhaps it is the wafted prayer of my little Edgar, that I shall return to my loved ones unharmed. If I do not, my dear Sarah, never forget how much I love you, nor that, when my last breath escapes me on the battle-field, it will whisper your name.

Forgive my many faults, and the many pains I have caused you. How thoughtless, how foolish I have oftentimes been! How gladly would I wash out with my tears, every little spot upon your happiness, and struggle with all the misfortune of this world, to shield you and my children from harm. But I cannot, I must watch you from the spirit land and hover near you, while you buffet the storms with your precious little freight, and wait with sad patience till we meet to part no more.

But, O Sarah, if the dead can come back to this earth, and flit unseen around those they loved, I shall always be near you in the garish day, and the darkest night amidst your happiest scenes and gloomiest hours always, always, and, if the soft breeze fans your cheek, it shall be my breath; or the cool air cools your throbbing temples, it shall be my spirit passing by.

Sarah, do not mourn me dear; think I am gone, and wait for me, for we shall meet again.

As for my little boys, they will grow as I have done, and never know a father's love and care. Little Willie is too young to remember me long, and my blue-eyed Edgar will keep my frolics with him among the dimmest memories of his childhood. Sarah, I have unlimited confidence in your maternal care, and your development of their characters. Tell my two mothers, I call God's blessing upon them. O Sarah, I wait for you there! Come to me, and lead thither my children.
- Sullivan

This letter may never have been mailed to the major's wife. Following his death, it was found in his trunk with his other personal belongings. It was subsequently reclaimed and delivered to his widow by Governor William Sprague.

⁓

Sullivan Ballou was a successful, thirty-two-year-old attorney in Providence, Rhode Island, and the former Speaker of the Rhode Island House of Representatives. After the bombardment of Fort Sumter in April 1861, President Lincoln called on the states to provide 75,000 militia troops to put down the Southern rebellion. Responding to the president's call for volunteers, Ballou enlisted in the 2nd Rhode Island Infantry, where he was elected major. It was while he was acting in this role that he wrote his infamous letter.

Major Ballou was born to a prominent French Huguenot family in Smithfield, Rhode Island. Unfortunately, his father died when he was still quite young; nonetheless, he was able to continue his education. As a boy, he enrolled in Nicholas Academy in Dudley, Massachusetts. As a young teenager he attended one of the finest boarding schools in the world, Phillips Academy in Andover,

Massachusetts. After his graduation from Phillips, he entered Brown University the following autumn. He then went on to study law at the National Law School in Ballston, New York. After his graduation, he was subsequently admitted to the bar in Rhode Island. Thereafter, he entered legal practice in 1853. Two years later, in October 1855, he married Sarah Hart Shumway, whom he loved deeply. Together, they had two sons, Edgar and William.

Ballou was active in public affairs. In 1854, soon after beginning his law practice, he was elected to the Rhode Island House of Representatives. He was chosen as Clerk of the House, and later as the Speaker. He was a staunch Republican and supporter of Abraham Lincoln.

Ballou promptly volunteered for military service and encouraged others to do so as well. He was commissioned a major in the 2nd Rhode Island Infantry Regiment. He was third in command of the Regiment, after Colonel John Slocum and Lieutenant Colonel Frank Wheaton. He was also appointed judge advocate of the Rhode Island militia.

The 2nd Rhode Island soon moved to Washington and joined the Union Army of Northeastern Virginia. On July 21, 1861, the regiment took part in the First Battle of Bull Run, or what was also known as the First Manassas outside Washington, D.C.

As a senior officer, Ballou was out in front of the troops while on horseback to better direct them. Unfortunately, this made him an easy target for enemy troops. He was hit by a cannonball from a Confederate six-pounder cannon, which tore off part of his right leg and killed his horse. He was carried off the field, and the remainder of his leg was amputated. The Union Army was defeated and retreated to Washington, and Ballou was left behind.

Ballou died from his wound a week after the battle and was buried in a nearby graveyard at Sudley Church. He was one of ninety-four men of the 2nd Rhode Island killed or mortally wounded at Bull Run. He was thirty-two at the time of his death; his wife Sarah was twenty-four.

The battle area was occupied by Confederate forces, and Ballou's body was allegedly exhumed, decapitated, and further desecrated by Confederate troops; his body was never recovered. In place of his body, charred ash and bone believed to be his remains were reburied in Swan Point Cemetery in Providence. Reportedly, this was a scandalous practice going on among Confederate soldiers to collect or unearth the remains of fallen Union soldiers and keep them as trophies. Confederates' quest for bones thus was connected to a bizarre history of the use, and misuse, of human remains. Although the practice started as a search for Union uniform buttons and other souvenirs, it became far more macabre. They started to collect bones and skulls which they claimed they would use as drinking cups. Bones from the Bull Run were taken as acts of domination and displayed as trophies of war in the South. It seems that the Rebel soldiers were both horrified and exhilarated by the bloody world of combat and transferred their mixed emotions into this collection of objects with violent histories.

Major Ballou's wife, Sarah, remained a widow and never remarried. She later moved to New Jersey to live with her son, William. She died at age eighty-two in 1917; her remains were buried beside her husband's.

Chapter 7
The South Awakens from its Long-Contented Sleep

Twin Oaks Plantation, Mount Pleasant, South Carolina, July 1861

The morning was already off to a hectic start as the missus was in a tizzy. Mr. and Mrs. Langdon were having their morning meal in the large, well-appointed dining room. The two sat at either end of a long, highly polished mahogany table. Tall candle sticks and a gay floral arrangement were carefully placed in the center of the table, which helped block Langdon's view of his wife, per his instructions.

Mrs. Langdon nibbled at her breakfast and complained throughout the meal. She didn't seem to find anything to her satisfaction. She had a boiled egg, fried potatoes, a piece of pork, and a corn cake, but none of it suited her.

"This food isn't fit for human consumption! The pork is dry, and the corn cake is gritty. How do you expect a woman of good breeding to eat such slop?" Mrs. Langdon slapped her right hand on the tabletop, soundly thumping the wood.

Two house servants were standing in their proper stations, up against the wall with hands folded before them. Hentie, the elder of the two, jerked backward and froze in her place, unsure of what to do. She was never certain how to best address the mistress' moodiness. Hentie glanced over to Octavia, the lady's maid, for guidance. Octavia had taken a few steps forward from her station against the wall to respond to the mistress' outburst. She used a soothing tone, almost as a mother would try to console a cranky young child.

"Well, ma'am, would you like me to see if the cook can make up some fresh Johnny cakes, perhaps some fritters and fresh fruit for ya? Or maybe I can see if she's bakin' some fresh bread for the midday meal. Maybe you'd like that?"

"No, I've simply lost my appetite. The potatoes are too cold, the pork too dry and salty and the egg is too bland. None of it is fit for a woman of my station."

Mrs. Langdon tossed her linen napkin onto her plate and rose from the table. William didn't even glance up as he reread an article in a week-old newspaper. His wife shoved her chair out in an angry, heaving motion while making a clicking sound on the roof of her mouth. As she rose from her chair, she shot an angry look over at her husband, who seemed to remain oblivious to her angst.

As she exited the room, her petticoats and stiff skirt swayed, rustling with her movements across the deep red oriental rug. Once her buttoned-up booted foot hit the wide-planked floorboards, her heels clicked as she progressed to the front stairwell.

Speaking to no one in particular, Mrs. Langdon announced, "I will be upstairs reading the Good Book and doing my morning prayers. I can ask the good Lord for guidance as to how I can better tolerate the burden I must bear . . . my mindless household servants and my petulant betrothed."

"Oh yes, ma'am. We'll make sure to let the ma'sa know," called Octavia.

"I guess one can't expect much more from ignorant darkies. They are only able to understand so much. Unfortunately, they can never understand the simplest things, nor can my beloved. Perhaps the Lord God can imbue me with more tolerance in my suffering," she huffed.

Octavia whispered a note of resignation to Hentie as she shook her head and rolled her large brown eyes. "Ain't nothing we gonna do right today. The missus is in one of her moods."

Standing at a safe distance from Mr. Langdon, the two spoke in hushed tones. Octavia stacked a few emptied dishes on the sideboard and reached under the tea cozy to ensure the teapot still had enough warm tea for her master.

"Well, I best clear this table and get things tidied up in case the missus changes her mind and walks back in here. She might start tossing the china. She's so unpredictable. You never know when she'll throw one of her tantrums!" Hentie quietly hissed as she quickly started picking up the dishes.

Hentie threw a glance over to her master to see if he was in a better mood than his wife, but he just continued to focus on the newspaper, squinting as he adjusted his spectacles. He moved his lips as he went through a list of names of those local soldiers killed or wounded in the most recent battle. So many men had sustained atrocious injuries, losing arms, legs, even eyes, and portions of their faces. The brutality of the Yankees enraged him.

Langdon abruptly burst out in anger. "Those damn Yankees! Why don't they just let us leave the Union? We'd be a lot better off. We have thrived in the South. We have more refined ways and have far more wealth than the North! Can't they see we have a superior way of life?"

"Yes, Ma'sa, it's been that way for years, don't them Yankees know that?" murmured Octavia as she placed another warm buttermilk biscuit on his plate with silver tongs.

"Undoubtedly, when this comes to its natural conclusion, the South will remain as it has for decades, strong and indomitable, just as God intended."

Hentie and Octavia exchanged a glance as Octavia carefully

poured her master another cup of tea. Octavia kept a steady hold on the heirloom teapot given to Langdon by his grandfather, a planter and merchant from Charleston. The porcelain clay used to make the pot was collected by an artisan named John Bartlam trained in Staffordshire, England, and then relocated near Charleston in Cain Hoy. His small business aimed to compete with the British Wedgewood luxury porcelain market. To increase its popularity, he used the palmetto tree motif on the teapot, so beloved by South Carolinians. Langdon never raised an eyebrow at his otherwise beloved pot and remained engrossed in his reading.

Octavia shook her head in agreement. "Uh huh, those Yankees, they just don't know any better. I guess they will just have to learn the hard way, Ma'sa."

As she turned her back on her self-absorbed master, Octavia shot a look at Hentie and gently shook her head. Consumed with events, Langdon didn't appear to notice the exchange.

Knowing her master would continue to be engrossed in the newspaper for some time, as was his morning routine for years now, Hentie spoke to her longtime friend and fellow house girl in a quiet voice. "Octavia, I'm going to take some of the dishes back to the kitchen house, then go upstairs and tidy the missus' room. Can you handle everything down here?" Hentie wiped her hands on her apron as she spoke.

"You go ahead," Octavia whispered. "Best attend to them things before the missus gets riled. I have two of the young ones from the kitchen house over here with me. One is five years old and can help. We can tidy up the dining room and the warming kitchen, then start things for the midday meal." Octavia shooed Hentie off with a wave of her hand as she spoke.

Hentie started to pile some dishes, cutlery, and glassware onto a tray for the kitchen house and exited the dining room. She toted the tray of items over to be washed and reused later in the day. While in the kitchen house, she spoke briefly with Nellie to unload some of her angst. Hentie had known Nellie since her first day at Twin Oaks some three decades earlier and had always felt safe sharing her thoughts with this woman.

"You best make somethin' to the missus' likin' for dinner. She is in a mood today. The master just ignores her and keeps on with his business. Can't say I blame him none. Don't know how I'd stay married to that woman neither." Hentie chuckled and waved her hand.

"Well, it sho' ain't the first time the missus been in a mood. I just do the best I can. I'm makin' a chicken for they dinner." Nellie nodded and winked.

"I wish you good luck, then."

Hentie scraped some of the leftovers onto a roughhewn wooden slab used by the slaves for plates. It was for a little barefoot Negro girl dressed in a cutout gunny sack in the kitchen house. Then she dropped a few bits into a hand-carved small wooden bowl for a little spotted dog that hung around. Hentie smiled as she gave the wooden plate to the young child and gave the bowl to the little dog. Young children generally ate with their fingers, as utensils were scarce since they all had to be handmade. The two had voracious appetites, gobbling up the scraps. They were the first morsels they'd been given that day. Hentie offered them both water to wash it down.

The child's mama worked in the cotton field during the daylight hours, so Nellie kept an eye on her. The enslaved little girl, not yet four-years-old, was still too young to do much work around the plantation, so her master must not have felt she deserved clothes yet. His general rule: you have to work to earn your clothes. If you do labor somewhere on the plantation, you get your annual ration of fabric at Christmastime. Maybe next year she would be old enough to be assigned work duties.

Tobias, another one of the enslaved house servants, suddenly appeared in the kitchen house doorway. The tall, fair, broad-shouldered young man nearly took up the entire threshold.

"Y'all have any leftovers for a hungry young man who just

finished helpin' out in the stable?" whispered Tobias as he eagerly scanned the worktable for a leftover biscuit.

"Now you know how that crazy mistress feels 'bout the enslaved snatchin' up the leftovers Tobias! You tryin' to get us both whipped?" hissed Nellie.

Quick as a rabbit, Tobias snatched up two biscuits and dashed out the door. "You ain't assistin' nuttin' if I'm stealin' 'em." He stuffed the biscuits in his pockets and ran toward the barn where he could safely devour them.

"Tobias! You rascal!" Nellie called after him; but it was too late. He was already half-way across the work yard.

Hentie had witnessed the exchange and whooped in laughter, slapping her leg and bending over as she continued to cackle. "Nellie, we too old to catch the likes of Tobias." She leaned her back against the kitchen house as she let the scene pass from her mind, smiling at the image of Tobias's large frame hustling away from Nellie with her raised wooden spoon and flour-covered apron.

Hentie took just a moment to stretch out her back and rest before heading back to the big house. For a fleeting moment, she wondered how her friend, Juba, who used to share a slave cabin with her, might be doing. Hentie had heard Juba was somewhere down in the town of Beaufort. Only about eighty miles south by water, but an insurmountable distance for a slave to travel on foot, or even by bantu boat. Hentie had been so close to Juba for a time. She had taken her newfound friend under her wing when she first came to the Mount Pleasant plantation. Langdon had bought her when he traveled north of Charleston some forty miles to Georgetown, South Carolina. William Langdon owned another plantation up that way with his brother near the town of McClellanville.

Juba had been brutalized while living at that former plantation. When Langdon first brought Juba to Twin Oaks, she appeared sad and dejected. She had short, cropped hair, a medium complexion, and her dress hung on her modest frame. Juba had horrific scars on her upper arm and chest that must have somehow been concealed on the auction block. Moreover, the slave trader failed to disclose to Langdon that Juba had just delivered her master's baby a few weeks prior, and his wife had insisted the woman be sold. Juba had been violated in so many ways while living in Georgetown, not only by her master, but also then ridiculed and abused by his wife. Langdon overlooked the burn marks on Juba's one arm and shoulder where the mistress had thrown boiling water on her.

Hentie had sensed Juba was full of dread and helped soothe those fears. Over time, Hentie helped bring Juba out of her melancholy with her steady, calm support. Then Juba met a field hand, Cuffee, a young, attractive Black man. He was muscular and seethed with virility. There was a spark between the two from the moment they first laid eyes on each other. Their magnetism took hold and the love that evolved helped heal Juba's soul. Eventually, at Big John's urging, Langdon let the two jump the broom and were recognized as man and wife, at least on his ledgers. Slaves were considered chattel property and legally barred from marrying. Jumping the broom was merely ceremonial.

One day, Juba and Cuffee's fate abruptly changed. Langdon had been in a tumultuous mood over the recent death of his enslaved Negro concubine, Doll Baby, who had been drowned by his own hand a few weeks earlier. While in the kitchen house speaking with the cook, he erupted into a rage. He began shouting and hurling objects. Juba rushed in to see what was going on. In her hurry, she accidentally sloshed milk onto her master from a pitcher she was carrying from the dairy barn. The already enraged Langdon called for harsh retribution for this trivial mishap. He had Juba whipped, and then sold her to a slave master in another county.

Hentie could still picture Juba as she fell to her knees and begged her master for mercy. "It was only an accident, Ma'sa! I'm so sorry!" She had crumbled on the floor and was sobbing as she begged, but Langdon just stepped over her as if she was mere trash that had carelessly been tossed on the floor. Duke, the plantation driver, had dragged her out to the whipping post.

Simon McBride was waiting for her outside with his whip hanging around his neck like a snake hungry to strike. His cheek was swollen with a wad of tobacco, and his speech was slurred from the whiskey he had serendipitously sipped earlier that morning. McBride lashed her hands to the pole, then tore open the back of her dress, fully exposing her flesh.

"There you go, nigga," McBride scowled as he spit a stream of tobacco juice and exposed his brown rotting teeth, grinning with anticipation.

Langdon watched as Juba was lashed to the post, but then turned away saying, "Stupid wench! A slave's misfortune is brought on by their own actions. They're stupid, ignorant dogs!"

With each blow, the razor-sharp whip had cut her skin and tore off bits of flesh. The velocity of the lash had enough punch to knock Juba several inches each time it struck. She grimaced in agony as she was pitched forward with each blow. The bright-red blood pulsed onto her light-blue calico dress darkening it as it flowed. Gradually, Juba's dress turned midnight blue, totally saturated with blood. After several minutes into the beating, she hung limply from the trauma, unconscious. Hentie thought it was probably better that way; Juba's pain was temporarily suspended.

Hentie shook away her thoughts and wiped away the tears that had started to roll down her cheeks as she recalled the incident. It would never be easy to visit Juba. All Hentie could do was pray Juba had a better life and that the same Lord God looked down on them both with compassion.

Turning to the task at hand, Hentie walked to the rear of the big house and entered the warming kitchen. She passed through the butler pantry and pushed on a panel that led up the back staircase to the bedrooms, her knees creaking as she ascended the steps. She patted her thigh as she progressed as if it might dispel the pain. She needed to focus on the work before her, not the aching in her aging joints as she moved upwards to the mistress' bedroom.

Once upstairs, Hentie nearly collided with her husband, Big John, as he moved swiftly from Langdon's bedchamber, smiling broadly.

"Morning, sunshine!" His face lit up and his cheeks glowed. "How you doin' this fine day?" He gently reached out to touch her elbow.

"You best stop that right now. You know the missus is as crazy as a bed bug and likely to have you lashed for your tomfoolery!" Hentie hissed as she pulled away from his touch, then glanced around to see who might be watching.

"Hentie," Big John just looked down, smiled, and shook his head. "Master sent you to clean out Fitzwilliam's room. Make sure it's all tidy. Master's hopin' Fitz will be coming home soon on leave and will need to rest. God knows what that boy been through."

Hentie tilted her head, warming to her husband, then asked, "When that goin' to happen?"

"Don't really know, but master is hopin' soon," answered Big John.

"Well, it will have to wait a bit. I need to attend to the missus and her room. She in a mood today, I'll do Fitz's room next." Hentie reached outward and smoothed her hand on Big John's broad chest.

"Master said to get rid of his old clothes he wore before he went off to the Citadel. He's a man now and a Confederate officer," Big John said. "He should be dressing more like a gentleman heading up this plantation. He said to give Fitz's old clothes to Tobias. Surprised he'll even acknowledge the two are half-brothers. Anyway, it's fittin' as he's his manservant, Tobias gettin' his old clothes."

"Soon as I'm finished with the missus' room. I need to make sure her bed's all made and clothes put up." Hentie bit down on her bottom lip.

Big John nodded, softly chuckled. "Yeah, I thought I heard her hollering a bit ago."

"I expect she'll be goin' for her drops by midday and ready to have a lie down on her feather bed." Hentie pulled out some fresh sheets and pillowcases from a hall cabinet as she remembered her next task.

"Mercy me, she is one difficult lady," Big John said.

The two parted, both looking back to get that last look at one another. Then Hentie tapped on the missus' door, drew in a deep breath, preparing herself for the missus' angst.

Mrs. Langdon sat in a high-back upholstered chair, jerkily rocking herself as she read at a fast pace from her Bible, mouthing the words. It was almost as if she was in a trance, muttering to herself, moving to and fro. Occasionally, Hentie could discern some of her words, but only intermittently.

"And then the Lord said . . . the rapture is coming . . ."

Having become an expert in how to stealthily move about a room, Hentie tiptoed across the immense space, past the magnificent mahogany framed bed with an elaborately carved pediment hung with ivory-colored bed curtains. The headcloth and valances were decorated with intricate embroidery, but the sides were less ornate, draped with netting, and served to create a barrier between the person reclining and the omnipresent mosquitoes of the South.

Oh no, the missus has been taking her drops again. Just look at this room. Hentie set the linens down on a side table, then walked toward a dressing table with graceful cabriole legs and began to straighten it. Garish necklaces laden with rubies, emeralds, pearls, broaches, and hat pins had been mindlessly tossed about. Talcum powder had been dusted across the precious jewels and the remainder of the tabletop, showering it with a white coating. Seemed like such a shame to see precious things most ladies would prize treated so carelessly. As Hentie continued to tidy up the room, she moved over to the mistress' armoire. She picked up the petticoats and cotton chemises that the mistress had dropped on the floor when she decided she was no longer interested in them.

There was a knock on the door and Hentie swiftly answered so as not to disturb the missus. It was Tobias. He stood tall in the doorway, looking so much like the master himself, as well as his son,

Fitzwilliam. All three were so tall, broad-shouldered, and fair with those unique pale green eyes. In Tobias's hand was a letter for Mrs. Langdon.

When the mistress heard the voice of a man, she looked up and broke into a smile.

"Fitzwilliam, my darling boy! You're home! Oh, thank the Lord. My prayers have been answered. You're home safe and sound."

In her excited state, she clumsily pushed herself out of her chair, propelling herself forward and starting to lose her balance.

"But ma'am, you're mistaken, I'm—" Uncertain about what to do next, Tobias froze.

Hentie took a step toward him, throwing out a hand to help balance the mistress, and then spoke to him in a hushed tone. "Tobias, play along, she's not in her right mind. She's been in her laudanum drops again."

The mistress continued toward him, stumbling, then eagerly threw her arms about him in a warm embrace. Her legs wobbled as she stood.

"Oh, my Fitzwilliam. I am so happy you're home." With his eyes wide, he looked to Hentie for direction. He knew that Negroes were forbidden to touch White people. Tobias caught Mrs. Langdon just as she started to fall toward the floor. He made sure he merely supported her with one arm around her waist. He then handed the letter to Hentie to take care of for the moment until the mistress was able to gain her bearings.

"It was brought to Twin Oaks by a military courier. The man said it's a letter from Fitzwilliam, apparently from an encampment somewhere in Virginia," Tobias said quietly to Hentie.

"I believe I heard the missus say her son was sent up that way, but I'm not sure what that means," said Hentie, looking puzzled.

The missus let out a moan but was still swooning and not following the conversation.

"Look, it's got a red seal on it. So, it can't be no death notice, or it'd be black. But the courier said to give it to Mrs. Langdon straight away, as it was real important like. I can make out a little bit, but not this writing."

"I wonder if somethin's goin' on up in Virginia. Maybe Master Fitzwilliam wants to tell his mama 'bout it," Hentie said quietly with one eyebrow cocked.

Tobias turned his attention to Mrs. Langdon who was still hanging on his chest. He looked into her face and said, "Mother, I must get back to my duties. I have to leave now. I will visit with you later today perhaps."

"No, I've missed you so much. Thank God you've come home to me. I don't want to let you go, not yet!" Mrs. Langdon insisted, almost like a small child, begging for Tobias to stay.

"Let me help you to a chair. You rest and I'll come back later. How would that be, Mother?" Tobias tried to manipulate the mistress into letting go of his neck and sitting so she would not fall.

Hentie added to Tobias's urging. "Ma'am, I'm sure you don't wanna keep yo' son from his official duties. He's a fancy officer now, 'member? I think I heard some of the horses coming up the lane to fetch him just now. He'd best go. He'll be back later, ma'am." Hentie looked deeply into the mistress' eyes and dipped her head to reassure her it was all true.

"Well, then if you must go." The misses' head began to roll again as she sat back in her upholstered wingback chair. It was as if she used up everything she had in those passing moments.

"I know you must be off, Ma'sa Fitzwilliam. You travel safe," Hentie announced loudly.

"Goodbye," the mistress slurred. She lifted her hand a couple of inches, then dropped it, and her head bobbed a moment before it fell back into the cushion of the chair.

Tobias swiftly exited the room, giving a quick nod and a wave to Hentie who looked down at her hand and the colorful envelope emblazoned with the Confederate flag. She stuffed it into one of the deep pockets on the front of her apron. She thought she would show it to her husband Big John later for him to review. *He can read. He'll know what to do.* Still puzzled by what it might mean, she let her mind wander a bit, curious as to how matters were on the war front.

Chapter 8
Farewell to the Ninety Days' War

The Battle of Bull Run (The First Manassas)

Emily Langdon started to put three-year-old enslaved children through a routine that she said would "make them grow likely for the market." First, she made them line up outside the big house and open their mouths wide while she spooned fed them a foul concoction made of garlic and other oils, including fish oil. Following this, so that they would learn to quickly move in response to their mistress, the children were forced to race around a large oak tree in the yard. Mrs. Langdon kept a whip dangling from her belt, which she freely used on any child whom she didn't think ran fast enough. The children referred to the whip as the blue lizard.

"All right all you niggra children, line up. Time for your medicine. It will make you grow strong and tall. Your submission to your medicine is a godly act. It is God's will that you submit yourself to His will and that of your master and mistress. It was His intention that you serve, even starting at a young age. That's why I have you pull weeds and tote water. It's God's will, you know."

Believing that he was being not only a good boy for his parents and his mistress, but for God himself, Titus would quickly jump into line. As the mistress barked out her orders, Titus kept his eyes on the blue lizard. He could tell when the mistress' temperament was about to change. She would start to touch the leather whip, fingering the very tip of it. Sometimes she would just put her flat palm on the handle as if she were warming up to grab it.

After pouring her putrid concoction down the throats of the children, she took several steps back. Titus would watch as her wide hooped skirt move to and fro and made a rustling noise. His heart would start to pound and legs quaked; he wanted to jump out from the line of children, much like a racehorse from the starting gate, because he yearned to please his mistress and be spared the dragon's sting. That was his earliest memory of the missus.

One hot Lowcountry summer morning when Titus was six years old, he arrived a few minutes late to the work yard. He had been up all night with a severe toothache. The barefoot little boy wore tattered breeches five inches too short with numerous patches sewn into them. His Negro cloth shirt was all but rags as it hung from his bony shoulders.

The enslaved workers were generally only given about fifteen minutes after the morning bell to be outside the slave quarters and ready to work. The young boy unsuccessfully struggled to make it out to the grounds on time that morning. He had tossed and turned all night with throbbing pain. The movements and snoring of the eleven others who shared his small two-room slave cabin only added to his inability to find rest. The remedies Rosa, the worker at the infirmary, had provided him proved ineffective. The tortuous pain persisted; it was only when Rosa finally gave him laudanum drops she had pinched from the missus that he eventually drifted off to sleep well after midnight. It was still dark out, not even five in the morning, when he finally dragged himself to join the lineup of other children.

The workdays of the enslaved started early and went from "day clean" until dusk or "first dark." As Titus stood between the other young workers, he held his small hand to his cheek.

"Where you been damn pickaninny niggra child? When that morning bell rings, you show up," shouted overseer Simon McBride, a stout man with leonine hair turning gray.

"Don't mean no disrespect, sir. This tooth been achin' me terrible!" said Titus.

"I don't give a damn what's been aching you. It's morning. The workday has done started, and you weren't here. I know what'll cure you of the pain in your tooth! A damn good lashing. That's the best way to cure a niggra's toothache! Won't mind his tooth at all now," the overseer said with an acerbic smile.

With that, the overseer ordered his underling Negro slave driver to whip Titus. The overseer's impetuous decision took all those around him by surprise; his words hung in the air. It seemed horribly cruel to whip a small child for having a dreadful toothache.

The driver, Sancho, quietly gasped when he heard McBride's order. The young boy was small for his age and rather frail looking. The driver was concerned that the child might not survive a sound lashing. Sancho hoped the overseer might leave the area so he could perhaps lessen the impact of the flogging. The driver was in a precarious position as a man of color who lived among the bondsmen in the slave community but was charged with enforcing the rules of the plantation and doling out discipline whenever ordered to do so.

Sancho, a man not yet forty with a powerful build, began to show off some of his bravado for the benefit of the overseer. He was nothing more than an ox or horse to McBride and Langdon, and he knew it. Sancho tore a cowhide whip from his waistband and began to stretch and pull at it to loosen it up. He circled the young boy and paced in front of the children, cracking the whip over his head while simultaneously berating the now visibly shaking child. His showmanship seemed compelling. McBride, still watching the proceedings, needed to consider the ordeal credible and sufficiently brutal, as he thought it necessary to maintain order and maximum productivity.

In order to ensure that the overseer found the performance adequate, Sancho puffed out his chest and began to circle the boy, his thick brows knitted together. He wanted the overseer to think he would carry out the lashing with all his might, so he began to bully the petite boy. He then rolled the whip up and snapped it to his belt, much like a snake lying in wait. Sancho reached down and jerked up the young Titus by the arm and shoved him forward, allowing him to fall to the ground with such an impact it knocked the air out of him.

Sancho shouted as he kicked the boy in the side causing him to emit a yelp, followed by a guttural moan. The boy rolled over onto his side and gasped for air. Sancho turned and walked over to a locked cabinet kept at the edge of the work yard that kept a collection of weapons and restraints, a whip about nine feet long, a cobbing board full of angular holes, various hickory sticks, more cowhide, lead, ropes, clubs, various shackles, and a chain. He withdrew a brass key from his Guernsey wool trousers and unlocked the trove of tortuous devices. He studied the weapons, pondering over them like he was trying to decide between apple pie or pumpkin. He drew out a long, leathery hickory stick, and in an instant, struck it with all his might against a leather saddle hung across a nearby fence post. *Thwap. Thwap.* He turned and smiled as if he were just warming up. He rolled his shoulder in a circular motion as if he were loosening up his muscles, preparing to land multiple blows on the young boy.

Titus began to visibly quiver, his forehead glistening with sweat. Tears began to flow down his cheeks. The other young children, watching the ordeal, took a step back. Some unconsciously reached for the hand of the person next to them as they gasped in horror, while others remained staring, their faces hanging agog.

"Sir, I didn't mean to oversleep. My tooth ached me so . . . it was terrible . . . my gums was bleedin' . . . it tasted awful."

Sancho landed a solid blow on Titus knowing that he needed to comply with the orders of his superior or face his own consequences. He landed another blow across the boy's back with such force, his flesh split open, and blood poured out. The boy cried out in pain. Some of the children watching the beating began to whimper, while others stood glossy-eyed as tears welled.

Enslaved Blacks never had the means to care for their teeth and often lost many of them early in life. McBride thought this to be fact but nonetheless wanted to make an example of the terrified boy. Feeling confident that his orders were being carried out, McBride strolled away from the work yard, mounted his horse, and rode out toward the cotton fields. Sancho landed a few more blows, but with less force. Then he began to go back and forth between striking the child and hitting other objects around the work yard until the overseer was just a dot on the horizon. He stopped once the workers had dissipated and moved on to their own chores. Sancho, feeling remorse for his deed, had no choice but to turn away, leaving the child on the ground, passed out from the lashing, and returned the hickory stick to its locked rack.

Once Sancho was gone, Rosa, who ran the plantation's infirmary, ran out to assist the child. She helped him to his feet, then tried to walk him to the infirmary, but his legs gave out, so she ended up carrying him. The child's mother, Ida, joined Rosa and tended to her wounded child as best she could. She had Rosa help cover the wounds with spider webs and strips of cotton cloth. They used salves and oils. The boy remained unconscious for hours from the trauma he sustained, which was just as well since he wouldn't have to endure all the enormous pain.

Later, the father's child, Moses, came and bent down over his son. His heartache and sense of helplessness were immeasurable. His body quaked with anger and sorrow, then convulsed as he wailed. Unable to control his emotions, he ran deep into the woods and screamed. Only God could help calm him now. He remained there a few days, unable to return to the horrid scene. As if to cover for him,

Sancho claimed he had him working on the far end of the thousand-acre plantation. Sancho contended it was best he worked out there by himself. The driver was in a precarious position. As a man of color, he had loyalty to the enslaved workers. He knew that the command of the overseer was excessive, but he was helpless to do anything but carry out the order. While the White overseers changed every couple of years, he would probably remain as the master's chattel property for the remainder of his life. He was locked into the control and the whims of the master. He and the others covered for Moses until he could accept his plight and return.

Titus spent a week dealing with his wounds. Despite the abuse he had suffered, the boy wanted to stay near his family on the Langdon plantation. After the beating, Moses and others worried whether the boy was marked for sale. The stock market crash of 1857 had hurt William Langdon's bottom line and those of other plantation owners. Langdon decided to sell some of his slaves, a move that many of the families in neighboring plantations made to recoup their financial losses. Plantation owners routinely bought and sold slaves like farm animals, anyway. Langdon made a ceremony of it.

On every New Year's Day morning, Twin Oaks slaves anxiously waited to hear who would stay and who would go. Sometimes people were just rented out for the year to another plantation, or sometimes to a business like the wharves in Charleston, or to help with the phosphate sulfur mining. Others might be sold off to a plantation farther south in Georgia, or as far west as Louisiana. So far Titus and his family had been safe, but that was always subject to change, and everyone knew it. At least for this day, Titus got to stay at Twin Oaks for one more year.

Hentie hurried about the big house, tidying up as she prepared for the midday meal. Langdon was particular about his dinner and always wanted it served promptly after touring the plantation grounds. He was out checking on the most recent crop of peaches, blueberries, strawberries, mangos, lemons, and vegetables, including tomatoes, spinach, collards, chard, cabbage, carrots, cauliflower, cucumbers, beans, pumpkins, peas, zucchini, and the special nut—pecans.

The second growing season had just ended. Many crops had two or three growing seasons in South Carolina, starting with the first planting in February. The Sea Island cotton wouldn't be harvested until around September; nonetheless, it was the most important commodity, so Langdon watched its progress carefully.

Hentie selected a table covering from the linen press for the long mahogany dining room table and smoothed it out across the expanse. She then picked out the china and cutlery and started to arrange it on the table. Hentie had been doing this task for decades now, ever since she first came to Twin Oaks. At this point, she even knew the mistress's favorite tablecloth, her preferred china for family, and the one for guests, along with the complementary flatware. Performing such tasks had almost become rote for her.

Hentie startled when she heard a horse and carriage clopping up the front lane. An unexpected guest was pulling up to the main house. She was puzzled by the arrival of a visitor so early in the day and wondered if he might be bringing bad news about the war.

The Federals had run with their tails between their legs after the firing on Fort Sumter. Ten states had since joined the Confederacy with others considering the move. The Confederate states possessed a considerable amount of land, and William Langdon believed that the South could easily stand as its own independent sovereign country due to its great wealth.

The buggy pulled up to the front of the house and a well-dressed, middle-aged gentleman, who was riding alone, hastily jumped out. An enslaved stableboy met him and took his rig back behind the mansion house to water and feed his horse. The driver turned and swiftly made his way to the front door of the mansion house and tapped on the heavy brass knocker. A well-mannered enslaved Negro butler, Samuel, answered the door and invited the guest into the main foyer. As he stood on the black-and-white marbled flooring, the gentleman addressed the butler in hushed tones.

"I would like to see Master Langdon. Is he available? I'd like to show him something," said the caller.

"Yes sir. You're a neighboring planter, correct sir?" inquired the butler.

"Just tell him it's Henry from down the road a bit. He'll know who I am." The man smiled and nodded.

Samuel, already having some familiarity with the man as a Mount Pleasant planter with other plantations in the region as well, waved the gentleman to the most comfortable chair in the sitting room.

"Please, sir, wait here in the parlor, and I shall fetch Master Langdon straight away." He smiled, nodded, and bowed, then turned and left the room to inform the master of his guest.

Hentie, overhearing the exchange, set another place setting on the dining room table.

In a matter of a few minutes, Langdon entered the parlor and shook hands with the White man whom Hentie recognized as Master Pinckney, a wealthy planter from a neighboring plantation in Mount Pleasant. Hentie let the men converse with each other for a handful of minutes before quietly entering the sunlit sitting room.

When there was a natural break in the conversation, she said, "Excuse me, master, but I see you have a guest. We're getting ready to serve dinner soon. Will Master Pinckney be joining us?" Hentie lowered her eyes and dipped in a brief curtsy as signs of submission.

"Yes, do stay, and you can show me the newspapers you brought with you, and we can sit and talk. I would love to learn more about what happened at Bull Run up in Virginia. I'm glad we're continuing to lick those damn Yankees," exclaimed Langdon.

"Yes, yes, William, I'd enjoy that, my friend. That's really why I came, to let you know the latest news. Awfully good of you to let me stay for dinner. I happen to know you have a wonderful cook here." Pinckney gave a hearty laugh. His belly shook as he patted his gyrating midsection. "I remember the wonderful dinner we had here last month. It was the best meal I ever had, absolutely scrumptious. The pork your cook made melted in my mouth."

"Well, let's go into the dining room, and you can read to me the newspaper articles you've brought. I'm anxious to hear them." Langdon leaned forward and put his palm on Pinckney's shoulder as the two strolled into the next room.

Pinckney glanced down at the most recent rags he had in his hands, folding them up to the most important articles. Once the men were seated, he adjusted his spectacles.

"This one is from a newspaper in Richmond, Virginia, *The Richmond Enquirer*. I think it gives the best account, as the reporter was right there with all the action." Pinckney looked over his spectacles and nodded at Langdon.

"Oh, good. Read that one first. I want to hear it." Langdon leaned forward with all the eagerness of a small boy.

Pinckney started to read:

> *Manassas, Virginia, July 22nd, p.m.*
> *Heroic conduct of Generals Beauregard and Johnson.*
> *Beauregard's Horse Shot From Under Him!*
> *The enemy opened their batteries at McLesh Ford, on Bull Run at 8:00 a.m. with heavy guns and rifled cannons. Several small field pieces were used, these being intended as a mere feint, for the purpose of drawing our fire. Our generals seeing through the ruse, did not respond. The enemy chose their own positions a few miles beyond Stone Bridge on Bull Run where the principal part of the battle was fought.*
> *The enemy attempted to turn, if possible, on our left flank, but the battle raged for four hours at that point.*

Langdon interjected. "Well, I'm glad to hear that our generals weren't duped by those Yankee dogs and saw through their trickery."

"Of course, they did, Langdon. Look who was on the field at the time—Beauregard! A brilliant West Point graduate. He was second in his class!" Pinckney pounded his fist on the dining room table, then slapped Langdon on the back while belting out his laughter.

Pinckney continued:

> *The fire on both sides was appalling. Men on both sides had never fought better,*
>
> *the enemy having largely the advantage in numbers and artillery. Between eight and four o'clock, our brave men began to waver, and the result actually hung in the balance, when Generals Beauregard and Johnson threw themselves into the thickest of the fight.*
>
> *General Beauregard crowned himself with glory. He had his horse's head shot off with a shell as the battle raged on with a tremendous fury. But our generals rallied our men and urged them onto victory. Reinforcements coming up just at the critical moment, the result being to turn in our favor, the enemy falling back in good order. . . .The enemy was totally routed and fled in great confusion for miles.*

"See that, Langdon? It was an ugly battle, but the Federals ran all the way back to Washington. Let me read you some more articles I have here." Pickney looked over to his friend, smiling, trying to reassure him that the War Between the States would come to a swift end and that the South would prevail.

Pinckney flipped through the various US newspapers he had brought with him, mostly from other Southern cities. He then went on to read newspaper articles from other well-known publications including *Harper's Weekly* of New York City, the first newspaper to release the news of the Battle of Bull Run. This highly regarded paper included several dramatic eyewitness illustrations, as they had been able to send a wartime illustrator to the front. Then there were other papers: *The Newbern Weekly* from North Carolina, *The Raleigh Register*, *The Charleston Daily News*, and *The Charleston Mercury*, all Confederate rags.

"So, you have read all these newspaper articles. You're a well-educated, astute, and worldly man. What do you think? Is the South winning the war so far? It certainly sounds like it to me."

"Of course we are winning, William! It's just a matter of time until we defeat the North. We have some of the best officers on our side that West Point has ever produced. Thank God, Robert E. Lee turned down Lincoln's request to lead the Union Army. He's a good Virginia boy and couldn't turn his back on his own commonwealth. Between Lee and Beauregard, it's only a matter of time, my good man!" Pinckney reached out and slapped the hopeful-looking Langdon on the back.

Relief washed over Langdon, and his body relaxed, imbued by Pinckney's blustery elevated spirits.

⁓

Hentie tracked down Big John out by the stables and showed him the letter addressed to Mrs. Langdon. She was curious as to its contents and feared it could carry bad news. Knowing that Big John had been taught to read as a boy when he lived in the Caribbean by his former mistress, she handed him the sealed envelope.

"What do you figure this is? Who's it from?" Hentie gazed upon Big John.

"Looks like Master Fitz's handwriting, but it's not as neat as it usually is, but maybe he's writing on a wobbly table or something." Big John held up the sealed vellum military stationery and examined it.

"Do you think we should read it 'fore we give it to the missus? What if it's bad news? She is already in a bad mood and taking her drops." Hentie asked.

"Maybe we should take it to Master Langdon, let him open it. Ain't nothing she can do against him but throw one of her fits," Big John chuckled.

"That's probably the safest thing to do cause if you get caught readin' it, that will be bad for us all." Hentie waved a cautionary finger at Big John.

"I reckon the master is in his study right now. Let me take this over to him. See what he says." Big John gave Hentie a nod and peck on her forehead as he turned to leave.

Hentie broke out in a warm smile and nodded back at him, her cheeks glowing. Her eyes followed him as he walked across the work yard to the house. Her attention was broken by the low husky laughter of the cook from the kitchen house.

"Sho' glad after all these years you two done jumped the broom and become man and wife. Best thing that ever happened round here, and you be knowin' it too," Nellie smiled and gave a belly laugh.

Heat rose to Hentie's cheeks, knowing that Nellie spoke the truth. It had taken years for Hentie to open her heart to Big John after all the trauma she had been through with her capture in Africa, the long Middle Passage, and the loss of her family. But eventually, she realized what a good, kindhearted man he was and that he would never hurt her or allow her to be hurt. Hentie merely nodded at Nellie and gave a tight-lipped smile as if no words were necessary. Hentie was blessed and she knew it.

Big John crossed the work yard and entered the rear of the big house, then walked down the hallway to his master's library. He found Langdon sitting behind his large, hand-carved desk and leather chair. The room was rather dark due to the deep-wine-colored draperies that had been drawn. The three club chairs covered in blue damask fabric and a burgundy silk settee were all covered in papers and a few old ledgers his master seemed to be organizing.

"Excuse me, Master. I hate to trouble you while you workin' away so hard, but the missus got a letter, and I thought you might want to take a look at it." Big John held out the letter toward his master.

"Well, why doesn't she read it? Is something wrong?" Langdon lifted his head with a quizzical look.

"The missus is feeling kinda poorly right now. She done took a bunch of those drops and—" Big John's voice trailed off.

"Oh, I see. Thank you for bringing it to my attention." Langdon jerked his head upward toward Big John's hand. As he extended the meaty hand in which he held the letter, his master retrieved it. Big John watched him carefully for his reaction.

"Hmmm." At first, Langdon smirked at the Confederate stationery that had been used. The stationery was printed with colorful ink of indigo blue and ruby red with a Confederate flag waving in the background. There were dozens of different varieties of patriotic stationery on the market, but this particular depiction was of the death of Colonel Elmer Ellsworth, a close personal friend of President Lincoln, whose demise had struck at the president's heart and was printed as a sign of defiance.

The dashing young infantry commander was the first Union officer to be killed in the war during his daring attempt to tear down a Confederate flag from a boarding house in Alexandria, Virginia, just outside the nation's capital. Ellsworth had already removed the flag and was quickly descending the steps when he was shot and killed instantly at close range by a Confederate soldier named Jackson. Moments later, Jackson was bayoneted by a Union officer. It was funny that Fitzwilliam should pick this particular scene for this stationery.

Upon closer examination, Langdon said, "Rather odd. This is Fitz's handwriting, but it looks a bit off." Langdon then broke the thick red wax seal and started to read it:

July 24, 1861
Near Centreville, Virginia
(Outside the District of Columbia)
Ever Dear Mother,

Once more with pleasure, I take my pencil in hand to write you to inform you that we are near Centreville, Virginia outside the Union capitol of Washington. Our general decided to take the fight to the Yanks and met them head-on here. We won't stop in Centreville long, perhaps move along later today or tomorrow. We will probably move south of where we are in Virginia. But where we will go to next, I cannot tell you. We had a hot time of it here, but Thank God I got out all right, safe and sound, with only a modest flesh wound to one arm. I know I am quite fortunate. The Lord must have looked down on me and smiled.

Our meeting with the Union troops outside their own capital will ever be a memorable day in the annals of America. There were wagonloads of spectators with their picnic baskets who watched the battle unfold. Next to the sacred Sabbath of our independence from Britain, it will be the eventful era in the history of the Republican Government. The military despotism of the North, proud, arrogant, and confident, has been met in the open field, and the true chivalry of the South, relying only upon the justness of their cause, though comparatively weak in numbers, has gained a victory that in completeness has never been paralleled in history since the American Continent first dawned from its ocean-girt upon the eyes of the longing discoverer. But the victory has been dearly won—purchased, indeed, with the heart's blood of thousands of the bravest and truest men of the Confederate states. The blood will not only cry aloud to the heavens for vengeance, but so fructify the soil of the South that here more than elsewhere will ever bloom and blossom the glorious tree of liberty.

Although the Yanks tried to deceive us in the early morning hours at Bull Run, the Union infantry, famous for their tricks, advanced with a large column under a Confederate flag and within fifty yards of the Confederate line opened fire with hot musketry nearly disseminating the Fourth Alabama Regiment. It was in fact, difficult to discern who was the enemy as we wore the same gray militia uniforms. Many units, if not most, on either side have not had the opportunity to acquire official regalia. The Rebs had to tie a white strip of fabric around their hats or use it as an armband so that we could identify ourselves from the enemy. It made it all quite difficult as the Yanks are often our own neighbors and, albeit, look quite a bit like us. The only person we could truly discern was Confederate General Beauregard on his mount. Throughout the battle he wore a straw cap with a black velvet band displaying the stars which proclaimed his rank.

A total of nearly nine hundred men died here, most of them, over 450, were Yankees. Upwards of three thousand were wounded, unfortunately, many of those injured were our boys. However, far more Yankees were missing or captured, around 1,300. A number of factors played into the high numbers. One is the rather old tactics we had still used of marching onto the battlefield in Napoleonic form, lined up so that the enemy can merely pick us off. We shall never do that again; it makes us too easy a target for the Union soldiers. Cannons can now fire at long range, over two miles, so we must use a different approach. But all of this will come with time as the Rebs successfully conclude this conflict and the South rises again as a new nation. I must close now as my unit is on the move. I hope to visit home soon. Until then, you and father will always be in my heart.

Your loving son,
Fitzwilliam

Langdon carefully folded the letter and returned it to its colorful envelope. He let out a heavy breath as he placed the letter on his desk and patted it. He paused before he spoke. "Big John, I believe this war is going to be a lot more costly than we ever imagined. Please make sure we are very careful with our harvest and all of our sales with local businessmen. We may need to rely on this money for some time to come."

"Yes, Ma'sa, I'll watch it real careful like. Don't know what's gonna come with this here war." Big John nodded.

"I'm lucky that you, Hentie, and the others are happy slaves. You understand our peculiar institution and realize we are doing a positive good here. We take care of you like a loving parent and consider you part of the family. The Yankees can't understand that. We planters in the South are the chosen ones."

"Yes sir, the good Lord made the planters the chosen ones. He allowed them to prosper, just like you, Ma'sa," Big John looked into Langdon's face and nodded as he spoke.

"Our society is far superior to that of the North. Our intellectual thought is far more advanced than that of the northern regions of our country. We have our protected colored servants in our homes. Our Negroes, who we see as our extended family members, do our physical labors, while we focus on higher thinking and advancing mankind. Can you grasp that, Big John? I know it may be beyond your means and ability, but try to understand we only hope to help our society to grow and develop as part of God's overall vision." Langdon tilted his head and looked with bated breath at Big John.

"Oh yes sir, I understand. You give us a job, a home, and put the clothes on our backs. You treat us niggras good, sir." Big John nearly choked on his words.

"Well, good, John. I'm glad you understand that. There may be tense moments in our future. I know I can count on you to remain loyal and by my side." Langdon looked down and smiled as he started to move papers around on his desk.

"Yes, Master, you sho' a good master, we all think so," Big John nodded again, playing with the edges of the hat he held in his hands as he inconspicuously backed out of his master's library and sauntered down the hallway back to the work yard.

Once he was a safe distance away from Master Langdon and the big house, kicking the dirt of the work yard, he muttered to himself, "Crazy White buckra, what he think? Doesn't he realize a Black man might want his freedom? Choose where he can live, who he can marry, and who owns his children?"

Big John walked on down toward the slave village, blowing anger out of his big barrel chest, then punched a stack of hay and muttered some more. "Does he think I want to stay here forever, waitin' on him and his crazy wife until the day I die? No sir! I want my freedom, and I will take it justa soon as I can! Let's hope them Yankee soldiers come up over the horizon one day and set all of us colored folk free." Big John punched the stack of hay once again, knocking one several feet across the work yard. "The very idea of being a free man and able to walk out the Avenue of Oaks makes me giddy!"

Big John knew he was too old to ever try running away from Twin Oaks plantation, but maybe someday one of the young, enslaved men could be someone with an inner yearning. Perhaps Cully. Many wanted to run, but few were triumphant. The successful fugitive slave had to be physically strong with great endurance for the long journey. He had to be fast, able to walk for miles, have a good sense of direction, be able to push ahead with little sleep and no food, have the endurance to swim, quick wits to hide, strength to fight, reflexes to kill wild animals, and so much more.

Big John knew he could never run and would better serve his people by gathering and sharing intelligence. Some wrongfully believed he was beholden to his master, but most knew better. He was just biding his time. He continued to help many, just as he had helped Cuffee, Juba's husband, reach her through the Underground Railroad down in Beaufort. Big John made the connections for him and got him a new pair of boots, socks, and a few other items. That's how Cuffee was able to travel so far and see his wife before he was killed by slave trackers. Unfortunately, he never got to meet his son, Issac. Big John paused and pondered a moment. *Issac. He's probably a grown man by now living down in Beaufort with his mama, Juba. I hope they're safe there.*

On this day, Mrs. Langdon decided to write to her cousin Sarah Chase who lived in southern Pennsylvania. The two had been quite close since they were small children when they lived close to one another in the Upcountry of the Carolinas and often shared their innermost thoughts. She worried about how the war was progressing and what might be the fate of her son, Fitzwilliam. She also gave passing thought to Sarah's son, Elliott. They had a bit of a spat months earlier but had since smoothed things over. Emily acknowledged she had been unladylike.

Mrs. Langdon sat at her writing desk and retrieved from her slope a medium-sized wooden box with brass fittings. First, she pulled out a sheet of her fine ivory vellum stationery made from a combination of bleached fiber extracted from cotton and linen rags. Secondly, she selected a fine-edged steel nib to attach to her dip pen. She had a collection of about a dozen nibs. To avoid smudging, she pulled out a blotter card and attached it to a handled block of wood. In the event that ink pooled, the card would be rolled over the writing to absorb excess ink. The blotter card holder had been a gift the previous Christmas and had Emily's initials etched on the handle. Lastly, Mrs. Langdon carefully withdrew a small glass inkwell and opened it. She chose to use violet ink, as she believed it reflected her mood. She and other women of the time had been using colored inks to make letters more vibrant and emotive. She delighted in trying out new colors and began to draft her letter:

July 30, 1861
Mt. Pleasant (Charleston), South Carolina
My Dear Cousin,

    Thank you for your favor of the 15th ultimo. I enjoyed your letter immensely. It lifted my heart so hearing from you. The summer's heat is upon us now and the intense humidity is so tiring. Reading a letter from you was like a cool breeze wafting over my face. Ordinarily, we would take refuge in the mountain air near White Sulphur Springs, Virginia, but my beloved does not believe he should leave the plantation now with gestures of war from the Yankees. I worry so about our succumbing to summer diseases. Yellow fever has been so rampant these past few decades. It even befell some of our Negro slaves who ordinarily have more resistance to such ailments.

    Fitzwilliam has been gone for weeks now. As you may recall, Fitz received an appointment as an officer shortly after graduating from the Citadel. In no time, it seems, he was promoted from a second lieutenant to a captain. It appears that many of the higher-ranking officers are of advanced years, having served in the War of 1812, while others served in the Mexican American War, so they have to promote younger officers rather quickly.

    My husband tells me that he has read of a great battle that recently occurred at Bull Run near the town of Manassas, Virginia. I believe many of our Confederate troops were there for this engagement. I hope the Lord protected our boys, both my Fitz and your Elliott, and forestalled any suffering for those he gathered up to himself. Each night I pray for the safe return of our sons and the swift end of this Yankee aggression. I am hoping that Fitz gains a furlough soon so that he may return to the plantation, at least for a brief respite. While I am grateful that our son is defending the Confederacy, I still must look upon the vacant chair at the dining room table and wonder where he is and if he is in harm's way.

It is quite warm now and I grow tired from the heat. I believe I shall retire for the night. I will soon write again in a different strain.

From thy affectionate cousin
Emily Trenholm Langdon

Mrs. Langdon held up the piece of vellum and blew on the ink to help it dry, then laid it down on her writing table. She decided to use an envelope rather than the cheaper form of mailing in which correspondence was sent upon a folded piece of paper, offering limited privacy. If one used an envelope, the postage was charged as a separate piece of paper. But never mind that charge. After folding the letter, she creased it carefully and slid it into the envelope.

She returned to her wooden writing slope and selected a stick of red sealing wax, then pulled a wax taper used to light oil lamps closer to her in order to melt the sealing wax. She carefully inspected the stick of wax to make sure it was scarlet red rather than black, which was used for mourning or announcing a death. Then lighting the wick, she let the bright-red wax drip down onto the paper. Suddenly, the scarlet liquid reminded her of blood that might be dripping from young Fitz, a possible victim of a Yankee sniper. Her mind shifted as images scampered across her memory from the brutal scene of the battlefield at Bull Run, the news of which she examined in the issue of *Harper's Weekly*. The artist's rendering had so meticulously displayed the brutality of it all. She imagined her son mortally wounded, then gasped and dropped the candle. Unable to stop herself, she began to bawl. "Poor Fitzwilliam," she cried out. Sobbing, she crumpled to the floor. She glanced over to the candle and wax seal. Fortunately, the flame had gone out, just as a life can so easily be snuffed out on the battlefield.

"This damn war! Why can't the Yankees just leave us alone? We just want to keep things the way they have been for hundreds of years. Why stop us now? It has worked so well for everyone. It's God's will that we live this way!" screamed Mrs. Langdon. She then turned and rested her elbow on her writing desk chair and continued to let the tears flow.

While Mrs. Langdon sat on the floor weeping, she heard the concerned voice of her lady's maid, Octavia calling out, "Oh Mistress! You okay? I's a'comin', I's a'comin'. You don't fret now!" Octavia's large frame moved steadily down the hallway over the creaking floorboards as she huffed down the hallway. "Almost there! I's a'comin'!"

The Battle of Bull Run, or the First Manassas, was the first major battle of the Civil War (July 21, 1861). Two inexperienced armies met head-on upon the battlefield, using the outmoded Napoleonic method of marching into battle in straight lines, making themselves easy targets for the enemy. The technology that had been developed by that time far outstripped the military methods still being used in the field. Canons could hit targets over two miles away, and firearms had improved with the help of the Industrial Revolution; parts could be machine-made rather than all the component parts having to be made one at a time by hand.

The battlefield was about thirty miles southwest of Washington. It caused angst for President Lincoln and his cabinet to have the fighting so close to the nation's capital. There were fears of the Rebels burning the city, much like the British had done decades before. The Confederate capital had moved from Montgomery, Alabama to Richmond, Virginia just two months before the battle.

The objective of the Confederate Army was to block the Union Army from advancing to Richmond, about ninety-five miles away, by defending the railroad junction at Manassas, an extremely valuable objective.

Believing that Union forces would soundly defeat the Rebels, wagonloads of spectators packed up picnic baskets and grabbed blankets and parasols to sit in the sunshine and watch the bloody spectacle unfold. This was the first real engagement, and the Federals hoped to swiftly defeat the Confederates, much like what had happened months before at Fort Sumter when the Federals were defeated in roughly thirty hours. The spectators had no idea what was about to unfold before their very eyes. Thousands of lives were lost on both sides of the battle. While civilians, congressmen, and reporters watched from nearly two miles away in a festive mood, whole rows of men were mowed down, limbs were blown off, and soldiers decapitated. There was much confusion on the field as to who was the enemy. Since there had not been a national army on either side, but local militias, there were no standard uniforms for all Union and Confederate soldiers. Moreover, there was confusion over the flags carried into the battle between the "stars and bars" versus "the stars and stripes." Following this battle, General Beauregard designed a new battle flag with white stars embedded in a blue St. Andrew's Cross on a red field, which became the familiar banner of the Confederacy. It was also the first time the eerie scream, which would later be known as the Rebel Yell, was first uttered by the Confederate soldiers.

At the end of the day, five thousand were killed, wounded, captured, or missing. Congress realized after this harrowing battle that the war was not going to last just ninety days as they had originally projected.[2]

---

2   In each but one (Shiloh), the Confederates named the battle after the town that served as their base, while the Union forces chose the landmark nearest to the fighting or their own battle lines, most often a river or stream. It is believed the Northern soldiers, who were more likely to hail from urban areas, were impressed with the geography of the South and chose names based on the territory.

Chapter 9
Issac Runs from the Confederate Encampment

Rural Areas of Southeastern South Carolina, Fall 1861

Issac had become despondent, dragging along with the Rebel troops. He was their hired bondsman, rented out by a local planter and forced to do their bidding. He was hungry and tired. As an enslaved Negro worker, he ate last after the soldiers had their fill; he got what was left over. Often, he ate nothing more than tainted gruel. At best, he had rice and a bit of salt pork, along with portions of hard tack.

He missed his home in Beaufort, South Carolina, where he had served Ashdale Plantation master, McKee, and his own mother, Juba. He had gained some privileges working near the big house out in the barn with the other stable hands, no longer out in the fields. Tending to the horses and livestock was much easier work than what he was now compelled to do; even acting as a field hand was easier than the continual monotonous laboring for the Rebel troops.

Issac had been rented out to a Confederate officer at a January 1, auction, "hiring day," as it was known. As the war approached, McKee gradually sold off bits of his inventory, including those human beings he considered expendable. Issac, a young Black man with a strong back, brought much-needed cash. All the enslaved workers attached to the regiment were Blacks who had been bought, rented, or seized. They endured hard work, much like the horses, helping to carry out the functions of the war machine.

Issac was on call twenty-four hours a day. He and the others were to prepare food, plate meals for soldiers, forage for food, fetch water, spread out beds, blacken shoes, gather wood, or pack haversacks, and handle whatever task needed doing. There were manservants, cooks, teamsters, laundry maids, and general hands who attended to the personal comfort of the men and cared for the animals. Issac marched with the Rebel soldiers for miles, hauling a pack or the gear no one else wished to carry. He was ever mindful that the enslaved were seen as expendable. Nearly all of them were homesick and physically drained; if they were injured, medicines were not expended on them, but saved for the Rebel soldiers. Many times, the Negro slaves were merely allowed to die, their bodies abandoned along the trail.

Issac sometimes ate the food that had been plated up for a wounded soldier, who was unable to eat it or subsequently died. On those days he might get a piece of dried fruit or some berries that had been gathered along the way or even chopped up meat. Issac had been reduced to taking the boots from a dead man to cover his tired, cut, and swollen extremities. The soles of his feet had been bare or covered with rags. It was a desperate act to take the boots from a departed soul, but he felt forced to do it. He had asked for God's forgiveness as he tugged on the soldier's boots, noticing the blood splattered all over the heel along with human hair and tissue.

Over the weary miles, Issac became even more disheartened, serving the very men who would kill those trying to set him free. He was torn between his need to follow the Confederates' directions while hoping they would fail. Issac experienced guilt over wanting them to die in battle, to be rid of them.

Issac had seen so many lives lost. Men butchered before his eyes. He once saw a man's head blown from his shoulders by the sheer velocity of a cannonball. The victim had been a mere boy, probably no more than sixteen. He thought that God had never meant for men to have this sort of firepower, the wherewithal to shred men without discrimination. To blow off limbs and shatter bones of those who could have been a neighbor. Someone that they might have shaken hands with, under other circumstances.

Issac had rarely been away from the McKee plantation or the main house in the city. Most of the people he had interacted with at the McKees' were other enslaved Blacks, including their driver. He missed his mother and the family of workers he had become so close with at Ashdale Plantation and the McKees' city house. Issac felt drawn back to his home, even though he wasn't sure what remained of it. He believed his mother may have been hired out as well, but he had no idea which regiment Juba had gone with, or where she might be. He could only hope that she received moderately humane treatment and was still alive. Issac knew that Juba was treated harshly by her former master, William Langdon, in Mount Pleasant. He was the ogre who mercilessly had Juba whipped, then sold miles away from her husband. But all that happened before he was born.

Issac wanted to be away from the bloodshed and toil of camp life. He wanted to be able to joke with the other enslaved men on the plantation and feel their camaraderie again. He longed to visit with his mama in the slave quarters adjacent to the big house on a Sunday afternoon and eat her good cornbread. Issac decided to slip away in the night. There were rumors circulating that the Federal troops were coming. He had overheard the men say that the Yankees outmanned the Rebel troops, and that they were better armed. The guns the Northerners possessed and the cannons they fired were far beyond what the Rebels had in their arsenal. The Confederates were afraid of being slaughtered; things were starting to look dismal for them.

The rattle of wagons hammered in his head as they bounced down the rutted roads, occasionally cutting tracks across fields. A few of the officers were on mounts, but most of the men were on foot, trudging along with a pack, blanket roll, cartridge case, tarp, rain jacket, utensils, and a dangling canteen. At the outset of their travels, the pack had everything they needed and weighed nearly thirty pounds, but as the trek continued, items were dropped. Men were willing to chance the possibilities due to their exhaustion. On occasion, Issac would pick up their discarded items thinking it might somehow benefit him one day. Being at the back of the long line of men and wagons, no one ever noticed his actions. They had traveled away from their fort near Hilton Head but were now returning. They felt confident they would make it back.

As dusk began to swiftly fall, it was as if a veil dropped around Issac, and he pulled back into his thoughts. He started to mull over his plans as to how he might escape. Issac believed he had figured out where he was after overhearing the discussions of the officers and glancing down at a map they held. The commander had displayed it so the officers could review it and better develop their strategy. Issac tried to act as normal as possible, showing a high level of tolerance for the men's insults and degrading acts. The soldiers loved to humiliate and belittle him just for sport. They spit in the leftover food that was handed to him to eat or tripped him as he was retrieving their tin plates. The sound of their roaring laughter carried all over the camp. Issac tried to ignore their comments, backing away slowly from them while bending at the waist and lowering his eyes as a sign of submission while knowing he had a knife tucked down in his boot, which he had serendipitously taken from an officer's portable desk.

The darkness masked the abandoned houses and empty fields, farms from which the inhabitants had fled, burying their silver and taking what livestock they could manage. Occasionally an ox or cow was seen wandering alone. Issac speculated as to how he could make use of what remained. Perhaps he could snap up food or a valuable tidbit he could use later should he have the courage to actually run.

Issac persisted with his compliant ways, always accommodating and pleasant to the White soldiers, while in his silent prayers hoped that a Yankee bullet would strike them dead. His thoughts would dart between wishing he could poison them and how he might appease their hunger. He tried to anticipate the needs of the men, particularly the officers, but he was on edge, fearful they might somehow know his inner thoughts and beat him for such notions. His movements sometimes jerked as his mind raced; fidgety thoughts, much like a squirrel running on the branches of a tree. He once dropped an officer's fork. He froze, afraid of a harsh reprimand or slap. But instead, the officer was recounting a tale to his cohorts and didn't even flinch.

Issac momentarily closed his eyes in thanks to God, calmly bent and picked up the fork, then turned and retreated to the site where the dirty metal plates and cutlery were stacked. Once there, he hung onto the side of a water barrel to regain his composure for just a few beats. He returned to his duties once again, retrieving empty plates and cups from the men. He ducked his head as a sign of respect when addressing the soldiers. He swallowed his thoughts and worked to control his agitation, his Adam's apple bobbing up and down as he did so. While grappling with his resentment, he collected more items that might be of use to him should he strike out on his own—a knapsack, a canteen, and a quilted jean cloth hat.

Issac hated working around the medical tent, the wounded men lying in agony, some dying as he walked past. The stench of dried blood, rotting flesh, and oozing pus was sometimes overwhelming. The screams of the men were heard all over the camp. Rudimentary tools and saws were used to remove shattered and worthless limbs. The appendages were stacked up like cords of wood, often disposed of in the closest waterway. Men were seen rushing this way and that from hastily assembled tents, scampering to get water, fetch bandages or avoid the horrific cries of the wounded. Issac would periodically see the doctors in blood-soaked aprons spilling out basins of blood, bones, and human tissue. Issacs's stomach churned at the sight of it. While he hated the White men, it pained him to see their suffering.

Issac had been listening carefully to the discussions of the Confederate soldiers for a few weeks now. He knew that the Federals were moving southward. They had scouts who had been sent out to monitor their movements and gather information; the Rebs were alarmed at what they had heard about the numbers of the Yankees. Officers' voices seemed to match the pulsating mood of the men. They were agitated and worried. There was movement on the water, and the Federals were creating even more havoc to lines of transportation by positioning themselves in Charleston Harbor. The Rebels had believed they were in relative safety down in the Beaufort area along the Port Royal Sound and the other waterways. But now the confidence of the Confederate stronghold wilted.

Suddenly, Issac was thrown from his thoughts of escape when an officer hollered over, "Boy, I need more grits."

Issac swiftly leaped to his feet and walked to the sergeant, careful to lower his eyes as he approached.

"Yes sir, you'd like more grits? I'll fetch them for you right quick."

Gently retrieving the tin cup from the officer's hand, with a swift bow at the waist, he turned on his heel to fetch more food for the officer. Hastily returning with a cup of the food, the officer did not even look up as he snatched the tin cup from Issacs's hand.

Following the evening meal, Issac collected the tin plates from the men, careful not to make too much noise. He mindlessly washed them in a pail of water adjacent to a nearby creek while he hatched a plan to escape. He filled a canteen after the dishes were clean and tucked it under the heap. He was careful to bury the rotting scraps of meat that even he wouldn't touch in order not to attract any animals during the night. He ensured the area was tidy and orderly.

Issac recovered the small items he had scrounged over the past weeks from a knothole in a tree adjacent to the creek bed where he had hidden the precious items—an officer's pocketknife, a few coins, and a pin he had removed from a dead man's uniform. Anything he could salvage from that evening's meal, he placed into his small haversack—a portion of bread, an apple, a carrot, and a few nuts. He even managed to snatch a bit of salted pork. He slid the knife into his trouser pocket, sure that he would need it at some point.

Issac was finally able to bunk down. He made sure to remain at a distance from the Rebel soldiers. As the moon rose, he could hear the men snoring. He kept his eye on the sentry posted at the edge of the encampment, the Rebel charged with repelling any insurgent Yankee looters or spies. Issac memorized where the lookout had been pacing back and forth. He carefully watched the speed of his step and when he turned, noting the timing of his movements. After an hour, when he felt confident the exhausted men were asleep, he began to head out. Then, when the guard was turned the other way, charged with adrenaline, Issac darted into the woods.

As he rushed into the forest, past the evergreen trees, his shirttail got hooked on a branch. While attempting to disentangle the fabric, he heard a Confederate officer call out.

"Boy, fetch me some water! That damn salt pork left my throat dry as dust. Boy! Boy, where are you?"

Panic shot through his body. *Damn, what do I do? Do I act like I wandered off to relieve myself or keep runnin'?*

"God damn it, boy! Get my water, boy. No niggra boy is allowed to sleep while tending to an officer!" The man's booming voice paused for a few beats, awaiting a response. Hearing none, he resumed his rant. "Where the hell are you, boy? You worthless darkie, you better not leave your post! I am warning you. You better answer me NOW!"

Hearing the ire in the officer's voice, he knew he would be whipped for his transgression. It would be days, if not weeks, before he would have another opportunity. Issac could overhear some of the men mumbling about his absence and what to do. Following this, a handful of men began to walk about the camp knocking over coffee pots and tin cups as they grabbed their boots and pulled on clothing. Then, Issac heard the sentry call out to his superior officer.

"Captain, I think the boy has run off!"

"Well, goddammit! Don't just stand there, go fetch him!" The officer's thunderous voice echoed through the woods, loud enough to scare a screech owl.

With his heart pumping, Issac yanked the garment, tearing the end of his ivory osnaburg shirt from the tree and bolted from the scene like a racehorse. Having some familiarity with the immediate area, he made good progress while men at the camp were still fumbling around, pulling on boots and lighting lamps.

The guard on duty seemed to be caught in the confusion, not knowing which way to go. He blindly fired off a round toward the woods, the shots ricocheting off a nearby oak and sending bark and debris flying. Issac threw up an arm for protection, stumbling at first, but then catching himself, his legs continuing to make steady strides to flee the Rebs. He sprung into a cluster of loblolly pines where he had a great deal of cover. It was almost as if the sound of the long rifle gave him an additional burst of energy, sending him forth much like the bullet coming out of the barrel. From there he went into the belly of the woods.

The heavy Jefferson boots he'd taken from a Confederate soldier pounded the ground under him. His anxiety rose as leaves crunched and dead twigs cracked under his feet. At one point, he stumbled into a deep hole, apparently dug by a wild animal, which sent him sprawling onto the ground. He landed with a thud and let out a low grunt as his chest hit the cold floor of the forest. Birds, frightened by his fall, suddenly took flight. Issac, momentarily stunned by the impact, remained motionless. Some of his possessions were sprawled over the forest floor. A sinking sense of terror paralyzed him. Meanwhile, his mind raced. Beads of sweat broke out on his brow and blood coursed through his veins as his heart pumped.

I have to get out of here. God, show me the way. I have to get away from the Confederate camp. God, be with me now. Send someone to guide me. Please show me the way.

Issac fumbled on the ground attempting to quickly locate the possessions. Frantically, he passed his hands over the earthy soil and crumbled leaves, locating everything he needed. He took in a deep breath and wiped the dirt and crumbled leaves from his hands. He started to feel the scrapes he had sustained on his palms when he had sprawled onto the hard earth. Allowing his eyes to adjust to the moonlight coming through the trees, he tried to orient himself. For a moment, it was as if the world about him froze. The sounds of the chirping crickets vanished, and the frogs stopped croaking. He took in the scents of the dark earth, the molted leaves, the rotting logs.

Guide me, dear Lord. Be with me now. Show me the way. I need your help.

He felt a sudden and inexplicable breeze pass by him. A chill ran over his body. He caught just a glimpse of a trailing white light that passed toward the edge of the woods. It could have been a moonbeam, but he believed it was God's hand directing him to his right, on down toward the water, guiding him out of the woods.

I'll lose the soldiers in the stream. They can't track me there. I gotta run. I just gotta keep running. I need your help now. God, put your speed in my feet. Get me away from here!

Issac was nearly a mile from the Rebel encampment before he slowed his pace. His adrenaline and God's good graces had carried him away from the Confederate soldiers. Fearful they might still be pursuing him, Issac knew he must keep moving. He was still somewhere near the town of Beaufort. However, before Issac could commence his journey in earnest, he had one stop to make. He wanted to visit the person who mattered so much to him. This man compelled his actions more than any other. Issac wanted to reaffirm his promise to this man before going on.

Sometime later, hours perhaps, he arrived at a darkened field on the outskirts of town. He knew the location well. It was where his father, Cuffee, had been buried after being gunned down by slave catchers. They had reluctantly turned over the body to his mother who had begged them for the right to bury her husband. The grave was marked with nothing more than a cross, perhaps a foot tall, which one of the enslaved had crafted to mark the site. There was also a small, handcrafted cross under the soil that topped the grave that his father, Cuffee, had carried in his pocket while alive. Juba had made a mark where it lay. Only Issac and Juba knew that it was there. He dug it up and added it to his rucksack.

As he stood before his father's gravesite, Issac knelt on one knee and humbled himself. He bowed his head and mumbled a prayer to God asking aloud for the strength to see him on his journey.

"Protect me, Dear Lord, as I begin my journey. Guide me on my travels and spare me from harm. I need you now, God. Please, please be with me and show me the way."

Then he spoke quietly to his father. He swallowed hard with emotion and tried to conjure up an image of him. He drew in a breath before he spoke.

"I know what they did to you. Mama told me the horrible things you went through to reach her. I know you two loved each other very much. She was pregnant with me when the slave catcher shot you down, but you didn't know it at the time. Mama still speaks of you. You were her only love. Papa, I ask that you watch over me now. Watch me on my journey; help me to stay safe from the White men and slave catchers. Because I swear to you, one day Mama and I will be free. Papa, I swear this on your grave. I will be a free man. All this hardship we have known will be behind us. I won't be owned by another human being. Neither will Mama. We will be free. I swear it. Our time is coming, Papa. I am telling you: freedom is a coming.

Be with me now, Papa. I need you more than ever."

Issac paused and then nodded in deference to his father and rose to his feet. Trying to picture the man his mama had described to him, Issac closed his eyes and tried to focus. He wanted so badly to feel his presence. Standing tall, he splayed his fingers and tilted his head back. With fierce concentration, he tried to conjure up an image of his father who had run away from his master to be with Juba but was gunned down just as he reached her. He would understand Issac's plight and why a young man would run.

Suddenly a chill ran through his body; it was as if the temperature around him had dropped several degrees. Frozen in fear, he slowly opened his eyes. Then, he saw his father clearly for just a few moments. Standing in front of him, nearly at eye level, man to man. He had on a brown woolen jacket, dark thick curls on his head, and almond-shaped eyes. His face looked kind. He radiated love and warmth. The apparition looked at him, his eyes blinked and then he nodded and smiled. Issac froze; the image looked just like what his mama had described to him. He wanted to call out to his father, but finding no voice, he could only reach out his hand to him. But then in an instant, the apparition was gone.

"Papa, don't leave. If ever I needed you, it's now. I need you to guide me, show me the way."

He paused then, not knowing if what he had witnessed had really been his father's spirit, or just his imagination, "Thank you, Papa. I will carry you in my heart always. Together, we will be free."

Issac felt a presence behind him, someone squeezing his shoulder and ruffling his hair, but then in an instant, the presence disappeared. He knew it was his father, saying his final goodbye and reassuring him that he would be by his side.

From there, Issac hurriedly turned on his heel and headed away from the site, toward a wooded area, which ran parallel to the road. The moonlight shone down on his path, illuminating the way. He knew he had to make good time and pumped his arms as he ran.

He pulled the energy from deep inside him. He moved like a deer, leaping over logs and jumping over the thicket.

At first, he felt as though he was running blind, just fleeing the Confederates and their encampment without direction. Then he paused and leaned against a tree, listening carefully to the sounds around him. An owl hooted overhead, and his breathing skittered from his lungs like angry bees. He closed his eyes and drew in a deep breath, trying to calm himself. Opening his eyes again, he tried to get oriented and think about the discussions he had overheard as to the Rebels' location and the next day's march they had planned. He ran his tongue quickly over his lips. His mouth was dry, and his heart was still pounding against his ribs. He calmed himself and concentrated on where he was going. *Think Issac. Think.* He tried to picture the map in his mind's eye and recall the discussion of the officers. Issac replayed in his mind the gestures the officers made as they talked about the progress of the Union troops, where they were encroaching, and how they planned to circle around them. He closed his eyes and ran over the discussion. *This way*, he thought. *The Union troops are this way*. Then hearing a man's voice in his head, *"That's right son, that's right. Head that way."*

With conviction, he turned his body toward the north.

Chapter 10
Flag Officer Samuel DuPont's Great Armada

The Eastern Seaboard, Giving Way to Port Royal Sound, Beaufort, SC

Fall had come late to South Carolina in 1861. It slowly rolled from the shorter days of October into November, but still no killing frost had arrived. Tender green plants lingered in the oblique autumn sunshine. The mighty oak trees draped with gray tendrils of Spanish moss remained steadfast as they had for hundreds of years. Lush marshes and hidden estuaries all along the waterways meandered southward, dolphins dipping in and out of the currents. Gentle breezes wafted in from the ocean, soothing the sailors' faces as they made their way toward Port Royal Sound. Overhead, an osprey, its wings spread wide, sailed effortlessly on the wind, so free in a land tainted by years of enslavement.

The fine long-staple cotton that grew in the unique, hot, moist climate of the coastal Carolinas had been brought there from the Caribbean and flourished, the soil bursting with white cotton boll weevils for weeks now. This cash crop had brought tremendous wealth to the planters of the region. All along the coast of the Sea Islands, enslaved Negro field workers were picking the crop that promised to be the largest in memory. Their dark-skinned figures in the waist-high cotton dipped and rose like sea waves as they tended to their work. Their traditional Gullah songs floated up through the air; they sang to the Lord God to help them endure their long hours of toil in the fields.

> *"O, walk 'em easy round de heaven,*
> *Walk 'em easy round de heaven,*
> *Walk 'em easy round de heaven,*
> *Dat all de people may join de band.*
> *Walk 'em easy round de heaven,*
> *Walk 'em easy round de heaven,*
> *Walk 'em easy round de heaven,*
> *O, shout glory till 'em join dat band!"*

Ardent Southern-rights groups believed the season's bounty was a sure sign that King Cotton was going to win the War of Northern Aggression for the Confederacy. But some of the more practical planters were undoubtedly wondering whether the cotton would reach the Liverpool markets and the textile factories of England. In the seven months since the firing upon Fort Sumter, an ominous quiet settled over the South Carolina Lowcountry. The silence was almost eerie, as if on tenterhooks. The Confederacy, having initiated a conflict against its own mother country, was still unsure how it would play out. Could the nation really be broken in two with limited loss of life and survive as two separate sovereign countries?

Local Southern militia groups drilled, and Confederate fortifications went up as hastily as feasible. On any clear day, one could see from the Charleston wharves the blockading Federal ships offshore patrolling the harbor waters. Otherwise, there were few overt signs of war.

The United States Blockade Board was created in June 1861 by Secretary of the Navy Gideon Wells at the urging of President Lincoln. There was an urgent need for a coaling station and suitable anchorage for the Union's South Atlantic blockading fleet. Since the fastest vessels were run by steam engines, coal was needed to keep the fires stoked and the ships operational. Some of the US Naval vessels had alternative power, both wind and steam, but coal remained vital to ensure their readiness. There were no suitable Yankee ports between Cape Hatteras, North Carolina, and Florida, making the trek abysmal. The Federals needed to do something to secure a new port at a midway point and move the conflict along to a decisive end. Ultimately, Port Royal Sound near Beaufort was selected due to its ideal location along the palmetto-studded coastline between Charleston and Savannah. Having the finest natural harbor on the Southern coast at that time, it could float all the navies of the world.

It was decided by Union authorities that a great flotilla would be assembled, first in New York Harbor, to be moved to some clandestine location. Newspapers carried reports of the large fleet, noting that it was to be sent to some undisclosed Southern location. Fears started to rise, but no one knew where the great armada would land. From New York, it sailed down to Virginia, where once again it was anchored for over a month. Speculation rose, however, the ultimate plan was cloaked in secrecy.

Finally, near the end of October, preparations to launch commenced, and it became apparent to even the casual observer that something profound was about to happen. The Federal's great armada with an Army-Navy expedition was about to sail down the Eastern Seaboard from Fort Monroe in Hampton Roads, Virginia, a fleet of more than seventy ships and fifteen thousand soldiers sent with the blessing of President Lincoln himself in hopes of putting a stranglehold on the rebellion.

The men on board were exhilarated, the very air charged with electricity, as the frenzied soldiers prepared to overwhelm the enemy. The event was a call to arms, the first combined amphibious assault of the war, executed in part due to the events that had occurred at Manassas in July of 1861. The assault on the Union Army at Bull Run propelled their joint Federal forces down the coastline in hopes of turning the war in its favor. This concentration of naval firepower had never been seen before and would not be seen again until the landing at Normandy, France, nearly one hundred years later.

Other vessels would join the Union's armada as it progressed, making the complement of ships a site to behold. The strike force of seventy-seven ships included twenty colliers, six supply vessels, several specialized craft to carry cattle and horses, and seventeen warships. Navy Flag Officer Samuel DuPont, later admiral, led the way.

Union Brigadier General Thomas West Sherman was on board one of the ships that followed. Sherman oversaw the Army's land forces, which included the infantry and cavalry. The "Other Sherman," as he came to be known, was renowned for having walked almost four hundred miles from his home in Newport, Rhode Island, to Washington, DC, to speak directly to President Andrew Jackson and to personally apprise him of the poor schools in his home state. The president rewarded young Sherman with an appointment to West Point. He performed well academically and graduated with a commission as a second lieutenant.

Major John G. Barnard led the Army Corps of Engineers, overseeing all the necessary planning, designing, building, and operating improvements. Having departed from Fort Monroe after a month of being tethered to its port, this move resulted in rumors across Virginia that a grand nautical scheme must be in the offing. The Confederates knew there was a plan to execute a decisive attack of some kind but did not know where the ships would land.

Samuel DuPont, dressed in a pressed woolen uniform with elegant tailoring, adorned with shiny gold buttons and encircling a snug waistline, progressed down the midsection of the *USS Wabash* with authority. His head uplifted, firmly planting each footstep as he strode across the deck, DuPont remained confident that he was about to engage in his finest moment as he traveled southward to seek his destiny.

"Men, I think the timing is right. I believe the hour is upon us. It is time we get underway to meet the enemy. We have planned this expedition long enough. Now is the time to act." DuPont poked his finger upward to emphasize his point that this was the moment to strike.

Shortly after five o'clock in the morning on October 29, 1861, DuPont ordered that the signal be given to get under way, and the *USS Wabash* began to move.

"Signal corpsman, fire the signal gun! Tell the fleet to move out! It's time to get underway," DuPont shouted.

Samuel Francis du Pont, ca. 1863.

The booming gun reverberated over the still, deep-water harbor of the Chesapeake Bay, echoing loudly off the stone walls of Fort Monroe. The sound carried down into the holds of the moored ships and into the bones of the anxiously awaiting young soldiers, eager to get underway.

A crash rang out, the last gang plank dropped to the pier. Then, with precision, sailors in their stiff blue uniforms with brass buttons untied the ships' ropes and tossed them into heaps, winding them like coiled snakes on the decks of the ships. Pursuant to directives, none of the Union sailors were to know where they were going until they were en route. The Federals were merely aware they were headed to Rebel territory. To keep the element of surprise as long as possible, Flag Officer DuPont ordered its disclosure to remain confidential until underway. Each ship's captain had been given a sealed envelope with the true destination and strict instructions not to break the seal until at sea.

Within an hour after the signal to commence had been given, the colossal flotilla in its entirety was on the move. The progression of the ships started a ripple of chatter across the nearby docks and progressed to the nearby towns.

"Look! They are getting under way!" shouted one young man down on the wharf clad in a brown jacket and wool tweed ivy cap.

"Yes! The ships are moving. Look! They're on their way now," hollered another man a few feet further down the wharf.

Boisterous cheers erupted from the men amassed along the railings, as well as the crowds on the seawall below. Women clapped and waved their hankies. Musicians from the ranks grabbed the instruments they had brought along for the voyage, forming spontaneous musical ensembles. They began playing various military tunes, such as "Battle Cry of Freedom" and "John Brown's Body."

On the three levels below deck, those sailors who tended to the holds were delighted to be underway. At last, they were off the leash and glad to be moving with a sense of purpose after being confined to a ship for a month. The lower levels of the ship were less than pleasant, with horses and livestock held in stables and all the provisions needed for weeks crammed into tight cells. There were carriages, tents, kits, crates of ammunition, and, of course, hard tack, the bland, thick cracker that could sustain a soldier for weeks, that is, if he could choke it down.

With his chest puffed out, DuPont turned to one of the Army officers on board, the much shorter Issac Ingalls Stevens, and said, "This is our finest day. Look at this flotilla. Impressive, isn't it? This is the largest group of ships ever assembled. Quite an assortment, I will admit, but we have the power within this fleet to choke the South, stemming their flow of supplies. All they have is their agricultural wealth. They can produce cotton, rice, corn, and tobacco. We, on the other hand, can produce machines, ships, munitions, and the tools that will enable us to win this war. If they can't trade with other countries across the Atlantic, they won't be able to gain the ships, cannons, and weapons they so sorely need. Only the Industrial North can produce those things."

As Stevens looked out over the waters, he saw such a discordant mix of vessels. The Union, having entered this conflict without a real navy, had to purchase or lease any seaworthy vessel available. The main column featured the forty-six-gun frigate: *The Wabash on which the two men stood. It was a sidewheeler capable of propulsion by steam or sails.* While shipbuilding had taken off at an incredible speed, the Navy was still sorely in need of augmentation. Floating around them was every description of craft—ocean steamers, coasters, sailing vessels, ferry boats, river steamers, and gunboats. Some of these boats had been nothing but timbers growing in the forest just ninety days before.

"Yes sir, we have the benefit of surprise with an armada that will overwhelm the Confederacy from the moment they see us come over the horizon. This will be a fine win for the North, just what we need after what happened after Manassas." Captain Stevens glanced down with a bit of shame in his eyes. The unusually short man stood only five feet, three inches tall, an apparent consequence of a congenital glandular disorder. His distinctive officer uniform had to be custom-made by his family's tailor to fit his diminutive physique.

Jerking up his head to disregard the notion of defeat, DuPont said, "As commander of the Port Royal Expedition, I think we will achieve a striking blow to the Southern rebellion. Our objective is to capture the fortifications at Port Royal Sound, as it is the finest harbor south of the Chesapeake Bay. It will give us a strategic advantage and serve the Union effort well."

Captain Stevens nodded in agreement. "It certainly will, sir. It will be a tremendous resource to us. The captain tucked his hands behind his back and strolled aside DuPont.

Captain Stevens was from the landed gentry who had settled in Andover, Massachusetts. Many of his family members were in the military and clergy. Stevens was an extremely bright man who had suffered a troubled childhood and a near mental breakdown following the death of his mother. Nonetheless, he went on to graduate at the top of his class at West Point with a particularly good math acuity, which often proved helpful in calculating movement in the field or on the seas. His brilliance, at times, was controversial, as he could be rather opinionated and polarizing. Despite his foibles, DuPont regarded him highly.

DuPont went on with great enthusiasm. "Did you know our naval ships can approach Port Royal by three different channels, the least of which has seventeen feet of water? Do you realize what movement that will allow our fleet? The entrance to this harbor is over two miles wide."

"Why, sir, that's tremendous," the captain regaled at the news.

DuPont continued. "There is more than ample anchorage. There are so many great resources we can draw on surrounding Port Royal and Beaufort. Port Royal Sound and its nearby islands Saint Helena and Lady's Island are the wealthiest of the Sea Islands. The area has beautiful mansions, plentiful plantations with rich soil and beautiful summer resorts. It's the Newport of the South. The plantations here are devoted to the precious Sea Island cotton, worth five times as much as all other cotton. We will seize it and use for our benefit!

"This will be a formidable distinction for us! What a stronghold this will make for the Union forces. We will be able to choke off the South's supply lines traveling by water from Europe, as well as their rail lines coming from elsewhere in the South attempting to deliver armaments and supplies to Savannah and Charleston. They will be reduced to using homemade bows and arrows! It will be such a blow to the Confederates. Jefferson Davis will cry himself to sleep at night!" Stevens burst out in laughter.

While the officers continued to chuckle on deck, there were those who were just happy to be alive. Below the decks of several vessels were runaway slaves who had come on board at Fort Monroe seeking shelter from the seceding states. Fortunately, they were granted sanctuary by commanding officers, but some of the men under their command were not as accepting about this arrangement.

The Navy had already begun enlisting men of color into their lower ranks as sailors for an extended period before this excursion. These lower-level sailors were known as the "bluejackets." There were several of them on the expedition. While the career Navy men were a bit more tolerant of having Negroes on the vessel, infantrymen were not. They considered the enslaved Negroes to be a burden, with more mouths to feed, and a means to deplete their supplies. Sometimes the tension was palpable between the enlisted and the living contraband of war. Nonetheless, the two groups managed to coexist. The standing order remained to accept them onto the ships and to do no harm to them.

Along with the contrabands were dozens of captured Confederate soldiers who had been held at the fort in Virginia and were now being transported for holding in South Carolina. They were resented even more due to their role in instigating the war.

As two of the enlisted soldiers strolled the upper deck of the ship, they looked down with scorn on the prisoners of war they held onboard. Resentful of the burden they bore, one of them kicked a bit of trash toward the prisoners and spit in their direction as they walked past.

Emitting a grunt, the other Union soldier said, "I don't know why we must feed these bastards. Given the chance, they would blow our brains out and kill our president. Why don't we just dump the trash overboard? It would leave more food for us and less of a stench onboard this ship."

His comrade nodded in agreement. "You got it right, mate. We should just throw the rotten bastards overboard and save us all a lot of trouble."

Tossing a cast-off tin can overboard to show how easily it could be done, he then smiled and jerked his head toward the prisoners. Meanwhile, his companion scowled at the chained and uneasy Rebel soldiers as if he were contemplating the notion.

The younger Yankee soldier went on. "Isn't bad enough we have horses, pigs, wagons, and crates of goods up to our asses, but now we have to take on runaway darkies and Rebel soldiers, too? It feels like we're carrying a damn circus on this ship, not readying ourselves for battle. I'm afraid I'll pull out a blasted carrot instead of a pistol in the heat of the battle," he complained.

"Yeah, and to top it off one of those damn newspaper reporters we have on board would be there to catch the moment and print it in the *New York Tribune*. Wouldn't your mother be embarrassed for you, lad?" The elder man slapped his comrade on the back and erupted in laughter. "It's too bad we don't have any photographers on board to capture the moment. We could put it on a tintype and set it in a case for her." He exposed his gnarly teeth, some of which were missing, some stained from years of chewing tobacco.

The solider, still a boy, rolled his eyes, then shot a disparaging look to the small group of newly liberated slaves huddled together on a corner of the deck.

The standing orders to provide comfort were interpreted differently depending on who commanded the vessel, their town of origin, and their persuasion. Some of the naval officers were quite kind, while others were barely tolerant. The formerly enslaved had no choice but to endure their treatment, whatever it might be, for the duration of the journey. Most did what they had been taught to do their entire lives—cater to the White man, act respectful, and seem grateful for any kindness shown.

As the fleet continued down the Atlantic Coast, their travels became more difficult. On November 1, they passed from North to South Carolina where the seas became angry with high swells. The wind increased to a gale force, and by midafternoon, DuPont ordered the fleet to disregard the order of sailing. Most of the ships managed to ride out the storm, but some had to abort their mission. A handful returned home for repairs, and a few were lost at sea. One gunboat had to jettison most of her guns to stay afloat. Three ships carrying food and ammunition were sunk or driven ashore without loss of life. A transport ship carrying three hundred Marines went down; most of her contingent were saved, but seven men were drowned or were otherwise lost at sea. But still the armada continued toward the great battle.

Chapter 11
The Battle of Port Royal Sound Commences

Somewhere near Edisto Island, Fall 1861

While the armada made its way down the coastline, the Rebel encampment carried on near the town of Beaufort. The escaped slave Issac was still running from the Confederate troops, trying to make his way to enemy lines so that he could join Union forces. Tired and disoriented, he pushed onward. Despite his exhaustion, he was sure he'd made the right decision to leave the Confederate camp. He simply couldn't take kowtowing to the Rebels any longer.

Issac had been traveling on foot for a few days, continually following the North Star. He wasn't sure how far he had traveled, but he knew he had been hugging the Atlantic coastline of South Carolina. He managed to feed himself on the bread, nuts, and salt pork he had swiped from the camp before he ran. He managed to pick some berries along the way as well, but his stomach rumbled with hunger.

Issac was sorry he hadn't managed to nick a compass before he left the Confederate camp. Now he questioned his whereabouts.

What if he never made it to the Union lines?

He had tried to travel under the cover of darkness, sleeping briefly in a tree or on a level, elevated plateau. The centuries-old oak trees, so prevalent in the region with their broad branches, offered the best sanctuaries. The massive, curved branches of the arbors, some of which were covered with the delicate green fronds of the resurrection fern, cradled him as if God intended it.

After two days of heavy rains, the sun shone on the beachfront. While Issac's boots were still damp, his clothing had partially dried out and stopped chaffing his skin. His throat was parched, and his mouth was dry; he felt weakened and a bit light-headed. He approached a creek bed to refill a canteen he had snapped up from a dead Rebel soldier. While crouched, he heard voices echoing down the adjacent waterway through the trees. The sound of men's voices startled him. He froze, fearful the Confederate soldiers he had abandoned were somewhere nearby. Fugitive slave laws were still in effect; if captured, surely he would be tortured, then killed. He fell flat to the ground, then crawled on his belly to a bush.

As he peered through the shrubbery, he was amazed by what was approaching him. Masts and expansive white sails contrasted sharply against the clear azure skies. As Issac crawled toward the larger body of water, he spied an entire fleet of ships. There were nearly a hundred of them all bearing the American flag. His weakness dissipated, and he became charged with adrenaline.

Union troops! The Federals are sending their forces southward!

There were ships of every sort; some were steam vessels, others relied entirely on their sails and the force of the winds. The lead vessel, *The Wabash,* was a magnificent frigate ship cruising toward Issac at an impressive speed, all of its sails billowing out like pillows of air. It was an impressive ship over three hundred feet long with a beam of over fifty feet, a full complement of crew of well over six hundred. Behind it were a variety of other ships, but none as inspiring as the lead vessel.

I'm saved! If only I can make it to these ships. How can I get out to these boats? The water's so deep. Not sure I can swim out there.

Issac sprang to his feet and began walking from the creek bed out to the larger body of water. He paced back and forth trying to assess the situation. How broad the water was; how far he would need to swim; how he would board a vessel; which vessel he should attempt to climb aboard. As he scanned the area, he spied a small bantu boat partially concealed by vines, but still afloat on the smaller tributary.

Lord God, you are with me, aren't you? You've given me the means to get out to those boats.

Issac swiftly made his way down to the small worn fishing boat, apparently left after a day of trolling on the water. Such a craft was often used by Negro fishermen to shrimp and angle fish. He had used them since he was a young boy. He picked up a paddle and began to head out toward the approaching fleet, careful not to move with too much haste as to put himself in danger. He knew the Yankees would not be looking for a Black man in a small boat. The larger boats might plow him over, but perhaps a smaller vessel at the rear of the cluster would allow him to board.

As the procession moved toward him, his stomach tightened as the first few vessels seemed to ignore him. There were no greetings or query as to his well-being.

Oh no, maybe I made a mistake coming out here. What if I put myself in harm's way?

But as the flotilla of ships moved past, the mood of those on board began to shift. Soldiers and sailors began to look down on him with concern. Some waved. Some called out.

Finally, Issac shouted to them, "Help me! Help me, please! I've run from the Rebel troops. I need your help! Please, help me!"

An officer in one of the smaller vessels waved him toward the ship, turned toward his crew members, directing them to assist the man. The crew members quickly threw down a rope ladder. Issac, grateful for their gesture, could have cried with relief. A broad, toothy grin spread across the starving wanderer, and he quickly paddled to the vessel. It was the most beautiful sight he had seen in days. Once he climbed aboard, he noticed other runaway slaves, which at least initially, gave him comfort.

A Negro sailor wearing a uniform blue jacket approached, nodded, and handed him a tin cup of water. "Welcome aboard, young man."

"Thank you. Thank you so much for picking me up. I wasn't quite sure where I was just now. I had run away from a Confederate troop. Master McKee had rented me out to the Rebel troops to serve them as a cook's aide. I hated it; I couldn't take it no more, so I left."

"Well, you'll be safe with us. We're going down to Port Royal, setting up camp there. It's going to be a big Federal encampment."

"The Union Army will seize Port Royal?" Stunned, Issac froze in place for a moment. This was both exciting and frightening at the same time, since his mother lived right next door in the town of Beaufort. Concerned, he blurted, "They must know there are Rebels all around there. Are they ready for this?"

"Oh, yes, we are more than ready. Just look at some of these big guns!" the sailor exclaimed as he pointed to a huge howitzer. "We have cannons that can fire for over two miles. We have guns on these vessels those Rebs have never seen before. They don't have the fire power or the men to put us down. They are in for the surprise of their lives!"

"Oh, Lordy! I can't believe this. The Yanks are coming to take over Beaufort and the whole Southeast port." Issac, so overwhelmed with glee, raised his hands skyward, then bent over and grabbed his knees. "I never thought I could see such a day."

"Nor did we, but here we are on our way to meet the Rebels head-on. I know there'll be a fight, but we'll whip em. I know it!" The Negro sailor grinned and bumped his elbow into Issac's ribs.

"God, let's hope you're right. Otherwise, we'll be blown to bits." Issac dipped his chin as he feigned wincing with pain.

"Oh, don't worry, mate, we'll be fine. You'll see." The blue jacket sailor slapped him on the back and smiled.

The armada stretched twenty-five nautical miles and stopped at Edisto Island before proceeding down to Port Royal Sound. DuPont had a signal officer from the Army Signal Corps, which served all branches of the military, transmitted a message via the recently developed wigwag system of signaling. Using one signal flag, the well-trained soldier gave notice to the other ships. This system of communication had just been developed the year prior and was already in constant use. At night, a kerosene torch was used in the same manner. This system was complemented by communication via telegraph. The Confederates had developed something similar, but it used different signals.

DuPont wanted to make sure that the men were ready and that the onslaught involving the two Confederate forts went off as planned. They would be trying new techniques of warfare, and he needed their attack to go as originally envisioned while in Virginia before leaving port. Because of the ships and supplies that had been lost or delayed while en route, DuPont wanted to rethink matters and modify his scheme accordingly.

DuPont and a landing party rowed up to the Sea Island of Edisto with maps, a compass, and other equipment in hand to go over their strategy once more. DuPont and his closest officers had a party of twenty in front of them and another landing party of thirty or so behind them to ensure their safety. There might be Confederate scouts or sharp shooters in the surrounding area trying to pick off higher-ranking officers.

Issac managed to finesse his way into joining the third group, agreeing to carry guns, ammunition, foodstuffs, and drink for the men to be consumed by the officers while on the island. He was eager to get a closer look at those in command and to understand what was about to unfold. Having been well-trained while at the McKee homestead, he fully understood how to conduct himself. He was careful to hang back a bit and to listen, but not speak. He was ever mindful of their cues, wishes, and desires.

He stood at the ready while the officers spread out a map of Port Royal Sound and talked about their strategy. He held a bottle of wine in one hand and a bottle of spirits in another. He had a tin cup tied to a piece of twine in his grasp. By his feet, he strategically positioned a basket of bread, hard tack, and beef jerky. He even managed to include some cheese brought on the journey from Virginia, and a pocketknife.

Eventually, one of the officers signaled him over and asked him to pour him a half cup of spirits to help embolden him for the attack. When he emitted a satisfied sound as it smoothly rolled down his throat and then slapped his chest, the other offices decided to join him. Issac efficiently made his way around the circle, serving every officer with a gracious bow and polite word. DuPont was impressed by Issac's respectful manner. He thought he might make use of this young man at his encampment.

The contingent continued to discuss the execution of their plans and the order of the ships as they entered Port Royal Sound. They weighed out the armaments each one carried and the virtue of each, careful to note that some of the vessels were not armed, but simply supply ships. Once all the officers felt satisfied and full from their refreshments, DuPont ordered the party back to their vessels. He turned and signaled Issac to join his men returning to *The Wabash*.

"Yes sir!" Issac almost leaped for joy.

I will get to see some real action. I can't believe DuPont has asked me to join him on the lead ship. What luck!

The men began to ready themselves for the battle. They knew that their flotilla was impressive, but one never knew what might happen in the heat of battle. They were relying heavily on the intelligence they had received from scouts in the area, particularly Blacks, who were feeding information to Union lookouts, but circumstances could change without notice. They had to be ready.

Men were scurrying about, starting to prepare the cannons and all the items necessary to keep them ready.

Issac asked one of the other Negro sailors in a blue uniform, "How many men does it take to fire that cannon? There are so many working on it."

"Boy, this takes five men to man it. It is a steady process to ready it, clean it and prep it, reload it, and fire it. No one can miss a beat. We all need to do our job and do it correctly each and every time. If a cannon misfires, we're all dead. We count on each other to do his job and to do it right!"

"I never realized the size of these cannons. They're huge!" Issac looked upon a parrot cannon in awe.

"Some of these cannons can fire over two miles, maybe even three. To hit with such power at a great distance, there must be a great deal of force behind it. It must be this big." Hurrying away from Issac, he waved him off.

⁓

It was half past nine in the morning on November 7, 1861, as the mighty armada approached Fort Mitchell. It was calm and clear as the ships entered the harbor in two defensive columns. The November weather was crisp yet temperate. The sun had risen with unusual splendor in a cloudless sky. Not a breath of wind marred the smooth surface of the water. DuPont became charged with electricity and turned toward his men. He was ready for the engagement.

Issac's eyes became wide at the monumental event he was about to behold. His jaw was agog as he looked over to the man he had spoken with earlier, the man now busy readying the ship for the imminent attack. Issac could not believe what was unfolding before him, what he sensed would be one of the great sea battles of the Civil

War. He also thought he might have a real chance to see freedom. As they approached, the ships prepared themselves; guns were turned and men ready to confront the enemy. As the crew scurried about, sailors shouted at Issac to join in and grab items for them. He was only too happy to oblige. He could feel his pounding heart rushing blood through his veins. The officers shouting commands and the rhythm of the soldiers loading the cannons functioned like a well-oiled machine. It added to the galvanizing mood of the men and the electricity that charged through Issac and those around him.

Issac looked up at the sails of *The Wabash*; it had a peculiar appearance as it approached Hilton Head Island. Never having seen a naval battle, Issac wasn't sure what the ships would do as they prepared to engage in a confrontation.

Issac asked a Negro sailor in a blue jacket uniform, "Why did our ship do that to her sails? They're all tucked up."

"She's got her sleeves rolled up. She's come for the fight." He jerked his head and raised his fist.

Issac carefully watched DuPont as he strode across the deck full of energy; he could almost feel the electricity surrounding him. At first, they would strike at Fort Walker, the larger threat that possessed more guns, then turn and attack Fort Beauregard to neutralize its threat. The plan as adopted by DuPont called for his fleet to enter the harbor at mid-channel. On the way in, they would engage both forts. After an initial pass of the forts in which guns would fire in rapid succession, the heaviest ships would then execute a turn to the left in column and go back against Fort Walker. Again, past the fort, they would once more turn in column and repeat the maneuver until the Confederate forts were neutralized. While the main fleet was engaged, five lighter gunboats would form a flanking column that would proceed to the head of the harbor and shield them.

DuPont planned to rely on the destructive agency of several gunboats, using overwhelming force and the terror inspired by it to send off a shower of iron hail in the briefest time in one spot.

What he hoped was the opposing forces, who were unprepared, would see it as Hell itself and flee the area. In short, DuPont was determined to go in, inflict the greatest amount of harm in the shortest amount of time on Fort Walker, then turn to the opposing fort. Officer Samuel F. Du Pont ordered his ships to keep moving in an elliptical path, bombarding Fort Walker on one leg and Fort Beauregard on the other.

This is a brilliant plan, Issac thought. *The Rebs can't defend themselves against this. Their forts weren't constructed for this type of maneuver.*

Suddenly a loud boom rang out, followed by white smoke curling up from the adjacent Confederate fort. Issac's body jerked at the sound, fearful of where the cannon fire might land. Adrenaline charged through him and the rest of the men on board as a shout rose up.

DuPont exclaimed, "Now we have the opening of the ball, men! Prepare to fire!"

Issac found himself throwing up his fist and shouting, "Yes! There you go, you Rebel dogs!" After months of having to serve them in the Confederate camp, he was charged for the fight.

The large guns required at least five men to manage them, as there were several steps that had to be taken in prepping, firing, and cooling the huge cannons. Once the firing began, shells were lobbed into the thick woodland areas where the Rebels were encamped. Initially, the Union ships fired a few shots to adjust their range, but then opened regular broadside fire.

The Confederate base at Fort Walker had twenty-one guns, including one ten-inch columbiad canon and six rifled thirty-two-pounders. Fort Beauregard had nineteen guns. The Confederates supported these forts with about three thousand men. The force was commanded by Brigadier General Thomas F. Drayton, an 1828 West Point graduate of a noble Southern family. He found himself and his men in an untenable situation and did not wish to concede to the Yankee forces, unless there was no other alternative. So, he and his men bravely held on as long as they could, but ultimately had to abandon the fort. The battle lasted less than five hours.

⌒

The Civil War pitted family members against one another. Some men were forced to make the difficult choices of which side to take. This harrowing decision was made by two brothers of a prominent Southern family, that of William Drayton, who had relocated from South Carolina to Philadelphia. One brother, Percival, had opined to be on the sea from boyhood and joined the Navy as a teenager where he served as a midshipman. He advanced through the ranks as he served all over the world. When the War Between the States erupted, Percival remained loyal to the Union and was assigned the commander of the *Pocahontas*, part of DuPont's expedition. This pitted him directly against his blood brother, Thomas, who commanded Confederate forces in the area.

Thomas Drayton had attended the United States Military Academy at West Point and was classmates with the president of Jefferson Davis. The two men remained lifelong friends. Thomas was appointed brigadier general and given the department at Port Royal. It was on this afternoon that he had to consequently face his own brother in heavy battle.

The bombardment continued on in this way until shortly after noon, when *Pocahontas*, delayed by the storm, put in her appearance. Her captain, Commander Percival Drayton, placed the ship in position to enfilade Fort Walker and joined the battle. Commander Drayton was the brother of Thomas F. Drayton, the Confederate general who commanded the forces ashore.

Early in the afternoon, most of the guns in the fort were out of action, and the soldiers manning them fled to the rear. A landing party from the flagship took possession of the fort. When Fort

Walker fell, the commander of Fort Beauregard across the sound feared that his soldiers would soon be cut off with no way to escape, so he ordered them to abandon the fort. Another landing party took possession of the fort and raised the Union flag the next day. Only eight were killed in the fleet and eleven on shore, with four other Southerners missing. Total casualties came to less than one hundred. Both brothers survived the ordeal. The area became a Union stronghold for the remainder of the war.

Chapter 12
DuPont Walks Through Beaufort; Robert Smalls Liberates Himself

Beaufort and Fort Royal, November 1861

The Federals took both Fort Walker and Fort Beauregard within a matter of hours. The two forts lie on opposite sides of the sound, Fort Walker on Hilton Head to the south and Fort Beauregard on Saint Phillips Island to the north. Fort Walker fell first. A landing force of sailors and Marines went ashore to the larger Fort Walker to seize it and check for any straggling Confederate troops.

Issac, eager and alert, offered to go ashore with the landing team. Issac pointed out he could help the soldiers by carrying a large bucket of tools and bags to collect items left behind by the Confederate soldiers as mementos. Flag Officer DuPont allowed him to go along to assist but directed him to be mindful not to interfere with any military protocols. Issac nearly burst with joy. He knew this would be an important event for the Black people around Beaufort and Port Royal if the Yankees succeeded in their mission to oust the Rebels.

The entourage of men used a smaller vessel to head out to the fort. Everyone was given a weapon before departing, including Issac. The officer in charge cautioned the men to remain alert, as Rebel soldiers might still be lurking about the fortification waiting to ambush them. Issac felt his heart pounding as they drew near the island fort, perspiration slowly trickling down the side of his head. He knew that a Negro might be picked off first from the rest of the group, just as a warning shot.

The crew quietly landed their vessel and using hand gestures, moved onto the beach in differing directions. Unable to locate any hidden Confederate soldiers, each man in turn called out the "all clear." They moved about freely then, snapping up mementos as they did so. Of course, items like revolvers and pistols were snatched up first, but the breastplates and belt buckles with the Confederate insignia were favorites, too. Then there were other items such as coat buttons, cannonballs, and the unique smooth-side canteens, which the men liked to collect as well.

Two men raised the Union flag at Fort Walker among cheers from the landing party and those on nearby vessels. The thunderous roar reverberated across the open water and through the riggings of the ships. One of the nearby vessels was the USS *Susquehanna*, launched in 1850, a sidewheel steam frigate and the first ship of the US Navy to be named for a river. The band on the ship played the "Star-Spangled Banner" to a cheering crowd of thousands of Union troops. The ordeal they had been through, including weeks on board cramped ships and tempestuous storms, was now worth it all. It was a grand achievement, especially after the beating they had taken at the Battle of Bull Run earlier that year.

Issac had become a valet and cabin boy to DuPont, and he had grown to garner a great deal of trust from the officer. When the landing party returned to the ship, Issac approached the commanding officer a bit tentatively and wearing a nervous smile. Noting the young man's anxiety, DuPont waved him over.

From a large bag, Issac withdrew an embellished Confederate officer's sword, about thirty inches in length, from a scabbard with *CSA* etched on the side, which stood for the Confederate States of America, and held it out. He proudly handed it to DuPont.

DuPont's eyes widened with surprise. "Oh my, this is beautiful! What a prize."

Issac then pulled out a second one. "Sir, I thought you would want two of these officer swords. You see, they still have fancy tassels and initials on them. It makes them extra special. Should be real special for you and your family, sir."

DuPont's mouth dropped. He was overcome with emotion and momentarily speechless.

Fully aware of the import of his moment, Issac drew on all the good manners he had been taught while serving under Master McKee, standing tall and steady before the commanding officer. He wanted to avoid an awkward pause, so Issac filled the void. "Sir, I thought you'd be wanting to remember this day and your family would as well. You served your country with honor. Every American will know that, and so will your family." Issac smiled broadly.

Commander Rodger, who had been in charge of the landing party, had been standing near Issac the entire time and presented DuPont with a palmetto flag he had seized from the fort.

Commander Rodger gave the flag officer a few moments to gather himself. Then, he nodded and took a step forward. "Yes sir. We thought you would want mementos of this fine day. Perhaps a sword for each of your sons and the flag for your cousin, Christopher Rodgers. It was your finest hour, sir. I'm sure your entire family, as well as the entire naval fleet, will forever be proud of your service to your country."

"Thank you, gentlemen. I'm grateful to you. I will treasure these for the remainder of my life, as I am sure my family will as well." DuPont extended his hand to Commander Roger, shook it, and then nodded to Issac.

The men standing around watching it all applauded the spectacular event. They all knew a historic victory had been achieved and that they had been part of a job well done. The locals would forever regard this military seizure as the "Great Skedaddle," and also the Day of the Big Gun Shoot," as all the area's planters and other White folks fled the area.

———

While the Confederate soldiers quickly retreated, enslaved workers from the nearby plantations on the Sea Islands were hiding out in wooded areas, celebrating.

"Yankees done come and brought God almighty wit dem!"

As the jubilant enslaved workers fled their masters' plantations, they sang:

> *Wake up, snakes, pelicans, and Sesh'ners!*
> *Don't yer hear 'um comin'*
> *Comin' on de run?*
> *Wake up, I tell yer! Git, up, Jefferson!*
> *Comin' on de run*
> *Bob-o-ish-i-on!*

Slaves watched the retreating Confederate soldiers head inland and many of their masters following. It was the best day of their lives. It was as if God had answered their prayers. They sat in the fields and feasted on all the foodstuffs left behind in the plantation houses.

A short distance away, city dwellers in the nearby town of Beaufort left in droves. The White slave holders forced their bondsmen to quickly pack up their valuables and bury the silver. For many Blacks, it would be the last act they performed for their masters. White aristocratic masters had either directly threatened their slaves at gunpoint or tried to frighten them with stories that the Union soldiers would sell them to the owners of Cuban sugar plantations, where the work would be much more grueling and their life expectancy far shorter. Some slave masters insisted that their closest house servants, who had seemingly up until that point been ever loyal, accompany them on their journey. Those who refused were shot dead, often without hesitation, despite years of loyal service.

In the town of Beaufort, there were Black bodies left lying in the street in front of mansion houses on Bay Street as reminders of their defiance. They had been gunned down and left after refusing to join their White planters as they fled their city houses. Many of the enslaved managed to take flight and hid in the woods, swamps, and fields. The escaped slaves remained there, uncertain as to what they should do.

Panic ensued among the local residents who could see the white sails billowing over the hundred-year-old oak trees, moving slowly along the Beaufort River. Their masts seemed to float along the waterways. The echoing sounds of the creaking of the wooden vessels could be heard along Bay Street and spilled over into the nearby streets. The townspeople of Beaufort froze to better hear who was approaching; they could discern an officer barking orders to prepare to anchor. Landing boats made splashing sounds that reverberated off the banks as they were dropped into the river. Townspeople knew the Union soldiers were just minutes from landing.

"The Great Naval Expedition" to Port Royal, SC, 1861

Fearful of what the Yankees might do to them, Whites scrambled into their wagons. They left what they could not carry. Women became hysterical, terrified that maiden ladies might be violated, and their throats slit. Their frenzy wafted out onto the streets causing panic. In their hysteria, the townspeople scurried away on foot, on horseback, or in wagons. Those who had beasts who would carry them cracked their whips and shouted for them to gallop out of the town.

DuPont came up the Beaufort River where he was struck by its beauty and serenity. Weeping willows and rambling old oak trees draped in lacey gray moss hung over the waterways. Huge, lovely mansion houses nestled against the waterfront. It truly was the Newport of the South, with its palatial mansions along the water's edge. Along with the erection of stately homes were also institutions of higher learning, libraries, and other cultural institutions.

DuPont and his landing party disembarked from their larger river vessel and were rowed ashore in a smaller landing boat. As they approached, the men could hear the panicked voices of the townspeople shouting at one another, the whinnying of the scared horses as their hooves pounded the ground, and the rushing wagon wheels as they rolled across the crushed shell-and-sand roads. Not wanting to confront the citizenry, DuPont ordered the men to pause for several minutes to allow the townspeople to clear the area. The men were armed in case they were confronted by injured Rebels left behind or White townspeople who had refused to leave.

They waited until the noise abated and a calm came over the area.

DuPont and his landing party walked down the main street as he and the other Union officers were struck by the signs of their panic everywhere. Debris was carelessly scattered about on the streets—a shoe here, a hankie there, a checkered towel which had wrapped a few freshly baked buns. As the landing party quietly and cautiously progressed up the main street of Beaufort, voices in the distance spoke a melodic language unfamiliar to them. They would later learn it was the Gullah tongue.

"I can feel them peering at us, can't you?" said DuPont to one of his officers.

"I'm sure the slaves refused to go. That's why they shot some of them down in the streets in cold blood." The officer pointed to the bodies of two enslaved workers lying along Bay Street. "They would rather have them dead than see them enjoy freedom. Their act of defiance must have been too much," responded one of the lieutenants.

Suddenly they heard feet scampering across the piles of leaves and dried twigs, fugitives escaping.

"The slaves are probably peering at us from inside those houses or behind some of those trees. The Negroes will just have to learn to trust us. I don't think we should chase them down. That would only add to their distrust of Yankees," announced DuPont.

"I think you're exactly right, sir," nodded a lieutenant as he strolled beside him with one hand on his side arm.

DuPont looked toward a wooded area and called out, "We know there are slaves here with us. You can come out when you are ready. We will not harm you. We're here only to fight Rebel soldiers, not Negro slaves. That is not our mission. We're here to bring this town under Union control, that is all." DuPont exhaled sharply as he looked about. He walked with authority, his back erect as he strolled down the street.

The men continued down Bay Street and then began to enter the mansion houses along the waterfront. Inside, they found that homeowners had apparently dropped what they were doing the moment they heard the Yankees were coming. As DuPont and a few of the officers from his landing party approached the first house, they noted the high tabby foundation which was braced by multiple sturdy chimneys. The house overlooked a long sweeping lawn with elegantly manicured gardens. When the officers first entered the stately home, a lieutenant noticed a lady's hankie had dropped in the middle of the black-and-white marble floor. The men stood for a moment and took in the elaborate entryway, noting the finely carved moldings, the thick mahogany doors with leaded-glass transoms, and heavy brass door fittings. The entry had a tall ceiling and a crystal chandelier that glittered.

As the officers entered the parlor, they were impressed with the finery of the room. It had outstanding paneled interiors, including hand-carved mantels and over-mantels, chair railings and wainscoting. The parlor was outfitted with two settees, overstuffed chairs, and button-back armchairs, all in rich colors, burgundy, navy blue, and forest green. A large tapestry decorated the wall with a Paris street scene, apparently acquired in France. The keys of a piano were exposed, the lid having been lifted and enabling the resident to play; sheets of music were scattered all about on the bench and floor below. In the adjacent dining room on a long mahogany table, a book lay open with a recent love note tucked inside. A glass of lemonade, half empty, sat on a sideboard, as if someone would be back momentarily to reclaim it. As one of the officers entered the warming kitchen, he saw that one of the servants must have just sat to catch a bit of a meal in between serving the family members. A dish of half-eaten food remained on the table—a bit of bread torn in half thrown on top of the plate, an apple slice beside it.

White folks had all fled for the Upcountry, save one drunken and confused man who unwittingly stayed behind. Mr. Allen, a rather frightened merchant. Reportedly, he was a northerner of Massachusetts birth who stayed on after the Union invasion and ended up doing steady business with the occupying forces. Eventually, the locals made up a poem about Mr. Allen:

> *Tis the last man at Beaufort*
> *Left sitting alone*
> *All his valiant companions had "vamoosed"*
> *No secesh of his kindred*

To comfort is nigh,
And his liquors expended,
The bottle is dry!
We will not have thee, thou lone one
Or harshly condemned-
Since your friends have all "mizzled,"
You can't sleep with them;
And it's no joking matter
To sleep with the dead;
So we take you back with us-
Jim lifts up his head!
He muttered some words
As they bore him away,
And the breeze thus repeated,
The words he did say:
When the liquor's all out,
And your friends they have flown,
Oh who would inhabit
This Beaufort alone?

Simultaneously, several miles away on Hilton Head Island, Brigadier General Thomas W. Sherman of Newport, Rhode Island (not to be confused with Major General William Tecumseh Sherman who would lead the famous and destructive March to the Sea) was commanding Union land troops. While Port Royal provided the strategic deepwater sound on the South Carolina coast between Charleston and Savannah, the surrounding land provided the Union Marines with the critical supply depot it needed and a base for military operations. The Union's optimal plan was to also cut off the nearby railroad to stem the flow of supplies from cities further south into Charleston.

Once the plantation owners left the area, the jubilant enslaved workers, free for the first time, ransacked the beautiful homes of the area. They whimsically played out the roles of their demanding masters and put on their finery and strutted about the mansion houses. Some pounded on pianos and organs and danced in jubilation. Black women tried on corsets and chemises for the first time, then fine gowns. They put combs in their hair and fluttered fans shipped from Paris. They investigated all the finery they had admired their entire lives but had been forbidden to touch, fearing they would be mercilessly whipped, or worse, torn from their families and sold down river. Always having been deprived of enough nourishment, they took foodstuffs, meat and spices, along with anything else they had admired all their lives. They became intoxicated just by the indulgences they waded in, the finery and all the accoutrements.

While this was going on, some White residents secretly returned to their fields to burn their valuable Sea Island cotton so that the Union soldiers could not profit from it. However, only a few managed to do so, and they were cut short in their efforts. Much of the famous cotton was later gathered and used by the Union forces, first sold on the open market and later made into uniforms.

Unfortunately, some of the Union soldiers also strayed from their encampments and entered the private homes of the planters. They plundered the abandoned homes and took anything they could find of value, and sometimes destroyed novel things left behind. Brigadier General Sherman was furious when he learned what the soldiers had done to private residences. He swiftly punished the offenders and issued orders forbidding the men from entering the homes of the local citizenry. DuPont was likewise incensed, punishing those who had pillaged and stopping any unauthorized travel by boat.

The commanding officers had not expected that the fleeing plantation owners would leave behind ten thousand slaves who were now seemingly reliant on the Union Army for support and direction. Unsure as to what to do, they quietly pondered the matter and set up an encampment on Hilton Head Island. What had once been an area of more than twenty working plantations, Fort Walker and little else, was suddenly converted into a working military community humming with activity. There were over fourteen thousand Union soldiers occupying the area and thousands more from the Navy, the Corp of Engineers, and other branches of service. Along with these soldiers were thousands of bewildered newly liberated slaves unsure of where to go or what to do. But a page had been turned. With the efforts of the different branches of the service, new buildings went up, as well as wharves and bridgeworks. It was becoming manifest; a new era had begun.

It was late spring of 1862 when Big John, Tobias, and Cully traveled to Charleston on a small river boat the master had recently acquired. The weather was warm, but the great heat of summer hadn't set in over the land. The boat they traveled in from Twin Oaks in the adjacent town of Mount Pleasant had been purchased by Master Langdon from a planter named Allston on nearby Waccamaw Island. His chief carpenter, an enslaved Black man, Thomas Bonneau, took great pride in his work and produced superior vessels. The craft, a river steamer over fifty feet in length, allowed them to haul a variety of goods down to the waterfront for trade. The trio was hauling cotton, rice, and indigo down to Charleston for shipment to England.

Eager to get into town to hear the most recent scuttlebutt, the men had Nellie make up a basket of food and drink to last the day. Little did they know the news they would hear when they docked in Charleston. Big John was a more skilled captain, but Tobias could easily pass as White, so he took the wheel at times so no questions would be asked. Cully, a slighter-framed young man, laughed at the other two as he stretched out in comfort the entire ride.

Once they arrived, stevedores on the waterfront were all abuzz about an enslaved Black man named Robert Smalls who had been working down on the waterfront in Charleston for the last few years. On the night of May 12, 1862, he had managed to escape with a Confederate vessel, along with the ship's enslaved crew and their family members. It was a miraculous story. How had a Black man managed such a feat? Men of color weren't supposed to know how to navigate the waters with such a boat, the signals to get by the Confederate check points, or a myriad or other matters that would have stymied anyone else.

Robert Smalls was a bright young man and a quick study. He was in his early twenties and had been rented out in the city of Charleston since he was a young teenager. He had been born in Beaufort to a planter named Henry McKee who owned a city house in Beaufort on Prince Street, as well as a nearby plantation named Ashdale.

Smalls' master, Henry McKee, also owned Smalls' mother, Lydia. Robert had been born on the floor of the kitchen house. It was believed by many that his master was also his biological father. It was common in the planter system for masters to have relations with their enslaved Negresses and thereby sire mulatto children. This was apparently the case with Robert.

Smalls was married to a woman named Hannah and they had two children. One was just a small infant. Smalls had hoped to buy his freedom one day, but it would be a long process. Smalls earned sixteen dollars a month from John Ferguson, the owner of the steamer which he had absconded with a few days before. Smalls had negotiated with his master, McKee, that he could keep one dollar a month from his earnings. He had always been thrifty and was careful to tuck away money. But he had grown anxious and didn't want to wait any longer. He wanted freedom for himself and his family now.

Smalls worked on the ship the *Planter* initially as a deckhand, then as a wheelman. The *Planter* was a steamer that was being rented out to the Confederates. Neither the Confederates or the Federals had possessed a standing army prior to the war, so one had to be quickly raised through any means necessary. For the most part, that meant renting vessels until the ships could be quickly constructed. The *Planter* featured two large, enclosed paddle wheels at port and starboard. From the outset of the Civil War, the Confederates had hired this ship as a transport to carry soldiers and military supplies. The *Planter* was known as one of the newest and fastest steamers operating in the area.

Earlier in the fateful day, the ship had picked up four massive cannons and a substantial amount of ammunition. There was a banded forty-two-pound rifled gun, an eight-inch columbiad gun, an eight-inch howitzer, and a thirty-two-pound rifled gun, along with a ten-inch columbiad gun carriage. This gave Smalls added incentive to not only seize the ship, but also the ammunitions to turn over to the Union Navy. Most escaping slaves rowed out to the Union troops. No one had ever captured a vessel of this size, turned it over to Union troops, and delivered such a bonus gift as priceless armaments.

⟿

"So, what happened?" Big John asked an older dockworker. Mingo, in a blue shirt with graying hair and a few missing teeth chuckled. "Dat Robert Smalls, he sure a sly one! He really outsmarted da White man this time! Ha!" The enslaved stevedore couldn't contain himself; he was so proud of Smalls and amused at the same time. "Dat sly dog, he done waited until all da White crew left da ship. Da married men went home t' dey wives. Da' single men went t' dey pubs. Smalls knew dey wouldn't be back. He waited jus' ta' make sure. He must've planned 'dis for a long time, learned all da Confederate signals ta' get out da harbor. Must be a half dozen check points, and he got past em all."

Another enslaved dock worker, Scipio, in a loose oatmeal-colored shirt broke in. "You know what else dat man did? He put on Captain

Relyea's straw hat and his coat. Dat stupid captain always left his hat 'n coat on da ship 'n Smalls knowed it. Da two men 'bout da same size. In da moonlight ya' can hardly tell da difference. Smalls practiced da captain's voice and signals, and by God, it worked! Damn it! Da man's brilliant!" He erupted in laughter at the notion of having fooled the White Confederate soldiers in such a spectacular way.

Mingo added, "Smalls got past all the check points, but it got scary out in da harbor. Da poor man out there wit' his family and seventeen other slaves. They still had the damn Confederate flag flying. They had to keep it up to get past all the Confederate check points, but someone should have thought to take it down before they approached a Union ship."

"Damn right! Dey was out dere, in da harbor with the Stars and Bars flying!" Scipio slapped his thigh and spun around.

Mingo went on with the story. "Dey made it past Fort Sumter, 'den Morris Island before dey took down de dang Confederate flag. Here dey was with steam and smoke belchin' out from the *Planter's* stacks, de paddle wheels churnin', and she's headin' toward a damn Union ship. Some fool finally think to go grab a white bedsheet off a mattress in da captain's quarters, another one right quick pulled down 'da Rebel flag. Da whole time, da Yankee cannons start turnin' toward the *Planter* and about to fire on them. Dey just 'bout to blow dem out da water!" Scipio explained, "I bet dey was about to pee dey pants! Dey had babies on board, all dey families was with em."

"Da Planter made it all da way out in da harbor and de cannons was turned on dem, da Yankee ship knew dey couldn't outrun da Planter, it too fast of an ironclad steamship. They had to stay and fight. The Yanks lieutenant in command ordered them to battle stations. Could you imagine how those runaway slaves felt about then?

"Dey made it all the way out into da harbor wit' a stolen ship and dey 'bout t' get blown t' bits? Smalls' woman a' holdin' da baby and dey 'bout t' meet dey maker afta' all dat plannin'," Scipio shook his head.

Mingo jumped in. "Yeah well, 'de angels musta been lookin' down on dem folks. A breeze of briny salt air came through 'bout then. Across the quiet harbor, 'de Yankee officer heard the voices of those on the Planter screaming 'Don't shoot.' Den he saw da white flag waving from 'de front of the ship. Right quick he ordered 'de gun crews to stand down. Dey was just 'bout to fire on dem firing at Smalls to stand down. Da lucky bastard. God smiled down on dem. Yep, He sho' did."

Scipio continued. "I heard da Yankee lieutenant hollered over to em, askin' who dey was and what dey intent was. Smalls hollered back and explained he was a slave and so was da others on board. Den he told em he had just stole da dang ship, a prize Confederate vessel. When 'da lieutenant ordered dem to come along side, da enslaved. Onboard all started to cheer and dance. Dey knew dey was free. Dey Yankees was gonna save em. What a glorious moment! Can't imagine how good dey musta felt right 'den."

"My God!" uttered Big John, "Amazing. He must have been planning that for months."

"I'm sure he was. He's a smart man ya know. Wish I'da been on that ship wit' him."

"Me too, me too," nodded Big John.

Robert Smalls would go down in history for his act of great courage and cleverness. He not only turned over numerous weapons to the Union forces, but also signal code books found onboard the *Planter* that proved invaluable to the war effort. At the time there was no electronic means to communicate between ships or land forces. The principal means was through flag signals or Confederate wigwag signals, which were coded messages transmitted across line-of-sight distances by an officer performing specific combinations of motions with a flag or flags. Each motion represented an alphanumeric character determined by a signaling code. At night, the Confederates used torches instead of flags. Before the Confederates realized the code had been compromised, the Union forces had been able to interpret signals sent from Fort Sumter, Fort Moultrie, and Morris Island to the Confederate headquarters stationed in Charleston.

Following Smalls' seizure of the *Planter*, he and a minister from the Beaufort area, or what later became known as "The Port Royal Experiment," convinced the president to allow men of African descent to fight as soldiers in the war. They had reason to fight for liberty for themselves and their families. Smalls was so convincing, Lincoln agreed. This surge in additional Union troops turned the tide in the war.

Smalls subsequently went on to act as a paid officer for the Union forces and headed a vessel. In early 1863, Smalls piloted the *Keokuk*, an experimental ironclad. Eventually, in late 1863 he was appointed the captain of the *Planter*, the very vessel he had commandeered after it had been refurbished, making him the first Black captain of a Union Army vessel. Meanwhile, he was cursed by the Confederate soldiers and lay citizens throughout the South. Smalls began to tour the United States and Europe delivering talks about his extraordinary act of courage. Eventually, he would serve as a five-term congressman during Reconstruction.

Harper's Weekly June 14, 1862

Robert Smalls between 1870-80

Chapter 13
Can the Union Army Recruit African American Men?

Mount Pleasant, South Carolina

Charleston was considered the spiritual capital of the Confederacy and therefore a prime target for the Union. So many acts of defiance had percolated up in this city; it was the heart of the rebellion and had been that way for decades, extending back to the Nullification Crisis of the late 1820s when John C. Calhoun challenged federal tax laws and contended the state of South Carolina had the ability to nullify an act of Congress. It was then that the term "state's rights" was coined and would continue to be used for over a hundred years even though it was without legal merit.

By May of 1862, the city of Charleston waited to feel the full wrath of the North. After all, it had hosted the Democrat convention in April 1860 and South Carolina's secession convention that December. A handful of months later in April 1861, the first shots of the war had been fired in the city's harbor. Then in the fall of that same year, Union troops had established a blockade just south of Charleston at Port Royal with the largest armada in history. On the heels of the Blockade, Charleston experienced a horrific fire in December of 1861. It had been a windy, chilly evening, and seemed as though the fires of hell had broken out to punish the Southern town. The devastating fire blazed through the streets, leaving a path of destruction roughly a mile long and several blocks wide, causing an estimated eight million dollars in damage and burning one hundred forty-five acres. Nearly six hundred homes, churches, and public buildings perished in the blaze. The destruction only added to the already sullen feeling of the citizenry.

Most Charlestonians had no doubt that the Union was itching for the city to feel its full wrath. By this time, the Confederates were so certain that an assault was imminent that they prepared to instate martial law in Charleston.

Fears among the White citizens of Charleston escalated when the Union Major General David Hunter, a West Point graduate from the nation's capital city of Washington (not yet referred to as D.C.) and ardent abolitionist, abruptly declared all enslaved Blacks residing within the Department of the South where he acted as commander (South Carolina, Georgia, and Florida) to be free effective May 9, and planned to arm them. This pronouncement bewildered even the military leaders in Port Royal and nearby Beaufort, including DuPont, who had continued to act as head of the Naval forces in the area. Hunter had made this pronouncement without authority from President Lincoln, and the declaration was subsequently rescinded by the White House due to promises the president had made to Southern leaders in an effort to preserve the Union.

Major General Hunter had previously requested permission from Secretary of War Stanton to enlist African Americans as soldiers. Hunter assumed that the secretary, having remained silent on the matter, was passive consent and moved ahead. Hunter thought, perhaps, there were political reasons for his silence. Hunter, being a man of action, trusted that the secretary of war had obviously approved or would have otherwise sent word via telegraph.

Hence, Major General Hunter issued on May 9, 1862, General Order No. 11, which read:

> *The three states of Georgia, Florida and South Carolina, comprising the Military Department of the South, having deliberately declared themselves no longer under the protection of the United States of America, and having taken up arms against the said United States, it becomes a military necessity to declare them under martial law. This was accordingly done on the 25th day of April 1862 Slavery and martial law in a free country are altogether incompatible, the person these states, Georgia, Florida and South Carolina – heretofore held as slaves are therefore declared forever free.*

After issuing this order, Hunter directed the Union troops under his command to start collecting prospective Black soldiers from the fields of the surrounding plantations. He directed them to round up "every able-bodied Negro between the ages of eighteen and forty-five, capable of bearing arms." Soldiers began recruitment the following day. Although some of the Black men were suspicious of their actions due to rumors still circulating that they would be sold as slaves to Cuban plantation owners, for the most part, they were willing to join.

After General Order No. 11, Hunter began enlisting Black soldiers from the occupied districts of South Carolina and formed the first such Union Army regiment, the First South Carolina (African Descent). President Abraham Lincoln quickly rescinded the order and directed the troops to disband. Lincoln was concerned about the political effects enlisting Black troops would have in the border states, driving some slaveholders to support the Confederacy. (Lincoln's own Emancipation Proclamation was announced about four months later in September, taking effect in January 1863.) Nevertheless, the South was furious at Hunter's action. Confederate president Jefferson Davis issued orders to the Confederate Armies that Hunter was to be considered a "felon to be executed if captured."

In the meantime, recruitment efforts in the north were going poorly. Union forces needed to move their men from the southeastern coast up to Virginia and nearby regions to focus on the fighting there. Draft riots were starting to break out in New York and other New England towns. White men complained that they were dying for Black people, and dying in large numbers as a result, while Black men did not have to fight and die. Meanwhile, Blacks wanted and needed to fight for their own cause.

Hentie was dusting the front parlor when she heard a rider coming up the Avenue of Oaks toward the mansion house. She glanced out the large front window, framed with ivory lace draperies. The man riding horseback appeared to be a mail carrier in his courier's jacket and mailbag on his mount. Hentie watched him dismount and approach the mansion house and proceed toward the portico. The large brass knocker on the heavy wooden front door announced his arrival. Samuel, the house butler, answered and spoke with the man. After retrieving the proffered letter, he showed Hentie the sealed ivory vellum envelope.

"Hentie, the man said this here letter is for the missus. You probably ought to take this on up to her. I believe she on up in her room," Samuel said and handed her the dispatch with its elegant handwriting. Hentie recognized the tight script with a bit of floweriness at the end of each word. It must have been penned by Sarah Chase, Mrs. Langdon's cousin in Pennsylvania. The two corresponded with some frequency, and when the mistress was under the influence of her laudanum drops, she freely shared the contents of each letter about her son Elliott, a Confederate officer, and her deceased husband, Julius.

As Hentie walked to the back stairwell, which the servants were always mandated to take except in special circumstances, she flipped it over and noted the red wax seal with the familiar stamp on it. She slipped the envelope into the front pocket of her house dress and ascended the stairs as she listened to the conversations being held on the level above.

Octavia was arguing with the mistress about where she last put her gris-gris. Mrs. Langdon was nearly hysterical. "I need my special necklace to ward off that evil woman. I know her spirit is circling me, the spirit of my husband's first wife is flying about this house. I feel it! That cold chill went up my back and I caught a whiff of roses again. It smells like tea rose perfume. I tell you; it was her! I know the Gullah charms are the only thing that can keep the spirits away. Now, find it!"

Hentie, having dealt with this issue many times before, jumped in to soothe the mistress. She had stuck multiple good luck charms and talismans throughout her room so she could always access one when needed, much like a mother would do with toys for a toddler.

Hentie reached into the lower drawer of a beautiful mahogany armoire that towered at the end of her bedroom suite. In it were many of the mistress' dressing gowns, corsets, and petticoats. Hentie had stuck one of the charms beneath a few pairs of the mistress' cotton drawers.

"Here it is!" Hentie held up the talismans and smiled.

"Well, thank the Lord!" Octavia exclaimed as her large round eyes looked skyward in relief and her body swayed to and fro.

Hentie made sure that Mimba, the plantation's Gullah conjurer, had constructed several mojo bags in similar fabrics and twine so that the mistress would never be the wiser. The charms probably didn't hold the same amount of magical protection that Mrs. Langdon was seeking, but that didn't matter. She believed it did, so it soothed her.

Immediately upon seeing the charm, Mrs. Langdon calmed and reached for the gris-gris. She put the charm around her neck and tucked it under the neckline of her dress. The two house servants glanced at each other and smirked while the mistress, full of happiness and glowing with delight, continued admire the small bump under her corset,

The missus had never fully recovered from an incident that had occurred years ago when Mimba had grown tired of Mrs. Langdon's mean, vengeful temperament and cast a hex on her. The hex caused the master's wife to have fits. She would crawl around the floor, barking and howling like a dog. A White doctor tried to treat her, contending the mistress was suffering from the blues and some form of anxiety. The doctor prescribed laudanum, a form of opium to treat the condition, and that was when the mistress' dependency on the drug began. She contended she needed it to treat her "nerves." That was over twenty years ago. But the barking and crawling around on the floor continued, so William Langdon asked Rosa, the herbalist who ran the infirmary, to summon a root doctor who practiced hoodoo. Rosa brought in Tiger Lowe, the best root doctor in the area. He made the mistress two conjure bags of ground rattlesnake rattles and told her to wear them under her armpits. Mrs. Langdon carefully followed the doctor's directions. Within a week, the fits ceased. Even though the missus found relief, Mimba, amused at her own handiwork, chuckled to herself for weeks.

While she was still in a good mood, Hentie decided to approach her with the letter.

"Madame, a letter just arrived for you. I assume you would like to read it right away," said Hentie as she pulled it out from her pocket.

"Oh, yes, of course." Missus Langdon extended her hand to retrieve it. "Oh, it's from my cousin in Pennsylvania! How wonderful."

The mistress broke the seal and then asked Octavia for her

spectacles, and began to read the letter aloud:

> *May 1, 1862*
> *Gettysburg, Pennsylvania*
>
> *My Dearest Cousin*
> *I received your very affectionate letter. It was so very kind of you. I am grateful that we have not allowed this dreadful conflict to come between us. While the War goes on in other parts of our country, thus far we have been largely untouched.*
>
> *I know that the draft for Union soldiers has gone into effect in some of the larger cities such as New York and Philadelphia. It has caused riotous behavior as white men complain that they have been dying for black people. It seems dreadfully unfair to them that black men don't have to go to war. I can't say I blame them. It has led to riots and the burning of certain black institutions, even the Colored Orphan Asylum in Philadelphia. Those poor negro waifs had nowhere to go now but to simply live on the street and scour the trash cans. Such a pity.*
>
> *We must trust this all to God's Divine guidance. My son Elliott has been assigned somewhere in Virginia; I am not sure where he is currently. The post takes so long from the battlefront. I pray that he is safely delivered back home at the end of this conflict. I know Fitzwilliam must be valiantly leading his troops somewhere in the South. I pray for him every day and for his safe delivery back home. I envision us all together again someday, as joyous and happy as we once were. I pray that day comes soon. Since I have nothing more of importance to write, I will quit, so adieu. God Bless you. May this conflict come to a swift conclusion – this is the prayer of us all.*
> *From thy affectionate cousin*
> *Sarah Chase*

"What a lovely letter," Hentie said. "How nice your cousin writes you like that."

"Yes, we've always been quite close. We used to spend summers together when we were children. Our mothers are sisters, and they too were very close. I believe they were only a year apart in age. We all lived in the Charleston area and received a proper rearing as young ladies. There were so many fine social events Sarah and I attended together as young ladies. Fortunately, we were always interested in different young suitors," Emily Langdon smiled as she looked off as if in recollection of those summer days.

"Well, that's good that she put you in a better mood, Missus Langdon. That cousin of yours is a real nice woman." Octavia looked at Hentie as if to say such an intervention came just in the nick of time.

Hentie walked about the room picking up the mistress' discarded items and fluffing pillows. Hentie looked at Octavia and tipped her head and cast a look toward the mistress' expansive bed, a magnificent mahogany frame with an elaborately carved pediment hung with heavy draperies. Dark wooden bed steps led to the immense, soft mattress made of goose feathers.

"Missus Langdon, I know you must be plum wore out with all this activity. Perhaps you would like to lie down for a little afternoon nap. I'd say you'd be deserving one 'bout now." Octavia looked down on the mistress with her large brown eyes, seemingly full of concern.

"Yes, Octavia, I think that would be a splendid idea. It's been such a busy day. A nice respite would do me good. Could you make sure my window is open so the fresh air can pass over me? It makes me feel so much healthier." She looked away at the willow tree gracefully bending and swishing in the breeze.

"Yes, ma'am let me get this window, then I'll help you get into a dressing gown." Octavia's full-figured body moved swiftly across the floor heaving open the large frame window, then scurrying over to the mistress' dressing area.

Without saying a word, the mistress turned her back to Octavia so that she could begin to undo all the buttons lining the back of her immense gown. Having completed this task many times before, Octavia moved quickly, helping the mistress disrobe, and removing several layers of undergarments.

Meanwhile, Hentie began on the other side of the room folding down the blankets and sheets on the missus' bed and fluffing her feather pillows. Eventually, the two house servants had Mrs. Langdon safely tucked in for a nap. The small brass servant's bell was placed on the nightstand so that she could ring whenever she awoke and gain assistance in dressing for the evening meal.

As the mistress began to fall into a deep slumber, Hentie and Octavia looked over to one another and broke out into a mischievous grin. They knew they could enjoy a small bit of freedom once she was asleep, so they tiptoed out of the room and quietly shut the door. Both stood frozen for a minute, listening for the mistress' beckoning to them, almost as one would wait for a baby to cry when awakened from a nap. Hearing nothing, they smiled and nodded at one another, then quietly crept down the hall, freezing momentarily when a board creaked. After pausing for a few beats, the two continued down the hall, opened the hidden doorway to the back stairwell, and descended the steps, giggling in hushed tones like two schoolgirls.[3]

---

3 As with most of the scenarios depicted throughout this novel and my previous one, *Gullah Tears*, the slave stories and depictions of the Civil War officers and soldiers have been taken from slave narratives, letters, journals, and recorded oral histories. The story of the hex placed on Mrs. Langdon which made her bark like a dog and the intervention of a root doctor which cured her, is based on an actual incident that occurred in the Sea Islands off the Coast of the Carolinas.

Chapter 14
Getting Settled in After the Big Skedaddle

In the Sea Islands of the Carolinas, near Hilton Head Island, Autumn 1861

Juba beat the dust off a weathered patchwork quilt. She was trying to help some of the refugees get settled into their makeshift shacks. The morning was full of cold, bright wind pouring off Port Royal Sound, with clouds blowing like windsocks. Juba paused and listened to the clatter of saber fronds shooting out from the palmetto trees and clattering on the recently constructed shacks. Some of the refugees managed to get into huts made of local timbers, while many remained in donated military tents. Newly displaced "contrabands of war," formerly enslaved workers liberated by the military, aimlessly scampered across the grounds of the compound as they tried to figure out where to go and how to begin their lives again.

Droves of the liberated had followed Union troops after they sailed into Port Royal Sound and set up camps in the neighboring town of Beaufort. They weren't sure where to go or what to do, so they clustered around the military encampments and hoped the Union soldiers would help them. It had only been a matter of a few weeks since the Federals had seized the area, so everyone, both Black and White, was trying to get used to their new circumstances. Initially, there was no formal leadership, no hierarchical chain among the emancipated Blacks. Several thousand were set adrift with no guidance or direction; they had some protection from the Union forces, but little else. If they left the safety of the area under Union control, they would be considered runaway slaves and taken under the control of Confederate forces or local authorities, beaten, and resold, or returned to their previous owner.

In the Beaufort area, Negroes enjoyed a haven of freedom and security which they had nowhere else in the South. The problem was that the Union troops had only limited supplies and foodstuffs. President Lincoln and the federal government hadn't given any guidance to the Union officers as to how to respond to the circumstances. It seemed no one in Washington had thought through what to do after the slaves were liberated.

DuPont's only objective had been to take control of Port Royal Sound so that a blockade could be established, thwarting the Southern supply line. It would be months before abolitionists, missionaries, and other humanitarians sent representatives to the area to provide help. Moreover, shipping additional supplies, such as clothing, food, provisions, and medicines, would take weeks, if not months to arrive. Blacks needed food, blankets, basic clothing, essential medicines, and common rations, such as meat, beans, oats, flour, and salt, basic items they used to receive from their masters on a weekly or monthly basis. But now they had to fend for themselves, which involved stealing whole hams, livestock, and items of finery from abandoned plantations.

"Them White folks sure never expected those Yankee soldiers to march right into Beaufort now, did they?" Juba chuckled, as she stuffed some straw into a bag to form a makeshift pillow. "Bet they never saw it coming so early in the war, but those ships sailed right into Port Royal Sound, didn't they?

"They sho' was surprised! Didn't see it comin' now, did they?" chortled Bessie, another newly liberated Black woman.

Juba went on to explain, "The master here in Beaufort been renting me out to the Confederates, but when they started to move further away from town, he brought me back home. Glad I was here when the Federals landed. It sho' changed my life. Glad I was here to be liberated. Might never have seen freedom any other way."

Bessie was helping Juba set up some cots and bedding for newcomers and started to reflect on the day the Union Army showed up in Port Royal. She lined up some pallets, topped with thin mattresses stuffed with hay and corn husks, then set about finding blankets.

"You should 'a seen my mistress when she heard the cannons firing." Bessie burst out laughing as she recalled the look on her mistress's face. "When she realized them Yankees were a comin' into Beaufort, whoo boy, she was fit to be tied. I thought she would pee herself right then and there! She thought they'd come in and rape the White women and steal all her jewels."

Juba whooped with laughter. "The master was so dang confident the Rebels would lick the North. He never dreamed they'd come into his hometown."

"I sho' bet he didn't!" Bessie slapped her knee as she let out a howl.

Juba said, "My mistress and the other folks in town had been havin' themselves an afternoon tea on they fine china when the commotion started. Mistress dropped her teacup right on her fine silk hoop skirt. Another lady spilled tea right down her fine white blouse wit' all kinds of lace trim on it. She said she bought it on her last trip to Europe."

Bessie chuckled, "I can just see it all now."

"All them White folks was taken completely by surprise." Juba paused, waved a pillowcase in the air, and bent over in laughter. "In all the missus' rushin' around, her cheeks got flushed with sweat rollin' down ruinin' all that fine face powder. Then her hairpins started fallin' out. She started lookin' nattier than a beggarwoman."

Bessie scooted out a chair and shoved a makeshift table with her knee, "I'll tell you what, it sure shocked the Rebs when that huge fleet of ships sailed into the sound. I bet their eyes popped right out de' heads! They never imagined the Yankees could have so many boats. Didn't they realize the South had seceded from the Union and started the damn war? What do they think the damn Yanks would do?"

Juba took a swig of water from an old military canteen, then held it in her outstretched arm for Bessie to take a drink. "I heard the Union troops had some new kind of weapons, too, cannons that fire further than ever before, clear across town. Can you believe that? Who would have thunk the Yankees could come up with that?"

"Thank ya. I could stand to wet my whistle 'bout now." Bessie took a long swig and handed the canteen back to Juba. "Those White folks in town had no idea what kinds of things those Yankees could make up North in dem factories."

Juba smoothed out a tattered patchwork comforter on a rickety army cot, pushed on it to make sure it was stable, then looked up at Bessie. "When the cannon fire started, the missus let out a shriek that made my hair stand up. I bet I gained three new gray hairs just from that first round and her screeching. Miss McKee told me to start pulling together all the silver and then to sew her jewels into her cape. The house staff was scurrying around like crazed mice, everyone in a panic."

Bessie nodded as she stuffed some old corncobs into a mattress. "My house 'bout the same way. Everyone tryin' to snap up valuables and such. The mistress was hollerin' and just 'a wailin'. We just grabbed a few clothes for the missus and master. Wasn't any time for nothing else."

Juba nodded. "That's about right. Cannons firing, rifles zinging right by me. What are you supposed to do? I saw the family across the street load up and get ready to pull out. And you know what? When that master finally got his carriage all loaded up, he ordered his butler, Samuel, to sit on the front of the rig, right behind his seat.

Bessie interjected, "Bet that master wanted to keep an eye on him. That's what he was up to."

"That poor, frail old Black man hesitated and got a questioning look. Out of nowhere, Master Hamilton landed a heavy slap on the old man's face. Samuel's eyes rolled around in his head. He spread out his hands to keep his balance, then shook his head tryin' to right hisself."

"Oh Jesus, bless that man."

"The master's nostrils flared like a horse at his old slave; he didn't think his ole' houseboy would defy him. It scared Samuel real bad when his master was a' actin' that way. I saw terror in his eyes. Samuel took a step back, then turned and started to run. That mean old White buckra pulled out his pistol and shot poor Samuel right in the back. He had worked for him his whole damn life and that bastard shot him in the back. Shot him dead, right then and there."

Bessie shifted her weight and put one hand on her hip. "Oh, my Lord! What did you do?"

"Well, I could see which way things were going, so I took off right then and there," Juba said. "I didn't live this long to get shot in the back."

Bessie paused and lifted up a short tent pole, pointing it at Juba. "And you know what that mistress of mine asked me to do in the middle of that mess?"

"No, what? What she want you to do?" Juba cocked her head as she folded a few old rags on top a small table.

"That fool woman shouted for someone to run back in the big house to fetch her new French ivory silk slippers with the little roses on em. They just come from Paris. She wanted them for Race Week to wear to all them fancy events held all week up in Charleston come wintertime. Can you believe dat?"

Juba burst out in laughter. "Stupid wench!"

Bessie paused and clucked her tongue against the roof of her mouth. "That's what that simpleminded woman was thinking of in the middle of a war! She wanted to show them new silk slippers off at those fancy balls and galas. That's what she worried about when them Yankees are busy firing cannons at us!" She dropped her hands to her sides, took a step back, and held her palm to her forehead.

Juba cut her eyes at Bessie and hissed, "I tell you what. Them White women just ain't got no sense sometimes. They start all that special tutoring and polite education for the delicate female mind when they twelve or thirteen years old."

Bessie leaned forward and nodded as she moved a small stool. "Dey sho' do, don't they?'

Juba laid out an old corn cob mattress and smoothed a worn and tattered quilt over it as she spoke. "Them White folks teach their daughters how to be a lady and carry on a conversation so as they can marry some rich planter. They show them how to flutter their fan and hold a teacup, but they never teach them no sense." Juba shook her head.

Bessie shouted, "You got that right! What do they teach them girls? Needlework, penmanship, manners, drawing, piano, Bible passages, and French, and only enough math so as they can count how many children they done had."

"That's for true!"

"How them simpleminded White women gonna run a house without dey servants to do for them? They ain't got no sense. Ain't never had to pluck a chicken, bake some bread, or even nurse their own baby." Bessie waved her hand at Juba and shook her head.

Juba sighed. "They'll likely starve to death if they got to wait for a White woman to cook 'em some supper! I bet they don't even know how to stoke a stove." Juba laughed out loud, then pulled out a gunny sack of clothes and started to sort through them.

Bessie went on with her story. "Anyhow, so when that fool woman asks me to fetch her silk slippers, I jump right outta the wagon and head toward the house. I says, 'Ma'am, I'll go fetch 'em for you. I'll be right quick about it too.' She says to me, 'Fine. That's real good, Bessie, you go fetch 'em for me.' And you know what I did?"

"What you do? Tell me you didn't get them shoes for no White woman, did you?" Juba leaned back with a puzzled look.

"I gave a quick curtsy real proper like, it bein' my last one, nodded my head and narrowed my eyes, then I took off. I ran in the front door of the mansion house, right past all the servants carrying out the missus' paintings, then I run right out the back door, through the work yard, and out the back gate. I just kept running till I was behind some trees. I turned and looked around, and I could hear that missus screaming my name, but the master shouted to the horses, and they pulled off. That dang woman was still hollering for her slippers."

"Ha! Good for you, Bessie!" Juba slapped her leg and burst out laughing.

"While that crazy woman was still hollering and carrying on with her foolishness, all the scared slaves just took off. They knew leavin' with the ma'sa was no good.

"Sure glad y'all realized that!"

"Thank the good Lawd, we was all out of range when the ma'sa startin' shootin' or he's so angry he couldn't hit the broad side of a barn by then. We all scattered in different directions. A couple of dem slaves nearly sprawled in the mud, but they managed to keep on goin'. Some of us hid behind buildings or took off for the woods. Everyone was so panicked I guess we was able to run faster than ever before. Thank goodness nobody was hit by a stray bullet."

Bessie fluffed an old feather pillow snatched from one of the White folks' mansion houses in town. A feather fluttered out between her fingers and floated off on a breeze. Her eyes followed it for a moment until it snagged on a young branch outside a new hastily built shack. Then, her attention returned to Juba.

"I know what you mean. When we started to hear the sharp crack of rifles get closer and closer, we just hunkered down in the woods. We didn't know what might happen next. Fear of the woods made my feet clumsy. I tripped over fallen branches, scratched my shins on the spiky brush, and bumped my head on low-hanging branches." Bessie looked down at her shins as she talked about that day.

"Musta been frightening runnin' like that." Juba shot Bessie a sympathetic look.

"I remember running by our old praise house, where we met for church on Sundays. Then I tumbled down a hill along the side of a cemetery, all scattered with shells, starfish, and things from the sea to honor our dead. I started to fret over running into a wild animal or a poisonous snake, cause we got all kinds here in the Carolinas. I prayed to God to protect me from such harm."

"You sho' got that right. We got all kinds round here." Juba nodded.

"Confusion all around me. To survive this, I couldn't let my mind threaten to strangle me. I tried to clear the worry from my mind, but then something pricked my ankle. I nearly jumped out of my skin. I never actually saw what bit me, but it swelled up real big and red." Bessie touched her one ankle as she recollected the incident.

"Oh my, I wonder what bit you?" Juba raised an eyebrow.

"Never did find out. But at least I had proper shoes on my feet. Some folks was barefoot with the constant pricks of stones, pinecones, and needles. They feet were all tore up. It coulda been worse. All I know is I lived, and I thank the Lawd for that."

Juba's jaw clenched and her eyes narrowed when she recounted one incident. "God bless me, I will never forget the sound of the mini balls zinging right by my head. Them bullets musta been just a couple of inches away when they hit a tree and all the bark burst off. Scared me to death. That exploding tree bark coulda been my skull!"

"Lawd Jesus!" exclaimed Bessie. "You musta been scared to

death." Bessie squared up two pallets adjacent to each other for a mother and her two small children.

Juba placed both hands on the back of a chair and leaned against it. "Oh, let me tell you, I was. I never thought my heart could beat so fast. After that, I heard the soldiers calling to one another. They would shout something, then pause for a moment. I didn't know what they were plannin.'"

"Did you even know if they were Rebels or Yankees? Good Lawd, you musta been terrified thinkin' your life was 'bout to end," Bessie shook her head and cut her eyes to the side.

Juba exclaimed, "I sure was! Suddenly, a bugle sounded. I didn't know what that meant. The soldiers were shoutin' to each other. Then there was this pounding of the galloping horses charging down the road. I thought, surely, we are all about to die."

"Oh my, how scary, Juba," Bessie held her hand up to her bosom.

Juba then calmed and changed her tone. "But then to all of us Black folks' surprise, the Rebs took off. It was all over right quick, just a couple of hours, I reckon."

Bessie nodded. "I know it was over pretty dang fast. The Rebs just weren't ready for the Yanks and all those ships. I knew the Union soldiers took over pretty quick."

Juba went on to explain. "We weren't sure what to do next. We didn't know how those Yankee soldiers would treat us, so we stayed in hiding for a long while. We still didn't know who DuPont was and what he would do to us."

"Yeah, you never know with the White folks what they gonna do," nodded Bessie. "Hey, we best go fetch some water for folks, so they have something to drink when they get here. I heard some refugees should be coming back from the fields soon. I'll grab these here two wooden pails. There's two more pails over there." Bessie pointed to the other side of the shack.

As the two women moved away from the shack, Juba could feel her body go limp with ease. She realized how tense she had been recounting the day the Union troops took over the town. For days, she had been so worried, not knowing what would happen to her, always on guard, always expecting a soldier to grab her or a stray bullet hit her. But here on the waterfront, with the salt air flowing over her and folks moving freely around, she could feel the soothing mood that had been cast over the area. She felt a smile teasing the corners of her lips. She turned to look out over the water and wonder where her son might be, and if Cuffee was looking down on them from Heaven above.

The two women headed out into the encampment for the Black contrabands. There was a lot of activity going on around them. A woman with caramel-colored skin in a long, dark-brown skirt and colorful headwrap was cooking a large kettle of stew over a large fire. The kettle hung from an iron hook that looked like it might have been part of a fancy iron gate at one point. They nodded to the woman tending the pot as she added in some vegetables.

"Afternoon. Whatever you cookin' sure smells good." Juba lifted her nose to the air and breathed in the delicious aroma.

"Makin' some Frogmore stew. Everybody's welcome to have a bit. You gals come join us later," the old woman smiled.

"We stop by in a spell after we've done carried some water back to the shacks for folks to drink and clean up with at the end of the day. We thank ya for ya offer." Bessie nodded at the woman and smiled.

Juba nodded, took a step closer over to Bessie, and went on with her story, "Like I said, we didn't know who this Officer DuPont was back then. All we knew was he was some Yankee officer out in front of the other men."

"Yeah, you never can tell what them White Federals gonna do. Some's good, some's bad." Bessie frowned and gave a disapproving look as she continued to walk down the beachfront.

"We watched him as he came ashore and began to walk up Bay

Street. They seemed so respectful to the dead and dying they found on the street. They's mainly the colored house slaves shot by they's masters, but there were a few Rebel soldiers. They tended to the ones who were still alive, even if they were Black. That didn't seem to matter to them. They still tended to their wounds."

"Well, that's good. Kind of surprised a White Yankee man would do that."

Juba nodded. "For months, White folks been telling us all kinds of stories about what the Federals would do to us, but it turns out, none of it was true. They didn't attack us or sell us for profit to the Cuban sugar cane plantation owners like them White folks said. They was just trying to scare us. It's done been more than three Sundays, and they ain't done nothin' like that yet. Don't reckon they's goin' to now."

"Just like always, White folks lyin' to us, so we stay and do they work!" Bessie said and then ducked her chin.

"But I got to admit, we didn't really trust them soldiers for weeks. It took a while for me to start to believe the Yankees were here to make sure we're safe and taken care of, and at least had some comforts. But they did make a lot of improvements around here, just like this water pump. They put this in, and sure makes it easier."

"Hard to trust White folks after all they did to us, Juba." Bessie lowered her bucket under the pump and filled it.

"I sure know the truth in dat! I had two bad masters in my life. First one up 'round Georgetown, 'bout sixty miles north of Charleston. Then my last master, in Mount Pleasant, just the other side the river from Charleston. He's the one near lashed me to death and then sold me a few weeks later in front of Customs House in Charleston. That's when Master McKee bought me and brought me down here to Beaufort. They tore me away from my husband. I knew I'd never see Cuffee again . . . and I loved him so much."

Juba lowered her wooden bucket under the pump as her eyes started to well with tears. She paused, trying to choke back her emotions, trying to focus on pumping the water. But all the pain she had pushed down deep in her soul could no longer be held back. She whimpered and tears spilled. She sucked in air while she tried to hold back the pain.

Bessie swallowed and gently placed her hand on her friend's shoulder. "Now girl, you listen, there ain't nothing I can do to make your husband magically appear here at this camp. He's with the good Lawd now and the two of them are watching over you and your son, wherever he might be."

Juba conjured that image: God Almighty and her handsome husband with his caramel-colored complexion and beautiful ebony curls looking down from Heaven, seeing all that was happening right now. If only he could hold her right now; she would give anything to be in his arms again.

The old wound tore open leaving a gaping hole. That longing for Cuffee could never be satisfied. She would never feel the warmth of his arms around her again, not ever. Sobs burst out of Juba, and she set down her pail. A look of shock, then horror came over Bessie's face. She had no idea Juba had endured such pain. Bessie squeezed Juba's arm, then lovingly rubbed her back for a few seconds.

Bessie spoke in a quiet, soothing voice while leaning into her. "Honey, now you let all that pain just come right outta you. Ain't no one round here but me. Them tears cleanse your soul."

Bessie stood with Juba for several minutes, patiently waiting and lending supportive words to her new friend, then allowed her time alone to gather herself. Bessie just turned her back to Juba and looked out over the water while Juba composed herself.

"Forgive me. I didn't mean for all that to come out of me like that." Juba took an old rag from her pocket and wiped her face. "I know we all have been through hard times here. I'm not the only one who's had pain in this life."

"Honey, you take your time. Gather yourself, then we'll head back." Bessie looked deep into Juba's eyes.

After several seconds, Juba looked out over the waterfront, drew in a deep breath, and picked up the two buckets. Then she began to tell Bessie her story.

"Cuffee and I jumped the broom together up at Twin Oaks plantation outside Charleston, just a matter of months. He was such a handsome man, and we were so in love. We didn't even know I was pregnant with Issac when the master sold me."

"Oh my. Cuffee never knew you was with child?"

"No, I was just startin' to suspect it and hadn't mentioned it to him yet. We been livin' on this plantation not too far from the city in a small town named Mount Pleasant. He was a field hand, and I didn't always get a proper chance to talk to him at the end of the day."

"Juba, I'm so sorry, that must have been hard."

"It was hard. All of it was hard. Our big plantation was down on the Wando River. 'Dat made it easy for ma'sa to send all da cotton down to the market in Charleston. I tell you dat ma'sa of mine was only concerned in makin' his money off da backs of his slaves. We wasn't no human beings to dat man. Nuh-uh. We jus' makin' 'da money for him."

"Oh girl, I know that musta been hard," Bessie stressed as she looked into Juba's eyes.

"Well, I have a son 'round here somewhere. Issac a man now. He run off when we were bein' rented out to da Rebel soldiers. Don't know where he at now. Just hopin' he's alive. I pray every night for him."

"You jus' keep prayin', girl. Lawd hears our prayers. He do now, don't doubt the Lawd God." Bessie raised her finger toward Juba.

"I know, I pray for my son and some folks from my old plantation. I ask God to keep my good friends Hentie and Big John safe from Master Langdon. He can be a cruel man. My friends, they's real good to me while I's up near Charleston. They was fine folks. I hope I gets to see 'em again someday, but I know it's not likely. Still, I keep hopin' and a prayin'." Juba looked over to Bessie and smiled.

As the two made their way down through the crowds of people, they had to split up and walk one in front of the other to get through without hitting folks with their buckets. Finally, they reached the shacks and surplus tents that had been set up. The area buzzed with activity with hoards of Black folks of all ages and skin tones. Many of them seemed to know one another and were jovial, while others sat by themselves and just watched as others passed by them. The place had a sense of community and provided a safe haven. For many it was a sense of calm for the first time in their lives.

Juba swung her head all around and then leaned over to Bessie and said, "I heard one officer say we had fifteen Negroes for every White man in these parts. So many slaves had been workin' in dem cotton fields. I wonder how many Black folks are here?"

"I don't really know, but I heard we got thousands here. People from plantations all over da Sea Islands, and they's at least fifty Sea Islands," Bessie smiled, "so I expect they's a lot!"

"Yep, a whole lot!"

"Juba, if you feelin' all right now, maybe we should go help that woman cook some supper for these folks. I know we could be cuttin' up some fruit and berries. I think some of the men went out and fetched some peaches and strawberries from 'da fields. There's gonna be lots of hungry folks tonight."

"You sho' got dat right!" laughed Juba.

The two ladies picked up their pails of water and began to head back to the encampment. Juba listened to the water gently lapping on the shore and the sound of seagulls flying overhead. As she drew in the sea air, she thought even if she lost Cuffee, she was lucky she was to have freedom and shelter here in the Sea Islands. She had folks she could rely on, and she knew she would have a bed and food to eat.

About that time a younger man, one of the new contrabands, ran toward them. He was a mulatto, and his cheeks were pink with excitement. "They celebratin' up at the camp. It's big doin's up there. They done caught dem a bunch of shrimp and all kinds of fish. Roastin' 'em all up. You best hurry!" He yelped with excitement, clumsily turned in the sand, and took off in the opposite direction.

Juba and Bessie turned to one another and locked eyes. They

burst out laughing as they shouted. "Like he said, we best hurry!"

The two scrambled as quickly as they could while struggling with their pails, sloshing water all along the way and roaring as they did so.

⸻

In November of 1861, when the Department of the South secured a beachhead at or near Hilton Head, they reportedly found more than thirty thousand Black residents who they would hire as laborers or enlist in the armed services. Although payment for services was at first inconsistent, the formerly enslaved laborers were now paid for their labor. Many were hired to harvest Sea Island cotton, which the Union Army sold or had used to make soldiers' uniforms. This cotton was initially sold as a commodity in the open market and then later sent directly to mills for processing into Union uniforms. He would later go on to be an early founder of Sears and Roebuck in Chicago, Illinois. The president of this retailing giant, Julius Rosenwald, would subsequently use some of his wealth to establish Black schools throughout the South known as the Rosenwald schools. Rosenwald first worked in his mother's clothing business in New York City, but then opened his own clothing firm in Chicago in 1885.[4]

In the 1800s and the first half of the 1900s, African American children did not hold a right to a free education or one equal to that of White children. Even after the US Supreme Court case Brown vs. Board of Education (1954), children of color often did not have access to schools or facilities that could truly offer them a decent education. In order to address this great need, between the

---

4 Over time, Sears & Roebuck, which first opened in 1893, decided to expand and carry clothing as well as household items in their general mail-order catalog. For the largely rural America, this shopping vehicle reigned supreme due to its lower costs, accessibility, and wide range of products. Consumers could buy watches, jewelry, buggies, bicycles, sewing machines, and even kit homes were available from 1908 to 1948.

years 1915 and 1932, Rosenwald provided schools to over 660,000 throughout rural Southern communities by way of challenge grants. Some of these schools are still standing, and efforts are being made to preserve this part of our history.

Four hundred and fifty Rosenwald schools were built in South Carolina between 1913 and 1940 at a cost of $2,892,360. Fourteen of these were built under the supervision of Washington's Tuskegee Institute in Alabama prior to the incorporation of the Rosenwald Fund in 1917. Nearly a century ago during segregation, the St. George Colored School was built in 1925 in St. George, South Carolina. It was one of two schools in Dorchester County. At least fourteen Rosenwald schools were built in Charleston County in the 1920s stretching from Wadmalaw Island to Lincolnville to McClellanville, according to records from the South Carolina Department of Archives and History.

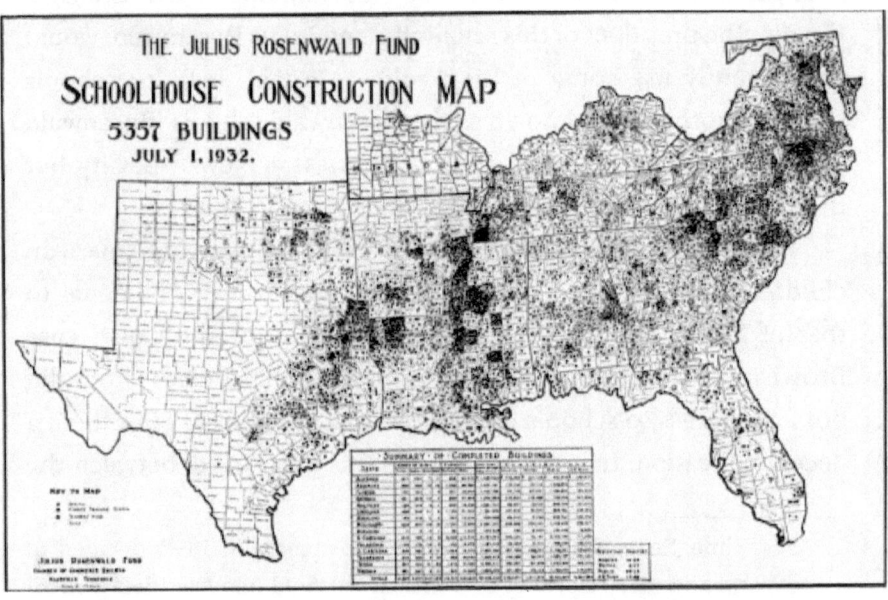

Fisk University, John Hope and Aurelia E. Franklin Library Special Collection, Julius Rosenwald Fund Archives

Chapter 15
Juba Meets Susie King Taylor from Savannah

In the Sea Islands of South Carolina, Spring 1862

Over the weeks and months, Juba began to develop friendships with some of the other formerly enslaved refugees. One such young woman, still in her teens, was Susie King Taylor from Savannah. She and her uncle had left the city shortly after it fell into Union hands. Susie was just fourteen years old when she arrived, but she was a hard worker, and smart. In the months to come she would become a formidable force and a leader in what would become known as the Port Royal Experiment, where the newly liberated enslaved workers would be taught basic literacy skills, money management, homemaking skills, good citizenship, and in many cases, how to run a small farm with the forty acres they were later given. Over time, Susie would emerge as a zealot in teaching young soldiers and the newly liberated of all ages how to read, write, cipher, and lift themselves up. Through the underground education system for Blacks set up in Savannah, she had been able to acquire far more education than not only the contrabands, but most of the White soldiers. Despite her youth, she was treated by those around the camp, both the Union officers and the Black contrabands, as one of the chief administrative collaborators working with the White missionaries. She commanded a great deal of respect and a fair amount of authority due to her role at Port Royal.

Susie's uncle had decided to seize the moment when Fort Pulaski in Savannah had been under attack in April of 1862. The entire city and surrounding area were in an uproar, so the uncle decided to take the extended family and leave the area. Along with the allure of freedom, the opportunity presented itself, so he grabbed it, taking Susie and her brothers. Her uncle had lived out in the country, but her grandmother, Dolly Reed, who served as Susie's primary guardian, had always managed to keep tabs on him through a network she maintained. Years before, Susie had been transferred from Master Valentine Grest's plantation on the Isle of Wight in Liberty County, Georgia, to his city house in Savannah. In so doing, Susie left the care of her mother, Hagar Ann Reed Baker, and started a new life in the bustling coastal city. It was a hard thing to leave her mother, never knowing if she would see her again.

On the day she left, Susie felt strange and hollow, unable to cry, unable to feel anything but an empty, extinguished place in the pit of her stomach. She knew going to the city was a good thing, but she was leaving everything she had ever known behind. Susie lost touch with her mother in the move. In Savannah, her grandmother served as her principal guardian, under the discretion of their White master. Reed refused to run with the rest of the family, as she didn't want to slow them down and increase the risk of capture.

As the settlement camps grew, a few natural leaders emerged. These folks tended to take informal supervision roles in the various sectors of the camp. Different quadrants, or sections of the encampment started, became recognized, and folks began to stake unofficial claims on certain tents, beds, and tables. These holds were respected by other refugees, much as they had done in their slave villages. However, along with these informally recognized claims, people also shared most everything they could, from small food items to homemade toys for small children. Some items were precious, such as a token gift given to someone from a parent, or a religious artifact or gris-gris. But for the most part, folks shared, knowing their generosity would come back to them. They believed that was how they would all get through this harrowing experience together and one day realize true freedom.

Around November, they were near the end of the growing season in the Sea Islands. Earlier in the morning, the sky had gone cobalt. When Juba first started to stir in her makeshift cabin, she could see through the slats that the sunlight had already started to wane. It had grown tinctured with an approaching storm, a common occurrence in the fall. Wind blew through cracks in the boards, coming thick with the smell of rain and oleander. Suddenly, thunder broke, and rain splattered across the roof of the shack. Fortunately, it abated as quickly as it had moved in.

Thank you, Lawd, I gots work to do today. And so does everyone else in dis camp. We gots to bring in the crops and every bit a food we can!

Juba decided they had best make haste and head out while a dry spell had set in.

Juba and Susie had taken a small, mule-pulled cart and gone to a nearby plantation to pick some of the fruits and vegetables still remaining in the fields. They brought two children with them to help with the ordeal, Samuel and Gemma. They held the baskets and a couple of burlap bags. They were both mannerly children, still dressed in raggedy clothing full of tatters and small patches. Juba wanted to outfit them in something better but had nothing to offer. Gemma was a lighter-skinned mulatto who had worked as an enslaved house servant in a mansion house on Bay Street. Samuel had a dark complexion and was rail thin. When enslaved, they didn't always get enough to eat through the allotments issued by their slave masters. It was not unusual for a master or mistress to withhold food as a punishment or to gain wanted information.

All of the surrounding plantations had been abandoned by the White plantation owners, along with their families, their overseers, and the Rebel forces, so Juba and Susie didn't anticipate any resistance. Nonetheless, in case they faced some unexpected intruder or a wild animal, they had taken some rudimentary weapons with them—an old pistol, a large hunting knife that had been sharpened to a fine edge, and other implements to cut the vegetables.

The weather was still warm, and the day was sunny. They moved along slowly on the dirt road scattered with ruts and potholes. They leaned into bumps as the wagon tilted to and fro all along their journey, splashing through some of the small mud puddles. The women sat up front on the bench while the children rode in the back of the rig. As they traveled down the road, Juba and Susie chatted.

Juba kept her hands on the reins while she queried Susie, "So how'd ya' get here from Savannah? Wasn't it under Rebel control?"

Susie explained to Juba what had happened to her in the months before her arrival in Beaufort. First, she had fled from Savannah after the Federals had attacked Fort Pulaski, just north of Savannah, right off the coast. All the uproar and commotion gave them the opportunity to flee. Initially, they went to Tybee Island, South Carolina.

"People were runnin' around crazy like," Susie said. "All you could hear was the roar of the great guns. You could barely think with all the bombing. All you could hear was those dang cannons for miles! With all the confusion, the White people weren't so concerned about us colored folks as they were about their own hide. We decided it was a good time to take off for the North."

"Oh my, I suppose it was a good chance to run, but wasn't it scary?" Juba asked. "Wasn't you afraid you'd get hit by cannon fire?"

"I 'member the cannons firing overhead and folks runnin' all over. Women were screamin' and cryin'. My uncle came and fetched me from my house. He took me and my five brothers to St. Catherine Island. It wasn't very far. I felt pretty safe there. The Union troops kept us safe. Then we went on to Big Tybee Island. Like I said, my grandma didn't want to come with us. She didn't want to slow us down. And my mama was never able to join us. She was way out on the master's plantation, way out there, fifty miles out. She didn't have a way to get to us."

"I suppose it helped, yo' havin' soldiers who could protect you. Dey had guns and could shoot back," Juba said.

Susie paused sullenly. "That Yankee Major Hunter said all of us colored folks were free. That's when they first started to call us contrabands of war. Said it meant the soldiers got to take us as the spoils of war, like a conquest or somethin'."

"Oh, I always wondered why they been callin' us that. 'Contrabands.' I've been called lots of names before, 'wench,' 'negress,' 'colored gal,' 'niggra,' 'Black bitch,' and 'girl,' but never a contraband," Juba chuckled.

"My uncle said it was a big thing that Major Hunter said all the slaves by the fort were freemen. But then we found out President Lincoln didn't go along with it. It took a while before the president finally agreed and let it stand."

"I know," Juba said. "I never am sure if we are free or not, or just kinda free while we here with the Yankee soldiers. It worries me some."

"Yeah, I know. Me, too," agreed Susie.

"The masters I've had in the past were brutal men. Look, I still have burn marks where the mistress threw hot water on me from my first plantation. Then I gots scars all over my back from the lash at my last plantation, Twin Oaks. That was because I accidentally spilled milk on Master Langdon." Juba pulled down her blouse from one shoulder to reveal hideous thick scars.

Susie gasped. "Oh, Juba, my Lord! I never seen such marks. I can't imagine what you musta been through. Guess I was more fortunate. I never got the lash."

There was a lull in the conversation while they both contemplated what Juba had just revealed. Their trek would take a while. The women looked about them before resuming their conversation, listening momentarily to the chatter of the children sitting in the back of the cart. Juba emitted a chuckle then looked toward Susie and smiled at the silliness of the children's conversation. They were arguing about how smart Br'er Rabbit was and whether he could outsmart Robert E. Lee. Gemma swore that Br'er Rabbit, trickster that he was, would find a way to elude a stupid Rebel.

Juba focused momentarily on the road before her and the rhythmic pounding of the mule's hooves, thanking the Lord for the beast's cooperation on their journey. As the wheels rolled through the sandy roads, Juba worked to avoid the ruts, as the small wagon jumped and bumped along. Juba took in the newly cleansed air; the brief morning rain had washed the earth just enough that it left a slightly dewy moisture. The treelined roads with tendrils of gray Spanish moss dangling in the breeze wafted a familiar scent that comforted her.

They weren't that far away by miles, but they would need to cross the freshwater of the Beaufort River before they could reach the plantation fields of Saint Helena Island. They took a turn in the road as they approached the waterfront. The dugout boats and other vessels ran frequently, but one never knew how long the wait might be to cross.

After a time, the women reached the water's edge. A thin haze had drifted in from over the river, and overhead the sun glinted in through it with a dull gold twinkle of sunlight. The wagon rolled up to the levee and Juba pulled the reins, signaling the mule to stop when the cart reached a level spot. She could see the deep waters passing just beyond it. Petals from hibiscus shimmered on the water. Chunks of leaves and bits of debris from the recent storm dipped and twirled in a watery dance. Juba fixated momentarily on its circular ballet, but then shook off the trance and turned to the task at hand. She clicked her tongue against the roof of her mouth to urge her body into action.

As the women approached the waterfront, they watched in awe as Black men in dugout boats with deep baritone voices were transporting folks across the waterways. The sight was something unique to the Sea Islands, and Susie had never encountered this form of transportation before. There were also larger transports that came periodically, but most folks relied on the riverboat men with their melodic voices.

Susie softly picked up the discussion with Juba, asking which way they were heading and keeping one eye on the boatmen. Then, turning her head in the direction of the dugouts, Susie whispered, "Who are these men with the boats?" She had never seen such large, well-muscled men, and they were all clustered around the dugout boats, some of which had been carved from huge cypress trees.

"Oh, they are just the boatmen, Susie. Ain't you never seen dugout boats 'fore? That's how we get around the waterways 'round here," Juba explained.

"Ain't never seen men THAT big. Why they sing like that?"

"The songs help them keep rowing all together with the same rhythm. They all do the same strokes, all at the same time. One man, the lead oarsman, he calls it out. Then the others follow." Juba nodded toward one man in a deep blue shirt.

Susie had been much more accustomed to wooden steamships with double paddle wheels that churned the water into whipped foam. On the huge timbers that had been hewn into towering masts were furled sails in neat white rolls at the base of a complicated spider's web of ropes and pulleys radiating out from the timbers. In these crafts were wheelhouses with men in starched blue uniforms barking out orders with precision. There was nothing like that here. Going between the Sea Islands was a lot different. The homemade crafts looked scary, and the men were bare chested as they worked the hand-hewn oars.

But then the melodic voices drifted up and began to soothe Susie's fears; it had the cadence she had known from her early youth. It was the singing and emotionally charged ring shout from her grandmother's church.

The women and the two children got onto the dugout with their small cart and settled in. Juba sat back and lifted her chin toward the sun, letting the breeze pass over her face. The two children passed a handmade toy back and forth to pass the time. Seeing how comfortable the others were, Susie decided to enjoy the ride. She glanced up at the patroon song leader, who nodded at her and smiled. Embarrassed at having been caught looking his way, she flushed and looked downward, afraid to look back his way the entire ride.

Susie later found out that these men who came to Saint Helena Island and the Beaufort area from the Gold Coast of Angola and Congo had a skillful form of rowing accompanied by important cultural words, melodies, rhythms, and harmonies. Their songs would later be used as freedom songs during Prohibition, two World Wars, and the Civil Rights movement.

The oarsmen sometimes modified their songs depending on who was being transported. Their messages became much more candid after the Great Skedaddle. Absent of White overlords, contrabands were much more open with complaining about their difficult working conditions and lifelong hardship as slaves. Boat songs sung previously under slavery were much more conciliatory. Through a hidden transcript, the enslaved complained of their weariness and sorrow. Oarsmen took advantage of the distractive sounds emanating from the oars, wind, and waves to insert their personal words and emotions regarding the often-unpleasant passengers they were forced to carry, the nearly unbearable heavy loads, and tortuously long hours of rowing.

Once on Saint Helena Island, Susie and Juba proceeded in their cart with the children. Juba seemed familiar with the roads and started on her way with confidence, pointing out a few signs and landmarks along the way, such as entrances to the Fripp, Tombee, and Coffin Point plantations.

"I know it's still early in this war and nothing is clear yet for us Black folks. It's been a year now since the Rebels fired on Fort Sumter," Susie said. "The conflict is a long way from over, but I am hopeful change is a' comin'. I don't think we are really freemen yet. I think we're only liberated while we are here with the Union soldiers. I heard that there's this new big man that President Lincoln brought to Washington. He's changing some things. It's been in the Black newspapers I been reading."

"You been readin? You read newspapers?" Juba's eyes widened. "You must be the only Black woman I know who can do that! So, tell me what's been changin."

"Secretary of War Edwin Stanton has been changing things. He's supposed to be a good man. Stanton is a lawyer by training and real smart. He doesn't support slavery. Stanton's the one who supported that idea of calling us contraband of war and allowing us to be liberated. That protects us, at least to some degree. We just have to stay in the area where the Union troops can protect us. We can't go beyond where they have set up picket lines or encampments."

Juba shook her head and went on to say, "'Course, nothing is for sure in the life of a Black woman. What else?"

"Anyhow, when we first left Savannah we traveled from St. Catherine's to Tybee Island, just north of Savannah. It's a bigger island. I think about thirty of us went there about two weeks later."

"Lots of movin' around. Musta been kind of scary," said Juba.

"It was. Not sure you could really trust where you was being taken. On the boat, Captain Whitmore, who was leading the Union troops on the ship, started to ask me all kinds of questions, like where I was from and if I could read and write. He was surprised when I told him that I could do both. He gave me a book and a pencil and asked me to write my name. Then he asked me to start reading from the first page of the book. He seemed impressed I was able to read with no trouble. I reckon he had never seen a Black woman do that before."

"I bet he was surprised! Where did you learn to read?"

"When I was living in Savannah with my grandmother, she would send us to a free woman's house. We had to wrap up our book and pencil in brown paper to conceal it. As my brother and I would get close to the woman's house, we would split up and go in separately, spacing out when we entered the house."

"Wasn't it scary doin' that?" Juba asked. "Up in Charleston you coulda been whipped to death for doin' that kinda thing."

"Well, we just watched ourselves every single day and got a routine down. We were allowed to learn a trade, just not book learning. This woman taught us to read, write, cipher, different things about history, and a lot of other stuff. I got to do that several years until she had nothing left to teach me. I guess I was about twelve or thirteen when I stopped going for lessons."

Juba looked at Susie in amazement, unable to grasp how a Black child could have schooling every day for years. Susie then stood, stretched her back, and continued.

"After that, I learned from others. I had a friend who was taught at a Catholic convent by nuns. Every day I would do lessons with her. Bernadette taught me everything she had learned in school. I learned about history, geography, and even a little Latin."

"Boy, you sure was lucky! I can't imagine anyone around Charleston gettin' away with something like that," Juba said. "The angels musta been smilin' down on you!" Juba looked upwards to the heavens to emphasize her point.

Susie nodded. "Yes, I was lucky in many ways. After Bernadette taught me what she had learned at the convent, I started practicing my lessons with the landlord's son. He shared books with me and taught me more complicated math skills. I never would have picked it up any other way."

Juba looked down and shook her head. "God musta had a plan

for you, Susie. He knew you would be coming here and helpin' with all us Black folks. Why else would you get all the book learnin'?"

Susie nodded. "Does make you wonder, doesn't it? I had to laugh to myself sometimes at how stupid the White buckra thought us colored folks were. Right before the war, White masters started telling us all kinds of tales to scare us into not leaving for the Union side. They told us those Yankee soldiers would harness us to carts and make us pull them all over, in place of their horses."

"Such wild tales those White folks make up!" Juba threw her hands up. "We can tend to their children, run their plantations, and keep their big house runnin' better than any of dem can manage, but we can't figure out that those White folks are lying to us? Tell me, who is the simpleminded?"

Susie continued. "I know, y'all managed to grow gold rice when they couldn't, the same with the indigo. And look at what the colored folks have managed to do with growing the Sea Island long-staple cotton. Only the warm, wet sea islands and the labor of us Black folks could have made them White buckra so stinkin' rich. They didn't do it. We did it for them. Now they think we're so simpleminded we're going to believe their wild stories. Tell me who is the weak-minded one? I don't think it's the Black man!"

Juba jabbed her index finger at Susie. "That's for sure. Remember it's the Black man who built all the mansion houses and plowed all the cotton fields. None of that was done by the hand of a White man. He didn't have the know-how."

Susie leaned toward Juba. "You hear those officers are going to start paying us Black folks for working in the fields? Did you ever think you'd see the day? Course, ain't nothing but chicken scratch, but it's still money we can use to buy things for ourselves. I ain't never had that before."

Juba nodded. "Yes, I did hear something 'bout that. I'll believe it when I get those nickels in my hand!"

"I heard we have one of the largest cotton crops in anyone's memory. The Union soldiers want us to harvest it and send it north to be processed and made into Federal uniforms. I don't care where they send it, as long as they're paying us to pick it and pack it."

"All kinda things goin' on 'round here," Susie said. "You hear the Federals brought a bunch of soldiers down here to train? I heard some officers say this is good training ground cause of the warm weather. Them new recruits from up North don't know what our hot weather gonna be like by August. They think it's heaven now cause we ain't got no snow. Silly fools! Wait till the mosquitoes bite! They'll think otherwise by then." Juba started to laugh so hard her body quaked.

"But you know what else? I heard folks are selling them soldiers all kinds of stuff. Folks are making pies and cookies. Them poor starvin' boys love it! All they been gettin' is hard tack, beef jerky, and gruel," Juba exclaimed.

Susie pulled the wagon into the plantation and drove it toward the peach orchard. "I think for now they'll be needin' us as laundresses. I don't know which is worse, working over those big pots with lye soap, or ironing those officer uniforms. Either way, you have to work with hot fires and have sweat pour down you. In all that heat, you have to work those heavy sheets and uniforms with ponches or dollie sticks. The sticks alone are heavy, like a heavy broom handle with a milking stool on it, swirling the dirty laundry around to get it clean. The muscles in my arms burned from all the work."

"Doin' laundry is a dang tough job!" Juba said. "You can pass out from that heat! I saw one of the laundry girls pass out right before my eyes. The summer heat 'n that boilin' pot was jus too much for her. Poor thing. She hit the ground, and that dang stick hit her right in da head. Dang good thing she didn't fall toward that boilin' pot!"

"Dang! You got that right! Poor thing!" Susie crowed. "I think ironing is the worst. You have to keep rotating the flat iron on the fire to heat it up, make sure you don't blacken it, then pick it up with some kind of mitt or you'll burn your hand like a piece of meat. I've gotten all kinds of blisters from doing the ironing. Took a few weeks to heal. They were deep burns." Susie rolled up her sleeve and held out her forearm to show her new friend the scars.

Juba motioned toward Susie's arm. "Oh, Lordy Jesus! My that musta hurt! I have a few burns myself, but nothing like that."

Juba pulled the wagon to a stop and secured it.

"We're here!" exclaimed the children as they jumped down from the back of the cart.

"Now, you chillen' each grab a basket or bag 'fore you take off toward the orchard, 'hear?" shouted Juba.

Each child took a basket, shoving one another in the process, and took off running.

Juba and Susie looked toward each other and rolled their eyes in exasperation. Juba tied the donkey to a tree. Then the two women grabbed the remaining baskets and burlap bags.

Juba smiled and chuckled at the children's shenanigans. "Oh, how I miss the days my son was a little boy and was running around. He had to work for the master, but at least I got to see him."

Susie jerked her head toward Juba and said, "Oh, I didn't realize you had a son. He around here?"

"No, he run off when we were rented out to the Confederate camp by Master McKee. It was before we come down here to the Union encampment. He done took off. Don't know where he at now." Juba looked down and shook her head.

"I expect he'll turn up. The Lord didn't let him live this long to let something bad happen to him. He'll show up. You'll see." Susie smiled brightly and nodded her head at Juba.

Juba drew in a deep breath. "Yeah, hard to say where my son might be. Could be somewhere 'round here and I'd never know it. I think there are something like sixty sea islands 'round here. The Union soldiers are spread out over four islands and the town of Beaufort. My son could be anywhere."

"Yep, lots of folks here. I think there are over thirty thousand refugees. Then there is the Navy, the Army, the Army Corps of

Engineers, the missionaries from the North, newspapermen, photographers, and God knows who else!" Susie said.

The women laughed before falling silent. They knew how hard it would be for Juba to find her son with everything going on, so many people trying to adjust to their new circumstances.

The two women looked about at all the loblolly pines on the outskirts of the orchards, their tree trunks so tall and narrow. An eagle soared over head, shrieking as it dove toward a rabbit that plunged into a thistle bush, just in time to miss its outstretched talons.

The two continued to slowly walk, lost in their thoughts, still contemplating their previous conversation and their trip to Saint Helena Island. It had been years since Susie had actually walked the grounds of a plantation. She had been a mere child of five years when she left the plantation of her youth and her mother's side. She looked about and drew in a deep breath. The air smelled different from Savannah's odor.

Susie had lived not too far from Forsyth Wharf. From the slave quarters at the rear of the big house, she could hear the clomping of the horses' hooves as the plantation's wagons made their way to the waterfront to unload their cargo. The fluttering breeze from the water would set the palmetto leaves clicking against the sides of the wooden building. From there, Susie had been able to see the huge stacks of cotton bales being readied for loading onto ships. The stevedores would shout to one another as they loaded the snowy bundles, the cotton wrapped in hemp bags seven feet long by two feet wide, most of it heading to the midlands of England to be processed in the textile mills.

As the women walked toward the peach trees, they eyeballed the arbors for those heavy with fruit, then began harvesting it. Samuel was agile and able to climb up and pick the ones the others weren't able to reach. The two women approached adjacent trees so they could continue their conversation.

Juba ducked her chin and said, "Well, I guess we should be

thankful we away from the lash of our masters, but I still hate ironing and doing laundry! Both is dang tough jobs!"

"Those men expect us to work as a laundress all day, then teach the Black soldiers how to read by the campfire. It's hard to turn them down though. They are so eager to learn. We sit with the spelling book by the campfire. I just drill them and drill them. They catch on real quick, too. I hear them testing each other. It's funny to listen to when they carry on with each other for not knowing how to spell a word. Makes me laugh. But it also kind of makes me proud how fast they catch on, too."

"Maybe sometime you can teach me some letters and words," Juba said. "I ain't never learned to read or write. Folks were scared to death to learn up in Charleston where I used to live. Masters were real mean 'bout things like that and lots more. And I ain't never had a chance down here in Beaufort. There's been no one to teach me." Juba shrugged and turned to fold some of the sheets.

"I'll teach you all in due time. All in due time," said Susie.

Later that evening, all the Black folks gathered around a couple of fires that had been set up to cook a fish stew and some rice. The refugees ate from hand-carved bowls and roughhewn platters. An encampment colonel, Thomas Wentworth Higginson, made sure that the refugees were given tin cups, but unfortunately there weren't enough to go around, so folks made do with what they had. It had always been that way for the enslaved to make do or go without. Fortunately, the Corps of Army Engineers had some tools the men could use to fashion larger platters, bowls, stools, and benches for Black newcomers to use.

After their hunger had been satisfied, a deep baritone voice started to sing a familiar gospel song. Colonel Higginson smiled and sat on a nearby stump. It was as if he had been waiting all evening to hear the Gullah and their traditional songs. From the breast pocket of this officer's jacket, he withdrew a small leather notebook and pencil, then leaned into the firelight and started to scratch out some notes. This Harvard-educated, former clergyman and ardent abolitionist was the first to lead a regiment of Black troops. He had the challenge and the privilege of turning a ragtag band of eight hundred formerly enslaved men into a disciplined Army unit. And these men did so with honor and bravery. While most of the country was skeptical as to how these men would perform under fire, the colonel felt with perfect confidence that they could be trained for combat, for they had more than the mere abstraction of the Union to fight for; they had their own freedom at stake. So, he waited patiently to hear their beautiful melodic voices with an upturned smile, knowing he wouldn't be disappointed. Shortly after the traditional evening prayers started, the singing commenced. This rolled into the call and response that was so familiar to the Gullah; a group leader called out a statement, usually an affirmation of some sort, and the group responded in unison. It was a custom that had gone on for generations with the Gullah, a blend of African roots and Christian tradition. In time, people rose to their feet, including Juba who had joined the group, holding hands with others in the circle for the ring shout. It brought all the folks together and their individual energy merged into one as they stamped their feet and gently flowed in a circular movement. It was a spiritual expression that White folks didn't often experience. But Juba, Bessie, and Susie all joined in and let the frenetic energy of the group flow through them. Their spirits merged and then rose up, creating an inner excitement in each individual. It was an exhilarating experience that left them all feeling renewed.

When Juba heard the deep, melodic baritone voice, it reminded her of Big John back at Twin Oaks. She remembered the first time she heard that beautiful rich voice of Big John sing the very same song:

Steal away, Steal away.
Steal away to Jesus!
Steal away, steal away home;
I ain't got long to stay here.
My Lord he calls me;
He calls me by the thunder.
The trumpet sounds within my soul;
I ain't got long to stay here.
Steal away, steal away,
Steal away to Jesus!
Steal away, steal away home;
I ain't got long to stay here.

Not much was good about being an enslaved worker under Master Langdon at Twin Oaks, but Juba had good friends with Hentie and Big John. There were more senior workers there that helped guide her along the way. Juba hoped they were safe and out of harm's way. She prayed they stayed in Master Langdon's good graces. Juba missed having good friends she could trust, rely on, and share confidences with. That security was gone now; she felt adrift. People were kind in this encampment, but one could never be sure of their true intentions.

Juba reflected on what a kind woman Hentie had been to her when she first came to Twin Oaks. Juba recalled how Hentie offered to let her sleep on a pallet in her slave cabin shortly after she arrived. When Juba retired one night, she found a handcrafted rose made of palmetto fronds on her thin hand-me-down pillow. It was such a sweet gesture from Hentie, but that was the way Hentie was in everything she did. She had endured her own heartache; that's probably why she was so sensitive to the pain of others.

Chapter 16
Harriet Tubman is Called to Serve in the Port Royal Experiment

Boston, Massachusetts, Early 1862

Harriet was suddenly thrown from her thoughts as the boat slammed against the Boston dock, jarring her entire body. She grabbed hold of the ship's railing and shook herself from her contemplative prayer. The modest boat she was traveling on was preparing to land among the larger, grander ships. There was a cacophony of sounds: shouts of arriving passengers to loved ones on the docks below, the bellowing horns of large ships, the dinging bells of small vessels, and the banging of crates being unloaded. Overhead, squawking seagulls, hungry and eager to retrieve any scraps thrown overboard, dove down toward the returning fishing boats.

Suddenly, Harriet's attention was flung over to the captain of the small steamer vessel, the *Saint Johns*, who was barking orders to the dockhands trotting alongside the vessel. Her attention then turned to their clacking boots on the wooden deck and their responses being shouted back and forth to the captain. They jogged with their outstretched arms, ready to catch the rope lines in order to moor the ship.

As the cool breeze glided over Harriet's face, she drew in a deep breath of the briny sea air and reminded herself that she was in Boston on business, not pleasure, about to meet with the governor. Surely the matter was something serious. His message was short and to the point.

> *Come to Boston immediately for a meeting in which we may discuss persons of African descent.*
> *John A. Andrew, Governor of Massachusetts. Boston*

As she waited for the boat to be secured, she anxiously shuffled her feet and tapped her thigh as she debated whether she was about to be praised or scolded for one of her escapades. She knew she took risks leading enslaved folks to freedom, but it was something she just had to do. It was her calling. Harriet continued to shuffle back and forth from foot to foot much like a youngster about to be walloped for breaking the rules rather than a forty-year-old woman who had faced all kinds of adversity. She feared she was about to be admonished for the last group she had ferried to freedom on the Underground Railroad. Would she be directed to cease all activities for the time being due to the war effort? She couldn't live with such an outcome. She couldn't stop her quest to bring others to freedom. She had been doing it for ten years now and had helped so many, well over three hundred. And she never lost a single soul.

With the mooring lines of the vessel securely tied and the gangplank in place, Harriet grabbed her worn military-style haversack and proceeded to the dock. As she did so, she shot a nod and a wink to a Black seaman who had long been an agent at this station, a man with whom she was very familiar. He lifted his head in recognition and gave Harriet a broad smile as she stepped off the boat. She pulled down her hat and lifted the collar of her jacket to give herself a more mannish appearance and to better conceal her identity. Even though she was wearing gentleman's pantaloons and a man's work jacket, she didn't want to take the chance of being recognized on the streets of Boston. There was a forty-thousand-dollar bounty on her head, a tidy sum in the mid-1800s. She stopped to knock some of the mud off her dark-brown brogans before proceeding down the wharf. She wanted to be as presentable as possible for the governor. He was a good man, an avid abolitionist who had always done so much to help her cause. He had been a longtime member of the New England Freedman's Aid Society, and she hoped to stay in his good graces.

Her thoughts floated back to the reason the governor might have called her to Boston.

Now what could that man want? I hope he ain't fixin' to scold me like I'm some young child. I know I had twelve folks in that last group I ferried up to Philadelphia. I know dat's a lot, but how could I split up two close families? They'd agreed to follow all my rules. And they done stayed true to their word and we all made it.

As Harriet made her way to the government building, she muttered to herself, wondering what was up with the governor and practicing her sweetest, most accommodating voice to greet him upon entering his office.

I hope he doesn't intend to try and stop me from carrying folks to freedom. He would never do that . . . would he?

The broad boulevards of Boston bustled with street vendors, hecklers, and women hurrying home to prepare the evening meal with whatever they had on hand. The muddy streets had ruts and were no longer the pristine boulevards of the past. War did terrible things to a city. No time to manicure the lawns and gardens. No money to patch cracking bricks or paint houses. There were other priorities now.

When Harriet finally arrived at the governor's office building, she paused and gathered herself, attempting to prepare for whatever outcome there might be. The tall, imposing granite building had several steps leading up to it and pillars on either side of the front doors. The official-looking building was imposing. Closing her eyes momentarily and asking for God's guidance and protection, she girded herself and crossed the street.

She walked to the back of the building, not wanting to be recognized and unsure how these White folks would regard a Black woman in their midst. She chose to avoid any confrontation. Taking the back stairwell at the rear of the floor to the second level, she bounded up the steps two at a time. When she exited the stairwell, Harriet paused for a moment to test the waters and sense the mood of those on the floor. She straightened her jacket, took off her hat, and smoothed her hair, taking on a more feminine appearance. Feeling some calm, she moved forward. Approaching the guard, she stated her business. The guard seemed puzzled, perhaps wondering whether Harriet was a man or a woman; nonetheless, she was permitted to proceed to the governor's office.

Harriet entered the large outer office with high ceilings and fine oriental carpets. The brocade draperies and high-back chairs were covered in contrasting colors of Chinese red and rich deep blue. The hues complemented the deep blue Massachusetts flag, as well as the American flag proudly displayed at the end of the room.

Coming first to the governor's outer office, she addressed the receptionist.

"Good afternoon. I'm Harriet Tubman. I've been called here by Gov'nor John Andrew. He done asked me to come to Boston to meet wit' him. I came as soon as I could." Harriet nodded to the woman and then took a step back.

"Oh yes, I am sure the governor will want to meet with you shortly. Please have a seat."

Still quite nervous about the governor's intention, Harriet anxiously paced the room and strolled over to a window to look out on the city below with all the peddlers and people going about their business. While her back was still to the governor's door, he burst out and beckoned to her.

"Miss Tubman, you are here! I am delighted to see you!" The middle-aged man with brown, tussled curls and kind, round eyes approached her with a warm smile. He quickly ran his fingers through his unruly locks and tugged at his gaping waistcoat. Harriet had forgotten what a round shape the governor had. It looked like domestic life had been good to him as he must have put on a least another stone in body weight, or well over twelve pounds.

Harriet smiled as thoughts danced across her mind. *Well, that's good. He's happy to see me. It can't be that bad, whatever I did.*

"Please, won't you come into my office? Let us have a chat," the governor suggested.

The governor walked toward Harriet with a kindhearted smile and gently guided her by the elbow into his office and then directed her to a seat in front of his desk. The office was well-appointed with a large mahogany desk covered with several stacks of papers and a few weathered volumes. Behind him were tall, dark bookcases with what appeared to be official-looking books, perhaps legal texts of some nature. A framed map of the state of Massachusetts hung on his wall. There was a lovely portrait of a woman in a garden leaning against an archway; Harriet wasn't sure who she was. Perhaps his wife?

"Please sit down. I have something very important I need to speak to you about. I am hopeful that you'll be inclined to grant my request."

Oh, Lord Jesus, what does this man want of me? I just knew it. He wants me to stop carrying folks to freedom. I can't do it. I just can't do it. I feel it's God Himself who has asked me to do this work. I can't stop now!

Harriet mustered a polite and measured response. "Oh, yes, Your Honor. You know I will do anything to help you, sir."

"Well, Harriet, this time I have a very special project for you. It's down in the Sea Islands between Charleston and Savannah. The federal government wants to see how efforts at Reconstruction, or integrating Negroes into society as freemen, might work. There is an area near Port Royal Sound and Beaufort, South Carolina that has been liberated. There are dozens of islands in the area, but there are a handful of the Sea Islands that are now under Union control. Were you aware of that?"

Harriet nodded and leaned forward. "Yes sir, I have some understandin', but don't know everything 'bout it. Word travels fast in our network. The Union control changed a lot for the black folks down there. I heard our navy done took control of da whole area."

"Well, they need more than just being liberated. President Lincoln wants to fully prepare the contrabands for full citizenship. He wants them to understand how to run a household, learn modern agricultural techniques, how to read, write, and cipher, how to care for themselves, gain an understanding of proper hygiene and good grooming, and things like that. He wants us to implement a comprehensive training program for the Negroes down there."

"Oh my. I wasn't aware of this, sir. How ya gonna do this?" Harriet's eyes had grown wide and focused on the governor's face.

"A great deal of work has been done already. You may have heard that the local planters left the area in what has been termed the Great Skedaddle. All of the local White residents abandoned their plantations and city houses. The Army, Navy, and Army Corps of Engineers successfully captured Port Royal Sound and the nearby town of Beaufort back in early November. There wasn't much of a fight, so only the fortifications were damaged."

"Well, dat's good. I'm glad there wasn't much bloodshed nor damage to dat area." Harriet nodded.

"The Federals have stationed an entire military force there. Numerous buildings have been built and improvements have been made. They are also making use of the abandoned mansion houses, converting them to administrative offices, officers' quarters, and hospitals. Others have been brought in to assist. Moreover, all the enslaved workers in the region were liberated. We've been making use of all the abandoned crops and livestock. We hope to eventually allow the Negroes in the area to take over and run the area themselves."

"Gov'nor, this is amazin'. I wasn't aware of how big this mission was gonna be. My, my. It's gonna take a lot of folks to carry out." Harriet held her hand to her chest trying to take in all these details.

"Well, what is being planned is kind of a social experiment. We want to help bolster the newly liberated slaves so that they can establish their own households and communities. We want them to lead productive, independent lives. They will have almost everything they need to sustain themselves. The government will supply the contrabands with all the necessities, such as food, clothing, tools, educational supplies, and housing. The manpower for teaching academic subjects and agricultural techniques, along with daily living skills, such as self-reliance, industry, uprightheousness, cleanliness, and order will be provided by Christian mission groups."

"Sir, this sounds like something incredible. You sure this can work?"

How are all these White folks fixin' to teach thousands of slaves with no book learnin' how to read, cipher, run dey own house and plant 'dey own fields with no tools and no seed? Dey gonna need more than missionaries with a few Bibles and luck.

"Yes, Harriet. I think it can. We want to get it started up now. We would like to get it operating fully during this calendar year, so we need to move forward quickly to get things in place. But we need strong people to go to the area to help with these efforts in guiding these newly liberated slaves. I thought of you. We have collaborated many times in the past; you're a capable woman. You've always been so willing to help the cause. I hope we can count on you this time." He looked over at her with his eyebrows raised and face full of hope.

"Well, I don't know. Would dis mean I'd need to go to that part of the country 'n live for a time?" Harriet sat back in her chair and paused.

There be a world of difference between me sneaking in and out of the South to rescue some colored folks and ferry them to freedom and me livin' there permanent like. Cause I bet no White man Union soldier gonna risk his neck for no short little Black woman like me. Dey just let dem Rebel soldiers skin me alive!

"Yes, Harriet, it would. We need good, competent people there to work with these newly liberated people and help guide them. These enslaved workers have been told what to do and how to do it all their lives. Now they will need to live independently. Run a house, have a bank account, budget their money, and read a newspaper. There will be others there to teach them to read, missionaries mainly from the northeastern states. They will bring classroom materials, books, and early readers."

"Well, that's good, sir, cause you know I can't really read. I never learned."

"That's fine, Harriet. You are a smart, talented woman in so many other ways. You have done so much already. But we need all your other various abilities, skills, spirit, and of course, all that energy."

The governor waited for a few beats, ran his fingers through his thick, dark curls, looked down, and adjusted his spectacles on his large nose. He then touched the knuckle of his right index finger to the dimple in the center of his chin, letting it rest there for a moment.

"Harriet, you are well aware that I have always had strong religious views, which have always been my compass. I know, too, that you are a godly woman. You are a prayerful woman. You have the force of all the angels behind you. We need God on our side and you as His Messenger and aide. We cannot fail with this experiment. These liberated slaves must be able to succeed. The rest of the country will be watching us. We need Him and you as his angel here on Earth to work with us. Please tell me you will do this."

The governor hesitated momentarily and looked deeply into Harriet's eyes. Unable to read her thoughts, he went on.

"You know I have fought vigorously for the rights of people of African descent for years now. I have always been earnest and sympathetic to their plight. A great deal of my legal practice was devoted to it."

"Yes sir, I know that, but—"

The governor interrupted. "I provided the legal defense for many fugitive slaves since the 1840s. I provided legal support to John Brown after the incident at Harper's Ferry. I have done what I can. But this work in Port Royal Sound is unique. It calls for someone like you with your talents, life experience, and culture. Quite plainly, we need a strong woman of African heritage to join our work. Please, please join with our efforts." With pleading eyes, he looked across his desk.

Then Governor Andrew sat back in his chair and prepared himself for Harriet's decision. He knew he was asking a lot of her—a woman hated by White Southerners being sent to a semitropical region where there was the risk of disease, the possibility of physical harm. She had no husband or children. That would help.

Harriet looked down and paused. She knew what this would mean. Her real work of helping the enslaved reach freedom would be put on hold indefinitely. However, she would be able to help those who had already been liberated gain fully functioning lives. Which was the better use of her skills?

"What if I don't like it? What if I can't work with them White military officers? Then what?" Harriet asked with defiance.

Can I trust them White folks down there? The governor is a good man and my friend, but he won't be there. I'll be on my own.

"Well, Harriet, honestly, I can try to work with their superior officers. Federal officials with the blessing of President Lincoln have reached out to me to help prepare the newly liberated Negroes. They have appointed me president of the Educational Commission for Freedman to ensure a sound transitional period. But I'm not sure I have the authority to reprimand a military officer." Governor Andrew shrugged. "So, I guess you can choose to leave if they don't respect your wishes, or they won't cooperate with you."

Harriet stared out a large window, seemingly focused on pigeons strutting along the window ledge. But then, she tilted her right ear upward as though she was listening intently to something, or someone. After several seconds, her gaze returned to the governor's hopeful face. She drummed her fingers on the arm of the large upholstered high-backed chair, which dwarfed her petite frame. Then, she cleared her throat and began to speak.

"I will want a letter from you telling them White officers who I am and that you sent me down there to do this here job. I gots to have that or they will never work with me. If you can get Mr. Lincoln to write me a letter, that would be good, too. I know them Union officers won't want to let some little colored woman run around their camp. I'll be needin' those papers so they trust who I am and don't give me no lip. I can't work with them if they won't work with me. Understand my point?" Harriet sat up in her chair, leaned toward the governor, looked him in the eye, and decisively nodded.

"Ah, well, I'll see what I can do." Governor Andrew nervously scribbled a note to himself, then looked up. "So, do I have your word?"

"Yes sir, you do. When do I leave?" Harriet stood up and looked into the governor's eyes with determination.

"Ah, well, I will have the details worked out and get back to you immediately. Does that sound acceptable?"

"I'll give your secretary the address of where I'll be staying while I am here in Boston. I can be reached there. I look forward to serving." Harriet smiled and the two shook hands.

With that, Harriet turned and left the governor's office.

Explanation of the Port Royal Experiment

Penn School on Saint Helena Island
(Courtesy of Library of Congress)

The Port Royal Experiment, as it would come to be known, was starting to come together. President Lincoln was concerned that the newly liberated enslaved workers in the Sea Islands near Port Royal needed time to prepare for freedom and citizenship. He wanted to ensure that they were educated, trained, and adequately prepared to live independent lives. It was conceived that missionaries and educators would come to the Sea Islands for a period of approximately two years to assist with this transition period for the contrabands. Some left early, as they couldn't stand the semitropical heat, risk of yellow fever, malaria, and other diseases, while at least one woman, Laura Towne, came in April 1862 and remained the rest of her life. A school that remained functioning until the late 1960s, the Penn Center, still stands. Corporal punishment would be banished. Inducement to work would be based on wages and the desire to better oneself and family. Wages were to be around forty cents a day or twelve dollars a month. The government would provide food, clothing, medical care, and housing, all of which would be shipped from the North. The shelter would initially be in the form of tents and then eventually prefabricated houses. One of the targets of the training was to enable the contrabands to learn modern agricultural methods that would be implemented in the region. It was surmised that such methods would increase productivity and the yields of various agricultural endeavors in the area. More importantly, it was hoped that at least in the short run, it would assist the government in running the program.

As the Civil War was still raging in other parts of the country, the Sea Islands were carrying on business and, seemingly, needed intervention so that exploitative forces from both the North and the South would not try to take advantage of the situation. It was feared the valuable Sea Island cotton might lure unsavory businessmen. Military leaders began to collaborate with local and national faith-based groups, many of whom also had missionary components and abolitionist beliefs. Representatives were sent by President Lincoln to introduce the idea of a free society where the formerly enslaved people had to work to succeed but would have protection and support from the government. Meetings were held at the Brick Baptist Church and a chapel on the Eustis Plantation on Saint Helena Island to share this idea with the newly liberated slaves.

Miss Laura Towne's School (The Penn Center)

The Brick Baptist Church, St Helena Island
(Taken by Author)

"The Liberty Bell", Penn Center
(Courtesy of the Library of Congress)

Gantt Cottage on the grounds of the Penn Center,
where Dr. Martin Luther King, Jr. drafted his "I Have a Dream Speech"

Dr. Martin Luther King, Jr. and the Southern Christian Leadership Conference often met at the Penn Center during the Civil Rights movement. The center served as a rare retreat where members of both races could meet peacefully without being threatened or harmed.

Chapter 17
The Weeping Time in Savannah

Mount Pleasant, South Carolina

Hentie scampered across the wide hardwood boards of the upstairs main hallway, careful to avoid those spots that might creak. She tried to curl into a protective shell, hunching her back to shield herself from the screeching voice of Mrs. Langdon. The missus' caterwauling echoed throughout the second floor, setting the nerves of all the enslaved house servants on edge. As Hentie glided along the floorboards, she overheard Mrs. Langdon chastising Octavia over trivial infractions, which she probably never committed. Hentie peeked in the narrow gap between the door and the wall to see just how crazed the old mistress really was now.

"Do you see this, Octavia? You have placed my favorite chemise in the bottom drawer! You KNOW it never goes there! What were you thinking? Honestly, you colored gals have the intelligence of a gnat! How did you ever expect me to find it in the linen press?"

Hentie glimpsed the missus stomping across the bedroom floor toward the huge mahogany wardrobe, the door creaking as she opened it. Hentie hunched her shoulders when she heard the grating sound, wondering what possible infraction the misses would find next.

"Why, you stupid niggra! Why isn't this saffron silk dress back on this peg? How can I find it if it's way back here?"

While quickly bending at the waist to show deference, Octavia responded in a fast-paced apologetic voice. "Well ma'am, you told me you hated that dress. You'd like to never wear it again. Said it reminded you of what comes outta little babies' bottoms . . . just a horrid color."

"Oh, that's ludicrous! Why would I say such a thing!" In exasperation, the missus hurled a fine china vase from France across her sitting room to punctuate her point.

Hentie winced at the shattering sound of porcelain.

The master is going to have a fit when he sees the missus has broken that vase. He bought it especially for her as a gift on his last trip to Paris. Octavia had better calm that crazy woman down and do it right quick!

Octavia stood in the middle of the room, trying to maintain her composure while using a soothing voice to defuse the situation. Her plump figure was outfitted in a crisp linen dress with a long white apron draped over it, a large white bow tied in the back. Her hair smoothed back in a tight bun was tied snuggly in a knot at the nape of her neck. Octavia's hands were folded in front of her at waist height, her fingertips pressing into the tops of her hands, leaving indentations in her flesh from the intense pressure of her powerful squeeze.

Hentie got a glimpse of the mistress starting to grab objects off her dressing table just as she darted by the doorway. Octavia let out a whoop and begged the mistress not to shatter her crystal jar of pearl face powder, as the mistress was so particular about maintaining a youthful complexion. Hentie knew the mistress would regret the act yet blame the enslaved workers for it. Hentie winced when she heard the mistress slam the fragile glass container into the wall and shatter it.

"Here, ma'am. Let me help you put on the outfit you wanted for this afternoon," Octavia suggested in a pleasant, upbeat tone.

"Octavia, what is this? I can't be seen out in public with a streak like this down the bottom of my dress! What will the ladies say with me appearing at a luncheon looking like some Black courtesan or mulatto whore?"

Hentie chuckled to herself at the thought of the insane Mrs. Langdon working as a lady of the night.

I doubt that this crazy bitch has any idea how to please a man, let alone get paid for it. She's lucky the ma'sa puts up with her and doesn't throw her ass outta this house!

"Well, ma'am, let me see. Maybe there is something I can do with it to clean that stain. If not, we can find you something else real pretty to wear."

"Well, if the laundress would just do her job properly, we wouldn't be in this fix, would we? It always boils down to darkies not doing their work! I wanted to wear that ensemble. The colors favor me so. But wouldn't you know it? Heathen savages let me down again!" The mistress stamped her foot as she ended her sentence.

Two beats later, Hentie reached the back stairwell, opened the door, and scrambled down the steps. When she reached the lower level of the big house and swung open the door to the butler pantry, she accidentally slammed into one of the other enslaved house girls named Sally, causing her to toss several storage tins onto the floor, which landed with a reverberating clatter.

Hentie, horrified by the act, froze and pressed her flattened palm against her mouth, afraid to make a sound. Both Hentie and Sally locked eyes and waited for the wrath of the mistress to befall them. Moments passed.

The two waited pensively to hear the booming voice of the mistress. Finally, they were able to discern that Mrs. Langdon was still upstairs in her bedroom continuing her hysterics. Hentie and Sally smiled then scurried about, quickly picking up the tins.

"Sally, I's sorry I made you drop all them tins, but I gots to rush. I gots to go fetch some food for tonight's supper. The missus is having fits," Hentie warmly squeezed Sally's arm, then kept moving.

Hentie rushed out of the backdoor toward the dependencies to fetch a ham from the smokehouse. Company was coming and the mistress wanted an elegant dinner table set for friends, complete with a large, delectable ham. If there was one thing that set the missus on edge and caused her to be more temperamental than usual, it was guests coming to the plantation. She still wished to maintain her status as an elegant Southern belle, quite competent to entertain her visitors with style. More importantly, the well-heeled visitors who would be traveling from Savannah had a daughter of a suitable age for marriage. Mrs. Langdon hoped the girl would be a good match for Fitzwilliam. With the help of a friend Mrs. Langdon had met at church, they conspired to set up this meeting in hopes of forging the union of two wealthy Southern families of good breeding. Fitzwilliam would be coming home to Twin Oaks from the battlefield for a visit, so it was a prime opportunity to arrange an encounter.

As she hastened over the still, dewy grass, Hentie glanced across the work yard and caught a glimpse of Cully, one the newer bondsmen, who now lived with her and Big John. The master had purchased Cully, a mulatto teenager, at a big slave sale over a year ago. Cully had developed some skills as a carpenter and was in the midst of constructing a worktable for the laundry house. He had mentioned it to Hentie earlier that morning before heading out to start the day's work. The long platform would be used to sort laundry and make lye soap, a tedious process that started with rendering tallow.

Cully was a good boy, still a young teenager, honest and hardworking. Big John had taken him under his wing, by agreement with the master. Fortunately, he had been able to convince Master Langdon he should purchase the young man at the end of the huge slave auction down in Savannah. Cully was available at a low price since he was one of the few remaining slaves at the conclusion of the two-day sale. Cully had a lame hand but was otherwise healthy and showed intelligence and an eagerness to learn a trade. The master, trusting Big John's endorsement of the boy, consented. Big John and Hentie invited him to live in their larger brick slave cabin with the master's approval and now considered him their own son. He had become a part of their close family unit, and they informally adopted him. As was the tradition in the slave village when a bondsman was left without kin, others such as Big John and Hentie became their family.

Hentie briefly slowed her pace on her way to the smokehouse when she saw another enslaved worker, Flora, a young mulatto woman with a caramel complexion who had been born farther inland in South Carolina. She wore a look of exhaustion on her face from her labors in the laundry house. Flora's indigo-colored head wrap and deep ivory Negro cloth shift dress were soaked with perspiration from her drudgery in the heat and humidity. The withered laundress stopped at the brick water well and took the handcrafted dipping gourd and lowered it into a bucket she had retrieved from the deep shaft. She smiled briefly and raised it to her parched lips when she recognized her son's fingerprint in one of the top bricks of the well. Her son, Moses, had only been five years old when he formed the brick and used his thumb to make his impression to wink at her and the other enslaved workers who viewed his handiwork. It was one of his first jobs at Twin Oaks. Master Langdon said he could have shoes and a set of clothes that winter because he had earned his keep that year through his labors.

But those clothes didn't save him from the yellow fever that passed through the following summer. He succumbed to the scourge, just as so many others did that growing season, and withered away. The master never allowed daytime funerals for the enslaved and surely wouldn't waive that rule for a young child with little utility. Starting at the row of wooden cabins in the slave village, the procession of enslaved workers started out after nightfall by using torches to light their way. They made their way to the Black cemetery at the back of the plantation to bury the boy's small cloth-wrapped body. They sang gospel hymns about the loss of yet another one of their own as they made their way to the burial site located well behind the big house. Flora wailed most of the way. Her grief at the loss of her boy was palpable. Her smiling boy had been so full of life. It seemed to her that some demon in the form of a deadly disease had come and snatched Moses up when she least expected it, like a malevolent spirit in a dark cloak, and carried him off. Something, or someone evil, came and stole a boy who had been so innocent and pure. She would never forgive God for letting that happen.

As the image of her son passed through her mind, Flora slowly took in the water, savoring it as it flowed down her throat, which was parched from working in the heat. The cool moisture rolled over her tongue and cascaded down her throat. She dunked the gourd again into the bucket, closing her eyes as she took a gulp.

Suddenly, an abrupt voice thundered from behind her; it was deep and gravelly. "Hey, you there! What the hell you think you're doin'?" The burly Irish driver dug the toe of his boot into the dirt, spit out a stream of tobacco, and wiped his mouth on his sleeve.

A stableboy responded nervously. "Ah, nothin', sir, just stoppin' ta' brush the dirt off me. Heading back ta' the stables now."

The crusty old driver shouted out the side of his mouth, "Maybe a few lashes will remind you as to when you can take a break, you damn pickaninny niggra!"

Hearing the slave driver shout at another worker, Flora jumped, and her eyes flapped open. She dropped the homespun ladle back into the bucket with a splash and exhaled as she readied herself to return to the scorching heat of the laundry house. The driver continued onward, and she urged her bedraggled frame onward in the direction of the laundry's boiling cauldron. Unable to stand fully upright, she trudged forward. She had only gone a few yards when she heard Hentie call out to her.

"Girl, you look like you best go back for another drink!" Hentie joked. "And this time you best throw some water on your face. You have to watch what you're doing when dealing with the laundry, hot boiling water, and lye soap. It can make your eyes swell shut, might even go blind with it. Make your hair fall out, too!"

"Yes, ma'am. I think you're probably right. That lye soap may be good for the master's white sheets, but it's not so good for my skin." She wiped the sweat off her brow and slowed to speak with Hentie momentarily.

"Be mighty careful. You go blind and ole' Rosa ain't got no remedy for that. No tea or salve can fix it."

"Dat' for true. I'm careful every day cause a' dat!"

Hentie jerked her head toward her adoptive son, Cully. He was in the workyard cutting lumber with a handsaw, "I think my boy Cully is making y'all a worktable. That'll help out a bit. Maybe you can spread things out a bit more."

"Yeah, I am hopin' so. It's a dang long hot day dealin' wit all dat laundry here. All da shifts, petticoats, chemises, and kecks, we's got mountains of it! Then there's all the sheets and heavy work clothes of the skilled slaves like the blacksmith. Their breeches are heavy!" Flora's eyes grew wide as she bent her shoulders downward.

"I know laundry is a hard job. But maybe the ma'sa will move you onto another work area. You just gotta keep your head up 'n hope for better things. That's the only choice we got."

"I s'pose your right." Flora slowly nodded.

"Look at my boy Cully. Sold at the big slave auction down in Savannah. He coulda been sent down Louisiana way. Ya' know they work them slaves to death down there. Thank the Lord, Big John saw him and got the master to bring him here."

"Yeah, he sho' was lucky," Flora readjusted her damp head wrap.

"Lord only knows what might have happened to a boy like dat with a lame hand. Seems like the folks down in the slave village have done accepted him. He's made friends with some of d'other young men down there too." Hentie smiled as she nodded at Flora.

"Yes, it's true, everyone likes him. He's a good boy. You and Big John were so good to take him in. I'm sure he's thankful."

"Well, thank you, Flora." Hentie dipped her head toward Flora.

"I can only hope for da blessins of da Good Lawd. Only so much us colored folk can expect in this life. Speakin' of which, I best getta move on, or dey driver will have me whipped. Maybe I'll see you at suppertime."

"Yes, I best carry that ham back to the house 'fore the missus has a fit!"

With that, the two turned and went off in opposite directions—Flora back to the laundry house and Hentie sped down to the smokehouse. She opened the door to the cylindrical brick building and stepped back, letting the light shine on all the hanging hams. She selected a large one she thought would please the missus, took it down off its hook, and hastened back to the kitchen house. She held up the robust ham for Nellie to view as she passed through the doorway of the small brick building.

"Here you go, Nellie. I fetched a nice ham for supper. I'm hoping the missus will like this one," Hentie announced as she lay the ham on the worktable.

"My, that does look like a nice one. It should make the missus happy," Nellie nodded her approval. "Now you best go fetch some of the other fixins I'll be needin', like the sweet potatoes, onions, and a mess of vegetables. I gots to make up a nice servin' platter."

"I'm on my way." Hentie turned to step across the threshold of the kitchen house when she spied Big John with another one of the enslaved workers, Henry. The two approached while she was still standing in the open work yard.

Big John nodded at Hentie as he exposed a toothy grin, then started to speak with his deep baritone voice, "We just walked past Cully. He's doin' a fine job with that worktable. I think the master and the women folk will be happy with it."

"Good, glad to hear it turned out well," Hentie nodded.

"That Cully's a good carpenter," said Henry.

"Yeah, he sure is. You should see the table he built for our cabin. Why don't you come round to our house at suppertime? I'm making some fresh Frogmore stew tonight. Good cornbread to go with it. You like that, don't ya, Henry?"

"Sho' do! I'll be there, 'fo' nightfall. You can count on me." Henry hustled off with a broad smile and picked up his pace.

That evening, Big John, Hentie, Cully, and Henry greeted each other outside the small slave cabin before they walked into the dwelling.

"My, you folks managed to get a fine place here," Henry said. looking around the brick cottage. "Ain't many other folks who get a shack this nice."

"Well, our place is a bit bigger, and we sure are lucky that it's just us three livin' here. I know a lot of folks have nine, ten, or more in their cabin. I guess I get special treatment since I work for the boss man. We are lucky to have so few. And we have more furniture. We have a table and chairs, beds, a hearth, and an oven."

"Thank goodness the ma'sa loves my husband or we wouldn't be so blessed," Hentie said as she wiped the table with an old kitchen towel. "Here, y'all get yourself some stew and cornbread."

"First, I think we should be thankin' the Lawd for havin' this wonderful friend and family, don't you think, Hentie?"

"Yeah, you're right John. I just knowing everybody starving this late in the day."

The four of them joined hands and formed a circle around the table and bowed their heads, closed their eyes, paused momentarily, and exhaled. Big John cleared his throat and began to speak with his deep velvety voice.

"Lawd, thank ya for all the bounty you brought to us. The food we have before us, our good friend Henry, our son boy, Cully, and my wife, Hentie. Thank you, Lawd for bringin' her into my life and making me whole. And thank you, too, for our son who made us a real family. If'n it be your will, Lawd, bring freedom to our people. Show us the way out of Egypt. Please Lawd, let us Black men be able to fight for our freedom. Let us join the Union troops and bring this ugly war to an end. You know them Knights of the Golden Circle, dem men be scoundrels planning evil things for this world. Stop them, Lawd, please stop them. Let us colored folk enjoy life here in America, and let us live full lives so we can do your work. Look down on us and guide us through each day. Bless us all, Lawd. Amen."

"Amen," said the others in unison. "That was real nice, John, let's hope the Lawd does bring freedom to us, real soon. You think the president will ever let colored men fight alongside White men?" asked Henry.

As they sat down at the table with their dinner, they heard others in the slave community outside and decided to join them. Many sat at tables underneath a grove of trees eating their evening meal. Hentie, Big John, and Henry overheard some murmurings about the war and whether Lincoln was going to let Black men sign up to fight with the Union soldiers. It was a hotly contested matter. They walked over and joined in the discussion. Cully, with his parents' permission, went off to join some of his younger friends.

It seemed like all the men in the slave village wanted to fight, as they had their own freedom at stake.

"I'd love to take down a Rebel. Shoot him right 'tween the eyes," said one field worker. "Give me the chance and I'll join those Yankee troops, that is if'n they let me."

"Well, I suppose that's the biggest question, if them Yanks goin' ta' let ya join or make you wait here until the Rebel soldiers come over that hill and set this place on fire?" Henry twisted a piece of hay in his mouth and looked at the young man who was so full of himself.

"I guess we're gonna see then, ain't we?" the young man nodded and strolled away, joined some others across the grove of trees.

Other folks were already finished with their meals and were singing or playing instruments. Two of them had homemade banjos. Henry, Big John, and Hentie decided to leave the group and grabbed a table by themselves at a distance.

Then in a hushed tone, Big John told them about all the newspaper articles he had been able to snatch up when he traveled on the waterway. He had been eagerly reading both the Negro newspapers and the traditional newspapers from cities like Baltimore. All were writing about whether the Union would allow Negroes to join the war effort.

At the outset, Lincoln had promised that he would not allow Negroes to engage in combat, but he had started to reconsider as more troops were needed to fight the war. Many Northerners were growing weary of Whites dying to free Blacks who, themselves, were not fighting for their own cause. Many businesses and farms in the North were failing because they had no one to run them. Riots were breaking out at draft boards in large cities.

Despite the willingness to fight, fears persisted among higher-level military officers that Blacks might not hold up under fire. Some believed that Negroes were docile by nature, not that they had been beaten into submission.

"I'm too old to fight in a war. I think I can better serve my people right here, keeping my ear to the ground. Snatching up what I can to help my people. Then passing along information on the waterfront. That's how the Underground works 'round here," Big John said to Henry and his wife.

"I expect you're right," Henry said. "What are two old men like us going to do out on a battlefield? I can't fight a muscle-bound, twenty-two-year-old with a sword. I'd get chopped to pieces. I'm better off doing what I can from here. Wait until the Yankees come to free us. I do what I can to go 'round the White man here. Break his tools, hide his treasures." Henry shot an affirming glance over Big John.

"Quiet resistance, that's what I do," Big John said in a low voice,

"I watch a lot, read a lot of the ma'sa's papers, gather information, and then share what I can on the Underground. When I can, I snatch up little things I know the boss man won't miss. I'm savin' it all up for someday when we find freedom. That day's a comin'. I know it."

"Well, you don't think I get away with what I can 'round that crazy old lady? I'll add a few more drops a opium ta' her little blue bottle. Maybe luck will come my way and she'll take a little too much one day, then we'll find that troublesome old hag in a heap," Hentie whispered with a chuckle.

"I think every soul on this plantation would dance and holler that day!" laughed Henry.

"They sho' would!" Hentie said. "When her doctor comes round the house and he drops it off to me, I smile and curtsy real nice like. I act real respectful like and lower my eyes. I tell the doctor that I'll take the bottle and hide it in a special spot for her. Give it to her only when she needs it real bad. Then nod at him again and smile real politely. He always smiles and tips his hat to me."

"That's my gal! That's how you do it," Big John chuckled.

"That evil woman deserves to die an ugly death with rat poisoning. She treat all our people so hateful. There's a place in Hell for her kind!" Hentie made a loud grunting noise as she jumped up from the table and quickly stormed away, her skirts swirling around her in her fury.

Big John raised his eyebrows in amusement. "She gets like that now and again. I don't think she likes the missus much."

"Oh really? You think?" Henry chortled.

The two men sat alone for a while and listened to the others sing and caught a bit of the others' conversations. After several minutes Hentie returned and sat next to Big John on a bench "Sorry 'bout that. Sometimes that woman makes my blood boil. I know there ain't much I can do but live with what the Lawd has given me."

"That's okay. We do the best we can. Someday, we'll be away from here. You'll see," Big John leaned in and kissed his wife, his massive body towering over Hentie's much smaller frame, "It'll be me, you, and our boy, Cully."

Henry posed a question to his two friends. "Tell me, how did you both come to have Cully stay with you? He's not blood kin, is he?" Henry tilted his head as he queried Big John and Hentie.

"Well, it's a sad story," Big John began. "Big plantation owners down near Savannah had to sell a bunch of slaves to pay their debts. They'd owned over eight hundred but had to sell off half of them. Held a big two-day slave auction at a racetrack in Savannah. So sad how they had to bust up all those slave families."

"Lawd Almighty, never heard of a slave sale dat big," exclaimed Henry.

"Yep, for generations Butler Island plantation in Darien had been working really well. The original master who owned the plantation rarely sold anyone off. They were close. They helped one another. They were a community." Big John raised his arms as if hugging the entire community and pulling them together.

Hentie added, "Yep, them poor folks didn't see this comin'. They thought they were safe with 'dat White man."

"No Black man is safe when he's owned by White buckra," Henry muttered.

"I heard 'em say at the slave sale that Master Butler was one of the largest slave owners in America," Big John said. "Major Butler didn't get along with his own children though. Ended up leaving all his property to his two grandsons. Well, those fools didn't know nothin' 'bout running a plantation. They were city boys and flitted the money away."

"It's not easy runnin' a big plantation. Gots to know what you doin'," Hentie added.

Big John rolled his eyes. "One grandson never even saw the plantation. He never fancied that kind of life. He just drew money from it. He didn't like livin' in the country, working with your hands and gettin' dirty. He chose to live in a fine townhouse in Philadelphia.

He was single and thought the flow of money was endless."

"Yeah, he like da money, not the smell," Hentie snorted.

"Yep, he just like gambling, drinking, and buying things for the pretty women folk," Big John chuckled as he winked at Henry.

"Stupid White buckra. Lose all that money the Black man worked so hard to earn. Slaves dey break dey backs workin' the land and makin' all dat money. Dirty bastard threw it all away." Henry shook his head.

"Yep, he gambled it away. Bank came after him to sell what he had left, had to sell off all he got from his grandfather."

"How terrible it must have been for them." Henry shook his head. "I can't imagine what it would be like to see all those people split up that way. How did they even get four hundred slaves down to the racetrack for sale in Savannah?"

"Well, when Master Langdon and I got down to the racecourse in Savannah, we were told the slaves had been brought down by steamboat and train. But our boy Cully told me later that the ones who were old enough to walk were linked together by chains and forced to walk part of the way. That's how they actually got to the place where they held the slave auction, on foot. They walked in tired, dragging those heavy chains." Big John paused for a moment. "Can you imagine what that was like for them, 'specially the little ones?"

Hentie blinked tears and patted her heart. "Them poor babies. The ones that was three, four, five years old. Bound together, knowing they was going to be ripped away from 'dey mamas. God bless their little souls. I know what it was like when I got snatched up in Africa, forced to walk in chains. But we didn't have little ones with us. We walked hundreds of miles to the African coast. They had less than that, but they was babies."

"Dey knew dey about to meet dey fate, get sent down river. Leave dey family forever." Henry looked away as tears welled.

The three friends took a long pause contemplating the emotional and physical pain of what those four hundred slaves endured.

"Them poor folks got there four days before the auction so as the

White buckra could look 'em over and pick out slaves they fancied. Those buyers pulled em out of the horse stalls so they could judge."

"White man wants to look over dey goods fore dey buy em, you know dat," Henry said. Wants dey field hand who can work all day long in dey fields."

"Most of em were forced to open their mouths so they could look over their teeth, just like you do with a horse to size him up. Sometimes 'da buyers make 'da slaves jump so they could see if dey were able-bodied and how hard dey could work them."

"Shameful to treat a human being like that," Hentie scoffed. "Course, I had to go through that after I came here from Africa. Been on that slave ship for weeks and weeks. I was weak and sickly. Stripped down naked in front of people down by Gadsden Wharf."

Big John grimaced. "Yep, they did the same thing here. Strip them down naked. Those White men poked and prodded them. They look at their lower parts, and make sure they could make them babies. Took them slave women to private rooms and fondled them, then they got to test 'em out, make sure they was to they likin', if you know what I mean."

"Women folk has it the worst," Hentie scowled. Yeah, and not all the families got to stay together. Cully told me he was pulled out from the others early on. They decided to treat him differently cause of his lame hand. He was split up from his family without a chance to say goodbye. Broke his heart. 'Member this was a sale to pay off debts, not keep families happy. The auctioneer could do whatever he wanted with them."

"Poor Cully," Big John said. "He knew he would be treated differently. He feared it the whole time, even 'fore they left the plantation, but didn't want to say anything to his mama because he knew it would break her heart. He tried to be brave throughout the whole thing. He just kept looking down and tried not to take in what was happening around him. Cully told me bout it afterward. We talk about it now and again."

"The master and I stayed for most of the auction. Over four hundred slaves, including twenty-five babies, was sold," Big John said. "Took 'em two days. Children was torn from their mamas and handed over to the highest bidder. Sad to watch."

"Musta been hard for Cully to sit and watch everyone being sold off, just waitin' his turn," Henry said.

"Oh, it was so hard for that boy. Cully was one of the seven who was left at the end of the sale with no bidders. You can see, he had a lazy eye that scared off some buyers. He also had a lame hand from it getting' caught in a cotton gin when he was just a boy. Tore up his hand bad. He had been right-handed but had forced himself to use his left hand. He's gotten good with it. You would never know he was originally right-handed," explained Big John.

"You sure right 'bout Cully. He uses both his hands real well. He just uses 'em differently," said Henry.

"When we first arrived at the auction, Master Langdon was more interested in buying a field hand. We looked over those young men we considered to be three-quarter hands or full hands. We initially passed over Cully. But then, I could sense the panic in Cully. My heart was achin' for the boy. After his whole family was sold, I saw him weepin' and begging the buyer to take him, too."

"Oh my, that musta been terrible." Henry shook his head.

"That lonely soul crumpled to the ground when he saw his mother being led off. At first, the poor boy couldn't pull himself back to his feet. I looked over at the master to see if I could help the boy. He nodded at me to go ahead and help. The auctioneer told me to lead the boy back to his stall and rejoin the other handful of slaves who weren't sold yet. I did my best to calm the boy and soothe his broken spirit."

Hentie put one hand on her hip, looked down, and shook her head, "That poor child must have felt so forsaken. Poor thing must have thought his whole world was comin' to an end right then and there."

"All alone and his heart a breakin'. Good thing you were there, Big John. God must have sent you his way."

Big John nodded. "I started to speak with Cully and learn all about him. He's a smart boy. I learned he had some good skills. One of the men at the plantation was teaching him a bit about saddlery and making leather goods. He had also started learning about carpentry and making furniture. I thought we could make good use of him here. I told Master Langdon we needed a boy like that to help at Twin Oaks. We made a deal with the auctioneer to buy a three-quarter field hand and Cully for one price. It worked out well for the master and Cully. Thank God the master listened to me. Hentie and I didn't have any children of our own. Now we have our own little family. Cully fit in real nice like with us."

"Well, let's hope Cully gets to stay with us," Hentie said. "You know that New Year's Day is not too far off. That's when the master and all the other planters either rent out or sell the slaves they think they can spare. The closer that day gets, the more I worry. Everybody does."

"I think we best hope that the master keeps all of us another year," Big John said. "We're past 1860 now. Planters made a lot of money from the Sea Island cotton, but even more from slaves. I heard the master talk about it with other planters all the time. The master stopped buying stocks and bonds and started buying more slaves. He calls us a 'reliable commodity' and safer than stocks or bonds. It's all about money. And that's what happened to poor Cully. Just a commodity to be sold to pay his master's debts."

"That poor brokenhearted child. I hope I can help him heal that heart and his broken spirit." Hentie took a couple of steps over, stood behind Big John and wrapped her arms around his shoulders, then leaned her head against his broad back, letting out a long sigh.

"That boy is in good hands with you and Big John," said Henry. "Thank the Lord for his intervention. God knew where he needed to be, right here with you two. We can all take good care of him." He smiled broadly and nodded at Big John and Hentie.

Nearly fifteen million Africans were captured kidnapped and sent to various places in the Americas between the 1500s and the 1800s. In 1808 the international slave trade was banned by federal law, but the practice still went on through black market trade, particularly between Cuba, Brazil, and states such as Mississippi, Texas, and Louisiana. The price of enslaved Africans kept rising after 1800 as bringing in new "saltwater" slaves became harder. Planters and those tradesmen who sold human commodities believed that enslaved workers would become even more valuable than ever as chattel slavery pressed further west into the American territories and southward into Central America.

By 1850, there were over 3.2 million slaves in the South, one-seventh of the nation's population. With the invention of the cotton gin in 1793 and Europe's growing appetite for King Cotton to feed their textile industry, plantation owners needed to acquire more slaves to keep their operations productive and perpetuate their luxurious lifestyles. Many scholars believe that it was the coalescence of certain events, principally the clamor for King Cotton, which spurred the Civil War.

The Industrial Revolution enabled the textile mills located in England's Midlands to go from making yards of fabric, to making miles of it. Moreover, the methods of dying fabrics dramatically improved, allowing manufacturers to offer a wider variety of colors and more colorfast textiles, ideal for clothing and upholstery. The Sea Island cotton brought to the Lowcountry from Barbados was regarded as the finest of all available cotton. It was softer, stronger, and had longer fibers, and hence, was worth five times more than other varieties of cotton. This made the planters of the Lowcountry region enormously rich, spurring them to cling to their way of life even more fervently. In the Beaufort and Sea Islands area, there was a flood of "saltwater" slaves who came to the area in the waning days of the international slave trade around 1800-1808 to address the need for human laborers to plant, tend, and harvest their precious commodity. The number outpaced all the other areas along the Gullah-Geechee corridor extending from Wilmington, North Carolina to northern Florida near St. Augustine.

By the early 1800s, cotton undergarments became available for the first time; this soft, absorbent alternative to scratchy wool was enthusiastically welcomed by all. Around this same time, corsets and women's underwear, or "drawers" came into being. European royalty, particularly Napoleon brought fashion into vogue. It continued with King Louis XVI. His first wife, Josephine, was known to buy up to nine hundred dresses a year and one thousand pairs of gloves. Marie-Antoinette, his second wife, would purchase a number approaching two hundred. Such lavishness spilled over to furnishings, including plush draperies and upholstered furniture. The textiles required to manufacture these goods had to incorporate the long-fibered Sea Island cotton for the stretch and give needed in such furnishings.

Southerners and those involved in the slave trade (often from New York and Newport, RI) had been reckless with their tremendous wealth and made American finances unstable in the 1850s. After the stock market crash of 1857, which had caused a run on the banks, planters started to get nervous about preserving their money. Aristocratic Whites considered enslaved workers a safer investment than stocks, bonds, or savings accounts. While there were some fluctuations in the value of an enslaved person of color, they were a relatively safe investment. Those involved in the slave trade were making more money than they had ever conceived in their wildest dreams. New insurance agencies and banks were established just to handle the previously unknown prosperity this new commodity had created. New York Life Insurance allowed planters to recoup three-quarters value of a dead slave. Aetna and US Life/AIG also provided insurance. JP Morgan and Wells Fargo permitted the use of enslaved workers as collateral. By far, the sale of human beings had become the most profitable endeavor known to man. But just as men garnered tremendous wealth, some squandered it away, as was the case with Pierce Mease Butler, grandson to the Revolutionary War hero, Major Pierce Butler, Sr.

Prior to his death, the Major Butler had owned the Butler Island Plantation and the St. Simon estate called Hampton Point. At one point, it encompassed ten thousand acres with one thousand slaves, but by the time of the sale his assets had dwindled somewhat. The plantation had been in the Butler family for over four generations. Located off the coast of Georgia, just north of Savannah, these islands were worlds to themselves. Major Butler, his parents, grandparents, and his ancestors from Ireland, rarely sold anyone off. The bondsmen worked hard under the task system but had their own stable slave village and some sense of unity and stability. Major Butler experimented with new methods of crop rotation and fertilization. He eventually became one of the largest plantation owners in America. However, all his industrious efforts and accumulated wealth were squandered away by his heirs.

On March 2 and 3, 1859, a two-day auction was held to liquidate the Butler family assets, nearly half of which were sold to satisfy debts. Over four hundred frightened bondsmen took to the auction block. It was the largest recorded slave auction in American history. It had been advertised in all the major newspapers throughout the United States. Postings and billets were distributed on ships and trains. The event netted $303,850 for the debt-ridden Pierce Mease Butler, grandson to Major Butler, a phenomenal sum at the time.

The heavily indebted Butler had never even seen his grandfather's plantation. He chose to live in a fine townhouse in Philadelphia. He had never been gainfully employed; instead, he enjoyed the high life, often womanizing and gambling. What he didn't squander, he used to finance bad investments. Businesses kept extending him credit, but eventually called in the loans. Four hundred thirty-six unfortunate souls, including twenty-five babies, were sold over the course of the two-day sale at Ten Broeck Racecourse in Savannah, their individual lives treated with no more respect than that of a horse or cow. American law, both state and federal, clearly provided for the disposal of human life for such a dastardly purpose.

Chapter 18
Emancipation Day

Beaufort, South Carolina and nearby Saint Helena Island, Autumn 1862

Inside a cavernous gray barn at the Smith Plantation in Saint Helena parish near Port Royal, Issac and the other recently liberated slaves worked to unload the cotton they had hauled in from the field. It was the fall harvest, and everyone was expected to help out to bring in the snowy white balls as they popped open. The prized Sea Island cotton brought in funds used to help out with the efforts being made with the Port Royal Experiment.

Issac hoisted a basket of freshly picked cotton onto the platform along with the other newly harvested crop. It was part of a magnificent snowy pile. The workers were keeping track of the bushels that were being dumped into a holding bin and weighing each sack as it was thrown onto the wooden counter inside the barn. As the cotton was added to the heap, another formerly enslaved worker marked the board as to the day's harvest. Issac was delighted that he could follow what was being marked on the board. He had started to learn the fundamentals of the alphabet, numbers, and basic reading. The work was being monitored by a White supervisor, a man who worked for the Treasury Department. For some reason, the military officers stopped coordinating the work, and the new men from Washington began ordering them around. Issac didn't like it; he thought they were slippery characters. One of the men, Frederick Eustis, started to pocket some of the money the contrabands were earning.

The cooler fall air was rolling in as the summer heat abated, dropping the temperature, but only by a matter of degrees. It still hovered well beyond the ninety-degree mark and was still hot and humid in South Carolina. It would be a few more weeks before the humidity would truly begin to subside.

One of the men from Issacs's troops, the First South Carolina Volunteers, the first regular Army regiment of freed slaves, stopped his work for a moment. His name was Amos, and he was from one of the local plantations. His Gullah accent was thick and sometimes difficult to understand.

He turned to Issac and said, "Hey, did you hear what da damn rebels say dey fixin' to do us colored soldiers ifin' dey catch us? said the soldier.

Issac paused as he was about to throw a bag of cotton onto a wagon and dropped it back on the ground, "What? What did you hear?"

The soldier took a step toward Issac and lowered his voice. "Dem Rebels dey are debbles. Pure evil. You know what dey fixin' to do?"

"Well, I suppose it can't be any worse than what the White buckra slave masters have already been doin' to us. What? Tie us to a whipping post and take a lash to our backs till the flesh is gone? They have been doing that for a couple of hundred years now, Amos."

"Yep, I expect yo' right 'bout that. But now dey sayin' dey gonna take us out en' shoot us. Tie us to a tree and blows our heads off. Not jus' us, but our White Yankee officers too. Da men like Higginson, jus' cause dey usin' Negro soldiers." Amos looked down and shook his head.

"What? How can they do that?" Issac exclaimed.

"Dey say dey gonna treat us Black folk like runaway slaves. Dey supposin' to take us to court, have us a hearin' and all, but dey have nuthin' for dem. Dey not messin' wit 'dat. Dem Rebels just been beatin' dey Black soldiers and shootin' dem in dey head out in dey woods. Dem White Rebel bastards. Dey ain't got no soul."

"And the Confederate officers know about it and allow it to go on? God have mercy!" exclaimed Issac. He kicked the dirt and threw down his straw sun hat.

"Dat be right. Dey Black men allowed to fight dey White Rebels, but if dey captured, dey tortured and shot. Dey say dey runaway slaves." Amos nodded.

"You know those damn Confederates, they are the ones that picked this fight. They started the damn war! The Southerners were the ones that said they could break off and make their own country. South Carolina has been sayin' that bullshit for the last thirty years. It's those White folks who want to keep all their money rolling through the South on the backs of the Black man. Keep us down, doing their work for them. They gonna see a new day a' comin'." Issac punched one of the large sacks used to collect cotton out in the field sending some of the cotton dust flying up into the air.

"You got dat right, Issac. You sure got dat right," nodded Amos.

"You know those damn Confederate soldiers forced my mama and me to serve them in their camps. The devil bastards. We had to wait on them all day long. I helped out with the cooking and serving of the men. I couldn't stand helping those bastards who were fighting to keep me a slave. I ran away from their camp." Issac looked down and kicked the dirt.

"Good fuh you." Amos struck his fist into the air.

"I stopped by my daddy's grave the day I broke away from the Rebel camp. He was gunned down years before by a slave catcher. I made a pledge to him. I promised my daddy right where his body lay, I was gonna see things change. Negroes weren't going to be treated like they were less than human," Issac shouted.

"Let's hope dat come true," Amos nodded and said, "Lawd bless you and yo' mama."

"I never even got to meet my daddy. That plantation owner up in Mount Pleasant, Master Langdon, posted a reward for my daddy as a runaway slave. He had a bounty on his head, didn't matter whether he was dead or alive. My daddy, he run from up near Charleston to see my mama down here in Beaufort. He must have been on the run for days. She was carrying me in her belly. My daddy didn't even know about it." Issac paced in circles as the anger rose up in him.

Amos thrust out his hand and tilted his head, "Lawd Jesus. Ma'sa put a bounty on yo' pa's head?"

Issac nodded. "He sure did, just cause he had a mean spirit. Langdon had them chase down my daddy and kill em. My daddy only wanted to see my mama. They loved each other. They jumped the broom and everything. That White bastard sold off my mama just cause she spilled some damn milk. Can you imagine that?"

Oh my, dat wickitty man," Amos pressed his hand to his chest, his fingers splayed.

"So, my mama and I were livin' down here in Beaufort when the war broke out. Master McKee rented us out to the Confederate soldiers, and we were working for them at some encampment around here. I had to cook and serve those bastards. They loved to harass me. I couldn't take it no more, so I ran," explained Issac.

"I don't blame you. I can't imagine waitin' on no rebel soldier. Slab'ry gone out as soon as da' Yanks come here." Amos said.

"Them days of forcing Black men to do the White buckra's bidding gonna stop now. Black men needs to be free!" Issac kicked an oak barrel holding freshly picked pecans sending a spray of them spilling over the edges. Still fuming, he just strutted away to the other side of the work yard.

Suddenly, a young Black man in worn clothing, perhaps in his early teens, came running toward them from the road, up through the field. He was screaming wildly and waving his arms. Those in the barn stopped working. Surely this boy had been sent to help someone in need. Perhaps someone was grievously injured. Issac quickly glanced around the barn to see what he might be able to grab if he needed to recover someone who had fallen into the water or faced some other fate. He quickly reached for a blanket and a rope.

When the boy reached the barn, he continued to holler, his words indistinguishable. Tears rolled down his face. Gasping for air, he bent over, placing his hands on his knees, trying to catch his breath. His chest heaved in and out. Everyone remained frozen around him, holding their own breath, as if their ceasing to take in the air would give more to the boy. Still breathing hard, he looked up to everyone and much to their amazement, he broke out into a broad smile.

"Mr. Lincoln . . . Mr. Lincoln . . . he signed it . . . he said we gonna be free! Just a few more months and all us Black folk gonna be free!"

"What? He did what?" Amos asked with a puzzled look on his face.

"He signed the paper. In January, we are all free," the boy shouted over his shoulder.

With that, the boy was off. His shrill cries rose up as he ran across the field to deliver the message to the others.

"We gonna all be free. Everybody gonna be free!"

Everyone started running in from the fields from all over the huge plantation, wondering what this was about, or whether this could be true. Perhaps the Rebels had started a cruel joke. Some of the workers walked up to the main house to seek confirmation. Word soon spread all across the fields and down to the road.

A rider came up, Corporal Robert Sutton with the First South Carolina Volunteers. His scarlet pantaloons and wide red belt were visible even from a great distance. He yelled, "Mr. Lincoln said we're all going to be free! He signed some paper that say come January, if'n the Confederates don't cease hostilities, we's gonna be free." Soon everyone gathered and started walking to find out what was going on. It was late September 1862 and there was much work to be done. They discovered from one of the officers that President Lincoln had issued the Preliminary Emancipation Proclamation. It mandated that if the Southern states did not cease their hostilities by January 1, 1863, his proclamation would go into effect and all the enslaved who resided in the Confederate states would be freed.

Issac, hopeful with the good news, began to wonder what a new life would be like for him. Life as a free man. He could live with his mother and not worry. Then he paused, wondering where she might be at this very moment. She had been gone so long. The Confederate troops had taken her away from Beaufort to work in their new encampment, wherever that might be. God only knew what they might have done to her. As others cheered, he stared off at the road, hoping somehow, she might make it back to him. Eventually she might be free to come back home, and he would see her making her way down that road. He knew he would recognize her right away, particularly the way she dragged her right foot a bit from the severe beating she got while she was owned by Master Langdon. But all of that would be behind them. They would have no more worry, no more pain.

At long last, January 1, 1863, had arrived. On this first day of the new year, the Emancipation Proclamation was to be read before a throng of nearly two thousand people. The proclamation signed by the president had now been ratified by Congress; it would be the law of the land. Dignitaries and people of importance were coming to officially recognize the president's document and celebrate the momentous occasion. In the Deep South, it was a relatively mild day with temperatures in the mid to upper fifties. There was a cloudless sky, a blue river, and the warm sun imparted a springtime atmosphere to the lively assembly of euphoric souls in the oak grove. Festivities were to be held outdoors throughout the day.

Those in attendance at Camp Saxton were primarily the formerly enslaved. The site had once been Smith Plantation but was now abandoned and subsequently named the Old Fort Plantation before being recognized as a military installation. The white tents of the First South Carolina Volunteer Infantry regiment were spread in an orderly array on the grounds of the plantation, located on a picturesque point a few miles from Beaufort. This would be the only site in the entire nation where those Blacks in attendance would have already been liberated. The enslaved up in Charleston, only seventy-five miles away, and other surrounding areas of the South, were still held in bondage.

But here on Port Royal Sound the mood of exhilaration rose up into the air and seemed to reach the heavens as a special thanks to God himself. In all other jurisdictions throughout the country, those enslaved had remained bondsmen up until this day. Even this historical document would only impact those Negroes in the South who lived in Confederate states and acted as part of the rebellion.

The enormous crowd of people hummed with excited chatter. Issac, along with the other newly liberated enslaved workers, gathered on the field at the Port Royal encampment where the First Carolina Volunteers (Colored) had been formed. He was now a soldier of this groundbreaking and momentous regiment. The air pulsated with energy and euphoria. The crowd of excited onlookers appeared as an endless field of wildflowers, all cloaked in brightly colored scarves and wraps. Many of the women wore gay kerchiefs on their heads. The scarlet trousers that the regiment wore added to the lively scene.

The formerly enslaved came from miles around, from all the surrounding Sea Islands in the vicinity, many by foot. Some were fortunate enough to come by horseback, cart, or wagon. Others ventured there by water, many in small bantu boats, but some were brought by steamer ships. There were several hundred who were fortunate enough to be brought by the little steamer *Flora*, as it circulated throughout the various Sea Islands picking up those who wished to attend.

There were White military officers, including General Saxton, the military governor of the area, his father, and Colonel Higginson, the commander of the very first regiment of colored troops. Dr. Seth Rogers, a surgeon with the First South Carolina Volunteers was in attendance as well. The military band was there, and several White calvary officers hovered around the outskirts of the crowd of Black soldiers and civilians. Along with these people were government officials, teachers, and northern Methodist missionaries, including Laura Towne and Ellen Murray, who had been teaching the contrabands, along with other Gideonites, as they had become known due to their religious convictions. There were also Black missionaries who established the Port Royal Experiment, Negro teachers, such as Charlotte Forten, well-educated and from Philadelphia, who had helped to educate and support the ongoing efforts, and Susie King Taylor. Susie had been a refugee from Savannah and worked in the Port Royal encampment as a teacher, laundress, and nurse. Frances Dana Barker Gage, a notable White woman from Ohio and active abolitionist and mother of eight–four of whom served in the Union Army–had come to support the Port Royal Experiment. She was serving in the US Sanitary Commission and as superintendent of one of the freedman's schools.

Harriet Tubman, of course, was right in the mix of people. The small gregarious woman was exuberant at the moment she had long awaited. She smiled and glowed with sheer happiness. Tubman had helped hundreds to freedom before this day, and now she got to see some of her people revel in their newly found liberty. There were even a few of the local plantation owners, including Mrs. Amanda Rose Fripp, the woman who had been present at the lynching of Christmas Luke near Twin Oaks plantation a few years earlier. She had helped to incite the violence back then but had grown to later regret it. It proved to be a harrowing experience, the first time she had seen such cruelty firsthand.

Mrs. Fripp had brought a basket of hearty food with her. Harriet

Tubman noted the one-time caustic slave owner to have seemingly had a change of heart. While Mrs. Fripp could never verbally acknowledge the wrongfulness of slavery, her gesture spoke volumes. Together, Harriet and Susie King Taylor approached her and warmly welcomed her to the celebration. Making sure that they stayed a few steps back and did not physically touch her, they drew her into the crowd.

"Mrs. Fripp, perhaps you might like to join Dr. Brisbane and the other gentlemen on the podium? I am sure you would be more comfortable seated in a proper chair. You 'member Dr. Brisbane, don't you? I'm thinkin' you folks had plantations right close to one another." Harriet pointed over to Brisbane, a rather lean man in a dark suit and balding head.

"Oh yes, it's been years since I have seen him. I should at least go over and show the courtesy of greeting the man after such a long time. Thank you for pointing him out. And Harriet, perhaps I can make use of myself here in Beaufort. Maybe I can help with nursing duties or perhaps teach at the Penn Center? I am an older woman now, but I should be able to do something worthy to help your efforts here." Mrs. Fripp tilted her bonnet-covered head, almost appearing as a young child waiting to be rebuffed, standing tentatively and awaiting a response.

"Why yes, Miss Fripp. We'd love to have another set of hands helpin' us out. We'll talk more later 'bout this. We thank you for your offer." Harriet flashed a wide toothy grin and immediately put Mrs. Fripp at ease, as well as Susie King Taylor, who wasn't quite sure how to address this longtime slave owner.

The ladies all moved on, Harriet and Susie escorted Mrs. Fripp up to the raised platform. Harriet made brief introductions between Mrs. Fripp and Dr. Brisbane, Colonel Higginson, and a few other White dignitaries. Feeling a bit out of place on the platform, she departed after a handful of minutes, but not before she heard a genteel woman invite the colonel and surgeon to Sunday supper at her plantation to discuss how she might better support their efforts in the area.

A stunned Harriet stepped off the platform astonished by what she had just overheard. She grabbed Susie by the arm and quickly walked away from the stage and said, "My Lawd, this is a glorious day. The debbel had done turned 'to a sab'ya 'o grace!" She then departed with Susie.

Meanwhile, Issac kept looking about, hopeful that in this throng of people, with so many there from all around, perhaps God would see fit to bring his mother to him on this most special day. Issac squeezed his eyes shut and sent up a quick prayer.

Please, God. Please. Let her come here to this celebration. Let her be a free woman with the rest of us. Please, God.

People continued to arrive as the officials took their posts. The crowd continued to drift in by whatever means available to them. They brought with them blankets, jugs of water, and whatever food they could spare. Organizers maintained a fire for a huge barbecue. Twelve oxen were being roasted for the glorious occasion. From the supply stores, foodstuffs had been brought, including hard bread, molasses, fruit, ripened tomatoes, okra, sweetened water, and tobacco.

A speaker's platform had been built by the Army Corps of Engineers for the occasion. White officials sat at an elevated large round table upon it. Those at the table included all of the White dignitaries, including, of course, Colonel Higginson, the Harvard-educated, dyed-in-the-wool abolitionist and former clergyman who fought to end slavery nearly all his life. He had ridden with antislavery riflemen in Kansas during the 1850s. In 1859, he helped raise money for John Brown's raid on Harper's Ferry. He had been in the Army just three months before he had been summoned to the Sea Islands to turn a throng of eight hundred formerly enslaved field workers into a disciplined Army unit.

The colonel was overwhelmed with joy and glowing with excitement. Before taking the stage, he warmly greeted the Black officers in his regiment, particularly Prince Rivers and Robert Sutton, grasping their upper arms and shaking their hands. The band of the Eigth Maine Volunteer Regiment stood behind the platform, playing various patriotic tunes and requests for mainly gospel tunes such as "Walk 'Em Easy" and "I Know Moon Rise."

> *O, walk 'em easy round de heaven,*
> *Walk 'em easy round de heaven,*
> *Walk 'em easy round de heaven,*
> *Dat all de people may join de band,*
> *Walk 'em easy round de heaven,*
> *Walk 'em easy round de heaven,*
> *Walk 'em easy round de heaven,*
> *O, shout glory till 'em join dat band!"*

> *"I know moon-rise, I know star-rise,*
> *Lay dis body down.*
> *I walk in de moonlight, I walk in de starlight,*
> *To lay dis body down.*
> *I'll walk in de graveyard, I'll walk through the graveyard,*
> *To lay dis body down.*
> *I'll lie in the grave and stretch out my arms;*
> *Lay dis body down.*
> *I go to de judgment in de evenin' of de day,*
> *When I lay dis body down;*
> *And my soul and your soul will meet in de day*
> *When I lay dis body down.*

Folks started to gather around a particularly large oak tree in a grove of trees knowing that the more formal part of the ceremony was about to commence. As the trailing moss swayed in the mild breeze, one was hauntingly reminded of the symbolism of the strength and wisdom brought by the mighty oak trees over the millennia. At half past eleven, the three-hour service started with a prayer by the

Army's chaplain. Then a few selected poems were read by a teacher. There was a brief pause, then three hymns were sung, the first of which was one of the troops' favorites:

> *I WANT TO GO HOME*
> *"Dere's no rain to wet you,*
> *O, yes, I want to go home.*
> *Dere's no sun to burn you,*
> *O, yes, I want to go home.*
> *O, push along, believers,*
> *O, yes, I want to go home.*
> *Dere's no hard trials,*
> *O, yes, I want to go home.*
> *Dere's no whips a-crackin',*
> *O, yes, I want to go home.*
> *My brudder on de wayside,*
> *O, yes, I want to go home.*
> *O, push along, m brudder,*
> *O, yes, I want to go home.*
> *Where dere's no stormy weather,*
> *O, yes, I want to go home.*
> *Dere's no tribulation,*
> *O, yes, I want to go home.*

Issac looked off into the distance, lost in thought; his mind faded to the last time he saw his mother, Juba. It was nearly a year ago, perhaps more. He could still picture her drab brown dress and colorful red headwrap. Her eyes had been tired, but her smile had been warm. He lingered on that thought.

Then, as if he was hearing her voice, "Issac! Issac!"

Issac, half thinking it was part of his vivid memory, turned toward the sound. And to his amazement, he saw his mother crossing the field. Weary and stumbling, while dragging her right foot a bit, she rushed toward him, crying as she called his name.

Issac thought his eyes were playing a trick on him. It was just a memory that had manifested itself as a vision. It couldn't really be Juba; certainly not. Frozen in place, he continued to stare at the woman.

But then she finally reached him, cupped his face in her hands, and kissed his cheek. "My dear boy. I've finally made it back to you. I didn't think my legs would carry me this far, but I made it." She threw her arms around his neck.

"Oh Mama, you're here! You're really here. Praise God you're here!"

Issac grabbed his mother up and swung her around. He couldn't believe that God had sent his loving mother back to him. The only real kin he had. The woman who had been stolen away from him was now back here in the flesh. Issac was grateful to God. So much good had come to him on that day. He now had to see the mission through; he had to make sure that the war would end, and he and his mother would know freedom for the rest of their lives.

As they stood there, Issac was sure that on his other side, he felt a warm hand squeeze his shoulder. When he turned to look, no one was there. He knew it must be the spirit of his father standing beside him, sharing the moment they all had waited their entire lives for. Not wanting to alarm his mother, he merely turned to him and smiled. When doing so, Issac briefly saw an apparition of his father as he had once before. He had dark, thick curls and wore dark blue linsey-woolsey breeches, a brown woolen jacket, and newer leather boots, just as his mother had once described to him. Rather than becoming frightened, Issac was comforted by the sight. He smiled warmly and nodded. In a few moments, the apparition disappeared. He must have wanted Issac to know he shared in this day, too.

Hymns were still being sung as Issac clung to his mother. His emotions took over, and tears rolled down his cheeks. He was so grateful to God that his mother was there, as well as his father's spirit, to share this monumental moment with him. His chest filled with emotion. Overwhelmed with joy, he emitted a few sobs.

Finally, the official proclamation was read by a former planter, Dr. W. H. Brisbane, from Beaufort, who had left the area, but then returned for this day. He began with the words, "I do order and declare that all persons held as slaves are, and henceforth shall be free . . ."

He gave a stirring reading of the document as he had come to see the wrongfulness of slavery as a young man and was forced to leave the land to which he had been born due to his views. He had taken his enslaved workers with him northward, where he granted them manumission and then later became a man of the cloth and ardent abolitionist. Those virtues for which he had valiantly fought for years, had finally come to fruition.

There was a brief break for a few minutes when Juba turned to her son as she thought of all those enslaved back at Twin Oaks in Mount Pleasant near Charleston like her dear friends Hentie and Big John. They were about seventy-five miles away and their lives were tremendously different now.

Juba lowered her head as she spoke. "Issac, I feel so sorry for the Black folks back at my old plantation in Mount Pleasant. They all still slaves I'm sure, Master Langdon ain't never going to give anything up until the Yankees march down the Avenue of Oaks on his plantation."

"I'm sure you're right about that. He was one greedy old master," nodded Issac.

"Charleston is still being controlled by the Rebels. The Yankees only control the harbor. All they can try to do is stop supplies from coming in, but I hear those runners get by them all the time. I wonder when they will see freedom. I hope it ain't much longer," Juba said.

There were people moving around up on the platform, and they started to speak out to the crowd again. Following this, Reverend French presented Colonel Higginson with a flag of his Black regiment. The flag, which would be carried as they rode into battle, had been made by a personal friend of Dr. Brisbane up in New England. He stopped and got it in New York on his journey to the celebration. Colonel Higginson was so moved by the gesture he was speechless as he unfolded the colors. As he held the flag up in his hands, the colonel began to wave it for all to see. Still trying to carefully choose his words and regain his composure, a strong, but rather deep voice began to sing. It was one single man's voice, a rather elderly man. As two nearby women realized what he was singing, their harmonious voices joined in, as if by impulse.

What they were singing became clear to the rest of the crowd. "My country 'tis of thee Sweet Land of Liberty . . ." Initially, it was only the newly liberated who were singing the lyrics, but then Whites began to join in. Colonel Higginson quelled the White people, harmonizing with the others by gesture as if to say, "This is their moment, let them revel in it. They could not have sung this ballad before now." They had sung with infinite depth and tenderness, inspiring all those who could hear the melodic voices.

The words written in Colonel Higginson's diary about the moment were as follows:

I never saw anything so electric; it made all other words cheap, it seemed the choked voice of a race, at last unloosed; nothing could be more wonderfully unconscious; art could not have dreamed of a tribute to the day of jubilee that should be so affecting; history will not believe it; & when I came to speak of it, after it was silent, tears were everywhere. If you could have heard how quaint & innocent it was!

Colonel Higginson then folded the flag and gave it to the two Black officers of the regiment—the tall, handsome Sergeant Prince Rivers who had endured some forty years of slavery on Henry Middleton Stuart's plantation along the Coosaw River near Beaufort. Rivers had served as a house servant and coachman and surreptitiously learned to read and write while enslaved. He was joined on stage by the brawny Corporal Robert Sutton, a man of great savvy and intellect, although due to his circumstances, was just learning to read. The men took a few moments to savor the gravity of it all as everyone looked on. They then stepped back from one another and saluted. The soldiers turned and with military comportment, left the stage.

A few more speakers followed and then the ceremony was closed with the regiment singing "John Brown's Body." This was followed by a dress parade and much merriment by all in attendance. A grand barbeque followed the more formal part of the proceedings.

The Smith Plantation, the site of one of the earliest readings of the Emancipation Proclamation. Where General Rufus Saxton had assembled a large populace on January 1, 1863. The Smith Plantation later became the Old Fort Plantation around 1800. During the Civil War, it was confiscated by the US federal government and utilized by Col. Thomas Wentworth Higginson and the First South Carolina Volunteers as Camp Saxton.
Photo courtesy of the Library of Congress

William Henry Brisbane, 1806-1878 from Beaufort County, South Carolina, the gentleman who read the Emancipation Proclamation at the ceremony.

By the President of the United States of America: A Proclamation.

Whereas, on the twenty-second day of September, in the year of our Lord one thousand eight hundred and sixty-two, a proclamation was issued by the President of the United States, containing, among other things, the following, to wit:

"That on the first day of January, in the year of our Lord one thousand eight hundred and sixty-three, all persons held as slaves within any State or designated part of a State, the people whereof shall then be in rebellion against the United States, shall be then, thenceforward, and forever free; and the Executive Government of the United States, including the military and naval authority thereof, will recognize and maintain the freedom of such persons, and will do no act or acts to repress such persons, or any of them, in any efforts they may make for their actual freedom.

"That the Executive will, on the first day of January aforesaid, by proclamation, designate the States and parts of States, if any, in which the people thereof, respectively, shall then be in rebellion against the United States; and the fact that any State, or the people thereof, shall on that day be, in good faith, represented in the Congress of the United States by members chosen thereto at elections wherein a majority of the qualified voters of such State shall have participated, shall, in the absence of strong countervailing testimony, be deemed conclusive evidence that such State, and the people thereof, are not then in rebellion against the United States."

Now, therefore I, Abraham Lincoln, President of the United States, by virtue of the power in me vested as Commander-in-Chief, of the Army and Navy of the United States in time of actual armed rebellion against the authority and government of the United States, and as a fit and necessary war measure *for suppressing said rebellion, do, on this first day of January, in the year of our Lord one thousand eight hundred and sixty-three, and in accordance with my purpose so to do publicly proclaimed for the full period of one hundred days, from the day first above mentioned, order and designate as the States and parts of States wherein the people thereof respectively, are this day in rebellion against the United States, the following, to wit:*

Arkansas, Texas, Louisiana, (except the Parishes of St. Bernard, Plaquemines, Jefferson, St. John, St. Charles, St. James Ascension, Assumption, Terrebonne, Lafourche, St. Mary, St. Martin, and Orleans, including the City of New Orleans) Mississippi, Alabama, Florida, Georgia, South Carolina, North Carolina, and Virginia, (except the forty-eight counties designated as West Virginia, and also the counties of Berkley, Accomac, Northampton, Elizabeth City, York, Princess Ann, and Norfolk, including the cities of Norfolk and Portsmouth[)], and which excepted parts, are for the present, left precisely as if this proclamation were not issued.

And by virtue of the power, and for the purpose aforesaid, I do order and declare that all persons held as slaves within said designated States, and parts of States, are, and henceforward shall be free; and that the Executive government of the United States, including the military and naval authorities thereof, will recognize and maintain the freedom of said persons.

And I hereby enjoin upon the people so declared to be free to abstain from all violence, unless in necessary self-deference; and I recommend to them that, in all cases when allowed, they labor faithfully for reasonable wages.

And I further declare and make known, that such persons of suitable condition, will be received into the armed service of the United States to garrison forts, positions, stations, and other places, and to man vessels of all sorts in said service.

And upon this act, sincerely believed to be an act of justice, warranted by the Constitution, upon military necessity, I invoke the considerate judgment of mankind, and the gracious favor of Almighty God.

In witness whereof, I have hereunto set my hand and caused the seal of the United States to be affixed.

Done at the City of Washington, this first day of January, in the year of our Lord one thousand eight hundred and sixty-three, and of the Independence of the United States of America the eighty-seventh.

By the President: ABRAHAM LINCOLN
WILLIAM H. SEWARD, Secretary of State.

Chapter 19
The Combahee River Raid

Beaufort and the Sea Islands region, Spring 1863

Harriet Tubman's eyes opened to the sounds of a rooster crowing. She gazed toward a nearby window, trying to rouse herself from sleep. It took a few moments for her eyes to focus. It was like her spirit needed to walk out of a haze to rejoin her body and allow her eyes to focus.

Must be havin' one my spells again. Lawdy, can't afford such nonsense today. My mind needs to be alert.

Harriet shook her head to dispel the lingering shadows in her mind. She rubbed the dent above her left eyebrow. It was the deep scar she carried from her youth when an overseer threw a lead weight intended for another enslaved child who had escaped his wrath and instead delivered a stunning blow to Harriet's skull. She was just thirteen. The overseer was never held accountable, and Harriet was blamed for defending a fellow enslaved child. As a result of those injuries, she experienced headaches and dizzy spells.

Nevertheless, the trauma brought her closer to the Lord, and she forged a special relationship with Him. It seemed He appointed her as one of His special angels on Earth. Following the incident, she started to receive special messages and visions, seemingly Divine in nature. Without fail, she carried over one hundred souls to freedom and never lost one.

Fortunately, Harriet was already reclining when this particular spell came on, but she wasn't always so fortunate. She really couldn't predict when an episode might strike; she could be anywhere. When she suffered a spell, she still had some sense of what was going on around her, but it would fade into the background. Reality would be covered in a fog of sorts. Other visions would appear with great clarity. Sometimes it would be which path to take in the woods, a path she had never seen before. Other times she heard singing so lovely Harriet was convinced it was the angels themselves. On very rare occasions, she thought she heard the voice of the Almighty Himself telling her of danger ahead or directing her where to go. He bolstered her and lent guidance in her darkest times when the situation looked the bleakest. Harriet never shared these messages with others; she would only say she figured out which way to proceed. Her scouts and even the Union officers learned to rely on Harriet, as her insight and intelligence, from whatever source she might derive it, was always reliable.

After several months of working together, General Hunter and Harriet Tubman formed an alliance. Hunter was a true-hearted abolitionist and a zealous advocate for people of African descent. Harriet didn't always approve of Hunter's renegade methods, but she knew his heart and his intentions were true. The two had collaborated on several projects and missions over an extended period and had grown to trust one another. The general took pause when she spoke, and he always seemed open to listening to her insight and advice. In all her time there, Harriet had never steered the general wrong, not even once.

Harriet shook off her thoughts and tossed back the white sheet that covered her petite but sturdy body. Determined to get a move on, she swung her feet onto the chilly, wide floorboards. She scurried about the room, picking up the items she would need for the day, and tucked them into her knapsack. She pulled out her clothing—a skirt, a petticoat, and a simple Negro cloth shirt she had freshened up with a pitcher of water and a basin already. After tidying herself up and pulling her hair back in a tight bun, she quickly dashed down the steps of the rooming house on Craven Street in the town of Beaufort. She rushed through the kitchen house at the back of the dwelling to grab a few items to eat then headed down to the waterfront so that she could get on one of the boats headed to the Union encampment at Hilton Head.

Harriet was on her way to request General Hunter's involvement in yet another undertaking. Harriet walked briskly across the grounds outside the officer's executive quarters. Taking two steps at a time, she bounced up to the platform and entered the anteroom.

Harriet nodded at the private in the outer office. "Mornin'. I'm here to see General Hunter. I'm anxious to meet with him if he's available."

"Let me check. I believe he is in conference with an officer right now, but I know he will want to see you." The private rose from his desk and promptly walked toward the general's door. After tapping lightly, he entered.

Standing outside the general's door, Harriet overhead the following conversation:

"Sir, Miss Tubman is here to see you. She is anxious to speak with you if you're available, General," announced the private.

A lieutenant interrupted. "Surely sir, she will have to wait this time. We need to finish our conversation. We've needed to finish our discussion for a week now."

"Lieutenant, please!" the general barked at the whining officer.

"But sir, I need to get your final approval before my men and I move out. I want to make sure you approve our strategy and plans, otherwise, we'll be stuck here."

In a blustery tone the general admonished, "Lieutenant, I don't have that much confidence in the intelligence you are relying on or your strategy, whereas Miss Tubman has never been wrong. Her intelligence has always been reliable and dead on. Her planning and approach have always been completely flawless. I believe it may be a better investment of my time. Thus far, I have never had a failed mission with her. I cannot say the same with you, sir. You're dismissed, Lieutenant!"

Harriet heard a chair scrape across the wooden floor and heavy boots hit the floor at a fast clip.

A few moments later, a red-faced lieutenant with flaming red hair exited the general's office and shot a scowling look at Harriet. She returned his glance with a nod, along with a satisfied smile and a small wave. The lieutenant stormed out of the anteroom and slammed the door.

"The general will see you now." The private stuck his head out of the door and waved Harriet into the office.

General Hunter rose to his feet as Harriet entered and greeted her with a smile. "Good morning, Miss Tubman. How are you this day? I assume you have something on your mind?" He shot her a quizzical look.

"Yes sir, I do. I just learned through my scouts that the Confederates are goin' to be pullin' back and movin' farther inland this summer. The Rebels are concerned 'bout disease coming into the wetlands, bringin' malaria, yellow fever, and typhoid. I know you'll want to have your own men look into this, but if it proves to be true, it might be a good time to send a mission in the area while it's unprotected."

"Miss Tubman, once again you bring me valuable information and advice. What are you thinking of?"

Harriet leaned both fists on the general's desk. "Well, sir, it might be a good opportunity to raid the abandoned lands and plantation fields. We could liberate the slaves that live on those plantations. We would go several miles into the interior up the Combahee River by boat. We can't do this on land. We'll have to use gunboats and vessels that can get closer to the riverbanks."

"Oh, I see. Couldn't that be rather risky?"

Harriet nodded. "I know there are mines and torpedoes planted along the river, but my scouts can figure out where they are, map them out for us, and leave markers. If successful, we could do a lot of good for hundreds of slaves. I am sure when the Rebels leave, there'd only be a handful of white overseers left behind. Most of those planters don't really live there, or if they had, they are long gone. I don't think we'd have much of a fight."

She knew General Hunter was always willing to take unorthodox measures to achieve a solid gain or victory. Harriet held her breath while he pondered the matter.

"Miss Tubman, I admire your spunk and your ability to gather good intelligence from your group of spies in the field. The former slaves you work with that know the interior have been such a great help to us. Let me speak with my officers and see what we can work out. I will let you know. Thank you so much for coming to me. It's an honor to work with you." The general rose and extended his hand.

Harriet shook it, nodded, and smiled broadly. "I will wait to hear from you then. I know we can do some good for a lot of scared folks. I feel it in my bones. This plan will work, General. I know it."

Both parties knew it would be arduous for Harriet's scouts to map out all the mines, then known as torpedoes, along the Combahee River. These rather simplistic ordinances were often made of nothing more than old beer barrels and cow bladders stuffed with gun powder and filled with air so they could be suspended in the water. The more sophisticated torpedoes were coal set in a block of cast iron and dipped in beeswax and pitch, then covered with coal dust to elude the enemy. But Harriet knew she had a team of local Black watermen who could do the job.

Before the Union forces could strike out on the mission Harriet had suggested to liberate the hundreds of enslaved workers on the rice plantations situated along the Combahee River, General Hunter was relieved of duty. He had taken a series of unfortunate steps that concerned his commanding officers. Hunter was replaced by Brigadier General Quincy A. Gillmore and other lower-ranking officers. Among them was Colonel James Montgomery, a forty-eight-year-old from Ashtabula County, Ohio, who had led antislavery partisans in Kansas. He was known as a "Jayhawker" or one of the "red legs," guerrillas who often clashed with pro-slavery groups and occasionally cooperated with John Brown in "Bleeding Kansas." Montgomery served as the colonel of the 3rd Kansas Infantry Regiment, which he led in ruthless strikes against Missouri slaveholders until given command of the embryonic 2nd South Carolina in Port Royal.

Around this same time, DuPont, now US Navy commadore, was asked by President Lincoln to focus his energies on Charleston Harbor, planning a strategic attack with ironclad ships. For months a group of men in Washington, including Captain John Dahlgren, who commanded the Washington Navy Yard, Secretary of the Navy Gideon Wells, his deputy, Gustavus V. Fox, and others debated how an attack should be executed. Eventually, DuPont was pulled from the Beaufort area and his reluctance ended up in his undoing.

On the night of June 1, 1863, Harriet Tubman and Union troops under the command of Colonel Montgomery decided to raid recently weakened Confederate lines. Just as Harriet Tubman's intelligence had reported, Confederate General Walker, who led the Rebel troops in the region, had moved a number of his troops away from the marshy lowlands of the area to healthier inland regions to escape diseases. Unbeknownst to the Confederate general, hundreds of slaves had received word through the Underground Railroad and Harriet's roughly fifteen scouts of an imminent rescue near the Union lines on the Combahee River. Harriet's scouts and spies had surreptitiously removed many of the torpedoes along the waterways and sketched out those that remained.

Harriet consulted with Colonel Montgomery before undertaking the raid and went over the details of the proposed plan. Harriet knew that Montgomery was a man of action and bravado, a known guerilla fighter. He was known to use uncommon tactics to achieve his objective of ending slavery. On the evening of June 1, 1863, Harriet asked that their approach be changed and to get to the Combahee by heading northeast, then northeast through the Coosaw River, thereby approaching their target through St. Helena Sound. It was a safer alternative to avoid torpedoes and sandbars. Montgomery agreed with her suggestion. Thereafter, the three ships: the *John Adams, Harriet A.Weed* and *Sentential* headed out on one of the most consequential missions of the war.

Harriet Tubman rode on the upper deck of the lead gunship and guided the Union troops of the 2nd South Carolina Infantry. In so doing, she was the first woman to lead an expedition under the command of Colonel Montgomery and his troops. Montgomery himself called her "invaluable," as she and her scouts had alerted Union troops about concealed enemy torpedoes along the waterways. With her were the Black troops from the Port Royal Sound region who acted as guides through the hazardous waters, enabling her to avoid sandbars, cypress swamps and marsh areas, and all the waterways that fed into them. Although Colonel Montgomery was the officer in charge, he rode on the lower deck below Tubman.

The boats traveled several miles inland to reach their destination from Beaufort into Colleton County, South Carolina. Starting out under the cover of darkness on June 1, it wasn't until the early morning hours of June 2, 1863, that they reached their destination. A total of three hundred troops were on board the ships involved in the mission headed by Colonel Montgomery and supported by Company C of the Rhode Island Heavy Artillery manning the ships' guns.

Whether her sense of direction was based on hard information or divine intervention, one will never know. In the dark of night, she managed to guide a strike force of nearly two hundred and fifty men through the winding river to a specific marshy spot. Late into the night, Union gunboats made an unexpected appearance in and around the Combahee rice plantations. They stopped at Tar Bluff, Nicholas Plantation, and Combahee Ferry where the Yanks repelled Confederate troops, then gathered up supplies. Then they landed around Middleton plantation. The unprepared handful of White overseers hastily fled the area, just as Tubman had predicted, leaving the unsupervised Black field workers to flee the area, without impediment. After the shrill piping of the gunboat whistles, which signaled the bondsmen, the Black freedom seekers knew their liberators had arrived.

The gunboats dispatched rowboats to pick up runaway slaves. The bondsmen quickly gathered up their few possessions and began to flee. Those seeking to escape started to run toward the ships, first in clusters, then in large droves. They poured onto the rice fields and ran toward the awaiting ships. The jubilation rose up, as cheers and laughter rose from the crowd.

Gullah women had baskets on their heads while hauling bags of goods. Mothers carrying babies and pulling small children by their hands cried tears of joy. Some of the new mamas had twins that they tied in sacks hanging around their necks. Men carried burlap bags of belongings and foodstuffs as they rushed to freedom. Jubilant enslaved Negroes hurried through the Federal pickets, blessing the soldiers and giving thanks as they scurried onto the vessels. Scampering toward the Union ships were squealing pigs, clucking chickens, and barking dogs. One woman brought two pigs, one white and one black, and they were taken aboard a vessel. They were later named Beauregard and Jeff Davis. Harriet and some of the soldiers laughed uncontrollably at the sight of one particular enslaved woman as she passed by with a wooden bucket on her head, rice still smoking in it as she had just grabbed it from an open fire, while one toddler hung onto her skirt and another clutched to her waist with his legs, one arm wrapped around her neck, digging into the rice pot and eating with all his might despite its heat.

Meanwhile, some of the enslaved, afraid of being left behind, jumped into the river and held onto the sides of the boats as they feared the gunboats wouldn't wait for them. They worried this was their only chance at freedom. The soldiers worried that the boats might capsize, and the oarsmen initially beat the hands of the fleeing bondsmen, but later relented. Somehow by God's grace, everyone made it back to the encampment and safety.

Some of the troops destroyed the improvements that had been made to the fields, breaking up the floodgates and dikes. Rice barns, mansion houses, and outbuildings were burned. Angry former slaves sought vengeance for all the hardship and brutality they had endured. This was done with the consent and approval of Colonel Montgomery, as it seemed like an equitable remedy. Embolden Blacks rounded up horses, livestock, goods, and other assets. All of this was taken down to the waterfront to be transported back to the encampment. This lush, fertile land in which the tidal rivers flowed was a valuable seizure for the Union forces.

Two Confederate cavalrymen watched on horseback from a nearby bridge, offering no resistance. They remained partially in the shadows, helpless to do anything but observe. The Union boats moved past them, and the songs of the newly freed slaves wafted up. The Rebs turned their heads away from the sound as if joyous sound slapped their face in an offensive manner, only adding further offense to the night.

Issac was on the second gunboat returning to the encampment. He leaned against the side with his long gun balanced on the floor of the ship, glancing at the full moon. He wondered if his dead father, Cuffee, might have been able to look down on him and see what had just happened. He knew his father would have been proud of him and delighted to see so many enslaved people freed in one night.

Suddenly, Issac heard the neighing sounds of a horse, then a nickering. It was somewhere on a ridge or hill above him; he spotted the outline of a stone bridge overhead. The moonlight divulged silhouettes of two men on horseback. He paused and scrutinized the images, discerning the outline of the two Rebel officer hats and their gear. Not knowing what the men might do, Issac aimed his rifle just slightly below the brim of the hats. He fired off one round, then a second, almost as if it were a reflexive act. The first body fell from his mount, then the second. *Must have been Papa guiding my hand. I doubt I could have done that all on my own.* Issac saw a brilliant star flash at him. It was almost a wink.

"I see ya, Papa," Issac whispered with a warm smile.

Meanwhile, those around him abruptly stopped and looked toward him.

"What was that?" an officer shouted to him.

"Saw two Rebel officers up on that overlook, sir. I took 'em out. All is quiet now, sir." Issac ducked his head to the officer as a sign of respect.

"Good job, son. Like your gumption!" the officer replied.

The calamity in the boats started to rise up again after the shots were fired as the fleeing bondsmen feared the return of the Rebel soldiers. The Union troops made attempts to calm the crowd but weren't sure what to do. Harriet decided to take matters into her own hands. In order to quell the chaos, Harriet, who did not speak the Gullah language, took her place on the deck of one of the ships. She began to sing a song popular from the abolitionist movement to soothe the crowd:

> *"Of all the whole creation in the east*
> *or in the west*
> *The glorious Yankee nation is the*
> *greatest and the best*
> *Come along! Come along!*
> *don't be alarmed."*

As she began to sing some well-known gospel songs in a hushed tone, the panicked fugitives began to shout "Glory!" But in a few minutes, Harriet's calming voice soothed them, and the refugees joined in song. As she continued to sing, a calm came over the group and the din began to dissipate. They were grateful to be on a ship, knowing they were being carried to safety.

The enslaved refugees clung to one another, hopeful theirs was a ride to freedom and a new life. They sent up thanks to God with gospel songs giving thanks to God for his grace that night. They threw up their arms in praise. Of those who escaped, about one hundred joined the Union Army and fought bravely for their cause, not only for the Union but for their people, all the African Americans who had been brought to this country against their will.

Harriet Tubman

Sketch of the Combahee River Raid

Harriet Tubman was born under the name of Araminta "Minty" Ross around 1820 or 1821 (exact date unknown) in Dorchester County, Maryland, on the state's Eastern Shore. Birth certificates were not issued to Negroes until well into the twentieth century, so her exact birth date is unverifiable. Harriet was rented out to a series of different slaveholders in her youth and experienced a very harrowing childhood.

When she was around the age of twelve, she was rented to a local farmer to help pull in the fall harvest. During the course of her work, she sustained a traumatic head injury while trying to protect a fellow slave who was about to be harmed by his overseer for leaving the field early. The overseer hurled a lead weight at the field hand but instead struck Tubman, breaking her skull. She was placed on the seat of a loom where she stayed for the remainder of the day and on into the next.

She was ultimately sent back to her slaveowner, Edward Brodess, with a report that she was "not worth a sixpence." It took months for Harriet to recover from her injuries. For the remainder of her life, she experienced what was believed to be narcolepsy and epileptic seizures of some type.

Prior to the incident, Harriet had grown into a strong, well-muscled enslaved field hand. She learned to love the land, where flora and wildlife reflected the seasonal change. Whippoorwills would serenade her on summer evenings, and during autumn, Canadian geese often squawked overhead during their southern migration. While working in the outdoors, she saw God's hand at work, and her faith strengthened. Harriet experienced an intensification of her Christian faith, a deep and abiding spiritual foundation that remained with her throughout her life, no matter what hardship confronted her.

In her later teenage years, she began to work for a local entrepreneur named John Stewart, who over a period of several decades had built up a thriving lumber business. Several of Harriet's family members also worked for this man. It seems that somehow through this connection in the lumber trade, Harriet met her husband, John Tubman, who also ran a local lumber business.

Tubman was the family name of wealthy Catholic Dorchester County planters who established an estate in the seventeenth century. According to records maintained in Dorchester County, Maryland, there were eight Tubman households, three of which were Black and five of which were White families. Harriet married a free Black man from the area when she was around age nineteen in 1844. It is unclear which household John Tubman was from and if he had been born free.

After several years as a married woman, Harriet eventually decided she could no longer endure life as an enslaved worker. This occurred when Harriet's slave master threatened to sell her "down river," just as he had sold her two sisters. Soon thereafter, she devised a plan to run away. Harriet wanted to remain married to Tubman and initially assumed he would join her. To her surprise, he refused. He didn't want to leave his business and his extended family who lived in the area. Although they had celebrated their union as man and wife, it was not legally binding, merely ceremonial.

It was during this time that she contemplated changing her name. Prior to her escape, she decided to take on a new name using her mother's first name of Harriet and her free husband's last name of Tubman.

Prior to her escape, she reflected on the knowledge she had acquired earlier in her life when she had worked near the waterfront for a shipbuilder. That is when she overheard Black dockworkers and stevedores exchange stories about the inner workings of the Underground Railroad system. They would garner a great deal of insight from the watermen who traveled up and down the Atlantic Coast and throughout the interior waterways.

Eventually, Harriet struck out on her own. She was enterprising, resourceful, and often, overachieving. She crafted disguises for herself that were disarming, first as an old woman wrapped in a shawl with a large sunbonnet, carrying two chickens, and secondly as a young lad with a newsboy cap. Drawing on the information she had accumulated on the Maryland shore, she headed to Philadelphia. The triangulated region covering southeastern Pennsylvania, part of Delaware, and northeastern Maryland contained the largest concentration of free Blacks in the nation immediately before the Civil War. Wilmington, Delaware, Baltimore, and particularly Philadelphia supported large communities of people of color. Philadelphia and its surrounding county had more than twenty thousand African Americans by 1847.

Harriet was a very likable sort. She was witty and gregarious and known as a great storyteller. She held an ebullient spirit and a strong will that served her well, as well as those who were entrusted to her. This enabled her to escape from slavery in 1849, and shortly thereafter she began her work on the Underground Railroad.

One of the symbols Harriet reportedly relied on to guide her on her journey was lawn jockeys, modeled after General George Washington's loyal enslaved groomsman, Jocko. Legend has it that this young, enslaved boy waited outside all night for his master to return from his crossing of the Delaware River. Jocko held on tight to a lamp and the reins of the horses, awaiting the return of his master. Unfortunately, the boy froze to death before anyone could come to relieve him. The Underground Railroad adopted these statutes to signal travelers. Depending on the colors of the garb they wore, it alerted a runaway slave whether the dwelling could offer a safe harbor or to keep moving as danger was afoot. Armed with this knowledge and good fortune, Harriet traveled some ninety miles on foot via the Underground Railroad, where she ultimately found shelter and protection in the free state of Pennsylvania. It was there that she initially began to use her new identity of Harriet, her mother's name, and dropped her name of Minty. Two years later, she secretly returned to her marital residence in her home state of Maryland. She discovered her husband had taken a new wife. She abruptly left, never to return.

Harriet Tubman had seemingly been called by God to lead

the enslaved to freedom and to prepare them for this next stage of life as free people of color. Her work in the fields of the Eastern Shore of Maryland helped her develop a strong, fit body despite her small stature. Along with this physical strength, she took on great religiosity and received visions she believed were Divine in nature. Some believed that she was so connected to God Himself, and many referred to her as "Moses." Harriet was quite clever and often very calculating. Although she was illiterate, she was quite bright. She memorized most of the Bible and often put special quotes in her messages or used Scripture passages as passcodes to ensure the identity of the Underground Railroad conductors. Harriet also carried daguerreotypes of Underground Railroad workers. Tubman's treasured pack of *cartes-de-visite* became her insurance policy. She would ask folks to name those depicted to test their credentials.

Harriet helped John Brown plan his 1859 raid of a Harpers Ferry arsenal located in Virginia. It was one of the major events that led to the Civil War. When Harriet first escaped from Maryland, she traveled to Philadelphia, later relocating to Ontario after the Fugitive Slave Act became US law in 1850. (The act threatened imprisonment for anyone caught assisting a fugitive and meant she was at greater risk of capture if she stayed in the US.) It was in Canada that she first met John Brown, an abolitionist who believed that if he armed enslaved people with weapons, it would lead to widespread revolts and an end to slavery. Harriet helped him plan his raid on a federal arsenal by recruiting supporters and sharing her contacts and information on escape routes in the region. Brown valued her knowledge and referred to her as "General Tubman."

Prior to arriving in Beaufort, Tubman had rescued around three hundred slaves. Her clandestine service continued for several years. In addition to her ability to safely deliver the enslaved to freedom, she became a skilled operative, garnering valuable information for the Union forces. Tubman's spying and scouting strategies were so effective and well-developed that she reportedly taught at West Point

Academy following the Civil War. At the end of her life, she lived in New York along the Finger Lakes and established a home for the care of the ill and the elderly adjacent to her house where she continued to provide care for them until her death.

While Harriet was in Beaufort, she married a Black Union soldier who was subsequently killed during the War. She also continued to serve the Union forces for over three years as requested by the Union's Department of the South. Despite having to take leave to visit family up North, Harriet was never provided with a pension by the War Department for her service. She filed a claim for eighteen hundred dollars in the State of New York under her new married name of Harriet Davis and cited her service during the war under the direction and orders of Secretary Edwin M. Stanton of the War Department, but her claim was denied and her employment as a spy went largely unrecognized. It was not until the death of her second husband, Nelson Davis, that she received any compensation, and at the time of his death, it was for his service, not hers.

Harriet was given recognition by Queen Victoria for her service and in 2020, the Military Intelligence Corps made her an honorary member.

The house Harriet Tubman stayed while in Beaufort, SC., adjacent to Robert Smalls' church, Tabernacle Baptist Church, Craven Street, Beaufort, SC 29902. (photos taken by author)

Genesis of the Civil War

The city of Charleston, South Carolina, is nestled where the Ashley and Cooper rivers merge and flow into the Atlantic Ocean. At the time of the American Revolution, Charleston was the fourth largest city in the colonies and the most elegant. She was loved and admired by both Americans and Europeans for her ambiance and charm, her culture and gentility. This beautiful port city was well placed in a semitropical climate that flourished with flora not seen elsewhere along the Eastern Seaboard.

The foundation of Charleston's wealth was a series of dominant cash crops—indigo, then rice, then cotton, each dependent on slave labor. Charleston's White elite lived in constant fear of those it kept in servitude to ensure its prosperity. This dread increased exponentially starting in the 1700s up through the 1800s due to slave uprisings occurring in the Deep South and West Indies.

Ultimately, the city, state, and political thought became enmeshed with the economic system and its reliance on imported African bondsmen. In the struggle to preserve it, Charleston moved from an open society founded on religious tolerance and the free flow of ideas to a closed society threatened by and hostile to the outside world. This led to secession and a bloody civil war against a nation it once loved.

At the zenith of the King Cotton boom, after persistent urging from the residents of Charleston, the state of South Carolina, through its legislature, chartered the South Carolina Military Academy, or "the Citadel," in 1842. It was connected to the Powder Magazine at Marian Square, which had been in existence for some time. There was also a second facility situated in Columbia, South Carolina, referred to as "the Arsenal," a sister institution to the Citadel. Many of the cadets attended the Arsenal for the first year of their studies and then transferred to the Citadel in Charleston. As the days led up to a tense confrontation between the Rebels of the South and the Union Army, the lads at the newly established Citadel became eager for a fight. Their impatience was fueled by a perception that the Yankees were interfering with their way of life and long-cherished traditions.

The Citadel was established due to the pervasive fear that a slave uprising was possible, if not inevitable. There had been the Stono Rebellion near Charleston in 1739, the Haitian Revolution of 1791, and other skirmishes. The Denmark Vesey planned insurrection of 1822 in Charleston was the most notorious scheme in which hundreds, if not thousands, conspired in the region. This failed insurrection was followed by the Nat Turner Rebellion in Southampton County, Virginia, in 1831 in which sixty White people were killed in a day-long rampage by fifty followers of Turner. Trepidation heightened even more following all these events and persisted for years. Charlestonians were horrified at the thought of having their throats slit in the middle of the night as had been experienced in other attacks. Due to the significant imbalance in the racial composition of the city, Whites were fearful that they could easily be overpowered since they were grossly outnumbered. Some of the residents of the finer homes along the lower peninsula started to put up high fencing with *chevaux de frise*—barbs or sharp spikes intended to impale anyone attempting to scale the wall to harm the White owners inside. The Citadel had not been in existence to thwart any of the above-referenced uprisings, but it is believed that its presence, along with other stringent measures, helped to quell thoughts of liberation by Negroes.

Despite their fears, White slave owners never seemed to question the propriety of their peculiar institution of slavery. Free labor was a critical element in maintaining their way of life, a life they believed they were rightfully entitled to enjoy. The South had accumulated great wealth through its burgeoning agricultural endeavors, which took hold with rice and indigo, then later shifted to cotton. As the abolitionist movement solidified around the 1830s, slaveholders and nonslaveholders alike remained steadfast in their convictions. Opposition was not tolerated.

Charleston residents who spoke out in support of Negroes were quelled either by shunning or overt violence such as beatings and the burning of their dwellings and outbuildings, forcing them to seek refuge elsewhere. The notorious Grimké sisters from Charleston, for example, emerged as abolitionists, proponents of women's rights, educators, and national speakers. They were forced to move north and joined the Philadelphia Quaker society. Sarah Moore Grimké, the elder of the two sisters, was extremely bright and articulate. However, since she was a woman, her father denied her the classical education her brothers had received. She was confined to studying French, embroidery, painting, the harpsichord, and the study of books in her father's library. She used her brilliance in her later years to deliver talks on the horrors of slavery and was among the earliest of the major American feminist thinkers. The sisters chose to break from their family, religion, and traditions and leave their home state of South Carolina. They later became outcasts, actively exiled, and threatened with death if they returned and dared to spread their notions of equality for people of color.

Their father, John Faucheraud Grimké, was a wealthy planter and slave owner who owned multiple plantations in the Lowcountry, as well as the Upcountry of South Carolina. Moreover, he was a lawyer, educated at Princeton University, and later studied law at Trinity College at the University of Oxford in England. He worked as a barrister, speaker of the South Carolina House of Representatives, and as chief judge of the Supreme Court of South Carolina. He sired fourteen White and mixed-race children with his wife and enslaved female house servants, a fact that Sarah Moore Grimké found abhorrent.

South Carolina's Reliance on a Slave Economy

Rice planting, which was not introduced until the 1600s, steadily increased after 1695. This skill was attributable to the ingenuity of the enslaved Gullah workers. Gold rice is a complicated and labor-intensive crop, requiring five stages and substantial manpower. After swamplands are cleared, ditches are dug, and banks, sluice gates, or 'trunks' are installed to control the flooding of the fields. Stobs driven into the ground to control erosion demanded great engineering skill, skills that the Gullahs of West Africa possessed, but the White man did not. Moreover, the planters could not stand the stench that pervaded over the hundreds of acres of rice fields and feared diseases, such as malaria and yellow fever associated with heat and stagnant waters, and often departed for months at a time leaving their plantations under the care of the enslaved workers and a few White overseers. By April or May, the aristocratic planters enjoyed the cooler inland sanctuaries, such as White Sulphur Springs or other resorts and returned only after the first frost.

Unloading the Rice-Barges.

Enslaved bondsmen working in rice fields.

By the mid-eighteenth century, the labor of rice plantation slaves in the South Carolina Lowcountry afforded their masters the highest per capita income in the American colonies. They continued to earn huge profits for their masters up until the Civil War. Their wealth was only surpassed by that of planters who produced Sea Island cotton in the region around Charleston and Beaufort. This staple crop was worth five times that of other varieties of cotton. During the 1800s, the United States supplied 97 percent of England's cotton, 90 percent of France's, 60 percent of Germany's, and 92 percent of Russia's. King Cotton was the largest American export of its time.

Larger plantations typically encompassed hundreds of acres, sometimes thousands. Many planters owned more than one plantation, some as many as five or six. Such estates were in the hands of a relative few aristocratic families who held the land, most of whom could trace their heritage back to British roots. Although they benefited the most, a symbiotic relationship took hold with all the other merchants, shipbuilders, warehousemen, shopkeepers, restaurateurs, clothiers, theaters, public houses, racecourses, slave traders, bankers, builders, and other service providers, even the churches who tended the aristocratic flock and sanctioned their inhumane treatment of enslaved as the "will of God." It behooved Southerners of every stripe to keep the highly profitable system running, along with its strident caste system, which kept people of color at the bottom rung; mixed-race slaves were a step above, then recent German and Irish immigrants. Many privileged Whites had grown up being taught that they had to keep their way of life, fearing the economic and social implications of change. Their lifestyle of grandeur was important to the planter society. To help cement their social status, one of South Carolina's oldest and most exclusive social institutions, the Saint Cecelia Society, was established in 1766 and still exists to this day. Members must be able to establish their worthiness and heritage from the British Isles through their paternal bloodlines. Even in modern times, exclusive events, including the debutante ball, are held on an annual basis.

Along the Gullah-Geechee corridor, the ratio of those of African descent to those of European descent was invariably lopsided, varying with the particular community. (The Gullah corridor is that strip of land extending from Wilmington, North Carolina, to St. John's County in northern Florida, heading inland about thirty miles and including the Sea Islands.) The term *Gullah* is used in South Carolina and northward, while in Georgia and southward the term *Geechee* is used. The ratio ranged from one White man to four Negroes, to as much as one to ten, or one to twenty. Due to the great need for labor to keep plantations running, an onslaught of slave procurement occurred in the last decade of the Transatlantic Slave Trade in the early 1800s, causing a profound uptick in human trafficking.

The Transatlantic Slave Trade, which brought abducted Africans primarily from regions of Western Africa to the New World along what became known as the Middle Passage, went on for hundreds of years. The principal point of departure for the newly enslaved people was Bunce Castle in Sierra Leone, a holding place, much like an archaic prison, now a ghostly ruin. It was one leg of the triangular trade route that took goods (knives, guns, ammunition, cotton cloth, tools, and brass dishes) from Europe to Africa, enslaved Africans to work in the Americas and West Indies, and items, mostly raw materials, produced on the plantations (sugar, rice, tobacco, indigo, rum, and cotton) back to Europe. From about 1518 to the mid-nineteenth century, millions of African men, women, and children made the twenty-one-to-ninety-day voyage aboard grossly overcrowded sailing ships manned by crews mostly from Great Britain, the Netherlands, Portugal, and France.

The Transatlantic Slave Trade was deemed illegal by a federal law, which became effective January 1, 1808. It prohibited the importation of slaves from outside the country but permitted the domestic slave trade across the American South. Between the sixteenth and nineteenth centuries, upward of twelve million enslaved Africans had been shipped across the Atlantic to the Americas.

From 1804 to 1808, over sixty thousand Africans came to Gadsden Wharf in Charleston, South Carolina, from the Congo and Angola. Census records reveal that the St. Helena Parish population grew by 90 percent due to this influx of newly imported West African slaves. St. Helena is one of the Sea Islands adjacent to Beaufort, which absorbed this new slave labor into its ever-growing economy as the Sea Island cotton production thrived. Planters and those associated with the cotton trade realized tremendous wealth. This upward spiral in economic gains impacted the entire region and spurred numerous investments in civic institutions, such as those for higher learning, libraries, and churches. Beaufort wanted to be known as a distinguished community, and local planters built grand homes, leading it to be known as the Newport, Rhode Island, of the South.

By the 1850s, the "Negro question" was dividing the country. The Episcopal bishop of Louisiana, Leonidas Polk, decided it was time to create a Southern university and seminary to influence their parishioners to fully embrace slavery. This man would later become a Confederate general. James Henley Thornwell, a Presbyterian clergyman and defender of slavery from South Carolina, said in a representative sermon, "The Rights and Duties of Masters," delivered in 1850, that, "In one word, the world is the battleground—Christianity, and atheism the combatants; and the progress of humanity the stake." Thornwell contended that slave owners were the only true Christians and adherent to the "ordinance of God." To compromise on the slavery question was a sin in itself. Reason did not enter into it. Southern preachers began to not only tell their flocks that God approved of slavery, but also that the abolitionists were atheists, socialists, and communists. The progress of humanity was at stake, and these Godless people had to be stopped. (This claim took hold despite the fact that the abolitionists were led in part by religious fervor, one of the principal groups being the Philadelphia Quakers.)

Southerners hoped that Britain would back their states should a conflict with the northern states erupt, as their cotton was critical to the textile mills that served as their principal export. They played this card for a long time to the British dignitaries, pointing out that the United Kingdom needed the South's cotton, rice, and other agricultural products. However, the South also needed ships, armaments, and other instruments of war from overseas markets to be viable war combatants.

The exodus of free Blacks living in Charleston began in the summer of 1860 and continued as emotions spilled into the streets. For many people of color, there was uncertainty as to where they should travel. Haiti, which had led a successful slave rebellion and expelled French rule, was the top choice for many. But there was a substantial number of mixed-race mulattos who had strong ties to both their Black and White family members. They were reluctant to leave all they had known behind. It was a deplorable situation with an uncertain future.

Runaway Slaves Who Sought Freedom

While escaping to the northern states and Canada was the most common way the enslaved achieved their liberty, some found other means. It is believed that at least fifty thousand slaves escaped by following the North Star to freedom. A vast network of safe houses and means of transport was developed through a network known as the Underground Railroad (UGRR). It was most prevalent and successful along the East Coast, particularly via the waterways, as it was relatively easy to conceal runaway bondsmen in the hull of a boat, and they could be moved along their route swiftly. Moreover, there were numerous Black men who worked on the waterfront to assist runaways: fishermen, stevedores, freight handlers, teamsters, ships caulkers, semi-skilled carpenters, longshoremen, ship chandlers, shrimpers, and oystermen.

Less documented were the bondsmen who managed to escape by heading southward from states such as Texas and Louisiana to northern Mexico. However, this trek was riskier as there was no formal network to assist fugitives. Moreover, large portions of the journey were in wide open areas susceptible to detection. Nonetheless, some managed to successfully make the journey and join colonies of runaways in northern Mexico, many of which had indigenous populations from America's East Coast who had fled the Trail of Tears.

A limited number of bondsmen were able to gain their freedom by buying it from their masters; they would pay what was considered the fair market value as with any other commodity. Most of the enslaved had one day off a week, Sunday. The particularly ambitious bondsman could accumulate money by running errands, taking on other tasks, or hiring themselves out with their master's consent, or even running a side business, such as selling baked goods or fish. After decades of earning small change, some slaves earned enough "Sunday money" to buy their freedom. However, most were not so fortunate.

The South Carolina legislature outlawed manumission by way of a will or other documents. At one point, any Black person who claimed to be free was forced to leave South Carolina or face possible re-enslavement.

While many are aware of those who dared to run north to freedom, what is less known is that formerly free people of color were stolen away from safe harbors in Union states and then sold into slavery. It is unknown how many suffered this fate at the hands of unscrupulous slave catchers. This kidnapping of free people of color was a practice that came to light for many through the biographical drama film *Twelve Years a Slave,* based on the 1853 memoir and slave narrative by American Solomon Northup. He was born in the State of New York as a free Black man but was tricked into traveling to Washington, DC, where he was drugged and sold into slavery in the harsh Deep South of Louisiana. He was held there under tortuous conditions for twelve years before he was rescued.

The laws of the South actually encouraged the enslavement of free black people. One of the fundamental precepts of American Constitutional law is that a person is presumed innocent until proven guilty. But in the South during slavery days, African Americans moving about the streets without proper documentation or a "ticket" from their master were presumed to be runaway slaves and were promptly incarcerated. The burden was placed upon the accused to prove that he or she was free. However, all American states and territories barred persons of color from testifying in court. As a result, the accused was forced to sit silently throughout an arbitrary hearing while false evidence was introduced, identifying the accused as a genuine bondsman. Moreover, the accused was mandated to pay for their accommodations while detained, as well as all court costs. Those accused who lacked such funds could, and typically were, sold into bondage to pay the money owed.

Significance of the 1857 Supreme Court Decision in Dred Scott v. John Sandford

In March of 1857, Supreme Court Chief Justice Roger B. Taney stood among a crowd of anxious spectators and reporters outside the old Supreme Court chamber located on the ground floor of the US Capitol. In the marbled halls outside the chamber, a restless crowd shuffled their feet with anticipation and nudged one another as they wondered how the Court would regard an enslaved man, Dred Scott, who had lived for a period of several years on free soil in a Northern territory.

The facts of this case centered on a Negro bondsman who had served his White master, a physician in the US Army named John Emerson, as he traveled through various states and territories. Due to Emerson's many reassignments with the military, they traveled from Missouri to Illinois and then onto the Wisconsin Territory. For a period of about seven years, Dred Scott remained with his master even though he was situated in a free state and then later a free territory. When they returned to Missouri, Scott filed a lawsuit seeking for the court to declare his status as a free man of color. Eventually the dispute made it all the way to the US Supreme Court due to its unique facts and the remedy sought by the plaintiff.

Chief Justice Taney was a Marylander and former slaveholder himself. With a drooping and worn facial expression and tobacco-stained teeth, he announced that Black people could never be citizens nor considered "as part of the people." It became clear Justice Taney was announcing national policy and not just the fate of one man, Dred Scott, and his family. The listeners realized the gravity of the moment and began to stir; with questioning faces, they looked at one another in awe. Taney went on to say, "Every citizen has a right to take with him into the territory any article of property. The Constitution of the United States recognizes slaves as property and pledges the federal government to protect it."

The great crisis had for several years been percolating over the expansion of slavery into the western territories, such as Kansas. National newspapers issued a torrent of editorial commentary. Newspapers such as the *Daily Picayune* of New Orleans that sided with Southern Democrats, later to be known as Dixiecrats, celebrated the landmark decision "so adjude[ing] the vexed question of the times as to rebuke faction . . . and consolidate the Union . . . for all time." *The New York Daily Times* saw the ruling as a revolution against the federal government. "Slavery," it maintained, was no longer local; it was national. Taney's decision sought to resolve a powerfully divisive issue that, it turned out, he could not control.

The mounting consternation between the North and South was also fueled by the 1857 recession that threw hundreds of thousands of Americans out of work and led Northerners and Southerners to blame each other for the suffering. Fugitive slave rescues, some violent and successful, followed the Fugitive Slave Act of 1850. In May 1854, just as the Kansas-Nebraska Act exploded in American politics, a man named Anthony Burns, who had escaped slavery in Virginia, was captured and detained in Boston, Massachusetts. In the two days following his seizure, a large, angry, multiracial crowd had gathered outside the courthouse. The crowd, which sought his release, was armed and crazed. They stormed the building but failed to free the young, enslaved man, even though they managed to kill a guard. Amid great controversy, President Franklin Pierce sent some fifteen hundred troops to keep order and ensure the return of the enslaved man who had been captured to his home state. On June 2, residents of Boston draped their homes with black banners. The streets were overflowing with crowds of onlookers, largely composed of infuriated abolitionists who shouted as Burns was marched by with a thick iron collar secured with a padlock and shackles binding his ankles. A thick chain of metal was threaded through the clasp of each lock. Burns was led like an animal down to the wharf where he was to travel by boat to Virginia. There he was later turned over to the head jailer of an institution reserved for runaway slaves. No doubt this was where

Burns faced a long, torturous flogging from which he never recovered.

The Burns case provided another sensational story to a nation already reading Harriet Beecher Stowe's best-selling novel, *Uncle Tom's Cabin,* which was published in 1852. The book had raised awareness and galvanized Northerners, as well as Southern critics, around the issue of the fugitive slave like no other work of literature ever had. The novel's central theme is that "conscience is no match for the coercive force of the market." The novel swept up the American imagination and played a critical role in widening the sectional divide between North and South. Over the following handful of years, the country descended into disunion, and then later, into a bloody civil war.

Key Figures: Robert Barnwell Rhett and John C. Calhoun

John Caldwell Calhoun (Born: March 18, 1782; Died: March 31, 1850), South Carolina's revered statesman, was a lawyer by training who rose to become US vice president and father of South Carolina politics. Born in the Upcountry of South Carolina to parents of Irish descent, he was reared with a firm hand. As a young adult, Calhoun made quite a striking appearance in a crowd. He had a long angular face with penetrating eyes. He was very tall for the era, at six feet two inches, with thick, stiff, black hair that stood straight up, making him look even taller.

Calhoun's father, Patrick Calhoun, was a farmer, surveyor, justice of the peace, and one of the largest slaveholders in the region, and believed in iron self-discipline. The elder Calhoun passed these characteristics along to his son. Both men believed in the severe physical discipline of their enslaved workers and viewed it as necessary to keep their home and large farm functioning smoothly.

Although John C. Calhoun only lived part of his life in Charleston, he was the pride of the city. Calhoun attended Yale in New Haven, Connecticut as an undergraduate where he led a very studious life and rarely engaged in the frivolous college social rituals. Following his graduation from Yale, Calhoun studied law at the Litchfield Law School in Connecticut. After graduating, he was an apprentice at the prestigious law firm of De Saussure and Ford in Charleston. From there he rose through the ranks, making himself known in social circles, in part due to his association with Christopher Edwards Gadsden, a former roommate from Yale who was from a wealthy Charleston family, and Floride Bonneau Colhoun, widow of John C, Calhoun's cousin, John Ewing Calhoun, from a wealthy Huguenot family with land holdings in South Carolina and Newport, Rhode Island. Floride was Calhoun's wealthiest relative and served as his love interest for a time. She traveled with him on various trips along the East Coast and accompanied him to various social functions.

From 1808 to 1811, Calhoun, now well into his twenties, attempted to launch his legal and political careers. While networking with other planters and powerbrokers, he also gave thought to taking a bride. Around this time, he visited Floride Colhoun at Bonneau's Ferry, her Cooper River plantation. There he laid eyes upon her namesake daughter who was at age sixteen, a blossoming young woman. The younger Floride was pretty, petite, and socially accomplished, having been reared to take on the social and household responsibilities of a planter's wife. Calhoun looked upon her now not as a little girl, but a desirable young woman and fell quite hard for her beauty. The two were later married on the grounds of Bonneau Ferry when John was twenty-eight and Floride was eighteen.

Ironically, Calhoun also had a relationship with a handsome girl named Nancy Hanks, whose family ran a stagecoach tavern in Slab Town, near Anderson, South Carolina, in the Upcountry. The ardent young couple became lovers. In the course of time, Mr. Calhoun hired a man and bought two horses to take Nancy to her relatives in Kentucky where she bore a son whom she named Abraham. Sometime in the interim, she married a man named Thomas Lincoln. Her son, Abraham Lincoln, later went on to become president of the United States. Reportedly, Calhoun traveled to Kentucky to see

Nancy and Abraham once and thought of them often. This account was recorded by a neighbor of the Calhoun family in Abbeville in 1909 and sent to the *Charleston News and Courier*. The oral tradition of this story went back for decades. The tavern existed and so did Nancy Hanks; however, the Calhoun family denied the story, claiming that the timeline did not match, as that she was already married to Thomas Lincoln and had borne a daughter to him at the time of Calhoun's alleged indiscretion.

Calhoun emerged as an outspoken proponent of the nullification of federal laws that he believed adversely affected the Lowcountry's interests. He urged limited federal government oversight and the perpetuation of slavery. He assumed that Black people were naturally inferior to Whites, completely ignoring that South Carolina's wealth had been built on the ability of Africans to transfer complex knowledge and technology of rice cultivation to the New World. They mastered nearly all the skills performed by White craftsmen, including constructing classic estates, outbuildings, furniture, ironworks, and other items to go into the homes of landed White gentry. Calhoun often articulated his belief that slavery was a godly service as it had taken heathen Negroes from the jungles of Africa to civilization in America, providing them with an opportunity at salvation, training in a vocation, clothing, and shelter.

In 1837 on the floor of the US Senate, Calhoun proclaimed, "I hold then that there never has yet existed a wealthy and civilized society in which one portion of the community did not in ort of fact live on the labor of the other . . ." Slavery, therefore, was indispensable to Republican government. He considered it necessary to elevate the condition of Whites. Calhoun believed that what slavery had done for Carolina could be done for the Union, but only if the South was allowed to get its own way.

Calhoun died in March 1850 while still serving in the US Senate. He was staying in a boarding house in Washington near the Capitol after having been felled by pneumonia weeks earlier, apparently related to the tuberculosis he had contracted sometime earlier. It seems he never fully recovered from his illness. Following his death, he lay in state in the Capitol rotunda for three days and was then transported initially by train, then by a steamer ship, the *Nina*, to Charleston. Once his remains arrived in the city of Charleston, his heavy sarcophagus was received by military guards and slowly moved by an assiduously decorated wagon. His coffin was then transported to Charleston's city hall and flanked by military officers and an honor guard, Captain A. M. Manigault and distinguished pallbearers, including Jefferson Davis. The funeral itself was tremendously elaborate. Modeled on Napoleon's, it manifested every bit of grandeur. The entire city of Charleston was draped in black and mourned their cherished statesman.

Despite the death of Calhoun, his dogma and fervor lived on; Rhett Sr. carried his idol's work, spreading his ideology throughout the South. In front of the Rhett home was a bust of Calhoun draped in black with a green wreath in honor of the hero.

Portrait of John C. Calhoun 1845

But even Calhoun was not willing to go far enough on secession to satisfy Robert Barnwell Rhett. For Rhett, a newspaperman, secession was an obsession. And he hoped that one day his home state of South Carolina would see reason, break away from the Union, and appoint him president of a new Confederacy. It was a moment he had plotted for most of his life. He whipped up the locals through his antagonistic editorials and then sat back and waited for the populace to explode into a frenzy. Even some of the most zealous advocates considered Rhett a fanatic, even crazed at times, who teetered on the edge of lunacy due to his seething desire to avenge the North.

The *Charleston Mercury*, a Charleston newspaper, had an element of spark found in every edition; its tone could range from anger or annoyance to withering sarcasm. It would bait the readers to stay engaged and emotionally excited. The newspaper was first run by the father of rather humble beginnings, Robert Barnwell Smith, who later took the name Robert Barnwell Rhett. He handed over the day-to-day affairs to his son, Robert Rhett Jr. when he was about age thirty, although the father continued to hold a strong influence over the paper until his death. The senior Rhett used the newspaper to strongly defend slavery, a right Rhett, Sr. believed was given by God himself. Slavery. Blacks were nothing more than human chattel, with the same rights as a horse or cow, was euphemistically termed by Southerners such as Rhett as their "peculiar institution of slavery."

Rhett Sr. held himself out as an aristocrat of British descent, although born a country boy of modest means and took the name of a distant relative who had acted as the governor of the Bahamas. Rhett, like the lawyer and statesman, John C. Calhoun, contended that slavery was "a positive good," as slave masters provided their bondsmen with food, clothing, and trade, no matter how meager or inadequate. Scores of South Carolinians and numerous others throughout the South were deeply influenced by their dogmatic, if not fanatical, approach and faithfully followed their radical ideas. Rhett, Sr. was a member of the South Carolina Southern Rights Association, an organization that promoted secession and the perpetuation of slavery. He was regarded as the greatest of the "fire-eaters," radical Southern secessionists who had long been committed to the disunion of the United States and the perpetuation of chattel slavery.

There were several Southern rights groups during the 1800s, the best known being the Knights of the Golden Circle, which has remained in existence up to the present. This group managed to raise thousands of dollars in gold coins and stashed their bounty in secret hiding places throughout the countryside (some caches are still being uncovered to this day) and raise several thousands of troops that ultimately merged with the South's Confederate Army. This paramilitary group, formed in the 1850s, was a branch of the Masons, adopting many of its customs, signs, and practices. The group's objective was to create a country based on a slave economy. Geographically, the newly formed country's ideal was to form a large loop or circle, which was to include the Southern United States, Mexico, Central America, northern parts of South America, Cuba, Haiti, the Dominican Republic, and most of the islands situated in the Caribbean.

Robert Barnwell Rhett
Lived 1800-1876

The Rhetts' newspaper was a uniquely valuable tool. Despite widespread illiteracy among Whites in the South at that time, those who could not read were bound to have their views shaped and influenced by those who could. Rhett, Sr. believed nothing was as powerful as a daily newspaper to impact the thoughts and opinions of its readers. Charleston, along with the rest of the South, tended toward an alternating cycle of indignation toward powerful federal government control and inertia in pushing back against the Yankees. Rhett sought to keep their blood pumping and radicalized in their politics, in favor of secession, but conservative in nearly everything else, such as sexual roles, social protocols, faith practices, and the like.

Rhett Sr.'s office, located at 4 Broad Street, was in the heart of Charleston, just one block south of the slave trading district centered on Chalmers Street. Although the slave trade was once performed in the open, ladies of good breeding objected to the sight of naked heathen Negros on the open streets of their fair city. Hence, walk-in slave trading parlors with a slave auction gallery, such as Ryan's Mart, were established between the 1830s and 1840s. This house of trade, intended to impress men of means, had a stucco façade with octagonal pillars and a central elliptical arch at the central entrance. Inside were holding pens for those awaiting sale along with a morgue or "dead house" adjacent to the auction floor for those who died from disease, injuries, or exhaustion prior to making it to the auction block. In the center of the building was a kitchen and at the back was a barracoon or jail for "those who needed to get their mind right."

Notifying readers when ships, including slave ships, were due into port, the *Mercury* made a significant amount of money on the classified ads it ran for the slave trade. Other means of advertising included broadsheets circulated far and wide, sometimes as far away as Texas.

Rhett Sr. emphasized the absolute necessity for White solidarity during those years leading up to the War of Northern Aggression. His newspaper painted a dire picture of the future under a Republican administration that championed the rights of Negroes. "The midnight glare of the incendiaries torch will illuminate the country from one end to another, while pillage, violence, murder, poisons, and rape will fill the air with the demoniac revelry of all the bad passions of an ignorant, semi-barbarous race, urged to madness by the licentious teachings of our Northern brethren." According to this view, the South would face a war of races, and slave uprisings would be inevitable as White women would be raped and ravaged by Black men, and the South would end up with a mongrel race.

By the middle of November 1860, South Carolinians were seething with emotion. It was during this fervor that South Carolinian Francis Pickens, who had been serving as a minister to Russia, returned home in an effort to quell emotions. His ship docked in New York, and on his way home to Charleston, he stopped in Washington and met with President James Buchanan. They held a lengthy meeting in which Buchanan implored Pickens to influence his fellow statesmen to exercise discretion, to influence them on behalf of moderation, and to cease threats to secede, at least while he was still in office. The inauguration was still pending as Abraham Lincoln had been elected to office on November 6, 1860. Lincoln had been a candidate of the newly created Republican Party, which officially wanted to limit the expansion of slavery.

As Pickens left the White House, a prominent New Yorker and well-known attorney, George T. Strong, stopped him and pulled him aside. He told him that his fellow Carolinians were making a laughingstock out of themselves before the rest of the country. He advised him to rein in his fellow brethren. The red-faced Pickens was momentarily speechless, but then thanked the gentleman for his kind advice and quickly departed.

While Pickens intended to bring calm to the situation, once he stepped on South Carolinian soil, he too became infected by secession fever. He modified his views and urged disunion. Soon thereafter he gave a speech in which he announced that he would be willing to "appeal to the god of battles . . . cover the state with ruin, conflagration, and blood rather than submit" to the wishes of the Federals. He told the crowd what they wanted to hear, hoping to pave the way to his subsequent election to the governor's office. It was where he ended up, fulfilling those very words he had invoked.

Now having become every bit the fire-eater that Robert Barnwell Rhett or John C. Calhoun had been, acting governor Pickens charged ahead. On December 20, 1860, four days after the gubernatorial contest, the secessional convention declared South Carolina to be out of the Union. The state was now sailing an uncharted and irreversible course.

Robert Barnwell Rhett sent an invitation to the other Southern states, inviting them to likewise secede as South Carolina had done and join the new Southern political union. He hoped he would be ultimately chosen as president of the Confederacy and was quite disheartened when he was passed over for the position.

The Origins of the States Rights Argument

Lawyer and South Carolina statesman John C. Calhoun introduced the idea that states had the power to nullify a federal law created by an act of Congress if state lawmakers believed it to be unconstitutional or adverse to their interests. It was a notion Calhoun articulated when Congress imposed a tariff that taxed British imports so heavily that the English demand for Southern cotton dropped considerably. This "Tariff of Abominations," as it became known, was a damning blow to the South Carolina economy. But this was only because this particular tariff affected the state's international trade with Britain on one particular commodity—cotton, a slave-dependent crop. At that the time, the textile mills in the Northern United Kingdom, primarily situated in Manchester, produced the vast majority of the yarns, cloth, and woven fabrics; moreover, it accounted for nearly half of all its exports.

Calhoun's assertion was perpetuated throughout the southeastern states that claimed states' rights outweighed those of the federal government, and lawmakers in a state such as South Carolina could thereby ignore an act of Congress.

Calhoun's prominence as a lawyer, statesman, and national leader, spurred courts in Southern states to declare federal laws null and void, even though such a declaration was entirely without legal precedent or based upon recognized law of any kind. Calhoun's bold action spurred what was known as the "Nullification Crisis," which he later conceded as being wholly without merit. The tariff was only the pretext, and disunion and the South's Confederacy were the real objects. It was directly linked to the slavery question.

By 1860, there were fourteen men in the country who owned five hundred or more slaves, and most of them lived in the Lowcountry.

Slavery was almost wholly the domain of the very wealthy. Three percent, however, held a considerable majority of the state's political platform and immeasurable sway with its citizens.

By 1840, the Southern states grew 60 percent of the world's cotton and provided nearly 70 percent of the cotton processed in the British textile industry. As a result, chattel slavery provided the capital and later the economic goods that spurred economic growth in North America. Moreover, because the Southern states specialized in cotton production, the North developed a variety of industries, services, and machinery, such as insurance companies, banks, shippers, and cotton brokers, which dovetailed with the South slave economy.

In 1830 and again in 1850, South Carolina held tariff conventions to determine the course for the much-loved state. Fortunately, on both occasions, the players backed down and decided to remain in the Union and submit to federal laws. But the ill will simmered.

For more than two decades following the Nullification Crisis, eleven Southern states had toyed with plans to secede from the Union and to expand slavery west into the Territories. The slavery question was at the heart of this turmoil. The Southern states were still based on an agrarian society and relied heavily on bondsmen to perform required physical labor in clearing swamps and marshland rife with alligators and snakes, along with the planting, maintenance, and harvesting of staple crops. Work started at "day clean" and ended at "first dark."

The Newly Formed Republican Party

In February 1854, political zealots of various stripes met in Ripon, Wisconsin, to form what would later become known as the Republication Party. These fierce politically minded activists were Free Soilers, Whigs, anti-Nebraska Democrats, and sundry antislavery advocates. They sought to fight pro-slavery forces and anti-immigrant nativists whose credo was "I know nothing." The Know Nothing Party, or Nativists, believed that all men were created equal except for Negroes, foreigners, and Catholics. Because of the splintering of the Democratic Party due to the slavery question, the newly formed Republican Party, and the four-way split, and favor fell Lincoln's way for the 1860 election.

The Democratic Convention of 1859

When delegates came to Charleston in 1860 for the Democrat convention by way of train, they were horrified at what they saw from their carriage windows; Negro slaves applying manure to the fields with their naked hands; men, women, and even young children involved with this putrid task. It was enough to set the Northern delegates back on their heels and question the institution of slavery. Overcome by the putrid odor of the rice fields and their stagnant waters, the delegates passed through counties such as Georgetown, north of Charleston, in the heart of the rice belt of the region. Delegates were dismayed by the living conditions of the enslaved they observed from their train car windows or train platforms. The Northern gentlemen had never taken in such a rancid odor that made one want to retch. The rice fields seemed to go on for miles and nary was a white face to be seen; only a few overseers were left behind in the already rising temperatures of late spring in the Deep South. The Lowcountry, being situated in a semitropical area, was already experiencing elevated temperatures and feverish humidity. Most of the plantation owners had departed for more pleasant surroundings, wanting to be away from the stagnant waters that tended to carry diseases such as yellow fever, malaria, and the like.

When the Democrat National Convention was called to order on April 23, 1860, in the city's Grand Hall of Charleston's South Carolina Institute on Meeting Street, a brief prayer was offered by a clergyman. In a matter of just a few beats, the assembly fell into heated bickering. Tempers rose along with the temperature of the semitropical city; the humidity joined the symphony of cantankerous shouting already rolling across the broiling streets with the pounding rain beating on the roofs with a mid-morning downpour. As tempers flared, the cacophony of heckling voices echoed throughout the chamber. Even the pigeons flew off from their usual perches to find relief from the rancorous sound.

William Lowndes Yancey of Alabama, an ardent fire-eater, took center stage and spoke in defense of wary White Southerners who believed the present and the future were slipping from their accustomed control. Yancy's voice blared across the hall, "Ours is the property invaded; ours are the institutions which are at stake; ours is the peace that is to be destroyed; ours is the property to be destroyed; ours is the honor at stake," Yancey added, "They would yield no position here until we are convinced we are wrong." It was evident that the Southern landowners, businessmen, and attorneys in attendance believed they were being judged as wrong-minded and hated it.

In Charleston, a majority report emerged from the 1860 Democrat platform committee. It was unambiguously pro-slavery, asserting that, "Congress has no power to abolish slavery in the Territories." Seemingly, they forgot that Congress held full federal authority in balance with the president and the US Supreme Court, the three branches of government. "We shall go to the wall upon this issue if events shall demand it, and accept defeat upon it," Yancey said.

A brief time later on the floor of the Senate chamber in Washington, Jefferson Davis, who would later become president of the Confederacy, announced to his colleagues, "We want nothing more than a simple declaration that Negro slaves are property, and we want the recognition of the obligation of the federal government to protect that property like all other."

A minority report in the Democrat convention took a more moderate position, suggesting the party avoid congressional action on slavery and support popular sovereignty. Although the preferred candidate of Northern Democrats for the presidential nomination was Stephen Douglas, who was viewed by Southerners as too yielding on the slavery question, they could not muster enough votes. Many of the more radical Southerners, full of pride and passion, departed the convention in a boisterous storm, having lost the platform vote 165 to 138. They were followed by Alabama, Florida, Mississippi, and Texas, who withdrew outright. They were then followed by South Carolina, Georgia, Virginia, and Arkansas. The report of the broken Democrat convention elated the newly formed Republican Party.

A Four-Way Presidential Field

Eventually, the mainstream Democrats reconvened in Baltimore and secured the nomination for Stephen Douglas, but it was a hollow victory. The party was fractured and limped along. The forces led by the fire-eater William Lowndes Yancey of Alabama had broken off for good from the Democratic Party, forming a Southern alliance and selecting Vice President John C. Breckenridge of Kentucky as their candidate for president. The Southern Democrats believed they were losing control and forged a fractious and wary splinter group. "Ours are the institutions which are at stake; ours is the peace that is to be destroyed; ours is the property that is to be destroyed; ours is the honor at stake." Yancey added, "[y]ield no position here until we are convinced we are wrong." The Southern Democrats believed they were being judged and hated the very notion of it.

Lincoln had been put forth as the candidate of the new Republican Party, and a fourth candidate entered the running, John Bell of Tennessee, a Constitutional Unionist moderate who represented the Whig remnant.

The Presidential Election of 1860

As the election of 1860 approached, tempers flared. To question slavery was to question the South's values, faith, and intelligence.

Lincoln knew that Americans would be willing to fight to preserve the Union, but not to enforce abolitionist beliefs. Despite his decades-long abhorrence of slavery, he now had to take on the mantle of a politician seeking office and hold a more palatable position that could reach a broader constituency.

Despite the lingering uncertainty, Lincoln had done next to nothing publicly, and precious little privately, to advance his own cause. Prevailing political tradition called for silence from presidential candidates. In earlier elections, nominees who had defied custom appeared desperate and invariably lost. Besides, when it came to the smoldering issue of slavery, the choice seemed clear enough. Although Lincoln had personally abhorred chattel slavery his entire life, in his political life he had to take a more palatable position. He was already on record as viewing slavery as "a moral, political and social wrong" that "ought to be treated as a wrong . . . with the fixed idea that it must and will come to an end." These sentiments alone had proven enough to alarm Southerners. But Lincoln had never embraced immediate abolition, knowing that such a position would have isolated him from mainstream American voters and rendered him unelectable. Unalterably opposed to the extension of slavery, Lincoln remained willing to "tolerate" its survival where it already existed, believing that containment would place it "in the course of ultimate extinction." That much voters already knew.

During the campaign, Lincoln confided that he would have preferred a full term in the Senate "where there was more chance to make a reputation and less danger of losing it."

On Election Day, Tuesday, November 6, 1860, Lincoln arose as he ordinarily did on a chilly autumn morning. He dressed in his usual attire of a formal black suit, first donning a stiff white shirt and collar, then winding a black tie carelessly around his sinewy neck. Next, he pulled on an ebony waistcoat and fastened the two rows of dark buttons. He collected himself before sitting on a side chair, then yanked on tight-fitting boots over his gargantuan feet, emitting a yelp when his heel hit the sole. Then the final touches came, a long ebony frock coat and his signature stovepipe hat.

Lincoln stayed in his office at the statehouse most of the

day, trying to busy himself with typical duties. He voted in the midafternoon. The usually sedate and self-composed Lincoln was observed by others in the statehouse tapping his leg and gazing out his window as if wondering what fate awaited him. He monitored the results through the evening hours and into the next morning via telegraph. In the wee hours of November 7, the returns added up to a Republican victory and his long legs carried him home to wake his wife, Mary, where he announced, "Mary! Mary! We are elected!"

Lincoln had won 53.9 percent of the popular vote in eighteen states that made up the North at that time. He won California, New Jersey, and Oregon with pluralities of the popular vote. In the Southern slave states, Lincoln only won 2.1 percent of the votes. Breckenridge, the Democrat candidate put forth by the Southern slaveholders, carried 44.7 percent. Bell was followed with 40.4 percent and Douglas followed with 12.8 percent. Lincoln's name wasn't even on the ballot in several Southern states such as Alabama, Arkansas, Florida, Georgia, Louisiana, Mississippi, North Carolina, and South Carolina. South Carolina did not bother to hold an election at all, and by way of the state legislature empowered the electors to give their votes to Breckinridge. By 1860, only one state, South Carolina, had ever used this procedure in a presidential election.

The Fallout from the Presidential Election

A few short weeks following the election of Abraham Lincoln as president, the city of Charleston had been abuzz with meetings nearly every night plotting their next move and how the upcoming Convention of the People of South Carolina would unfold. The convention was intended to take into consideration relations with the federal government. Robert Barnwell Rhett, Sr. was giddy with excitement. The ordinance he had promoted for years was finally being considered just blocks from his office. He held hope against hope that he would be the one that would lead a new Confederate nation as president.

"The Succession Movement"
New York: Published by Currier & Ives circa 1861, The Library of Congress

After several days of deciding bureaucratic parliamentary procedures and finer points on how they would be recognized as a sovereign country, the delegates to the convention finally got down to voting on secession. There was little to debate. An ordinance of secession was penned; the document itself was beautifully crafted and succinct. The roll call to obtain a vote of the 169 convention delegates who unanimously voted to secede from the Union took less than ten minutes. As a result, on December 20, 1860, the delegates of South Carolina, amid marching bands, fireworks, and flag-waving rallies broke from the rest of the country to form their own new sovereignty.

Depicted are: John Durant Ashmore Milledge Luke Bonham William Waters Boyce James Chesnut, Jr James Henry Hammond Laurence Massillon Keitt John McQueen William Porcher Miles
In the public domain

In short order, the *Mercury* newspaper had a special edition circulating on the streets of Charleston with Rhett's splendid news. A banner headline read *The UNION is DISSOLVED!* Church bells rang, the Citadel cadets fired artillery salutes, and businessmen suspended trade to celebrate in local taverns and public houses. The officers of the lower guard house stretched a line from their station to city hall and used it to hang a banner that featured a palmetto with a rattlesnake coiled around it, cannons on either side. The names of the fifteen Southern states surrounded the palmetto, along with the words, *Hope, Faith* and *Southern Republic.*

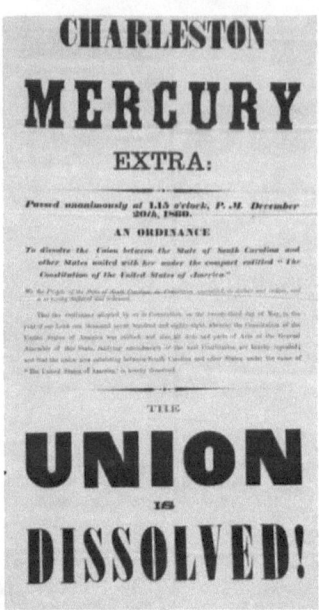

The first published Confederate imprint of secession, from the *Charleston Mercury*

Leading Charlestonians, lawmakers, planters, businessmen, and others in favor of perpetuating slavery voted in favor of the momentous document. That afternoon, the ordinance was rushed to a printer who was persuaded to prepare a final copy by that evening. On that eventide, a long line of dignitaries marched east on Broad Street, then turned north on Meeting toward Institute Hall, or what would later become known as "Secession Hall." This new Italianate building stood adjacent to the Circular Congregational Church and was Charleston's largest public venue, as it seated three thousand. Nonetheless, it couldn't hold all those who wished to witness this momentous occasion. At approximately 7 p.m., the delegates lined up to sign the document, in alphabetical order of their districts, tapping their toes and tugging on their beards as they waited their turns. It took over two hours for all the signatures to be scrawled across the parchment.

When Robert Barnwell Rhett Sr. took his turn to sign the

document, he seized the moment. With great aplomb, he captured the attention of the crowd and played it for all it was worth. Rather than merely bending over the table to sign the parchment, he dropped to his knees and bowed his head. Then pausing for the swarm of people to take in his moment of near swooning, he waited for a tittering to go through the crowd. His body trembled at this momentous occasion and his hand quaked as he grasped the pen. He had waited decades for this moment, and he was romancing the crowd with the notion that they might appoint him their leader and president of the about-to-be-formed Confederacy. With great flare, he dipped the nib of the pen into the jar of black ink, then carefully tapped it on the edge of the orifice. After pulling back his hand and pausing, he lowered his hand and scrawled his signature across the document. He then dropped his pen and lowered his head as if to ask for God's special blessing for his act.

Soon after that, the official document was complete. After nightfall, at approximately 9 p.m., the president of the assembly read from the freshly signed parchment, slowly enunciating each word. When he came to the word "dissolved," the crowd could no longer contain themselves. A roar was sent up that shook the building and reverberated throughout the halls. It went on for a handful of minutes and only ceased when the euphoric crowd lost breath. South Carolina had officially left the Union.

A handful of days following the vote, the committee of delegates drafted a report recounting the history of the country and what the South believed was increasing hostility on the part of the Northern states toward the institution of slavery, which in turn had led to their disregard of South Carolina's state sovereignty. The report was heavily laced with rhetoric about their need to perpetuate slavery with twenty references to the "peculiar institution." It was believed that federal laws that once supported human bondage were now being used against the institution and the heart of the South.

The president of the assembly went onto say, "These states have assumed the right of deciding upon the propriety of our domestic institutions and have denied the rights of property established in fifteen of the states and recognized by the Constitution; they have denounced as the sinful the institution of slavery."

As if a rebuke by God himself, both buildings where the proceedings had been held, including the large ornate Secession Hall, were later destroyed by fire in December 1861, one year after the Ordinance of Secession had been signed.

South Carolina state delegates later ratified the Confederate Constitution in the halls of the building on April 3, 1862, thus making South Carolina the first state to formally secede from the Union, what some would later consider an act of treason. However, President Lincoln, hoping to hold the Union together or at least reunify it at some point, carefully chose to term this act of defiance as a "rebellion," as a conciliatory gesture. Moreover, he promised Unionists or undecided residents of the seven seceded states that Union armies would take "the utmost care . . . to avoid any . . . interference with property." Americans from both the North and South knew exactly what kind of "property" the president was delicately referring to in his pronouncement; he would "avoid interference with," chattel slavery.

"Remains of the Circular Church and Institute Hall where South Carolina signed the Ordinance of Secession to leave the Union".

The citizens of Charleston were charged to an electrifying level as a result of the events that occurred earlier in the day on December 20. Their frenzy had them pouring out into the streets; their exhilaration was palpable. A few days later, they issued a statement blaming the situation entirely on the North's hostility to the institution of slavery. Within the document signed on that day, the Article of Succession, it was made clear that the perpetuation of slavery was the primary intention and long-term goal. It was delineated in each and every objective of their principal document. Whenever states' rights were mentioned, it was tied back to its impact on slavery, such as the fugitive slave laws, states' rights (tied into taxation for slave-produced commodities such as cotton), and dislike of Abraham Lincoln who was seen as supporting the rights of Negroes.

At the time of the Civil War, nearly all of the officers were West Point graduates, including Ulysees Grant and Robert E. Lee. For newly minted officers, following their graduation and appointments as lieutenants, many Southerners formally resigned from the

US Army to accept positions with the enemy Confederate Army. Unfortunately, they later killed US Army soldiers, some of whom they had held personal relationships with; some were even kin. Even worse, they abandoned the United States of America to fight for a new nation dedicated to one overarching principle, the degradation of an entire race of people.

Alexander H. Stephens, the Confederate vice president, addressed a secessionist audience in nearby Savannah, immediately following the events in Charleston. Approximately one hundred miles apart, the citizens of the two cities were in lockstep. Stephens called "African slavery . . . the immediate cause of secession. The new government's foundations are laid, its cornerstone rests, upon the great truth that the Negro is not equal to the White man: that slavery, subordination to the superior race, is his natural and moral condition."

Eleven Southern states seceded to protect and expand an African American slave labor system. Unwilling to accept the results of a fair, democratic election, they illegally seized US territory through calculated violent acts. Together this disgruntled group formed a new Confederacy, in contravention of the US Constitution, which many had already sworn an oath to uphold. West Point graduates such as Robert E. Lee resigned their commissions and committed treason, abrogating an oath sworn to God to defend the United States. They were not romantic warriors for a doomed but noble cause, but traitors to a country that had given them so much. They fought with all their might against their brothers and their own kin. They pressed on for four years during the bloodiest war in American history, taking more lives in such a brutal manner than all other American wars combined. Three million American men fought in this war; men sent into the country roads, corn fields, and peach orchards of the US slaughtered their own brothers. Young men who had never gone more than twenty miles from their homes were now traveling across the country, that at least initially, seemed like a great adventure. However, it turned out that the weaponry had become too advanced for the old military tactics still in use at the time. Well-disciplined men marched in straight lines into the meatgrinder. As a result, over two percent of the total population of the country was lost. It is estimated that at least 618,222 men died in the Civil War, but these numbers may be underrepresented. (Confederate statistics are not exact since many records were destroyed.) More than twice the number of men died from disease than were actually killed on the battlefield, usually from such illnesses as dysentery, diarrhea, tetanus, gangrene, and blood poisoning. Moreover, there were other transmittable diseases not associated with wounds and injuries, such as measles, typhoid fever, yellow fever, malaria, and pneumonia, which soldiers contracted in camps. These diseases killed at least 224,480 Union soldiers and 164,000 Confederates. The advanced technology used during the Civil War precipitated a substantial loss of life. Canons and guns could fire farther than ever, and a more highly effective bullet known as the minnie ball came into use. This small missile proved to be the single most deadly weapon in the entire war, causing over 90 percent of all wounds.

Hence, Lee and his comrades killed more US Army soldiers than any other enemy, ever.

The convention held in Charleston in December of 1860 resolved that any attempt by the United States to build up federal fortifications would be regarded as an overt act of war. President Buchanan in an attempt to appease the South had promised to maintain the status quo. However, he did not share this promise with his own military command situated immediately outside the city where the Ordinance of Succession had been executed, even though a telegraphic message could have sent the word. Buchanan was biding his time until he could slither out of the White House and leave the more challenging work in the hands of the newly elected president, Abraham Lincoln, when he assumed office.

Union officer Major Robert Anderson commanded the US Army forces in Charleston Harbor at the time. An experienced military officer and West Point graduate, he feared that the Rebels might launch a possible ground attack on the vulnerable Fort Moultrie, located on an outer area of the city by a strip of land on Sullivan's Island. The major chose to take evasive action to avoid a possible assault due to its proximity and accessibility. The fortification, constructed of palmetto logs, had been originally built in 1776 to protect the city of Charleston from British troops and did not appear to be sturdy enough to withstand a bombardment.

The relatively small band of soldiers under his command persisted in their fears of a brutal assault by the Confederates, the Citadel cadets, and the local militia, if not the local citizens themselves. Anderson, believing that his small unit of just eighty-five men might be sacrificed in such an event and the command of the harbor lost, chose to preempt an attack by moving to the federally owned nearby Fort Sumter that was situated in the center of the harbor and less readily accessible. Hence, the men quickly and stealthily packed up the unit under the cover of darkness and destroyed the armaments left behind. Anderson hoped his efforts would be to preserve the peace and avert a conflict. Although he was a Union soldier, he was from Kentucky, married a woman from Georgia, and had at one time owned slaves, he did not wish to ignite hostilities. However, he was wholly unaware of the sitting president's assurances to the Confederate leadership. The men made this move with only four months of food provisions and an uncertain future.

Nonetheless, the Charleston newspaper owner and ardent fire-eater, Rhett continued to try and whip up emotions in the *Mercury* newspaper when he asked, "Will South Carolina sit quietly with folded arms, and see a fort garrisoned by our enemies?" (Referring to the Union soldiers encamped for the United States military at Fort Sumter.) His ploy seemingly worked to inspire his readers.

Major Anderson requested that the federal government hastily send reinforcements, supplies, and additional armaments. In response, Union forces attempted to deliver a shipment of much-needed supplies to the encampment at Fort Sumter, but their efforts were thwarted.

The dwindling food supplies spurred a crisis. The men encamped in the middle of a harbor were forestalled from hunting and foraging outside the grounds since the fort was isolated on a man-made island constructed of seashells and granite from Northern quarries.

Throughout this time, Rhett Sr., used the *Charleston Mercury* as a platform to call for the war to get underway and for Yankee blood to be shed. The *Charleston Courier* newspaper had a far wider circulation and cautioned moderation as the tension heightened. Nonetheless, Rhett Sr. continued to beat the drum, calling South Carolinians to take up arms. Despite his goading, Governor Pickens wished to exercise discretion. He hoped Anderson would abandon the fortress. During this same time, Confederate Secretary of State Toombs wanted no part of firing on Fort Sumter. "Mr. President," he told Jefferson Davis, the newly elected executive who had just taken office on November 6, 1861, "at this time it is suicide, murder, and we will lose us every friend in the North. You will wantonly strike a hornet's nest which extends from mountain to ocean, and legions now quiet will swarm out and sting us to death. It is unnecessary; it puts us in the wrong; it is fatal."

President Lincoln and his cabinet had wavered on whether to force such a delivery of goods and munitions to Major Anderson, who was now holed up at Fort Sumter, as it might be seen as an act in preparation of war. The cabinet recommended foregoing the supplies and the attempt to soothe the South. Union General Scott advised Lincoln to abandon the fort; he reckoned it was now impossible to resupply without a big fleet and twenty-five thousand troops. Northern troops had been besieged by six thousand eager South Carolina militiamen and a semicircle of artillery batteries; it would require a major assault to put them down. Most members of Lincoln's cabinet agreed. The president wrestled with the issue for a few days but could not bring himself to abandon his troops and let them perish on the isolated Fort Sumter. He ordered those supplies to be sent to them.

Thereafter, a loaded vessel embarked to supply the men who

were being starved out. However, instead of sending a warship, the president sent a merchant steamship with a wooden hull, side paddle wheels, and two masts, thinking it would be less of a provocation. The *Star of the West* was a 228-foot ship originally built in New York City in 1852 for Cornelius Vanderbilt to use for commercial purposes. When the ship arrived in Charleston Harbor on January 9, 1861, the Rebel guns manned by young, spirited Citadel Academy cadets at Morris Island and Fort Moultrie fired on the ship, scoring several hits. The cadets, eager for a fight, were under the command of General Pierre G.T. Beauregard, who only served to add to their fervor. Not wishing to provoke a war, Union officer Anderson did not retaliate. He hoped his inaction would quell their spirits. However, the ship was prevented from reaching Fort Sumter. Union soldiers, already running critically low on supplies, were left without foodstuffs and other critical supplies.

Those shots fired that January day were technically the first of the American Civil War, even though they did not provoke a Union response.

A bold Governor Pickens promised in the last days of February that Fort Sumter would be taken. He wrote his wife in Texas that he had five hundred men ready to storm Anderson's little island. While in a drunken state, he made a fiery speech to the Citadel cadets in which he reiterated this promise and seemed to invite them to the charge. Pickens urged that Beauregard's command be expanded to include the entire coast, thus relieving the governor of this responsibility.

On March 4, 1861, Abraham Lincoln was sworn in as president. He and most other Northerners wavered on the question of war with the Southern states. They would go to war to keep the nation intact and to uphold the Constitution. Unionists contended that secession was illegal, a rejection of democracy and the rule of law. Secession would be a coup carried out by those enriched through slavery, either directly or indirectly, for their own nefarious purposes.

Abolitionists, who had gained momentum throughout the 1830's on up through 1860, called on the government to make war against lawful human bondage, arguing that slavery was not only inherently evil but also the root cause of the Southern states' drive for secession. They contended the nation could never be truly united as long as the institution endured. They were aware of certain Southern rights groups such as the Knights of the Golden Circle, a breakaway group of Southern Masons, who hoped to create their own country along with Mexico and other Caribbean Islands to form a new nation in which slavery could flourish.

Those more impatient for action finally prevailed. While skirmishes persisted over the weeks following, it was not until early April that the Confederate bombardment upon Fort Sumter commenced. After midnight on April 12, 1861, a party of Confederate emissaries rowed out to deliver to Major Robert Anderson an ultimatum from the Confederate Secretary of War Leroy P. Walker. The Confederates mandated that Anderson had until 4 a.m. to surrender, otherwise, the South Carolina batteries would open fire upon the federal fortification. Anderson refused to surrender and in a gentlemanly tone said, as he escorted his visitors back to their vessel, "If we never meet in this world again, God grant that we may meet in the next."

However, after a thirty-four-hour bombardment, Anderson surrendered Fort Sumter. The fort was engulfed in flames, much of it destroyed. Anderson had not fired a single shot. Miraculously, despite the hours of steady cannon fire, no lives were lost. The only casualty was a Confederate horse.

After the firing commenced on April 12, the governor was jubilant. Instead of being cursed, he was applauded. Although he had little to do with the battle, he took as much credit as possible. He puffed with pride as he spoke to the masses below from his balcony of the Charleston Hotel.

The *New York Times* soberly editorialized shortly after the firing on Fort Sumter, "The curtain has fallen upon the first act of the great tragedy of the age." The war that the fire-eaters had hungered for was now at hand. The glorious days of the Carolinians were now numbered, but in the closing days of April, excitement and joy ruled the Palmetto State, although Pickens' new popularity would prove to be ephemeral.

It was a bloodless opening to the grimmest war in American history. Entirely unimaginable before it began, the war was the most defining and shaping event in American history. Why have succeeding generations obscured the war with bloodless gallant myth, blurring the causes of the war and its great ennobling outcome—the freeing of four million Black people and their descendants from bondage?

From the Union perspective, this great war was spurred by man's greed, the desire to make a tremendous profit off the backs of people of color, and to continue a Southern empire previously unknown, one that not just planters benefited from, but also all the businessmen, craftsmen, and others that served them. Any White person could make demands of a Black man, and he had no recourse. Under the Black Code, it was unlawful for people of color to use force to defend themselves. The Negro was not even recognized as having the status of a person or human being, a legacy that lingered for decades, rendering Black people unable to vote, hold an office, sit on a jury, testify at a trial even if they were a victim of a crime, or buy a house. Some would say this curse persists.

It is time we come to terms with this legacy and all the residual effects of it that remain to this day. For too long, the history of the United States has been distorted; American textbooks have been full of half-truths about race-based slavery and the precipitating factors that led to the Civil War, a war that cost more lives than all wars put together and still divides our nation. Our country is fractured; hate groups spew bitterly divisive fabrications intended to inflame public sentiments. The Lost Cause Mythology is rearing its ugly head and we as a people need to educate ourselves as to the truth of our nation and our people. We have not learned from our bloodstained past; we are merely repeating it again.

Acknowledgments

In the long course of writing a book, one meets many people and incurs many debts, which are, in many cases, life-altering. I have been on a journey of discovery for almost nine years now, learning about the Gullah culture, the history of the Lowcountry, race-based slavery, and its residual effects on the Deep South and the nation as a whole. It has been challenging and one of my most satisfying life pursuits. Unearthing all the details and reasons the slave-holding states seceded, the history of the Civil War, and the unfolding of the Port Royal Experiment was an incredibly challenging and Herculean task. There was so much I did not know and so much we all still must learn. Through this book, I hope to give the reader a fair and equitable portrayal of our shared history, packed with facts, however painful, that reveal the truth of what happened here in the Charleston and Port Royal Sound area during the Civil War. Most of the people referenced in the book actually lived and worked in the area during the period; for them, I used their given names. A handful are fictional characters based on actual people who owned plantations or were bondsmen who resided in the area.

A very special and heartfelt thank you goes to my loving husband, Mark Niccum, who has been my stalwart support and the go-to man who has provided me encouragement and sustained me when I have struggled. I could always rely on my life partner to help me through so much and listen to so many ideas for this book and future books in the sequence. Due to the toll that research of this kind takes, I cannot imagine getting through the process without his encouragement that has sustained me through my darkest hours. He demonstrated an unflagging commitment to this book and my well-being. He listened to me read aloud drafts or sections of it, rendering compassionate feedback. I will always be thankful to my daughter, Allie Moorman, who assisted me with great skill and insight. Despite her hectic life, she took the time to read excerpts, assisted me with research, and provided advice. Without the support of both of you, this work would never have come to fruition. Like all classic heroes, they arrived on the horizon just in time to save the day and my sanity, allowing me to march on and complete this work.

So many people have given freely of their time and energy to help me gather important historical information that formed the essence of this book. It has genuinely taken a legion of librarians, archivists, local and regional historians, colleagues, and friends over a period of years to see this work come to fruition. This work could never have been realized without the insight and guidance of Pamela Main, who helped me expand, improve, and clarify my manuscript. Since I am an untrained writer, her professional insight and guidance were invaluable to me. I was fortunate to also have the benefit of a few beta readers who lent valuable insight due to their familiarity with the region, the Gullah culture, the history of the Lowcountry, and their command of the English language (a failing of mine having grown up as a poor inner-city youth). My undying gratitude goes out to Josette Grimsley, Tomilee Harding, and Ifetayo White.

Thanks to the many kind and considerate professionals and volunteers who have generously given their time and assistance and have made this project a great road to travel. In particular, I would like to thank Mr. James White of Worley International, Colonel Riccoh Player (Retired) USMC, Barbara Catenaci, Executive Director at the Heritage Library on Hilton Head, Richard Thomas, local historian, Caroline Bailey, former Volunteer Coordinator at the International African American Museum, writer Walter Curry, Jr., Ed.D., author and advocate Greg Estevez, and the librarians at the St. Helena branch library for Beaufort County. So many from the Gullah culture have given me insight into their culture and their experience, many of whom lived in Beaufort, Saint Helena Island, and Charleston. I particularly am grateful to those who took the time to review my manuscripts and provided edits and additional insight. Thank you for enabling me to go out and tell the truth about important, if not critical, events in our history.

Discussion Questions for Book Clubs

1. What do you imagine life was like for Big John, William Langdon's valet and trusted enslaved servant at Twin Oaks plantation? He was very bright and literate but had to kowtow and pretend as though he was merely following the master's good decision-making.
2. Emily Langdon, the mistress at Twin Oaks plantation near Charleston, enjoyed a privileged lifestyle due to her husband's success as a planter and slaveholder, yet seemed so unhappy. Why do you think that was so?
3. How were enslaved workers in Beaufort, South Carolina, impacted on the day of the "Big Skedaddle" when Union Officer DuPont's great armada sailed into Port Royal Sound? What thoughts and emotions might they have experienced?
4. What did you find most impressive about Harriet Tubman? Do you think she had a special calling?
   - Did Harriet genuinely serve with the Union troops? If so, why wasn't Harriet Tubman's military service recognized by the US government and subsequently awarded a serviceman's compensation? She spent three years attached to the Union Army in Beaufort-Port Royal Sound area and led the Combahee River raid. She even had to formally request leave when a family member became sick, and she returned home to Maryland. She only later received widow's benefits for her second husband after many years of disputing her claim. Was this a just outcome?
5. Robert Smalls was a significant figure during the Civil War for enslaved and free people of color, as well as Union troops. Reflect on his stellar act of seizing a ship and sailing to

freedom. Think of the detailed planning that was required of Smalls during the Civil War era Charleston to liberate not only himself but about a dozen others.

- Bear in mind that Smalls was a twenty-three-year-old illiterate enslaved man who managed to seize a 147-foot wheel vessel, the fastest Rebel ship in the region while running a gauntlet of Confederate checkpoints to deliver an extremely valuable vessel and its massive guns to the United States Navy. Through his daring action, he not only liberated himself and his crew, but his wife and two young children along with others. His bravery was in newspapers all over America and Europe. He ultimately served as a Union captain of the *Planter*, the Confederate ship he had previously commandeered and toured the world appearing to audiences.
- Might Small's actions have impacted White attitudes about African Americans who were regarded at the time as "simpleminded and passive creatures by nature?"

6. Reflect on the meeting between President Lincoln, Robert Smalls, and the minister Mansfield French who had been entrusted to carry a letter from Union Army Brigadier General (later military governor of the Department of the South) Rufus Saxton.

- What role did Robert Smalls play in changing the president's mind about the use of African American soldiers? Did that meeting prove to be pivotal?

7. How was Emancipation Day and the reading of the Emancipation Proclamation in Beaufort, South Carolina, unique from all other sites in the United States? What do you think it was like to be there and experience the event with nearly two thousand others?

Questions for College Classrooms

1. In the first chapter of the book, the lynching of a Black man occurred, something that was common throughout the Deep South. A lynching tree has existed in Charleston for decades. There are many others throughout the Charleston area. It was cut down in the 1970s, but then a new one was promptly replanted. Lynching is a practice that has gone on for decades. At one time as part of "Sambo art," Americans would send friends and relatives postcards of scenes of Southern lynchings depicting the Black victims hanging while a crowd of White onlookers smiled and pointed. Why was this tradition perpetuated well into the twentieth century and photos of the act sold for a profit?
2. What was the Charleston "sugar house?" What was its intended purpose? For twenty-five cents, a slaveholder could pay a jailor to get his slave's "mind right." This dungeon of terrors existed in downtown Charleston for one hundred and fifty years near where the Medical University of South Carolina (MUSC) hospital complex now sits. Ironically, no one in Charleston recalls it or ever talks about it. Why do you think this is so?
3. Why didn't President Lincoln want to use Black troops as Union soldiers? What was the political motivation to enter into an agreement with Confederate President Davis not to use Black troops? Why did he ultimately decide to use Black troops and muster South Carolina Volunteer ("Colored") troops?
4. Our current police departments are modeled on the antebellum slave catchers as characterized in the book. These men checked for identification, slave badges, "tickets," or travel papers. In recent years there have been many confrontations between law enforcement and people of color. What is causing the

underlying tension? Consider current calls to "defund the police" or spend more public funding designated for police departments on mental health workers who might be better able to defuse domestic violence situations or calm those with mental health disorders. What do you think might improve the dynamics and volatility of these situations?

5. Many jurisdictions still have "sundown laws" on the books as part of their city or county ordinances; others still engage in police practices consistent with the historic Black Codes of the South, which required people of color to be off the streets at a designated hour. Why do you think this is so? What needs to be done to rectify this practice? Should action be taken, or will it dissipate on its own?

6. A lot of animosity still lingers with regard to the Civil War or the War of Northern Aggression. Does it matter which side started the war? Should it matter that the South drafted the Articles of Secession and fired the first shots of the conflict? What about the Rebels desecrating graves after the first battle? What about the Confederate statutes and memorials that started to be erected at the end of Reconstruction (around 1890 to early 1900s) in an effort to reassert White supremacy?

7. Conversely, much like the United States dropping the atomic bomb on Hiroshima, the Union Army resolved to bring a swift end to the war after four years of brutal fighting and thousands of deaths on both sides. Sherman planned and executed his March to the Sea to bring a decisive end to the war. Was that a legitimate way to succinctly end the fighting? Many Southerners still harbor resentment regarding the destruction that was wreaked. Some say it took five generations to recover.

8. For a handful of years now, scholars and political pundits have been concerned that a second Civil War may be brewing, and

the Lost Cause mythology has been rearing its ugly head. Recently, a congresswoman suggested that the red states should "divorce" the blue states. On January 6, 2021, in a well-planned attack, members of far-right groups who were determined to overthrow a legitimate government stormed the nation's Capitol. The members of various extremist groups maimed and killed law enforcement officers and sought to harm, if not slaughter certain members of Congress and the vice president in an attempt to throw the presidential election. Such violence has never been seen by fellow Americans in recent times.

Select Bibliography

Afrika, Llaila Olela. *The Gullah: People Blessed by God.* Buffalo, New York: EWORLD, Inc., 2000.

Alexander, Michelle. *The New Jim Crow: Mass Incarceration in the Age of Colorblindness.* New York: The New Press, 2010.

American Battlefield Trust. *Battle Maps of the Civil War, The Eastern Theater,* Volume 1. Princeton: Knox Press, 2020.

American Heritage. "The Magazine of History," Ketchum, Richard M., Editor in Charge. *The American Heritage Picture History of The Civil War Volumes 1 & 2.* New York: American Heritage Publishing Co., (Doubleday & Co.) 1960.

Ash, Stephen V. *Firebrand of Liberty: The Story of Two Black Regiments That Changed the Course of the Civil War.* New York: WW Norton & Co., 2008.

Ashton, Susanna. *I Belong to South Carolina: South Carolina Slave Narratives.* Columbia: University of South Carolina Press, 2010.

Baker, Daniel and Gwen Nalls. *Blood in the Streets, Racism, Riots and Murders in the Heartland of America.* Centerville: Forensic Publications, 2014.

Bakke, Eileen Harvey. *L. Brantley Harvey: His Civil War Letters & Family History.* Arlington: self-published, 1993.

Bailey, Anne C. *The Weeping Time.* New York: Cambridge University Press, 2017.

Bailey, Judith and Robert I. Cottom, Editors. *After Chancellorsville: Letters from the Heart, The Civil War Letters of Private Walter G. Dunn & Emma Randolph,* Baltimore: Maryland Historical Society, 1998.

Barney, William L. *The Making of a Confederate, Walter Lenoir's Civil War.* New York: Oxford University Press, 2009.

Barrett, John C. *Sherman's March Through the Carolinas.* Chapel Hill: University of North Carolina Press, 1956.

Bartlett, Irving H. *John C. Calhoun, A Biography.* New York: W.W. Norton & Co., 1993.

Baumgartner, Alice L. *South to Freedom: Runaway Slaves to Mexico and the Road to the Civil War.* New York: Basic Books, 2020.

Benét, Stephen Vincent. *John Brown's Body.* New York: Rinehart and Company, 1927.

Berlin, Ira. *The Long Emancipation.* Cambridge: Harvard University Press, 2015.

Billingsley, Andrew. *Yearning to Breathe Free.* Columbia: University of South Carolina Press, 2007.

Blair, William Alan. *A Politician Goes to War: The Civil War Letters of John White Geary.* University Park: The Pennsylvania State University Press, 1995.

Blight, David W. *Beyond the Battlefield: Race, Memory and the American Civil War.* Amherst: University of Massachusetts Press, 2002.

Blight, David W. *Race and Reunion: The Civil War in American Memory.* Cambridge: Belknap Press, 2001.

Bonekemper, Edward H. *How Robert E. Lee Lost the Civil War.* Fredericksburg: Sergeant Kirkland's Press, 1998.

Bonner, Michael Brem and Fitz Hamer, editors. *South Carolina in the Civil War and Reconstruction Eras.* Columbia: The University of South Carolina Press, 2016

Bonner, Christopher James. *Remaking the Republic: Black Politics and the Creation of American Citizenship.* Philadelphia: University of Pennsylvania Press, 2020.

Boyle, Kevin. *Arc of Justice: A Saga of Race, Civil Rights, and Murder in the Jazz Age.* New York: Henry Holt & Co, 2004.

Bostick, Douglas W. *Charleston Under Siege: The Impregnable City, Civil War, Sesquicentennial Series.* Charleston: The History Press, 2010.

Bradshaw, Jr, Timothy. *Battery Wagner, The Siege, The Men Who Fought and the Casualties.* Columbia: Palmetto Historical Works, 1993.

Branch, Muriel Miller. *The Water Brought Us: The Story of the Gullah-Speaking People.* Orangeburg: Sandlapper Publishing Co., Inc, 2000.

Briggs, Amy. Executive Editor, Julius Purcell, Deputy Editor. "General Grant, From Cadet to Command," *National Geographic HISTORY*, July/August 2022, 76-91.

Brinson, Claudia Smith. *Stories of Struggle: The Clash Over Civil Rights in South Carolina.* Columbia: The University of South Carolina Press, 2020.

Brown, Alphonso. *A Gullah Guide to Charleston: Walking Through Black History.* Charleston: The History Press, 2013.

Budiansky, Stephen. *The Bloody Shirt: Terror After the Civil War.* New York: Plume Books, 2009.

Burton, Milby E. *The Siege of Charleston 1861-1865*. Columbia: University of South Carolina Press, 1970.

Burton, Orville Vernon with Wilbur Cross. *Penn Center, A History Preserved*. Athens: University of Georgia Press, 2014.

Camp, Stephanie M.H. *Closer to Freedom: Enslaved Women & Everyday Resistance in the Plantation South*. Chapel Hill: The University of North Carolina Press, 2004.

Campbell, Emory S. *Gullah Cultural Legacies*. Charleston: Book Surge, 2008.

Carr, Caleb. *Personal Memoirs of Ulysses S. Grant*, New York: The Modern Library, 1999.

Carhart, Tom. *Sacred Ties, From West Point Brothers to Battlefield Rivals: A True Story of the Civil War*. New York: Berkley, 2010.

Carse, Robert. *Department of the South, Hilton Head Island in the Civil War*. Columbia: The State Printing Company, 1961.

Catton, Bruce. *Grant Moves South, 1861-1863*. New York: Little, Brown and Company, 1960.

Catton, Bruce. *Grant Takes Command, 1863-1865*. New York: Little, Brown and Company, 1968, 1969.

Chernow, Ron. *Grant*. New York: Penguin Books, 2017.

Chestnut, Mary. *A Diary from Dixie*. Boston: D. Appleton and Company, 1905.

Clark, C., Grybowski, K., Lee, C., *Harry I Was?* Mount Pleasant: Patriots Point Institute of History, Science & Technology, 2018.

Cobb, James C. *Away Down South: A History of Southern Identity*. New York: University Press, 2005.

Coker, Michael D. *The Battle of Port Royal: Civil War, Sesquicentennial Series*. Charleston: The History Press, 2009.

Cone, James H. *The Cross and the Lynching Tree*. Maryknoll, New York: Orbis Books, 2011.

Cornish, Dudley Taylor. *The Sable Arm: Black Troops in the Union Army, 1861-1865*. Lawrence: University Press of Kansas, 1987.

Craney, Glen. *The Cotillion Brigade*. Columbia: SC: Brigid's Fire Press, 2021.

Crawford, Eric Sean. *Gullah Spirituals: The Sound of Freedom and Protest in the South Carolina Sea Islands*. Columbia: The University of South Carolina Press, 2021.

Creel, Margaret Washington. *A Peculiar People: Slave Religion and Community-Culture Among the Gullahs*. New York: New York University Press, 1988.

Cross, Wilbur. *Gullah Culture in America*. Winston-Salem: John F. Blair Publisher, 2008.

Curriden, Mark and LeRoy Philips. *Contempt of Court, The Turn-of-the-Century Lynching that Launched a Hundred Years of Federalism*. New York: First Anchor Books, 2001.

Curry, Jr, Walter B. *The Thompson Family: Untold Stories from the Past*. Columbia: Renaissance Publications, 2018.

Dabbs, Edith M. *Sea Island Diary: A History of St. Helena Island*. Spartanburg: The Reprint Company, 1983.

Dattel, Gene. *Cotton and Race in the Making of America: the Human Costs of Economic Power*. New York: Ivan R. Dee, 2009.

Dell, Pamela. *Memoir of Susie King Taylor: A Civil War Nurse*. North Mankato: Capstone Press, 2017.

Delbanco, Andrew. *The War Before The War: Fugitive Slaves and the Struggle for America's Soul from the Revolution to the Civil War*. New York: Penguin Random House, 2018.

Dickey, Christopher. *Our Man in Charleston: Britain's Secret Agent in the Civil War South*. New York: Broadway Books, 2015.

Dobak, William A. *Freedom by The Sword: The U.S. Colored Troops 1862-1867*. Alexandria: St. John's Press, 2016.

Doctorow, E.L. *The March*. New York: Random House, 2010.

Domby, Adam H. *The False Cause: Fraud, Fabrication and White Supremacy in Confederate Memory*. Charlottesville: University of Virginia Press, 2020.

Dougherty, Kevin. *The Port Royal Experiment: A Case Study in Development*. Jackson: University Press of Mississippi, 2014.

Doyle, Don H. *The Cause of All Nations*. New York, Basic Books, 2015.

Eisenschiml, Otto and Newman, Ralph. *The Civil War: An American Iliad*. New York: Smithmark Publishers, 1994.

Emilio, Captain Luis F. *A Brave Black Regiment: The History of the Fifty-fourth Regiment of Massachusetts Volunteer Infantry 1863-1865*. Columbia: Arcadia Press, 2017.

Evans, David. *Sherman's Horsemen: Union Cavalry Operations in the Atlanta Campaign*. Bloomington: Indiana University Press, 1996.

Faber, James M. *Invaders in Our Town: The Battle of Gettysburg Through the Eyes of Some Who Lived It*. Gettysburg: Thomas Publications, 2013.

Feiler, Andrew. *A Better Life for Their Children: Julius Rosenwald, Booker T. Washington and the 4,978 Schools That Changed America*. Athens:

University of Georgia Press, 2021.

Fleetwood, William C. *Tidecraft: The Boats of South Carolina, Georgia and Northeastern Florida, 1550-1950.* Tybee Island: WBG Marine Press,1995.

Foner, Eric. *The Fiery Trial: Abraham Lincoln and American Slavery.* New York: W.W. Norton & Co., 2010.

Foner, Eric. *The Second Founding: How the Civil War and Reconstruction Remade the Constitution.* New York: WW Norton & Co., 2019.

Foote, Shelby. *The Civil War: A Narrative (3 book set) Fort Sumter to Perryville, Fredericksburg to Meridian, Red River to Appomattox.* New York: A Random House Book, 1963.

Foote, Shelby. *The Civil War: A Narrative, Fort Sumter to Perryville.* New York: Vintage Books/Random House, 1958/1986.

Fordham, Damon L. *The 1895 Segregation Fight in South Carolina.* Charleston: The History Press, 2022.

Fradin, Dennis Brindell. *Bound for the North Star: True Stories of Fugitive Slaves.* New York: Clarion Books, 2000.

Frazier, Herb. *Behind God's Back: Gullah Memories.* Charleston: Evening Post Books, 2011.

Frazer, Herb, Bernard Edward Powers, Jr., and Marjory Wentworth. *We Are Charleston: Tragedy and Triumph at Mother Emanuel.* Nashville: W. Publishing Group, 2016.

Garrison, Webb. *Amazing Women of the Civil War.* Nashville: Rutledge Hill Press, 1999.

Garrison, Webb. *Civil War Curiosities, Strange Stories, Oddities, Events and Coincidences.* Nashville: Rutledge Hill Press, 1994.

Gates, Jr., Henry Louis, Editor. *Lincoln: On Race and Slavery.* Princeton: Princeton University Press, 2009.

Gates, Jr., Henry Louis. *Life Upon These Shores: Looking at African American History, 1513-2008.* New York: Alfred A. Knopf Publishing, 2011.

Gates, Jr., Henry Louis. *The Stony Road, Reconstruction: White Supremacy and the Rise of Jim Crow.* New York: Penguin Press, 2019.

Georgia Writers' Project. *Drums and Shadows: Survival Studies Among the Georgia Coastal Negroes,* 1940 Athens: University of Georgia Press, 2018.

Geraty, Virginia Mixson. *Gullah Fuh Oonuh (Gullah for You): A Guide to the Gullah Language.* Orangeburg: Sandlapper Publishing Co., 1997.

Ginzburg, Ralph. *100 Years of Lynchings.* Baltimore: Black Classic Press, 1962.

Glatthaar, Joseph T. *The March to the Sea and Beyond: Sherman's Troop's in the Savannah and Carolina Campaigns.* Baton Rouge: Louisiana State University Press, 1995.

Goodwine, Queen Quet Marquetta L. *Webe Gullah/Geechee: Cultural Capital & Collaboration Anthology.* Scotts Valley: Kinship Publications of Gullah Roots Productions, Create Space Independent Publishing Platform, 2015.

Gordon-Reed, Annette. *Estebanico's America:* "The Neglected Origin Stories of Black America." *The Atlantic.* June 2021, pp. 62-68.

Gorman, Amanda. *The Hill We Climb: An Inaugural Poem for the Country.* New York: Viking, 2021.

Grant, Ulysses S. *Personal Memoirs.* Caleb Carr, Series Editor. New York: The Modern Library, 1999.

Greene, Harlan, et al. *Slave Badges and the Slave-Hire System in Charleston, South Carolina, 1783-1865.* Jefferson: McFarland & Co., 2004.

Greenidge, Kaitlyn. *Libertie, a Novel.* Chapel Hill: Algonquin Books of Chapel Hill, 2021.

Grimsley, Jr., Major General James A. *The Citadel: Educating the Whole Man.* Charleston: The Citadel, The Military College of South Carolina, Nov. 4, 1982.

Griswold, Francis. *A Sea Island Lady.* New York: Beaufort Book Co. with William Morrow & Co., 1939.

Hadden, Sally. *Slave Patrols, Law and Violence in Virginia and the Carolinas.* Cambridge: Harvard University Press, 2001.

Hall, Stephen G. *A Faithful Account of the Race: African American Historical Writing in Nineteenth-Century America.* Chapel Hill: The University of North Carolina Press, 2009.

Hancock, Cornelia. *Letters of a Civil War Nurse,* 1863-1865. Edited by Henrietta Stratton Jaquette. Lincoln: University of Nebraska Press, 1998.

Hansen, Joyce. *Between Two Fires, Black Soldiers in the Civil War.* New York: Franklin Watts Inc., 1993.

Harris, Leslie M. and Daina Ramey Berry, editors. *Slavery and Freedom in Savannah.* Athens: The University of Georgia Press, 2014.

Harris, John. *The Last Slave Ships: New York and the End of the Middle Passage.* New Haven: Yale University Press, 2020.

Harris, Leslie M. and Daina Ramey Berry, editors. *Slavery and Freedom in Savannah.* Athens: The University of Georgia Press, 2014.

Harvey L. Brantley: His Civil War Letters and Family History. Arlington: Eileen Harvey Bakke, 1993.

Harwell, Richard B. *The Confederate Reader: How the South Saw the War.* New York: Dover Publications, Inc., 1957.

Helsley, Alexia Jones. *Beaufort, South Carolina: A History.* Charleston: The History Press, 2005.

Hersch, Jenny and Sallie Ann Robinson. *Daufuskie Island.* Charleston: Arcadia Publishing, 2018.

Hicks, Brian. *City of Ruin, Charleston at War, 1860-1865.* Charleston: Evening Post Books, 2012.

Hicks, Brian. *Sea of Darkness.* Ann Arbor: Spry Publishing, 2014.

Hicks, Brian. *In Darkest South Carolina.* Charleston: Evening Post Books, 2018.

Higginson, Thomas. *Black Soldiers, Blue Uniforms: The Story of the First South Carolina Volunteers.* Tucson: Fireship Press, 2009.

Higginson, Thomas Wentworth. *Army Life in a Black Regiment.* New York: Norton Company, 1984.

Higginson, Thomas Wentworth (Late Colonel 1st South Carolina Volunteers). *Army Life in a Black Regiment.* Collector's Library of the Civil War, Boston: Osgood & Co. (reprinted from 1870 edition), 1982.

Higginson, Thomas Wentworth. *Slave Narrative Six Pack 7.* Los Angeles: Enhanced Media Publishing, 2017.

Hill, Karlos K. *The 1921 Tulsa Race Massacre: A Photographic History.* Norman: University of Oklahoma Press, 2021.

Historic Beaufort Foundation. *Guide to Historic Homes and Places.* Revised 10th Edition. Beaufort: Historic Beaufort Foundation, 2014.

Holland, Rupert Sargent, Editor. *Letters and Diary of Laura M. Towne: Reconstruction Era Edition.* Charleston: Palmetto Publishing, 2019.

Holzer, Harold, Editor. *The Lincoln Mailbag: America Writes to the President, 1861-1865.* Carbondale: Southern Illinois University Press, 1998.

Holzer, Harold & Craig L. Symonds. *The New York Times Complete Civil War, 1861-1865.* New York: Blackdog & Leventhal Publishers, 2010.

Hughes, Langston, Milton Meltzer, C. Eric Lincoln and Jon Michael Spencer. *A Pictorial History of African Americans,* 6th Edition. New York: Crown Publishers, Inc., 1995.

The Humanities Council & Bernard Powers, Jr. *African Americans Who Shaped South Carolina.* Columbia: The University of South Carolina Press, 2006.

Hunt, O.E., Captain, United States Military Academy, et al. *The Photographic History of the Civil War, Volume 3, Forts and Artillery, The Navies.* Secaucus: The Blue and Grey Press, 1987.

Hurmence, Belinda. *My Folks Don't Want Me To Talk About Slavery.* Winston-Salem: John F. Blair, Publisher, 1984.

Jacoway, Elizabeth. *Yankee Missionaries in the South: The Penn School Experiment.* Baton Rouge: Louisiana State University Press, 1980.

Jaquette, Henrietta Stratton, Editor. *Letters of a Civil War Nurse: Cornelia Hancock, 1863-1865.* Lincoln: University of Nebraska Press, 1998.

Johnson, Charles. *Middle Passage.* New York: Penguin Books, 1990.

Jones-Rogers, Stephanie E. *They Were Her Property: White Women as Slave Owners in the American South:* New Haven: Yale University Press, 2019.

Jordan, Winthrop D. *The White Man's Burden: Historical Origins of Racism in the United States.* Oxford: Oxford University Press, 1974.

Joyner, Charles. *Down by the Riverside: A South Carolina Slave Community.* Urbana: University of Illinois Press, 1984.

Karp, Matthew. *This Vast Southern Empire: Slaveholders at the Helm of American Foreign Policy.* Cambridge: Harvard University Press, 2016.

Kemp, Sandra Rose Morris. *The Journey for Justice.* Meadville: Christian Faith Publishing, 2019.

Kendi, Ibram X. *Stamped From the Beginning: The Definitive History of Racist Ideas in America.* New York: Bold Type Books, 2016.

Kendi, Ibram X. and Keisha N. Blain. *Four Hundred Souls: A Community History of African America, 1619-2019.* New York: Random House, 2021.

Kilmeade, Brian. *The President and the Freedom Fighter: Abraham Lincoln, Frederick Douglas, and Their Battle to Save America's Soul.* New York: Penguin Random House, 2021.

Lee, Fitzhugh. *General Lee.* New York: D. Appleton and Company, 1894.

Leech, Margaret. *Reveille in Washington 1860-1865.* New York: Harper & Bros., 1941.

Lepore, Jill. *These Truths.* New York: WW Norton & Co., 2018.

Lineberry, Cate. *Be Free or Die: The Amazing Story of Robert Smalls' Escape from Slavery to Union Hero.* New York: St. Martin's Press, 2017.

Longstreet, James. *From Manassas to Appomattox: Memoirs of the Civil War in America.* New York: Barnes & Noble, 2004 (reprint from 1896).

Lonn, Ella. *Desertion During the Civil War.* Lincoln: University of Nebraska Press, 1998.

Mallory, Tamika D. *State of Emergency: How We Win in the Country We Built.* New York: Black Privilege Publishing, 2021.

Martin, Chlotilde Rowell. *Winds of Change in Gullah Land.* Mansfield: Bookmasters, Inc., 2003.

Martin, Valerie. *Property: A Novel.* New York: Vintage Books, 2003.

McDaniel, W. Caleb. *Sweet Taste of Liberty: A True Story of Slavery and Restitution in America.* New York: Oxford University Press, 2019.

McDonough, James Lee. *Shiloh—in Hell before Night.* Knoxville: The University of Tennessee Press, 1979.

McPherson, James M. *The Negro's Civil War: How American Blacks Felt and Acted During the War for the Union.* New York: Ballentine Books, 1965.

McPherson, James M. *Battle Cry of Freedom: The Civil War Era.* New York: Ballentine Books, 1988.

McPherson, James M. *Tried by War. Abraham Lincoln as Commander in Chief.* New York: Penguin Books, 2008.

Meacham, Jon. *And There Was Light: Abraham Lincoln and the American Struggle.* New York: Random House, 2022.

Miles, Suzannah Smith. *Writings of the Lowcountry: Reflections on the South Carolina Coast.* Charleston: History Press, 2004.

Miles, Tiya. *All That She Carried: The Journey of Ashley's Sack: A Black Family Keepsake.* New York: Random House, 2021.

Miller, Randall M. *Dear Master, Letters of a Slave Family.* Athens: Brown Thrasher Books/The University of Georgia Press, 1990.

Mills, Harold W. *The Confederate Secret Service: An Analysis of the Intelligence Community of the Confederate States of America.* Murrells Inlet: Covenant Books, Inc., 2018.

Mitchell, Patricia B. *Confederate Camp Cooking.* Chatham: Mitchells Publications, 1990.

Mitchell, Reid. *The Vacant Chair: The Northern Soldier Leaves Home.* New York: Oxford Press, 1993.

Mitchell, Reid. *Civil War Soldiers: The Expectations and Their Experiences.* New York: Simon and Schuster, 1988.

Morris, J. Brent. *Oberlin, Hotbed of Abolitionism: College, Community, and the Fight for Freedom and Equality in Antebellum America.* Chapel Hill: The University of North Carolina Press, 2014.

Morris, Brent J. *Yes, Lord, I Know the Road: A Documentary History of African Americans in South Carolina, 1526-2008.* Columbia: University of South Carolina Press, 2017.

Nolan, Alan T. *The Iron Brigade: A Military History*. Bloomington: Indiana University Press, 1961.

Oakes, James. *Slavery and Freedom: An Interpretation of the Old South*. New York: Alfred A. Kophf, 1990.

Oakes, James. *Crooked Path to Abolition: Abraham Lincoln and the Antislavery Constitution*. New York: Norton Company, 2021.

O'Neill, Connor Towne. *Down Along with That Devil's Bones: A Reckoning with Monuments, Memory, and the Legacy of White Supremacy*. Chapel Hill: Algonquin Books of Chapel Hill, 2020.

Oppenlander, Annette. *Everything We Lose, A Civil War Novel of Hope, Courage, and Redemption*. Columbia: Oppenlander Enterprises LLC, 2018.

Perry, Lee Davis and J. Michael McLaughlin. *It Happened in South Carolina: Remarkable Events that Shaped History*, 2nd Edition. Guilford: Morris Book Publishing, 2011.

Perry, Mark. *Conceived in Liberty: Joshua Chamberlain, William Oates, and The American Civil War*. New York: Viking Press, 1997.

Philadelphia Protestant Episcopal Book Society. *The 1861 Union Soldier's Prayer Book*, 1102 & 1104 Sansom St., Philadelphia: Henry B. Ashmead, 1861.

Pinckney, Roger. *Blue Roots, African-American Folk Magic of the Gullah People*, 2nd Edition. Orangeburg: Sandlapper Publishing Co., 2003.

Pollitzer, William S. *The Gullah People and Their African Heritage*. Athens: The University of Georgia Press. 1999.

Porter, Horace. *Campaigning with Grant*. New York: Time-Life Books, Reprint from 1981 from 1897 first edition.

Porwoll, Paul. "In My Trials, Lord, Walk with Me." *What an Antebellum Parish Register Reveals about Race and Reconciliation*. Charleston: Saint Andrews Parish Church, 2018.

Queen Quet, Marquetta L Goodwine. *WEBE Gullah/Geechee: Cultural Capital & Collaboration Anthology*. Columbia: Kinship Publications, 2015.

Reynolds, Jason. *Stamped: Racism, Antiracism and You*. New York: Little, Brown and Co., 2020.

Rhodes, Robert Hunt. *All for the Union: The Civil War Diary and Letters of Elisha Hunt Rhodes*. New York: Orion Books, 1985.

Robertson, David. *Denmark Vesey: The Buried Story of America's Largest Slave Rebellion and the Man Who Led It*. New York: Vintage Books, 1999.

Rodenbough, Theo. F. Brigadier-General, United States Army (Retired), Editor. *The Photographic History of the Civil War*, Volume 2, *The Decisive Battles, The Calvary*. Secaucus: The Blue and Gray Press, 1987.

Rodenbough, Theo. F., Brigadier-General, United States Army (Retired), Robert Lanier and Henry W. Elson, Editors. *The Photographic History of the Civil War: Armies & Leaders, The Calvary, The Decisive Battles*. New York: Random House, 1997.

Rose, Willie Lee. *Rehearsal for Reconstruction: The Port Royal Experiment*. New York: The Bobbs-Merrill Company, Inc, 1964.

Rosen, Robert. *A Short History of Charleston*. Columbia: University of South Carolina Press, 1992.

Rosen, Robert. *Confederate Charleston: An Illustrated History of the City and the People During the Civil War*. Columbia: University of South Carolina Press, 1994.

Rosen, Robert N. and Richard W Hatcher III. *The First Shot*. Arcadia Publishing, Charleston, 2011.

Rosengarten, Theodore. *Tombee, Portrait of a Cotton Planter: The Plantation Journal of Thomas B. Chaplin (1822-1890)*. New York: William Morrow and Company, Inc., 1986.

Roth, Ron. *The Civil War in The South Carolina Lowcountry: How a Confederate Artillery Battery and a Black Union Regiment Defined the War*. Jefferson: McFarland & Company, Publishers, 2020.

Rowland, Lawrence and Stephen G. Hoffius. *The Civil War in South Carolina: Selections from the South Carolina Historical Magazine*. Charleston: Home House Press, 2011.

Russell, Preston and Barbara Hines. *Savannah: A History of Her People Since 1733*. Savannah: Frederick C. Beil, Publisher, 1992.

Saini, Angela. "The Story of Human Difference: Race is a Social Construct, Not a Biological Trait: That is the Scientific Consensus-So Why Do Many Still Doubt It?" *National Geographic*, Sept. 2021, pp. 15-18.

Salaam, Yusef. *Better, Not Bitter: Living on Purpose in the Pursuit of Racial Justice*. New York: Grand Central Publishing, 2021.

Sears, Stephen W., Brooks D. Simpson and Aaron Seehan-Dean, editors. *The Civil War: The First Year Told by Those Who Lived It*. New York: Literary Classics of the United States, Penguin Books, 2011.

Seidule, Ty. *Robert E. Lee and Me: A Southerner's Reckoning with the Myth of the Lost Cause*. New York: St. Martin's Griffin, 2020.

Sessarego, Alan. *Letters Home IV, Life at the Front: Original Letters and*

Photographs from America's Civil War. Gettysburg: Americana Souvenirs & Gifts, 2003.

Sessarego, Alan. *Letters Home V, GETTYSBURG! Original Civil War Soldiers' Letters and Photographs.* Gettysburg: Americana Souvenirs & Gifts, 2003.

Sessarego, Alan. *Letters Home, Antietam, Gettysburg, Chancellorsville: A Collection of Original Civil War Soldiers' Letters.* Gettysburg: Americana Souvenirs & Gifts, 1996.

Shaara, Michael. *Gods and Generals.* New York: Ballantine Books, 1996.

Shaara, Michael. *The Killer Angels.* New York: Ballantine Books, 1974.

Siebert, Wilbur. *The Underground Railroad: A Comprehensive History.* Columbia: First Rate Publishers, 2015.

Simpson, Brooks B., Stephen W. Sears and Aaron Sheehan-Dean, editors. *The Civil War: The First Year, Told by Those Who Lived It.* New York: Literary Classics of America, 2011.

Sinha, Manisha. *The Slaves Cause: A History of Abolition.* New Haven: Yale University Press, 2016.

Smallwood, Stephanie E. *Saltwater Slavery: A Middle Passage from Africa to America Diaspora.* Cambridge: Harvard University Press, 2007.

Smith, Andrew F. *Starving the South: How the North Won the Civil War.* New York: St. Martin's Press, 2011.

Smith, Clint. *How the Word is Passed: A Reckoning with the History of Slavery Across America.* New York: Little, Brown and Company, 2021.

Smith, Clint. "The War on Nostalgia: The myth of the Lost Cause is passed down like an heirloom. *The Atlantic*, June 2021, pp. 52-61.

Smith, Derek. *Civil War Savannah.* Savannah: Frederic C. Beil, Publisher, 1997.

Smith, Shawn Michelle. *Lynching Photographs.* Berkeley: University of California Press, 2007.

Stampp, Kenneth M. *The Peculiar Institution: Slavery in the Ante-Bellum South.* New York: Random House, 1956/1984.

Stampp, Kenneth M., Editor. *The Causes of the Civil War.* Englewood Cliffs: Prentice-Hall, Inc., 1959.

Stampp, Kenneth M. *The Era of Reconstruction, 1865-1877.* New York: Alfred A. Knopf Publishers, 1966.

Stackpole, General Edward J. *They Met at Gettysburg.* Harrisburg: Stackpole Books, 1956.

Starobin, Paul. *Madness Rules the Hour, Charleston, 1860 and the Mania for the War.* New York: Perseus Books, 2017.

Still, William. *The Underground Railroad Records: Narrating the Hardships, Hairbreadth Escapes, and Death Struggles of Slaves in their Efforts for Freedom.* New York: Penguin Random House, 2019.

Stokes, Karen. *A Legion of Devils, Sherman in South Carolina.* Columbia: Shotwell Publishing, 2017.

Stubbs, Tristan. *Masters of Violence, The Plantation Overseers of the Eighteenth-Century Virginia, South Carolina, and Georgia.* Columbia: University of South Carolina, 2018.

Swanson, James L. *Manhunt: The 12-Day Chase for Lincoln's Killer.* New York: Harper Collins, 2006.

Tadman, Michael. *Speculators and Slaves, Masters, Traders, and Slaves in the Old South.* Madison: University of Wisconsin Press, 1989.

Taft, William H., former President of the United States, et al., *The Photographic History of the Civil War, Volume 1, The Opening Battles, Two Years of Grim War.* Secaucus: The Blue & Grey Press, 1987.

Taylor, Amy Murrell. *Embattled Freedom: Journeys through the Civil War's Slave Refugee Camps.* Chapel Hill: University of North Carolina Press, 2018.

Taylor, Candacy. *Overground Railroad: The Green Book and the Roots of Black Travel in America.* New York: Abrams Press, 2020.

Taylor, Susie King. *Reminiscences of My Life: A Black Woman's Civil War Memoirs.* Boston: Self-published by the author, 1902.

Thomas, Dean S. *Ready...Aim...Fire! Small Arms Ammunition in the Battle of Gettysburg.* Gettysburg: Thomas Publications, 1981.

Time-Life Books, Editors. *Voices of the Civil War, Gettysburg: Tell My Father I Died with My Face to the Enemy.* Alexandria: Time-Life Education, 1995.

Troiani, Don. *Regiments and Uniforms of the Civil War.* Mechanicsburg: Stackpole Books, 2002.

Trotter, William R. *Ironclads and Columbiads: The Civil War in North Carolina and the The Coast.* Winston-Salem: John F. Blair, Publisher, 1989.

Trudeau, Noah Andre. *Gettysburg: A Testing of Courage.* New York: Harper Collins, 2002.

Trudeau, Noah Andre. *Voices of the 55th: Letters from the 55th Massachusetts Volunteers.* Dayton: Press of Morningside, 1996.

Tucker, Glenn. *High Tide at Gettysburg: The Campaign in Pennsylvania.*

Gettysburg: Stan Wright Military Books, 1958.

van der Linden, Frank. *Lincoln: The Road to War.* Golden: Fulcrum Publishing, 1998.

Walker, Margaret. *Jubilee.* New York: Houghton Mifflin Company, 1966.

Walker, Timothy D. *Sailing to Freedom: Maritime Dimensions of the Underground Railroad.* Amherst: University of Massachusetts Press, 2021.

Ward, Geoffrey C. with Ric Burns and Ken Burns. *The Civil War: An Illustrated History.* New York: Alfred A. Knopf, Inc, 1994.

Wells, Jonathan Daniel. *The Kidnapping Club: Wall Street, Slavery, and Resistance on the Eve of the Civil War.* New York: Bold Type Books, 2020.

West, Emily. *Chains of Love: Slave Couples in Antebellum South Carolina.* Urbana: University of Illinois Press, 2004.

Westwood, Howard C. *Black Troops, White Commanders and Freedmen During the Civil War.* Carbondale: Southern Illinois University Press, 1992.

Wilkerson, Isabel. *Caste. The Origins of Our Discontents.* New York: Random House, 2020.

Wilkerson, Isabel. *The Warmth of Other Suns: The Epic Story of America's Great Migration.* New York: Vintage Books, 2010.

Willet, Robert L. *One Day of the Civil War: America in Conflict, April 10, 1863.* Washington, DC: Brassey's Inc., 1997.

Williams, Eric. *Capitalism and Slavery.* Chapel Hill: The University of North Carolina Press, 1944, 1994.

Williamson, Joel. *After Slavery: The Negro in South Carolina During Reconstruction, 1861-1877.* Hanover: University Press of New England, 1990.

Willis, Deborah. *The Black Civil War Soldier: A Visual History of Conflict and Citizenship.* New York: New York University Press, 2021.

Williams, Lou Falkner. *The Great South Carolina Ku Klux Klan Trials 1871-1872: Studies in the Legal History of the South.* Athens: University of Georgia Press, 1996.

Williamson, Joel. *After Slavery: The Negro in South Carolina During Reconstruction.* New York: Norton & Co., 1975.

Wink, Jay. *April 1865: The Month That Saved America.* New York: Harper Collins, 2002.

Wise, Stephen R. *Gate of Hell: Campaign for Charleston Harbor, 1863.*

Columbia: University of South Carolina Press, 1994.

Wise, Stephen R. and Lawrence S. Rowland. *Rebellion, Reconstruction and Redemption, 1861-1893. The History of Beaufort County, South Carolina, Volume 2.* Columbia: University of South Carolina Press, 2015.

Wood, Amy Louise. *Lynching and Spectacle: Witnessing Racial Violence in America, 1890-1940.* Chapel Hill: The University of North Carolina Press, 2009.

Woodward, C. Vann, Editor. *Mary Chestnut's Civil War.* New Haven: Yale University Press, 1981.

Works Progress Administration (WPA) interviewers; thirty-four former slave interviewees. Edited by Norman R. Yetman. *When I Was A Slave; Memoirs from the Slave Narrative Collection.* Mineola: Dover Publications, Inc., 1941.

Wynne, Lewis N. and Robert A. Taylor. *This War So Horrible: The Civil War Diary of Hiram Smith Williams.* Tuscaloosa: University of Alabama Press, 1993.

www.ingramcontent.com/pod-product-compliance
Lightning Source LLC
LaVergne TN
LVHW041739060526
838201LV00046B/862